I0778319

The
SECRET *of* EDEN
and the
NEW WORLD

J. Andrew Jackson

First published by Takin Five LLC 2022

First edition

Print ISBN: 979-8-9860474-0-9
ePub ISBN: 979-8-9860474-1-6
Paperback ISBN: 979-8-9860474-2-3

For Julie

PREFACE

As Americans, we take much for granted. Somehow, many believe that we have basic things such as protection from enemy attacks, fertile soil, and abundant natural resources, such as food and fresh water, simply because of good fortune. Most don't give a second thought as to why this land was granted to our forefathers. Many have fought and died for everything that we have. For many, the subject of our fallen forefathers is more of a cliché than a meaningful thought. If they delved into America's founding, which started before Columbus even set sail, they would understand that circumstances seemed to line up perfectly for the early explorers. Was this luck or divine intervention?

Generations later, an untrained and poorly armed set of militias defeated the world's largest military. Estimates state that as little as three percent and maybe as high as ten percent of men of the Colonies participated in the Revolutionary War effort. Also, there was little in the coffers to pay for the war effort. So how did the Patriots pull off this miracle victory? I believe that there was divine intervention. I think that the Founding Fathers believed this as well.

What makes America different? Often, you hear that America's Constitution is remarkable. Why is that? Every nation has a Constitution or at least a set of rules that governs its people. The difference is that America's Constitution and Bill of Rights are based on rights handed down from the Almighty. No Group or Government has the authority to take away our rights. Our

Constitution and Bill of Rights were written to protect us from tyranny. Most Constitutions are written in the context of what the government allows its citizens to do. America's Constitution is written based on what the government is NOT permitted to do. This distinction makes this nation special.

In fact, the Founding Fathers explain this in the Declaration of Independence with this beautiful sentence:

"We hold these truths to be self-evident, that all men are created equal, that they are endowed by their Creator with certain unalienable Rights that among these are Life, Liberty and the pursuit of Happiness."

This statement is at the core of everything that we do as Americans.

Furthermore, the Bill of Rights was written from the viewpoint that "No government shall infringe on the Right to Free Speech, the Right to Bear Arms, etc." The poorly educated masses in the United States do not understand this distinction. Some think that the government has the authority to take away our rights. I know it's not a popular opinion, but I believe a test of a person's knowledge regarding our Constitution should be taken before a Voter ID Card is issued. This would help erase many of the misunderstandings. At least everyone would have the proper foundation for electing our leaders. I believe that our Constitution needs minor adjustments as technology and world conditions change. The Constitution has accommodations for these eventualities. The Founding Fathers wrote a nearly perfect document because they were guided by the Almighty. Many will ask, "What about Atheists or non-Judeo-Christian religions such as Islam." Well, it protects their beliefs and rights as well. It is not written just for Christians and Jews. It is for all Americans.

Does this mean that the Almighty has abandoned the rest of the world? The answer is no. America's role in the world is to help secure peace and happiness for all less fortunate nations.

America was born because many of the nations of the world were governed by unjust leaders. During the middle ages, these leaders were in control of almost every country throughout the known world. In Europe especially, any new thoughts on science, mathematics, and religion were censured by the rule of the Church in conjunction with the various Kings. Anyone who offered a differing opinion from the Church was labeled as a heretic and was punished with prison or worse. As a result, many chose to speak only in the clandestine world of art and coded messages. This spurred the search for a new land.

Throughout ancient history, there was always a belief that a special place existed where resources were abundant, and free thought could be pursued. Plato talked about a place that he called Arcadia. Many great thinkers such as Leonardo Da Vinci and Sir Francis Bacon believed that the New World was to be the "New Atlantis." Some believed that the New World was to be the "Shining city on top of the hill" that Jesus spoke of in his famous parable of Salt and Light in the Sermon on the Mount. The Founding Fathers believed that America was this allegorical city. In the parable, Jesus said that all eyes would be on this city to set the example of how to live a righteous life. This city was to be a beacon of light for the entire world.

America is a place where anyone, man or woman, can succeed based on their own merits instead of their family's surname. It was founded to be free of Kings or other such nobles. It is where a man such as Abraham Lincoln could rise from his meager beginnings to attain the highest office in the land. This freedom is not free. It requires great leadership. Our Constitution and Bill of Rights give us the proper tools to manage such a nation.

In many ways, America has succeeded in its sacred mission, and in many ways, it has failed. America has defended the world against the many despots that have tried to conquer their neighbors. When a conflict is truly righteous, America always prevails. When America enters into a conflict to gain land or commodities such as oil, a loss or stalemate is witnessed. When America listens to those who are part of the Military-Industrial Complex that President Eisenhower so eloquently warned us about, then the war is neither won nor lost. The only victors are those who provide the arms and the implements of war. Their victory is that the war is perpetual, and their bank accounts will continue to grow.

My story is about the mandate that the Almighty has given America. The mandate comes by way of a Secret that was given to Adam after he was cast from the Garden of Eden. The Secret was handed to Adam with a set of rules that, if followed, would return mankind to the Garden of Eden and grant access to the Tree of Knowledge. During the time of Noah, the Almighty was so upset with humanity that he unfurled a catastrophe that wiped out nearly all of humanity. Noah had been pre-warned of the flood by a handful of Angels, who his great grandfather Enoch had named the Watchers. After the floodwaters had receded, the Watchers selected three of Noah's grandchildren, Peleg, Tytea, and Joktan, to be the Guardians of the great Secret. Peleg and Tytea become man and wife and are soulmates for all of eternity. Their cousin Joktan is always at their side. They would die and then be reincarnated every time the Secret was in jeopardy. On the contrary, Satan had selected one of Noah's other grandsons, Canaan, to be the adversary to the Guardians.

The story is revealed to a teenage boy named Nathaniel Briggs, or Nate as he is known by his family, in pre-Civil War America through his Dreams. The Dreams show in great detail all of the trials and tumultuous times that the Secret endures throughout its history. His first set of Dreams details the Knights Templar as they search for religious artifacts under the Temple of Solomon in Jerusalem. Along with other priceless artifacts, they uncover the Secret of Eden.

The next set of Dreams occurs roughly three hundred years later and finds the Secret of Eden to be in the possession of the Clan Sinclair in Rosslyn, Scotland. The walls begin to close in on Henry Sinclair, the Laird of the Clan Sinclair. His protection from the English and French Kings evaporate after the death of Robert the Bruce. He knows that he must follow the mandate of the Secret of Eden and move the Secret and its accompanying Treasure to the New World. The new home of the Secret of Eden is to be what we now know as Nova Scotia.

This is Book One of my story. It is a story of good versus evil. It is an adventure that takes place during the most significant times during the middle ages. It is a treasure hunt that also includes a love story between soulmates that have been together in each lifetime since the time of Noah.

Book Two, The Secret of Eden and the Founding Fathers, will show how the Secret interacts and guides many of the Founding Fathers, such as Benjamin Franklin, George Washington, Samuel Adams, and Alexander Hamilton. Once again, Nate Briggs sees the story of the Founding Fathers and the Secret of Eden through his Dreams. This time, two of the Guardians are his great grandparents, Hannah and Jeremiah Briggs. The third Guardian is one of the most famous men in American history. The two soulmates, Hannah and Jeremiah, share an extraordinary time together through times of great joy and also times where they are in great peril. Once again, the Guardians protect the Secret and reveal it to the Founding Fathers. Is this the mandate the Founding Fathers require for the revolution and the founding of a new nation?

Book Three, The Secret of Eden and the Civil War, will show how the Secret leads President Abraham Lincoln through his battle with the great scourge of slavery that has threatened to split the young nation. This story is a recounting of Nate Briggs' own life as he discovers his role with the Guardians. Nate meets and becomes a close confidant of Abraham Lincoln and tells the Great President of the Secret of Eden.

The story tells the harrowing tale of Nate as he is involved with the Underground Railroad, the Emancipation Proclamation, and the many battles of the Civil War, such as Gettysburg and Antietam. It is a classic love story of our soulmates set to the backdrop of 1860s America.

Book Four will tackle the issues of the twentieth century,

such as the Great Depression, World War I and II, the Cold War, and the countless other wars that America seems to find itself engaged in. Once again, the Guardians will find the Secret of Eden in great danger. The soulmates will help define their generation. They will be part of what was indeed the "Greatest Generation." This will happen as the adversary is closing in. Will all be lost? Will the Almighty unleash his fury just as he did in the time of Noah?

Book Five will be set in the future. Once again, the Guardians will be called on to protect the Secret. Our soulmates will be tested in a time when love and marriage are frowned upon. Children will be born in laboratories. The days will be dark until the Guardians arrive on the scene.

Will America have lived up to its mandate? Will greed and selfishness govern the masses? Will automation and robots replace the workers? How will the people survive? Will the people of this land be worthy? Will the just and righteous prevail? Will the Secret of Eden finally be revealed and the Secrets of the Universe be revealed? Stay tuned!

ACKNOWLEDGEMENT

I have always wanted to be an author. As a teenager, I wrote several essays which won some accolades. Unfortunately, I was drawn away from this passion by sports, school, and just life in general. Not to mention, I was heading to Engineering school. There are not too many Chemical Engineers looking to write historical fiction stories.

After college, I was hired into a position that required me to travel extensively for the better part of fifteen years. During this period, I became an avid reader. I read everything that I could get my hands on from Stephen King, Tom Clancy, Robert Ludlum, and Michael Crichton. In addition, I often returned to the classics that I read in my youth, such as *The Great Gatsby* and *To Kill a Mockingbird*. I thank the outstanding teachers who guided me through these classics.

F. Scott Fitzgerald's use of symbols such as the green light on Daisy Miller's dock that represented hope for Jay Gatsby, which was central to the story. Or the all-knowing eyes of Doctor T. J. Eckleburg as they looked upon the contrast between the wealthy travelers against the backdrop of sheer poverty and depression. In *To Kill a Mockingbird*, Harper Lee told the story of racism in the American south while still developing wonderful characters that stood on their own such as Scout, Jem, and Atticus Finch. Harper Lee developed the character Boo Radley, simply based upon gossipy townspeople. She very carefully introduced the real Boo at the end of the story. He was just a misunderstood man who had nothing but love in his heart for the children of the story. The overwhelming theme of not prejudging anyone until you get to know them yourself screamed off the pages. These stories are far more than just fiction novels. Margaret Mitchell wrote the masterpiece, *Gone with the Wind*, which was a love story written so elegantly against the backdrop of the American Civil War. Her messaging throughout the story was masterful.

I would never dare to compare myself to these legends, but nonetheless, I used their styles and message delivery methods as an inspiration while developing my story. All of these masters inspired my Secret of Eden series. As I would write about a particular scene, I would think back to these authors and how they so easily captured these feelings and sentiments of the times that were seemingly going on in the background.

During these early 2000s, I found myself studying writing techniques as much as taking in the stories themselves. This is about the time when my favorite author, Dan Brown, burst onto the scene. The way he defined the historical backdrop in great detail was awe-inspiring. His use of third-person omniscient narration is a work of art. Most authors avoid this style because it can often confuse the reader. Dan Brown used this style to keep his stories moving and suspenseful. I didn't dare attempt this myself. Maybe someday, but now I will keep it simple.

Being a first-time author, I have many people to thank. Far too many to mention here. My acknowledgments will be longer than the novel. I can go back to my grade school teachers, who taught me to look for the underlying messages hidden within a story. During my days at Shrine High School, I had a teacher named Pete Ferguson, who seemingly was barely older than his students. Pete did a great job of helping me understand the classics. I still consider Pete to be a friend today. Pete always thought that I was never paying attention. The simple truth is that I was paying attention. His thoughts on American Literature are still with me today.

Last but not least, I would like to thank my wife, Julie, and my kids, Melissa, Nick, and Rachel. Through the whirlwind of owning a business, I have put you guys through the trauma of loss and hardship. For this I am truly sorry. Fortunately, we mixed in some good times as well. The good news is that we are not done yet.

Many of my friends will never understand how Julie truly opened my eyes to the supernatural surrounding us every day. My life changed the day that she convinced me to read a book by a noted Psychiatrist named Dr. Brian Weiss. My eyes were forever opened to the reality of reincarnation. Julie and I attended a conference in Chicago where Dr. Weiss explained Past Life Regression Therapy. Through hypnosis, I learned of a past life memory that shocked me to my core. What I saw that day was not imagination. It was not a Dream. It was a look into a past real-life situation. The character that I saw will be a dominant person in my second book, *The Secret of Eden and the Founding Fathers*. The story around this character is fiction, but his being was a past manifestation of myself.

Julie also introduced me to a very gifted lady named Felicia Armstrong. She has gifts that I cannot explain. During my first meeting with Felicia, she described scenes from my childhood that I had never told anyone else. She very quickly realized that my soul had a gaping wound caused by my father's death some thirty years ago. I knew this to be true. She told me to write a letter to my Dad. I took it one step further. I wrote an entire book (and hopefully an entire series) for my Dad. Everyone that knew my father understood that he was an avid student of history. There are times when I first read one of my completed chapters that I have the sensation of "Where did that come from?" I truly believe that my Dad is with me, telling me what to write.

CHAPTER ONE

FORETELLING

EDUARD AND MICHAEL returned to the task at hand. The tunnel under the Sphinx was not completely clean and secure. At the end of the tunnel, the cavern reminded the men of the cavern under the Foundation Stone back at Solomon's Temple. Both caverns were natural and were used to hide a secret so powerful that it could shake the earth to its core. Unfortunately, that is where the similarities ended. Once the lanterns were all lit, they looked around and found nothing but an empty cavern. The floor had not been leveled, whereas the flooring of the Well of Souls back at Solomon's Temple was made of marble. They focused on the western wall. They figured that if it followed the layout from above where the Great Lion, or the Sphinx as it was known, is looking west, they would find the seal.

They went over the entire wall, looking for loose clay. Nothing was immediately found. Then, Eduard looked down and noticed a small pile of clay dust. He went from ceiling to floor above this dust pile, looking for an imperfection. Finally, Eduard held a lantern high up on the wall, and there it was. The Secret Seal of Solomon. It was covered with dust that had fallen from above. He called Michael over and informed him that he had found the Secret Seal.

Jacques said, "There is no time for celebration. The battle has started. Our brother Templars have set a fire ring that the Muslims will have to cross. Arrows are flying everywhere."

Eduard's attention then turned to the opposite wall. Michael went over with a lantern. He began to do the knock test on the opposite wall. The wall seemed like solid Bedrock. Near the floor, he noticed a rough surface. This was different from the rest of the wall. Eduard grabbed a trowel and scraped what looked like chunks of dried clay. He noticed rocks under the layer of clay. The rocks were perfectly selected so that the fit was perfect. No mortar was necessary. Michael had seen several other sites where perfectly fitted rocks had formed a wall over the years. The rocks went to a level that was about four feet above the ground. Michael noticed that the rocks were perfectly cut in straight lines. He had never seen rocks that were cut so perfectly.

Michael said, "These rocks were not cut by any artisans that I have seen. The Watchers must have cut them."

Eduard instructed the Squires to get some tools and break down the wall into pieces. Eduard and Michael returned to the tent. They wanted some fresh air for a minute. They were both anxious for the Squires to get the wall removal done. Both men had a drink of water from a canteen. The clay dust felt like it was everywhere. They could now hear the battle. The clash of sword against sword was unmistakable. They ran down the tunnel to see if the wall had been removed. It was halfway down. Eduard jumped in and began ripping the rocks away. A few minutes later, the opening was exposed.

One of the Squires lit a lantern and entered the cavity. His face was full of shock. Michael said, "What do you see?"

The Squire said, "I am not sure. I have never seen anything like it."

Michael said, "Let's get a few of the Squires in there and see if you can pull it out." The Squires lifted the box and carried it out into the open. It was a shiny silver rectangular box-like container that had what looked like a keyhole perfectly cut into its top. It was made of a metal that these men had never seen before. There was no lid. It was just solid all the way around."

Hamid said, "Is this the Secret of Eden?'

Michael said, "Yes. This is the treasure of all treasures. Someday, when mankind has become worthy, the Secret will open up and provide all the answers to the universe. It will answer the questions that mankind has pondered since the time of Adam and Eve."

Jacques suddenly could smell the fragrance. It was his greatest moment, and her spirit was with him.

Eduard ordered the Squires to carry the box out of the tunnel and load it onto a cart.

Michael said, "Hamid, you, your sons, and Mufti are welcome to go with us."

Hamid said, "This is our home. We do not want to leave here. However, if the Muslims ask us what we are doing, we will tell them the truth. We are part of an Archeological dig team that is exploring underneath the Sphinx."

Michael said, "Thank you from the bottom of my heart. I'm sure your father, Maat, is very proud of you." He then handed Hamid a satchel that contained at least three times the gold coins he had promised.

Meanwhile, Eduard and Jacques were waiting up top outside the tent. The Squires had just loaded the silver box onto the carriage. Eduard covered the box with blankets. Michael came topside and jumped on the carriage. Jacques decided that he would help clear the way for the carriage. The battle was now in front of them. Eduard remained back, giving the workers instructions to cover up the cavern they had found and to bury all of the dug holes. After giving instructions, he realized that he had waited too long.

Meanwhile, Jacques had a sword in each hand. He was cutting down the enemy right and left. Arrows were flying just over his head. He could hear them as they sped right by his ears. The fragrance was still with him. Jacques believed that she was somehow protecting him. They were now approaching the Nile. He could see the carriage directly ahead come to a stop. Michael was ordering the Squires to load the silver box onto the lifeboat. They did so, and the boat immediately left the shore. Jacques could see that Michael had been hit. The lifeboat was heading directly for the Command ship. It was finally out of the range of the arrows. Michael was slumped over in his seat, but he was still moving.

Jacques experienced great happiness, which was followed by a great sadness. Why was he so sad? Perhaps Michael would survive. Jacques had just delivered the Secret of Eden to safety. It was his life's mission. Then it struck him. Eduard had fallen. Jacques could sense that Eduard had passed. He circled back towards the Sphinx. He came across Eduard lying on the ground.

Jacques jumped off of his horse and looked at Eduard's face. He was dead. He threw Eduard's body over the front of the horse and then jumped on and rode towards the Nile. The last of the lifeboats were leaving. He screamed for them to wait. They had formed a Phalanx which protected them from the arrows. This gave Jacques enough time to carry Eduard's body to the lifeboat. Jacques looked out to the Command Ship and saw the silver box being loaded onto the ship. They had succeeded in protecting the Secret of Eden. He then climbed into the boat, and they began to move. Jacques looked back at the shore and saw pure evil. It was Abdul. He was standing there laughing. Just then, as if ordered by the almighty, an arrow went right into Abdul's eye. Jacques experienced a sense of relief. His relief was too soon, however. Just then, out of the corner of his eye, he saw an archer release an arrow. The arrow was moving ever so slowly towards him, and finally...

✠

Just then, Nate's father, Andrew, shook him until he was awake. Andrew said, "Nate, it was just a Dream. There is nothing to be frightened of."

Nate sat there bewildered. Once again, the Dream that he just had was so real that it was as if he was an actor within this dreadful play.

CHAPTER TWO

FAMILY VALUES

MANY THINGS IN this life cannot be explained. Since the dawn of man, many have tried to explain death. Virtually all societies have claimed that some type of afterlife exists. This claim was more about easing the pain of death on the living than about what awaited the deceased. Some have always believed that people would behave poorly if they thought everything ended at death. Many cultures have promised an afterlife that sounds wonderful for that particular culture. The Vikings believed that if a warrior dies on the battlefield, he will travel to Valhalla, where he will be seated at the table with the gods along with warriors who fell before him.

The Vikings believed that conquest and pillaging were a sacred duty. Christians believe that if one lives a pious life of giving to the less fortunate along with regular prayers, that person will earn a spot in Heaven. Is one culture right and the other wrong? They all promise a journey to a place that is befitting their culture. They all promise, one way or another, an afterlife that is similar to the world that Sir Thomas More described in *Utopia*.

All these belief systems are both correct and incorrect. Few understand what happens at the time of death. The understanding of life after death is the lesser part of this story. Understanding the Secret of Eden is far more important. Nathaniel Briggs, or Nate as his family calls him, is not sure he wants to participate in this tale. Fortunately or not, Nate is one of the rare people that are granted a glimpse into the afterlife and this great secret.

He was born Nathaniel Mayfield Briggs on January 20, 1840, in Detroit, Michigan. His mother, Sarah Mayfield Briggs, and his father, Andrew Briggs, are the parents of eight children. His parents were both born at the place that was simply known as the Compound. The Compound is located in southern New York State on the Susquehanna River. It was the combination of a plantation and Milltown. It was co-owned by Samuel Adams and Peter Adams, cousin, and brother, respectively, of the second U.S. President John Adams. The Adams Trading Company, which was in many ways its own town, was a prosperous business during the colonial days. The Compound was far more than a milling and lumber town during the American Revolution. At its core, it was one of the centerpieces of the American Revolution. It will never be remembered that way because everything there was done in secret, never to be recorded. Still, those involved knew that the Compound was as important as Philadelphia and Boston. Once the Revolutionary War had ended, the Compound's value began to deteriorate. Even though it was owned by one of the most prominent families in America, it had outlived its usefulness because the lumber business had become highly competitive. In addition, the farming business was spotty because of severe weather. The Revolution and the subsequent battles with the English were a thing of the past. Hence, Nate's parents looked for greener pastures, as they say.

Nate's father's closest friend, John W. Hunter, traveled west to Michigan in 1828 to trade for furs and explore the new land. He traveled via the waterways of Lake Erie, Lake Huron, and Lake

Michigan before heading inland to evaluate farming prospects. He marveled at the crystal-clear blue waters of the Great Lakes. He spoke in great detail about the shores of Lake Michigan. He said it had sand dunes on the Michigan shoreline from end to end. He declared that it was the most beautiful place he had ever seen, which says much because he traveled extensively throughout Europe as a child. On this journey, he traveled across the lower part of Michigan. He had heard that it was not farmable because most of it was a wetland. While he discovered many inland lakes, he also discovered vast prairies that were perfect for farming. Once he arrived at Fort Detroit, he wrote to Nate's father to tell him that he had found the land of plenty. He went on to say that the land consisted of rolling hills with fertile soil. One of the main attractions that drew Mr. Hunter to Michigan was that navigable waterways surrounded it. In fact, the Great Lakes could now reach the Atlantic due to the creation of the Erie Canal in 1825.

Nate's great grandparents, Jeremiah and Hannah Briggs, lived at the Compound for their entire marriage. Few knew that Jeremiah and Hannah worked very closely with the Founding Fathers. Jeremiah managed the Compound for his father-in-law, Samuel Adams, and was one of the Sons of Liberty.

The Compound was ideally located because of its proximity to the Susquehanna River. The great river led to the Chesapeake Bay and beyond. In Jeremiah's day, great value was placed on being near navigable waterways. By the time Nate's father was of age, the lands in the northeastern United States were seemingly crowded. You could no longer lay claim to the tillable ground because most of it was claimed after the Revolutionary War. Many Patriots were given large patches of land in return for their military service. The lands in the east were also surrounded by mountains, from the Adirondacks down to the Shenandoah Mountains. The terrain made the weather unpredictable. This made the land tough for farming. The land in the former Michigan Territory, which became a state in 1836, was wide open and ready to be settled. Many Michigan pioneers were overwhelmingly of New England origin, including transplants from upstate New York. This was comforting for Nate's parents. They were still Puritans at heart. Due to the new settlers' heritage, Michigan was at the forefront of the antislavery crusade and reforms during the 1840s and 1850s. This despicable practice offended Nate's parents, Sarah and Andrew. The move to Michigan was an easy decision because of its abolitionist leanings.

John W. hunter established a farming community in a place that became known as Birmingham, Michigan. Some say that it was given that name because it reminded them of its namesake back in England. It was a day's ride from Detroit, which was a growing seaport. In 1839, the railroad tracks connecting Pontiac and Detroit added a stop at Birmingham. This meant that you could have a day trip to Detroit anytime you wanted. Two steam locomotives stopped at Birmingham daily. You could reach the Eastern U.S., Europe, and beyond from Detroit. Andrew and Sarah had moved to a twenty-acre farm a few miles west of Birmingham in 1830. While loving their new home, Andrew and Sarah were still New Englanders at heart. As had many others, they moved to Michigan because Michigan represented freedom and opportunity. The wars with the British seemed like a thing of the past. Treaties had mostly settled the conflicts with the Indian Tribes. Andrew was also a great outdoorsman, and Michigan was very bountiful with respect to Deer, Elk, and other game. Politically speaking, Michigan was uncharted waters. There was a mix of transplants from both New England and Central Atlantic Coast states such as Virginia and the Carolinas. From 1837 to the 1850s, Michigan politics were decidedly Jacksonian and Democratic, out of loyalty to President Jackson for supporting Michigan's statehood.

Nate's grandparents, John and Mary Williams Briggs remained at the Compound until that fateful day in 1835. A fire had started at the sawmill and quickly spread to the entire community. The region was under the grips of a major drought, as the story goes. Once the fire started, it was over quickly. The Compound had burned to the ground and was never rebuilt. John and Mary barely escaped with just the clothes on their backs. Mary was from Hanover, Pennsylvania. Most of her family was still there, and she knew that they would always be welcome. They traveled to Hanover and would spend the rest of their days there. The family never believed the accidental fire story. They knew that the Compound had many secrets. These were secrets that no one spoke of even amongst family. The entire Briggs family found that it was much easier to go through life if the Compound's secrets were never discussed. The mysterious building at the Compound that was known as the Hall of the Freemasons had been the subject of many rumors. Supposedly, this building was one of the main meeting spots for many of the Founding Fathers. There was never any evidence of this, even though some of the Compound's elders would swear to it. The younger people just assumed it was embellishment. It was similar to the stories that many of the Inns in the Colonies had claimed that either George Washington or Benjamin Franklin had slept there. While it made for fanciful stories, most of it was not based on any facts. Either way, Nate's parents and grandparents believed that the fire was intentionally set to hide some things that certain people wanted to keep hidden forever.

Nate was part of a very close-knit and loving family. His favorite memories were just of simple times, such as sitting around the fireplace after supper. His father, Andrew, had plenty of stories. Many involved Jeremiah and Hannah's numerous tales of glory. Even though Nate heard them a million times, he still loved hearing them. The amazing part was that they were a little different every time, depending on whether his father had wine with supper. Nate was especially close with his older sister Jane even though she lived in her own home. Jane had known a local boy named Jonathon Willits her entire life. He was the son of a wealthy landowner and tavern owner, Elijah Willits. Jane and Jonathon were married when they turned eighteen and remained in the Birmingham area. She founded the first schoolhouse in the city and was its first teacher. Before the new Schoolhouse, Nate and his siblings would travel every weekday to nearby Pontiac for school. Nate and Jane had a bond that was very hard to explain. No one would believe it even if they tried to explain it. Yet, seemingly, they could read each other's thoughts.

Nate led, what most would say, was a very ordinary but happy life until the Dreams started. Then his life changed forever.

CHAPTER 3

THE DREAMS

THE DREAMS STARTED when Nate was roughly twelve years old. The Dreams that Nate had were not like the normal Dreams that everyone has where sights and scenes are unclear, purposes are vague, and for the most part, are meaningless. Instead, his Dreams were very clear. The Dreams were so real that it was like Nate was simply watching the events take place, and other times he was an active participant. They were like watching a replay of something that had happened a long time ago. Some were scary and involved very treacherous scenes where people were killed. Others were more mundane. Even though he felt that he was part of the action, Nate could not change the outcome no matter what he did. The Dreams covered hundreds of years from what he could tell. The languages spoken varied dramatically. Somehow Nate understood what was being said even though he didn't understand the spoken words.

The Dreams sometimes were very short, like a matter of seconds, and other times they seemingly went on forever. If a Dream was too much to handle, he could bring himself out of it. He would simply force himself to wake up. Many times, Nate would cry out during the night, which would wake up everyone in his house. Nate's mother spoke with Birmingham's only Doctor, Dr. Robert Garrett, about Nate's difficulty with sleeping. She didn't know about the Dreams. Nate had not told her yet. Jane was the only one that knew about the Dreams. The Doctor asked what he was reading before he went to bed. She replied that Nate typically didn't read before bed. The Doctor's basic response was that he thought that Nate would grow out of it. He went on to say that there were Doctors in New York and Boston that could probably give her some answers. She responded, "We can't go to New York or Boston. I have my other children and a farm to tend to." He understood. He said he would ask his colleagues if anyone knew of anyone who practiced in this specialty closer than the East Coast.

The Dreams would come and go. A few times, Nate went a month or longer without any Dreams. Then they would return with a vengeance. Jane suggested that maybe Nate should write them down. She said, "You may have a better understanding of what this all means once you write the Dreams down." The problem was that he was not getting much quality sleep on the nights that he was having one of these Dreams. Nate was always tired. The last thing that he wanted to do was light up a lantern and write what was seemingly a short book. The other problem was that Nate shared a room with his two brothers. They were not thrilled about being woken up while Nate was writing. The only solution was to go sit in front of the fireplace and write. Sometimes when the weather was chilly, Nate would build a fire. This became a place of comfort for Nate. He would end up there more nights than not. Anyways, sitting in front of the fire sipping tea became his favorite pass-time. Often, Nate would take a few minutes to visit the horses. This helped Nate to collect his thoughts.

Nate continued to record his Dreams for the next two years. He began to notice patterns and repeat Dreams. Did these

Dreams mean more? Did any of this mean anything at all? He was constantly asking himself these types of questions.

The stack of papers detailing Nate's Dreams became very large. He was very protective of his recorded Dreams. He didn't want anyone to read them. One problem was that the Dreams were very random. There was no telling when one recurring Dream would happen. So he decided to organize the Dreams by subject matter and by best guess of chronological order. Some Dreams took place in Europe, at least he thought so, because of the languages spoken. Many were in Jerusalem. Other Dreams were definitely from Scotland. The Dreams were not as clear as the notes depicted. The Schoolhouse had many books that described the times and events surrounding his Dreams.

Without additional information, the notes would have been hard to follow. As Nate would read about a specific event in a history book, it was like he already knew what had happened. Somewhere deep in his mind, he already had the whole story. There were times when Nate realized that recorded history was different from what really happened. This made Nate question what he was learning in school. In the past, he would consider written history to be fact. His Dreams taught him that recorded history was only from the author's viewpoint. Even though he had his doubts about the accuracy of his school books, he would use some of the basic facts from the books to give the story the proper historical context. This gave his story much more credence. However, he continued to find differences between his notes and the recorded history. He found many instances where the story was either incomplete or completely wrong. It made him wonder how many stories from the ages were incorrect.

Nate knew that many of our laws and customs were based on history. How would our societies and nations be different if only a different person had recorded the events? Throughout history, Kings have decided which version was going to be recorded. One such occurrence was when Emperor Constantine gathered a group of religious scholars in what was known as the First

Council of Nicaea in 325 AD. These scholars reviewed all known writings and stories on the life and times of Jesus Christ. At the conclusion, they settled on what is referred to as the New Testament. Many other writings were not included. Looking deeper into the findings of the First Council of Nicaea, it was determined that the relationship of Jesus Christ to the Heavenly Father was divine. This was known as the Nicaean Creed. It has become the foundation of all Christianity.

Did the discarded stories offer a different viewpoint? Would our Christian beliefs be any different? It made Nate wonder. Supposedly Constantine was not even a Christian until his deathbed conversion by Baptism. He had lived much of his life as a Pagan. Although he was a non-believer, he played an influential role in the proclamation of the Edict of Milan in 313, which declared Christianity would no longer be a crime in the Roman Empire. Many believed that this was because an increasing number within his own family had converted to Christianity. How many true stories were left out of the New Testament because they did not fit Constantine's narrative? He, like many other Roman Emperors, had significant plans of expansion. It was much easier to get the commoners to comply if you were flying under the flag of a united version of Christianity when going through an expansion. How many beliefs that have been passed down through the ages were simply incorrect? How many non-truths were perpetuated through the lens of conquest?

Jane helped Nate organize the notes. She wanted them to read like a written novel. She thought it would help anyone who read the notes to understand what Nate was going through. When they finished placing the notes in chronological order, Jane was astonished at the story being told. After Jane read them from start to finish, she said, "No wonder you weren't able to sleep at night."

Jane was astonished to learn the depth of Nate's Dreams. They were so explicit in their detail. Some were a Dream within a Dream. Nate was experiencing these characters so vividly that he felt like he was that person that was in the Dream. Nate also spoke of how the characters had Dreams similar to the Dreams that he was having. How was this possible?

Many would read this story and claim that it was nothing more than a boy's imagination run amuck. Jane knew better. She also had a very dark and deep secret. Somehow Jane was also experiencing something supernatural. She waited for the right time to tell Nate her secret. Jane had been holding this secret for a long time. She had not even told her husband, Jonathon. Finally, after giving it careful thought, she told Nate, "You may find this equally crazy, but as I read these stories, I discovered that somewhere deep in my thoughts, I know that your Dreams are real. As unbelievable as it may be, I remember most of what you are saying. I think I may have also been there witnessing the Dreams with you. How could this be happening?"

Nate was shocked. He said, "You are also having these Dreams?"

Jane said, "Not exactly. My recollections are just thoughts or intuitions that come to me. I didn't realize this until I read your notes in the proper context. I felt as though I could have finished some of your sentences. My intuitions are much stronger in the Scottish Dreams than the Knights Templar Dreams for some reason." She continued, "I have someone that I would like to have read the notes. She has a special gift." She would say that this person had a different way of looking at things. Once she said that Nate knew who she was talking about. There was an older woman in town that many thought was a witch. She dressed oddly and had unique decorations in her yard. Her name was Felicia. Nate was not sure how this crazy old lady could help.

Anyways, the following two stories are a stunning recollection of Nate's Dreams. The first is a tale of a Knight who lived during the late 11th Century and early 12th Century. The second tale is about a Senior Aide to a Scottish Nobleman during the late 14th and early 15th Centuries.

The Knights Templar Dreams

CHAPTER 4

THE KNIGHTHOOD

THE FIRST SET of Dreams takes place somewhere near Paris, France, during a tumultuous time where wars were seemingly going on all over. This era was scarred by Kings and an over-bearing series of Popes from the Church in Rome that sought to control the entire planet.

The Dreams started with a scene where the main character, who is named Jacques Courtier, was having a terrible argument with presumably his parents. They were a middle-class family living on a small farm near Paris. They were devout Christians. The debate centered on Jacques joining the Seminary and moving to one of the many Monasteries located within a day's ride. He strongly disagreed. Jacques felt that he had a calling to be a Knight. He regularly had intuitions that sometimes came in the form of a Dream, and sometimes it was just a thought. Jacques never told anyone, but he felt that these Dreams were guiding him. These Dreams and intuitions told Jacques that he was destined to become a Knight.

Furthermore, he was guided by a spirit that would speak to him in his Dreams. She was more than a friend. He was as close to her as he was to anyone in his awake world. Many times, he hated waking up. He just wanted to be with her. Yet, he could not speak about this to anyone. No one would understand. She would say that fate was going to guide him through his decisions. She was almost saying that his life was already preordained. How could this be? Jacques seemingly could change the course of his life and not follow the path that fate had intended for him. Fortunately, Jacques followed her guidance at every turn.

Jacques would see a specific type of Knight in nearby towns that intrigued him every now and again. They looked very powerful and had an elegance about them. He knew in his heart that being one of these knights was his destiny. These Knights wore a white robe with a large red cross on it. They were called the Poor Fellow-Soldiers of Jesus Christ, or Knights of the Temple, more commonly referred to as Knights Templar. The Knights were highly respected throughout Europe and the Middle East. These men took vows of poverty, chastity, and obedience and were renowned for their fierceness and courage in battle. They were a combination of warriors and monks. Their mission was to protect Christians as they made their pilgrimage to the Holy Lands. It was said that two Knights could defend an entire road. Their skill sets were legendary. The order was founded after the battle for Jerusalem with the Muslims during the year 1099. Jacques's point to his parents was that, in many ways, he would live like a monk, but at the same time, he would be a Christian warrior. His spirit guide, as he referred to her, showed him a vision in one of his Dreams where he was a Senior Leader within the Knights Templar and was leading his forces into battle against the attacking Muslim Army. Jacques strongly felt that this was his calling. The secret that he could tell no one was that even though a Knight could not marry, he would still have this woman with him in his Dreams. Jacques was not sure if this broke one of the cardinal rules of the Templars, but he would make sure to never speak of this to anyone.

It had become abundantly clear through the ages that Christianity had many enemies. Supposedly, all of these religions were based on peace. It was hard to see this through the death and destruction that had been reported from all over the Middle East and Europe. Jacques often wondered how these supposed religious leaders would reconcile this with the Creator on their deathbed. The Roman Catholics believed that you could simply go to Confession and be forgiven of their sins. Somehow Jacques didn't think it was that simple.

Jacques followed his intuition and joined the Templars. He met with a Knight and told him that he would like to join the order. The Knight very sternly told Jacques, "This vocation is a lifetime commitment that requires that you pass a very stern set of tests." The Knight continued, "There is a very intense training program that results in several deaths every year. Many determine during the training that the Templar lifestyle is not for them. You can opt out before you make your final vows. Once you make your final vows, you are in for life."

The Templars had many professions within their ranks. They were trained in many vital professions such as Accounting, Construction, Education, Historian, Archeology, and of course, the art of being a Warrior.

Finally, Jacques met with his parents and told them of his decision to join the Templars. They were disappointed at first but respected Jacques' decision. He immediately began the training. The first stage was completely physical. He was in pretty good shape, so he prospered during this phase of the training. Jacques befriended one of the other trainees during the physical stage. He was trying to become a Banker. It seems that the Templars had founded the modern banking system. One of the underlying facts is that Templars were incredibly wealthy. The banking system was based on a credit system backed up by gold. After it was determined that it was not safe to travel with vast amounts of gold. The Templars created a solution. The problem for travelers and pilgrims who wished to visit the Holy Land was that legions of robbers and outlaws thought nothing of killing you and stealing your gold. The credit system was based on notes issued by the Templars to travelers while their gold stayed on deposit with the Templars. When they made it to their destination, there would be a Templar building where the traveler would trade their credit certificate for gold. The Templars would charge a very expensive fee for this service, but, as they reminded their customers, they had arrived at their destination safely with their fortune still intact. This was one of the ways that the Templars built their empire. It became apparent that the non-warrior assignments were some of the most coveted. The Leaders of the Templars always possessed multiple skill sets. They were first trained as warriors but could become architects or bankers if they chose that profession.

There was an unbreakable set of stipulations, known as the Latin Rule. The Latin Rule had to become your guiding force going forward. It required the Knight to be Chivalrous above all else. Jacques had previously thought that the concept of Chivalry referred to a medieval sense of romance and gallantry. But he soon learned that Chivalry referred to military conduct, martial arts discipline, conduct as a warrior, and religious piety.

The physical training was very intense. It involved pushing the body to limits you didn't think were possible. The training involved many forms of hand-to-hand combat. Jacques learned how to use leverage and make an opponent's greater size a liability for them. His life of working on his parent's farm had prepared him for this physical challenge. In battles, Jacques could handle most of the other trainees with ease. He was smaller than most of the other men. He used his size and quickness to his advantage. The next aspect of training involved riding horses. Jacques had been riding since he was a young boy. His parents always had at least four horses. He was a natural with them. He had heard it said that any boy who doesn't know how to ride a horse by age 12 was only fit to be a Priest.

The next physical training involved jousting. Jacques had never jousted before. Unfortunately, this is where most of the injuries occurred. During the previous year, a trainee died while jousting. No matter how much training and preparation a trainee had done, there is no feeling like that of a horse traveling at you full speed with a lance aimed right at your midsection. One wrong move, and you will be dead. The idea is to break your opponent's lance or shield or completely knock them off their horse. Jacques never thought that this event had practical value. However, it did accomplish to tell the trainers exactly who is both willing and brave enough to stay engaged. Many would back off or steer the horse away from the contest. The ones who stayed engaged were the true warriors.

After Jacques completed the physical training, he was awarded the best in class award. The next training involved academic evaluations. The religious training involved the teachings of Jesus Christ. Jacques had to know not only the four Gospels but were regularly queried about the Letters written by St. Peter, St. Paul, as well as the communications that had taken place in the years following the Resurrection of Jesus Christ. One little-known fact of the Templars is that they had to have the ability to convert non-believers when encountered. They were the warriors for Jesus Christ and had to understand the Lord's message clearly.

At this point, most of the trainees decided on their life's path. Jacques chose to be a warrior. The decision was simple. His spirit guide had shown him the vision of himself in battle. Jacques was not meant to be a Banker or a historian. He was destined to be a warrior. He had no less respect for his friends who went down more academic avenues. Everyone seems to have their own destiny. The Trainees, at this point, took the vows of poverty, chastity, and obedience. Several decided that the life of a Templar was not for them. This was the only point at which you could leave the Templars. After this point, any breaking of your vows would result in serious penalties, including death. After the vows were taken, the Squires, as they were called, were separated into their various professions. The Squires were still considered to be in training for another two years. The title of Squire was a fancy name for someone who was basically a servant to the tenured Knights. This included everything from serving them their food to tending to their horses. A Squire was thought to be nothing more than a packhorse by some. The title of Knight of the Temple was earned. This part of the training was the toughest because it was mental. Couple this with the fact that you had already committed to your vows. The only exit was to start over in another Templar profession or death. To start over was a drastic choice. You would be already marked as a failure.

Jacques had one advantage over the other trainees because his spirit has an extraordinary mission. He was the guardian of an ancient secret. His spirit guide had shown him how becoming a Knight would draw him very close to this secret in his Dreams. She often referred to him as a Guardian of the Secret of Eden.

CHAPTER 5

EDUARD

DURING THE GRUELING dog days of training, Jacques had become close friends with a fellow trainee named Eduard. It was like they knew each other somehow. The two often tried to figure out how they knew each other. It didn't make sense. Jacques was from the area near Paris, and Eduard was from the ancient city of Marseilles, a port city on the Mediterranean Sea. Neither had traveled far from home before joining the Templars. It was nearly impossible for them to have known each other. Jacques always thought back to his Dream, where his guide told him that others share the same destiny. Was it possible that he and Eduard were somehow connected? The sad part was that he and Eduard would part ways once their training was finished.

Eduard was a fierce competitor, but his passion was history. Eduard often said, "You always can be a Warrior. By being a Historian, you will get to see faraway places and study other cultures." He was trying to convince Jacques to continue their journey together. Jacques also loved history. He knew that something deep within him understood history more than most. Somehow he felt that he lived through the events that the Templar Masters were teaching him. Eduard felt the same way.

After one of their lengthy discussions about their common thoughts, Jacques and Eduard both returned their focus on the task at hand. That was the task of preparing for their futures. Jacques always reminded Eduard, "Becoming a Warrior means living in vast faraway places spreading the word of Jesus Christ and protecting his servants. Going to faraway lands was not just for Historians." Eduard wanted to become a Historian so that he could understand the societies that existed in the time of Christ. Even though the two young men were seemingly headed in different directions, they both knew somehow that their paths would cross again.

Jacques understood that there were no coincidences in his life. Everything had a purpose and was driven by fate. He knew that this somehow included Eduard. Jacques knew that the truth would come out at some point in the future. He and Eduard were somehow connected.

CHAPTER 6

LIFE OF A SQUIRE

THE LIFE OF a Squire usually lasted two to five years and required an act of valor to move up to the status of full Knight. When at a Templar Facility, Squires were assigned to a Knight and, in some cases, two Knights. This meant that they would serve the Knights every need. They would launder their clothes, serve their food, and empty their chamber pots daily. While on a mission or a patrol, the Squire carried the Knights weapons and supplies. The Squire was only allowed to take a small bag for his belongings. The Squire was also responsible for the Knight's horse. The horse was to be saddled and ready for battle at a moment's notice. Once in battle, the Squire was responsible for taking the Knight's horse to the rear of the fight. The horses were considered a valuable asset and had to be kept out of harm's way. The Squire was also responsible for setting up the Knight's tent.

If a Squire had performed admirably during the battle on a particular day, he was given the honor of carving the meat at that evening's supper. As a Squire's stature had begun to rise, he was invited to partake in the battle. This is where Jacques shined. Many of the Knights took notice of his exceptional horse skills. The Knights didn't understand that he had an advantage over the other Squires. He had a spirit guide to steer him in the proper direction. He seemingly knew exactly what to do at every turn.

After about six months of being a Squire, the opportunity to shine presented itself to Jacques. The Knights had been traveling with the faithful on their pilgrimage from Paris to Jerusalem. Only the wealthy could take the sea route by boarding a ship at the port of Marseilles. Most Pilgrims could only afford the long and arduous route of traveling on foot through Europe and Western Asia. This route was full of thieves and Muslim Armies.

There was one late afternoon in particular where all seemed calm. For most people, a quiet afternoon would be a welcome event. For a Templar Squire, all could change in an instant. They learned in their training that if you were standing guard, you needed to expect anything. This was very nerve-wracking. At times the slightest noise could be misconstrued as an attack.

As the Knights were in their tents preparing for supper. The Squires were taking turns standing guard. When it was Jacques's turn, he began walking back and forth, looking for anything that moved or made any unusual sounds. He took this assignment very seriously. One wrong move and his career as a Knights Templar Warrior would come to an end. Jacques's advantage as a Warrior was that he had a secret spirit guide. Jacques understood that he needed to trust his intuitions. He knew that they were coming from his special friend. She was never wrong.

On this particular day, the intuition started with the hair on the back of his neck standing up. Next, it was almost like someone whispered in his ear, "Turn your head." He saw an attacker heading right for him when he turned his head. Jacques reacted very quickly and got into a defensive position. The attacker lunged forward with his sword, but Jacques managed to get out of the way. The attacker missed wildly. As the attacker went by,

Jacques swung his sword at the attacker's back. He managed to make contact and cut through the fabric of the cloak that the attacker was wearing. As the attacker regrouped for another attack, Jacques pivoted very quickly and caught the man off guard, and was able to thrust his sword through his mid-section. This all seemed like it was in slow motion. Jacques was relieved that he fended off the attacker. Unfortunately, his relief was short-lived. Just then, he noticed that the camp was under attack. The attackers were too numerous to count. The Knights were out-numbered. They were Muslims Warriors. Many of the Knights had battled the Muslims numerous times. They knew their tactics. Jacques was able to sound the attack horn while he was retreating to our compound. The Knights were streaming out of their tents with swords ready to engage. The attackers had no idea how well trained the Templars were. There was no time to mount the horses. The Knights slashed their way through the enemy's first line. All of the Squires had a judgment call to make. They were not supposed to engage the enemy unless ordered. Jacques could see that the Knights would take severe casualties if he didn't act. Many people had described Jacques as a natural-born leader. He screamed as loud as possible for the Squires to draw their swords and join the battle.

One of the Muslims was lying near Jacques. He was dying. He looked up at Jacques and, with his last dying breath, said, "Protect the Secret of Eden." He said this in French, which startled Jacques. Was this delirious talk on his deathbed, or was there a deeper meaning here? Jacques would have to think about this later. There were more pressing matters to attend to. Jacques grabbed the dying man's sword with his left hand and ran towards the battle. Jacques relied on his training and began taking out multiple Muslims. Just then, he saw the Templar Commander being surrounded by four Muslims. Jacques quickly attacked and took out two of them. The Commander made quick work of the other two. Jacques made eye contact with his Commander, who gave Jacques a nod that not meant "Thank you and Job well done." The battle ensued for some time. The numbers were now even. The remaining Muslims were no match for the combined forces of Knights and Squires. The battle was nearly at an end when several Muslims were retreating. Jacques went to get a horse to give chase to the attackers. The Commander ordered him to stand down. The Commander explained, "It Is more important for them to take the message back to their leaders that we were a fierce enemy and that they were no match for us."

Soon thereafter, the Squires began to clear the battlefield. One Knight and three Squires had been killed in the battle. The enemy had lost seventy-four. The Commander called everyone to the clearing at the center of the Camp. He began by leading us in prayer for the loss of our brave comrades. The Commander then said, "You all performed admirably. Although, the Squires took it upon themselves to join the battle even though they were ordered to stand down. Who ordered the Squires to join the battle?"

Jacques stepped forward and said, "I did, Sir."

The Commander went on to say, "You had a very busy night. I am thankful that you saved my life, but we have orders for a reason." He continued, "Under what authority did you order the Squires to take up Arms."

Jacques replied, "Sir, I had to make a split-second decision. I felt that if the Squires didn't join the battle, we would have taken many more casualties."

The Commander said, "You have disobeyed one of our rules of Engagement."

Jacques said, "I am very sorry, and I take sole responsibility for the actions of myself and the other Squires. But, unfortunately, my decision was made in the fog of war. The other Squires probably were unaware of who gave the order."

The Commander glared at Jacques and said, "I will deal with you later." The Commander then dismissed all of the Knights and Squires.

Jacques had returned to his tent after the Knights prepared the deceased for burial. The Muslims were given a proper

Christian burial. The Fallen Knight and Squires were wrapped in linens, and a team would depart in the morning for the journey back to France for a proper Templar Burial. Jacques thought to himself, "I had disobeyed a primary order. The good news is that I am still alive."

Jacques thought about his punishment. He would probably be transferred back to France to face a prison term, and then upon release, he would find another role to fill within the Templar community. What Jacques feared most was how his parents would react when they heard that their son was in prison. Then, all of a sudden, the monastery wasn't sounding so bad.

Several hours had gone by, the second in command of the Camp appeared at the entrance to Jacques' tent. He said, "The Commander wants to see you at once." Well, here it comes. Jacques's desire to be a Templar Warrior was coming to an end. Jacques thought about his response on his way to the Commander's tent. The best plan was the simple truth. Jacques thought, "I reacted, and we were able to fend off the attack. I would do it that same way again."

When Jacques arrived, he was ordered to take a seat. The Commander was not there. He waited for an eternity that was probably only thirty minutes. Finally, the Commander arrived. He asked Jacques to give him the rundown of what happened. From beginning to end. Jacques told him the entire truth except for the Secret of Eden comment from the dying Muslim. He still didn't have any idea what the Muslim meant. "How was a Muslim who probably had been in the Middle East his entire life speaking French?" Jacques thought.

Jacques continued to discuss the battle without mentioning saving his Commander's life. The Commander finally brought it up. He said, "While I appreciate your timely entry into the melee, I need to remind you that our orders are bigger than any one of us." Jacques sat there quietly while the Commander wrote a letter. After finishing the letter, he said, "I am ordering you back to France. I want you to accompany the bodies of our fallen heroes. You may read the letter if you wish. The team is heading back to France at sunrise. You are dismissed."

After returning to his tent, Jacques sat paralyzed while thinking about the day's events. He left when the supper bell rang. The battle caused the Templars to eat their supper much later than usual. Even though Jacques was physically and emotionally spent from the battle, he still had to serve the Knights their supper. Several Knights knew what had happened and told him to sit down. One of the Knights said, "You don't need to serve anyone on this night." They knew that rules were broken, but lives were saved. After supper, Jacques quietly returned to his tent to begin packing for the long journey.

He sat down and thought about reading the letter. The Commander said that he could read it if he wanted to. He figured that he should probably read the letter so he would know how to defend himself against the charges. He opened the letter and began to read. The Commander wrote, "Today we came under attack from a group of Muslims. The battle was fierce, but the Templars prevailed. About halfway through the melee, several of the Squires joined the fight. The Squires performed admirably. I am very proud of our Knights and our Squires. They performed just how we trained them. Unfortunately, we lost one Knight and three Squires. They each died a hero's death. I hope that God Almighty will accept our fallen into the Kingdom of Heaven. In conclusion, I would like to recommend the Squire, Jacques Courtier, for full Knighthood. His bravery and fast decision-making is exactly what the Knights need."

Jacques couldn't believe what he was reading. The Commander was recommending him for full Knighthood.

Jacques traveled back to France. It was a long and arduous journey. When he arrived at the Templar Headquarters, they were ready to have the Funerals to honor the heroes.   Even though Jacques was back in his home country, he was still dumbfounded regarding what the Muslim had said about Protecting the Secret of Eden.

CHAPTER 7

CLARITY

ABOUT A MONTH or so after Jacques arrived in Paris, he was fully Knighted. The Founder and Grand Master of the Templars, Hugues de Payens, presided over the ceremony. Jacques's parents were able to attend. They were finally on board with his decision to join the Knights. It was a glorious day for the three other Squires that were granted this title. As fortune would have it, Jacques' friend from his training days, Eduard, was one of them.

The two young Knights spent much time together as they awaited their new assignments. Even though Jacques was classified as a Warrior, he still had a significant interest in history. They would spend hours discussing the birth of humanity. For some reason, both men were drawn to this story. As a historian, Eduard had access to many of the manuscripts that told the ancient stories. Many of these stories were not included in the Holy Bible for some reason. The men had to speak of the Book of Enoch in private. It seems that the book possessed knowledge that the Church wanted to remain hidden. In fact, all known writings of Enoch were held under lock and key by the Church. The fact that Eduard was a historian granted him access to review the ancient scrolls.

One evening after prayers, the two men sat at a table near the stables where no one could hear them. It was their last night together before Eduard departed for his new assignment in Giza, Egypt. Eduard said, "Before I head to Egypt, I must tell you something that I have learned. What I am about to tell you must stay hidden. I am forbidden to speak of it to anyone outside of the Templars. I don't believe that forbids me from speaking of this to another Knight, though. Having said that, I still think it would be wise to keep this information to yourself." Jacques agreed.

He continued, "I had the opportunity to read a translation of the Book of Enoch. The original was written in an ancient Hebrew dialect, but as fortune would have it, one of the Jewish Scholars working in Jerusalem also spoke French. He kindly translated Enoch's book for us. It told of a supernatural tale of a group of God-like creatures that Enoch called the Watchers. Enoch claimed that the Almighty sent these Watchers. Their task was to watch humanity and determine if they were living by the rules that God had handed down. Enoch even claimed that he was taken to a place that was not of this earth to speak with the Watchers. He was warned that mankind was on the wrong path. The Watchers said that a great cataclysm would befall on the humans that would wipe out all of humanity except for a few righteous people. They also wish to save the animals that roamed the earth."

Jacques said, "This sounds like the lead-up to the story of Noah."

Eduard said, "Yes. You are correct. This story sparked great interest within me. I needed to know more. I spent much of my spare time with the old Jewish Scribes. After a while, they took me in their confidence. They told me of a legend that had passed down since the time of Adam and Eve. Being a historian, naturally, I wanted evidence of such a story. The problem was that very few people could read or write in ancient times. Most recorded stories had been handed down from generation to generation as folklore. I was very disappointed because I felt drawn to this story for some reason. One day as I was leaving Jerusalem for my trip back to Paris, one of the old Jewish Scribes came up to me and said, "I have not been candid with you. I have a gift that allows me to see into the souls of others. I prayed on it, and then I decided to share a great secret with you because you are one of the Worthy. You are one of the Children of the Flood."

Eduard said, "Worthy? What exactly am I worthy of? I am just a Squire that is hoping someday to be a Knight. Also, I was born and raised in a small fishing village which never had any flood that I can recall."

Next, he said something that shocked Jacques to his core. Eduard recalled what the scribe had said, "The flood that I refer to is the Great Flood. You are a descendant of Noah. You have been chosen to be a Guardian of a Great Secret." He handed me a scroll. I looked at it and instantly recognized that it was written in Cuneiform."

Jacques said, "Cuneiform?"

Eduard responded, "Yes, Cuneiform is one of the oldest written languages. It was believed to be written by the Sumerians several thousands of years ago." He continued, "The Scribe said, "Please take this scroll. Its message will lead you to a great treasure that accompanies the great secret.""

Jacques said, "Isn't the treasure itself the great secret?"

Eduard said, "I will get to that, but first, I must tell you that after we left Jerusalem, we briefly stopped at Giza to review some artifacts that had been discovered by our brother Knights, who specialize in Archeology." He continued, "I asked one of the Archeologists if there was anyone who could translate Cuneiform. Several days later, he introduced me to an older Egyptian man named Maat. Maat looked at the text and said, "This describes an ancient legend that contains guidelines from the Creator on how mankind must conduct himself. The Watchers are the ones who will be watching. If the Creator's wishes are followed, then a secret will be revealed that will answer all of the questions about the Creator and his universe."

Jacques said, "This is quite a discovery that you have uncovered."

Eduard said, "The problem is that this is all we have. I don't know where even to start looking for this secret. All I have is a name. Maat referred to it as The Secret of Eden."

Jacques nearly fainted. He quickly thought back to the dying Muslim who told him to protect the Secret of Eden. He decided to wait to tell Eduard about this encounter. First, he needed to get some answers. Jacques knew that answers would be tough to come by. Then it struck him like a lightning bolt. He would turn to his spirit guide.

CHAPTER 8

THE SPIRIT GUIDE

ommunicating with one's spirit guide was not as clear-cut and achievable as you might think. Jacques would often try to sleep in his spare time just to be with her. Many times, he would wake up and not remember anything except her. Even when the spirit guide came to him lately, it was for lighthearted moments. The subject of saving the world from a cataclysm was not part of these Dreams. Even though he was frustrated because he needed answers about the Secret of Eden, he was happy because his Dreams showed happy times with his spirit guide. Each Dream showed him and the spirit guide as a married couple during a different time period. In each Dream, she was beautiful but different. In one instance, they were in the time of Abraham. Another Dream would have them being together during the Exodus. In other Dreams, he was a Celtic Chieftain, and she was his wife. In each carnation, she looked different, but Jacques knew it was her. He could sense her soul, and she could sense his. These two souls had an attraction that defied explanation. In some Dreams, they had grown up together as children. In other Dreams, they would meet by happenstance. Seemingly, if their life had taken a slight turn, they never would have met. Somehow, the chance meeting always happened. Sometimes they had children. Other times they did not. In one lifetime, which was in Constantine's reign, they had a son. There was a familiarity about him. In other lifetimes this same soul appeared as a friend or a brother. The spirit guide and this person were present in all of Jacques's Dreams. What is the significance? What lay ahead for Jacques? He pondered this question daily. Unfortunately, he was no closer to getting any answers regarding the Secret of Eden.

This went on for six months or so. Finally, Jacques got to the point where he was no longer worried about the Secret. He was solely focused on being with her. This all changed one morning. Jacques sat quietly, eating his breakfast. He began thinking about the Dreams. What was his spirit guide trying to tell him? Was there something that Jacques needed to know about her? Or was it something else? Why did the other person keep showing up in the Dreams? Was it relevant? There was a familiarity about him. He looked different in every lifetime, but the soul was the same each time. Then it hit him. The familiar feeling was not from the Dreams. It was from the present. The man was Eduard. This brought a smile to Jacques' face. Once again, their meeting was by chance. They happened to be in the same cadet class. They were immediately drawn to each other. It seems that Jacques, Eduard, and the spirit guide were intertwined in an eternal story.

Now that Jacques understood that he and Eduard were connected. His attention returned to the Secret of Eden. He needed a breakthrough. He needed hard evidence that he could turn over to the Templar Leadership. Jacques knew that this Secret could not fall into the wrong hands. One thing about the Dreams that he tried not to dwell on was that there was always an adversary. There was a tragedy that often ended with the death of one of them, and in other Dreams, all three were killed. The good news was that they would all reappear in another life.

CHAPTER 9

THE ASSIGNMENT

IT HAD BEEN a year since Jacques arrived back in Paris. The Templars were still in their infancy as far as the organization went. Hugues de Payens had only founded the Knighthood twenty years ago. Their rapid growth came from the credit system they had developed as they helped travelers protect their gold and silver. They charged substantial fees for this service. No one seemed to mind. Even the wealthy Europeans traveling by sea to the Holy Lands used the Templar credit system. This growth gathered the attention of the various Kings and the Pope.

Even though Jacques was classified as a Warrior within the Templar organization, his leadership capabilities were evident to all. He quickly rose through the ranks of those stationed at the Paris Headquarters of the Templars. This included Hugues de Payens. Even though it had only been one year, Jacques was considered part of the Grand Master's inner circle. As a result, he was included in many Templar growth and strategy discussions. One such discussion was that of Jerusalem. The Holy City had only recently been liberated from the Muslims in what many called the first Crusade. The Templars had captured Jerusalem in a fierce battle. However, peace was short-lived because the Muslims were constantly engaging in counter-insurgency attacks. The Templars could fend off the attacks for now, but the threat was growing. As a result, the Templars had to deploy a more significant force to the Holy Lands.

One day Jacques was invited to a private supper with the Grand Master. Jacques was honored by the invitation. He was the youngest Knight within the inner circle. The meeting started with small talk about events happening with the Templars in Paris such as Cadet training and French politics. The Grand Master finally addressed the reason for this meeting. He said, "I wanted to meet with you to discuss the situation in Jerusalem."

Jacques said, "As you wish. I only know what I have discerned from your council meetings."

The Grand Master replied, "There is much you don't know. One of our secret motives for securing Jerusalem is that we have evidence that many of the artifacts surrounding the death of Christ are still hidden near or underneath the Temple of Solomon. Our historians and archaeologists have discovered documents that describe the wine goblet in which Jesus celebrated the last supper with his disciples, as well as the burial cloth, crown of thorns, and cross of Jesus Christ may be hidden under the Temple. We believe that there are other artifacts from the Old Testament located there as well. This includes the Golden Menorah from the Exodus and maybe even the Ark of the Covenant. We fear that the Muslims may soon learn of these artifacts and will once again focus their war efforts on the Al Aqsa Mosque, as they refer to it."

Jacques said, "Sir, excuse me for being so bold, but I believe the best course of action is for us to mount a secret campaign under the Temple to retrieve these sacred artifacts and move them to a more secure area where we can more easily protect them."

The Grand Master said, "That is why I summoned you to this

meeting. You have stood out as a great strategist in your short time here in Paris. I would like you to lead this operation."

Jacques said, "Thank you, sir, for this great opportunity. I will do my absolute best to secure these treasures."

The Grand Master said, "We must keep this operation a secret. Everyone will understand why the Templars will have a significant presence in Jerusalem, but they will not know about our clandestine mission. This includes the Pope. Once we make the discoveries, we will notify him, of course, but if we notify him now, he will insist that his guards conduct the mission. Therefore, I have far more confidence in our Knights being successful."

Jacques said, "I fully understand. However, I do believe that we must include our top archeologists and historians in this endeavor."

The Grand Master said, "Yes. I am planning a meeting for next month where we will develop the plans. This will give the Knights that are stationed elsewhere time to travel back to Paris. At this meeting, I would like you to layout your plan."

Jacques said, "I have one request. There is a historian Knight by the name of Eduard La Fonte that I would like to have as part of this mission. I know him well. I believe that he will add much to this team."

The Grand Master said, "As you wish."

The next day, messages went out to the leading archeologists and historians, including Eduard that they were ordered to travel back to Paris at the request of Hugues de Payens.

CHAPTER 10

THE PLAN

THE MONTH HAD passed very quickly. Jacques had spent most of his time putting his team in place for this most sacred mission. He tried to communicate with his spirit guide but was seemingly unsuccessful. In fact, many of his Dreams were more like nightmares. They depicted battles with his adversary. Most involved his own death, as well as his adversary's death. These were dark days for Jacques. Was this some type of warning? He was able to deduce that he was tasked with guarding a secret in all of the Dreams, whereas his adversary seemed to have different motives in each setting. For instance, in one Dream, the adversary fought for land that his tribe had lost. In another, he was a ruthless Egyptian guard who persecuted Jacques's spirit simply because of his faith. From the adversary's perspective, there was no connection between each Dream. Whereas Jacques's character was always protecting the same secret.

The team that the Grand Master had summoned began to arrive in Paris. One by one, they came to greet the Grand Master.

He told each of them that they were being reassigned to a special project that was to be led by Jacques Courtier. Some were shocked that such a young Knight was placed in charge of a mission that required the best minds in the order. This was a topic of whispering throughout the headquarters.

Jacques was seated at the table in the makeshift office that he had created adjacent to the armory when the door opened, and Eduard walked in. The two men very warmly greeted each other. Eduard said, "Congratulations on your new assignment. I will very proudly be a member of your team."

Jacques said, "Thank you, dear friend. I cannot speak of it yet, but we have a monumental task at hand."

Eduard said, "Then we will not speak of it yet, but I can't help wonder if there is a divine presence that keeps bringing us together."

Jacques said, "Who exactly have I offended in the heavens to keep getting stuck with you." Both men shared a hardy laugh. Jacques continued, "Actually, I insisted with the Grand Master to include you on the mission. Many think that both of us are too young for this mission, but I'm not sure how much age plays into this endeavor."

Eduard said, "Well, thank you for your kind recommendation. I will not let you down."

Jacques said, "You never have." Jacques didn't mean to say this, although he was thinking it. This was a comment that could have taken the two Knights down the road that led to the Dreams, but Jacques had decided to stay away from this discussion for now. Jacques quickly changed the subject. He said, "I believe your caravan is the last to arrive. The Grand Master has requested that we dine together after evening prayers."

Eduard said, "Until then, I will get myself settled. I have been assigned a Squire. I haven't had a Squire assigned to me since I was Knighted. Although a Squire may have slowed me down at Giza."

Jacques said, "I feel the same way, but I have found that having

a Squire has allowed me to worry about the larger tasks at hand."
As a result, the two men parted ways for the time being.

Later that evening, the summoned Knights gathered in the Dining Room adjacent to the Grand Master's office. The Grand Master greeted them and said, "Tonight is for celebration. After tonight, you all will be asked to join a very sacred but dangerous mission. We will not speak of this mission tonight. Tomorrow, after morning prayers, we will meet at the Church of Saint-Germain-des-Près. We are meeting at St. Germaine's because I feel we can meet in complete secrecy there. What you will hear then must be kept secret from everyone, including Brother Knights, Priests, Monks, and any laymen you may contact. Tonight, I would like to hear an update from every one of you about your current mission."

Everyone looked stunned. The Knights Templar in itself was a secret society. What could be so special that only this select group of Knights were worthy of the Grand Master's trust? The Knights that sat at this table were mainly Historians, Archeologists, and a few Builders. The easy conclusion was that the Knights had found something extraordinary.

After supper was completed and each Knight had given their update to the Grand Master, the Knights all took a few minutes to speak with each other. Many were old friends and hadn't seen each other in a great while. Eduard called Jacques over to meet someone. Eduard said, "Jacques Courtier, I would like you to meet Michael la Pierre. Michael is the Archeologist I have been working closely with at Giza."

Jacques said, "The Grand Master speaks very highly of you. Congratulations for being selected for this mission."

Michael said, "Thank you very much. I am like a young boy filled with excitement over what this secret entails."

Jacques said, "Then you will not be displeased."

Eduard said, "Jacques, if you recall our last discussion regarding the Eden scrolls, Michael is the one who found them. He has much to add to our discussion."

Jacques smiled and said, "You have great timing, but I must ask that you must save this conversation for tomorrow. It may be relevant to our discussions at the Church of Saint-Germain-des-Près." Both men smiled and quickly changed the subject.

— 45 —

CHAPTER 11

CHURCH OF
SAINT-GERMAIN-DES-PRÈS

THE CHURCH OF Saint-Germain-des-Près was known as the Abbey to the local Parisians. It was built in 540 AD and was subsequently named after Sainte Germanus, which was later changed to Germaine. It has been destroyed and rebuilt several times since its inception. The Vikings had ransacked the Abbey and attempted to burn it down during the 9th century. As a result, it was seemingly always in a state of rebuilding. The Grand Master had selected the Abbey for the secret meeting today because it was closed to worshipers while it was being rebuilt. Also, the catacombs that line the caverns under the Abbey would be a perfect place for a secret meeting. The Grand Master had posted Knights at each of its doors and gave them strict instructions not to let anyone pass that wasn't on the pre-approved list.

Jacques, Eduard, and Michael entered through the rear of the Abbey. They marveled at the artwork and tapestry that adorned the Abbey. Michael said, "Numerous Saints have walked these same floors that we now walk."

Jacques said, "Yes. I was raised hearing the stories of how Saint Germaine gave the Abbey's excesses to the oppressed. At the time, he was just a monk. His fellow monks became very angry with Germaine. They claimed that the Abbey would give away its total wealth if Germaine was allowed to continue. While the monks were not necessarily happy, The King of France, Childebert I, was very impressed. Germaine was later named the Bishop of Paris. King Childebert I was a Frankish King of the Merovingian dynasty. The legend of the Merovingians is that they were said to be descendants of Mary Magdalene. Some even made the heretical statement that Mary had been married to Jesus and that they produced a daughter named Sarah who started the Merovingian bloodline." Jacques continued, "Who knows if any of this is true. One thing for certain is that none of us should ever mention that story in the presence of a Priest. You may find yourself being burned at the stake."

Eduard joked, "What story?" All three men laughed.

The three joined the other Knights in the cavern that was directly below the altar. The relics of St. Germaine were in a nearby catacomb.

The Grand Master greeted everyone by saying, "Welcome Knights to this meeting. I will get right to the point. We believe that we have learned of the approximate whereabouts of the wine goblet in which Jesus celebrated the last supper with his disciples, as well as Jesus's burial cloth, the crown of thorns, and his cross. We believe that there are other artifacts from the Old Testament in this same location. This includes the Golden Menorah from the Exodus and maybe even the Ark of the Covenant. Our historians and archeologists have discovered documents that describe their locations. We believe that these items are hidden beneath the Temple of Solomon in Jerusalem. You are here because you are assigned to the search team. This mission must be held in utmost secrecy. We are not to discuss this with fellow Knights, Priests, Monks, or anyone else for that matter. If we make a discovery, I will notify the Pope myself. Our cover story is that we will be in Jerusalem in strength to fend off any Muslim attacks. Our goal is to locate these items and move them to a more secure location. The Muslims will attempt to retake Jerusalem sooner rather than later. You are ordered to travel to Jerusalem with a legion of our Warriors in the upcoming days. Jacques Courtier is in charge of this mission, and he will report directly to me. I know you will have many questions, but please hold off until you arrive at the Temple and are in a secure location. Knights, you have been chosen for a most sacred duty. It is your time to shine for Jesus Christ."

The meeting was over as quickly as it started. The Knights dispersed. Jacques had asked Eduard and Michael to stay for a few minutes. He then asked the Grand Master for a few minutes of his time.

The three joined the Grand Master at the table that was set up in the cavern. Jacques said, "Eduard has uncovered something very interesting that may pertain to Solomon's Temple. Eduard please elaborate."

Eduard said, "While on my assignment in Jerusalem, I was befriended by a group of Jewish Scholars who accepted me because they could see I was only interested in history and not involved in anything political. They allowed me to read a translation of the Book of Enoch. The original was written in ancient Hebrew, so they translated it. As luck would have it, one of them spoke French. It told of a supernatural tale of a group of God-like creatures that Enoch called the Watchers. Enoch claimed that these Watchers were sent by the Almighty. Their task was to watch mankind and determine if they were living by the rules that had been handed down by the Almighty. Enoch even claimed that he was taken to a place not of this earth to speak with the Watchers. He was warned that mankind was on the wrong path. The Watchers said that a great cataclysm would befall the humans that would wipe out all of humanity except for a few righteous people. They also wished to save the animals that roamed the earth. Obviously, Enoch was speaking of the Noah Story."

Eduard continued, "This story sparked a great interest within me. I needed to know more. So I spent much of my spare time with the Jewish Scribes. After a while, they took me in their confidence. They told me of a legend that had passed down since the time of Adam and Eve. Being a historian, naturally, I wanted evidence of such a story. The problem was that very few people could read or write in ancient times. Most recorded stories had been handed down from generation to generation as folklore. One day, as I was leaving Jerusalem for my trip back to Paris, one of the older Jewish Scribes came up to me and said, "I have not been totally honest with you. I have a gift that allows me to see into the souls of others. I prayed on it, and then I decided to share a great secret with you because you are one of the Worthy. I said, Worthy? What exactly am I worthy of? I am just a Squire that is hoping someday to be a Knight. He handed me a scroll. I looked at it and instantly recognized that it was written in Cuneiform."

The Grand Master said, "Cuneiform. Is that Sumerian?"

Eduard responded, "Yes, Cuneiform is one of the oldest written languages. It was believed to be written by the Sumerians several thousands of years ago. The Scribe then said, "Please take this scroll. Its message will lead you to a great treasure that accompanies the great secret."

The Grand Master said, "You have this cuneiform scroll with you?"

Eduard said, "Yes." He then handed the Grand Master the ancient scroll. He unrolled it to discover a series of lines that meant nothing to him.

Eduard continued, "On my way back to Paris, I briefly stopped at Giza to review some artifacts that had been discovered by my brother Knight here, Michael, who specializes in Archeology." He continued, "I asked him if there was anyone who could translate Cuneiform in Giza. Several days later, Michael introduced me to an older Egyptian man named Maat. Maat looked at the text and said, "This describes an ancient legend that contains guidelines from the Creator on how humanity must conduct himself. The Watchers are the ones who will be watching mankind. If the Creator's wishes are followed, then a secret will be revealed that will answer all of the questions about the Creator and his universe."

Eduard gave the Grand Master a minute to digest what he had just been told. He then said, "I will let Michael tell the rest."

Michael said, "I had heard of the term Watchers somewhere before. I couldn't quite place it. Then I remembered. We had found some carvings near one of the Egyptian tombs that spoke of the Watchers. The message was written in hieroglyphics. I had this message translated. It said, "The message of the Watchers is near Abraham's keyhole."

Eduard said, "We believe that Abraham's Keyhole refers to a hole that has been carved into the Foundation Stone."

The Grand Master said, "Is this the stone on which Abraham was about to sacrifice his son Isaac?"

Michael said, "Yes. The Foundation Stone is within the area where we believe Solomon's Temple once existed."

Jacques noticed that Eduard had omitted the part about being one of the Children of the Flood. This was a secret that only Jacques and Eduard would know about.

CHAPTER 12

THE SECRETS OF SOLOMON'S TEMPLE

T HE GRAND MASTER had sat and listened to Jacques, Michael, and Eduard tell what they had learned about what they called the Secret of Eden. He finally said, "This is a fantastic story. We must dig deeper. Any story that claims to know the secrets of the Universe is worth our time. Let me think about this for a few hours. Please report to my study after supper this evening. We will discuss this further."

As Jacques returned to his office near the armory, he thought to himself, "I believe that I am somehow connected to this story. The answers probably lie in my Dreams." He longed to see his spirit guide so he could gain some clarity on this issue.

✠

After supper, Jacques, Michael, and Eduard met the Grand Master in his study. The Grand Master started the meeting saying, "The tale that you three told was obviously not what I expected to hear today. But, first, I would like to understand what we know about Solomon's Temple other than what we know from the Old Testament? Surely, the Torah must have more information?"

Eduard responded, "I have created some notes from my days in Jerusalem. Therefore, I believe that I can summarize our knowledge succinctly."

The Grand Master said, "Please do."

Eduard started at the beginning of his notes. He said, "The Israelites regarded the Temple as the intersection between Heaven and Earth. It was believed that God lived there to be amongst his chosen people. Solomon was the son of the warrior King David from the Biblical David and Goliath Story. Solomon was born around 990 BCE. David had accrued a vast wealth of gold and silver, which Solomon used to build the Temple. The Temple was dedicated to Yahweh, the God of the Hebrews as described by Moses, in the Book of Exodus. The Temple was said to be the home of the fabled Ark of the Covenant, which held the two tablets that were inscribed with the Ten Commandments. The Ark was stored in a place referred to as the Holy of Holies. Only the High Priests were allowed to see it. It was believed that it had special powers that could defeat any of the enemies of the Israelites. The Temple was destroyed in 587 BCE by the Neo-Babylonian Empire king Nebuchadnezzar II when the Babylonians attacked Jerusalem. The Second Temple was erected in 516 BCE. The Second Temple lasted until Christianity took a foothold in the region. The Final destruction occurred in 70 AD when the Romans burned it to the ground. The First and Second Temples Site was known after the first century AD as the Temple Mount. The site was taken over by Muslims in 705 AD. The Muslims built a Mosque on the site of the Temple Mount, which was later known as the Al-Aqsa Mosque. Muslims believe that Muhammad was transported from the Great Mosque of Mecca to Al-Aqsa during his infamous Night Journey. Islamic tradition holds that Muhammad led prayers towards this site until the 17th month after he migrated from Mecca to Medina when Allah directed him to turn towards the Kaaba in Mecca. Muslims, Christians, and Jews have battled over this land ever since. The area is still described as The Temple Mount by Jews and Christians and the Dome of the Rock by Muslims."

The Grand Master said, "This is why we have had many battles over this small patch of desert."

Eduard continued, "It was also believed that the original Menorah was buried there. The common belief was that the Ark of the Covenant had been moved hundreds of years ago. Stockpiles of gold and silver are also rumored to be there. When Christianity was first beginning, the ancient city had tunnels underneath that are thought to be the home of many Christian artifacts. As you can see, this land held a special significance for many people and religions."

The Grand Master said, "Several years ago, we defeated the Muslims and took over Jerusalem because it is the most important city within Christendom. The artifacts were always on our minds, but that was not the primary reason for our Crusade. Our goal was to form a Templar Headquarters in Jerusalem. The Knights have sworn to protect the Holy City from any would-be attackers. We do have some knowledge about ancient secrets that are buried underneath the First Temple. Now, from what I am hearing from you three, these secrets could change humanity forever."

The Grand Master finished by saying, "Please add this task to your already monumental task list. I will expect updates monthly on your progress."

CHAPTER 13

JERUSALEM

ACQUES HAD BEEN settled in Jerusalem for several months when the first Muslim attacks started. When he made the trip to the Holy Land, he had one hundred warriors and squires assigned to him. The goal was to give the impression that the mission was to protect Jerusalem from attack. However, very few understood that the real mission was to find the Christian artifacts and investigate the Secret of Eden story further. Eduard and Michael returned to Giza because they felt that there were more leads to follow in Giza regarding Abraham's Keyhole.

Jacques knew that the Muslim attacks would eventually come, but it somehow became more real when the loss of life occurred. The Templars easily fended off the Muslim attack, but several Knights and Squires were lost in the melee. Jacques had brought several very well-seasoned Warrior Commanders with him for this mission. He tasked the senior Warrior, Martine de Vossier, with protecting the Holy City. The two met after the first attack. Jacques asked him for a report. Martine responded, "As I would expect, the Muslims are probing us. So these minor attacks are meant to assess our strengths and weaknesses."

Martine came up with a new strategy. He explained, "We have a significant army stationed in the port city of Acre. The Muslim Army is assembled in the north. We should have our forces in Acre attack the Muslim Army. This will take the focus off Jerusalem, which will allow you to complete your mission without the constant threat of attack."

Jacques agreed with the strategy. He said to Martine, "Travel to Acre and discuss this strategy with the Acre Commander. He can easily cause a change in focus for the Muslims. This will force them into a defensive posture." The following day Martine departed with two dozen warriors heading for Acre.

Jacques succeeded in sending a message that he had a significant presence of warriors stationed in Jerusalem when in reality, he had an army of academics. These Knights were a collection of master masons, architects, builders, religious scholars, historians, and archeologists. The Warriors were, of course, here to protect the mission, but they were also there to help with digs. The Templars were here basically in secret. If Christian Artifacts were found, the Church in Rome would be notified. There was no plan to turn over any findings. That would be a decision made by Templar Leadership back in France. Every one of the Templars understood what these artifacts were. They hold a special place in the hearts of all Christians. Whoever possessed these items would undoubtedly possess great power. The one thing that only a handful knew about was the belief that the Temple of Solomon housed ancient artifacts that explained the meaning of life. No one alive has ever seen these artifacts, but many insist that they are mentioned in the histories of ancient civilizations.

✠

Jacques's team has been working on the secret mission since their arrival earlier this year. Everything from troop movements to horse management was done in secret. The horses were stored in Solomon's stables and barely saw the light of day. The support team mainly made up of Squires, had to sneak out under disguise to obtain supplies and Food. The Archeologists have centered their searches in three areas: The Old City near Golgotha or place of skulls as it was commonly referred to; The Tunnel System under the area of the 1st Temple; and the Arch of the Dome. Jacques had assigned three Commanders to manage the task. Each had an enormous task ahead of them.

Eduard and Michael had just arrived from Giza. They had unearthed some new clues. Jacques placed Michael in the lead role of the Golgotha exploration, whereas Eduard was in charge of exploring the tunnel system under the Temple.

CHAPTER 14

ALCHEMY

SIX MONTHS HAD passed since Jacques first arrived in Jerusalem. His patience was beginning to wear thin. There had been no discoveries yet. As instructed, he sent an update back to the Grand Master. He gave updates on the skirmishes that had taken place with the Muslims but said little else. He decided that he needed to get some fresh air. The air within the caverns was awful. There were days when he wouldn't see any daylight. He needed a change. He decided to go for a walk in the Old City part of Jerusalem.

As Jacques walked through the Old City, he marveled at the fact that so many cultures had coexisted there. It was seemingly peaceful, but everyone knew that one incident could turn the city into a powder keg. As he had done in the past, Jacques liked to walk through the marketplace where merchants sold their wares. Every time he walked through there, he couldn't help but think of the New Testament story of how Jesus overturned the Merchant stands in the Temple courtyard. He wondered, how would Jesus have reacted to having three major religions calling this city home? Jacques purchased some fruit to take back to the Temple. He didn't buy any clothing because you were taught to travel lite as a Knight. Everything was very colorful, though. There were even items that had traveled the Silk Road from China. He often wondered if the Templars would start traveling east towards China to spread the message of Jesus Christ. It was said that there was much war and strife in the Far East. There were ruthless Warlords between the Middle East and China.

Every time he visited the market, he passed by the Alchemist Tent. He never went in, although he was always curious. Many considered Alchemy to be part of the Occult. Others had said that these stores were just a place to buy holistic aids for any ailment that you may be having. As he thought earlier, he needed a change, so he decided to visit the store. After all, many would think that his Dreams are a vision from the Occult. Why not keep an open mind.

As he entered the establishment, he could see jars everywhere that were filled with many substances. He thought, "How do they keep track of it all." Finally, he made his way to where the Merchant was. She was a relatively young woman who was wearing a very colorful gown. She welcomed him. She said, "Good Morning, Sir Knight. Are you looking for anything in particular?"

Jacques noticed that she spoke fluent French. He wasn't sure if this was her native tongue or if she was speaking French just because she saw the Templar tunic. Jacques said, "Yes, but I don't think what I am looking for will be in any of these jars."

Just then, an elderly woman entered the room and nearly fainted when she saw him. The younger woman said, "Mother, are you okay?" She led her mother to a chair and then poured her a cup of water.

She apologized to Jacques. She said, "My Mother has been having dizzy spells lately. Even though I have many cures here in my store, I don't have a fountain of youth."

Her mother called her over. She complied, and her mother

whispered into her ear. The younger woman then said to me, "Do you know who you really are? My mother says that you are a very old soul. She says that you are a guardian of a great secret."

Jacques said, "I have no idea what she is talking about."

She apologized and said, "My mother must have mistaken you for someone else."

Jacques said, "Thank you for your hospitality, but I must take my leave." He quickly left the establishment and walked around the marketplace for at least another hour. He thought to himself, "How did this old woman know any of my secrets? I have only heard the term guardian in my Dreams. That is what my spirit guide has called me." Finally, curiosity got the best of him. He went back to the Alchemy Tent.

The young woman greeted him again. She said, "My mother was sure that you would be back."

Jacques smiled and said, "Your mother seems to know me."

She said, "She knows your soul."

"May I have a word with her? I mean her no harm." Jacques said.

She walked over to her mother and spoke quietly. She returned and said, "My mother would be honored to speak to you. She has never met a true guardian before. My mother's name is Mary." She pulled up two chairs and set them next to her mother.

"Mary, it is very nice to make your acquaintance. How do you know so much about me?" Jacques asked.

Mary said, "I was born with a gift. I can communicate with the spirit world. You are on a great mission that has spanned many lifetimes. You and your friend are guarding a secret that is as old as mankind but has purposely been hidden. As a result, only the Worthy will receive the message of the great secret. Your mission is to make sure that it remains safe as you have always done."

Jacques could have denied everything, but this woman could see right through him. He said, "I understand this because of my Dreams. I have a guide that comes to me in my Dreams. She is a very beautiful woman. She seems to tell me the same message that you are telling me. Do you know who she is? How can I see her again?"

Mary laughed and said, "You can speak to her right now. She is standing right next to you. She has her hand on your shoulder." Jacques looked around and could see nothing. She then said, "Soon you will be reunited with her where you will spend many more lifetimes together as you have already spent many lifetimes together in the past. She is your soul's companion. Some call her your soulmate. Together, you and your soulmate will join your friend to protect the secret. The three of you are Children of the Flood. Some will also refer to you as the Guardians of the Secret of Eden."

Jacques felt a warmth go through his entire body. It was as if she passed right through him. He could smell the essence of the perfume that he had experienced in the past Dreams. He had never been with a woman, so he was unfamiliar with perfumes. The older woman was reading his mind.

She said, "Whenever you smell this essence, you will know that she is nearby."

Jacques sat in stunned silence for several minutes. He thanked both women. He offered the younger woman three gold coins. He said, "Please accept this. You have given me happiness beyond that which any secret or sacred discovery could give me." She thanked him, and he left the establishment.

CHAPTER 15

THE BREAKTHROUGH

J ACQUES RETURNED TO the Temple with new vigor. He had realized that his Dreams were not just his imagination gone awry. He had confirmation that he was indeed connected to the treasure, and more importantly, he had a special spirit guiding him. Mary had called this spirit "His soulmate." All of his problems seemed much less important all of a sudden. At some point, he would have to speak with Eduard about their connection to the Secret of Eden.

As he approached the place called Golgotha, Jacques' thoughts returned to the search for the artifacts of Jesus Christ. Michael noticed Jacques, and he said, "I believe we have had a breakthrough." He further explained, "To our good fortune, the Romans were known for documenting everything that went on within the Roman Government. One of the Squires was going through the Roman archives here in Jerusalem when he found some documents that referred to the supposed burial place of Jesus." He continued, "At the time of Jesus's death, the Jewish laws had forbidden any burials within the city limits. The problem was that the city had expanded after the death of Christ. Therefore, many of the previous searchers were mistakenly looking outside the new city limits." He continued, "The Squire found an ancient Roman manuscript that was an order that Emperor Constantine had issued that sent a team of representatives to Jerusalem to look for artifacts associated with the death of Jesus Christ. The team returned to Constantine and documented how in around 125 AD, the Roman Emperor Hadrian had built a small Pagan Temple over the sight where Jesus had been buried. Hadrian had built the Temple to display dominance over early Christian worshipers.

Further manuscripts showed that Eusebius, Bishop of Caesarea, had the Pagan Temple razed. Excavations beneath it revealed a rock-cut tomb. The top of the cave was sheared off to expose the interior. This site was marked on the document. It was further documented that it appeared that the tomb had several tunnels extending from it. The tunnels had been sealed off."

Jacques said, "This is wonderful news. Let's return to my office where we can speak in private."

The two Knights returned to the Temple. Jacques said to Michael, "Your mission is to be carried with the utmost discretion. I feel that unfriendly eyes were watching us as we walked around what we now believe is the burial chamber."

Michael detailed his plan. He said, "My team of builders, archeologists, and architects had reviewed an outcropping that was approximately 100 feet away from what the Romans believed was the burial chamber. They had determined that the outcropping was not natural. Therefore, they believe that a second chamber may have been created."

Jacques asked, "What makes you certain that the tunnel extended that far?"

Michael replied, "The soil was recessed in several areas leading to the outcroppings. This was conclusive evidence that the tunnels had collapsed."

Jacques said, "Why would they build a tunnel and then block it off? Unless someone purposely blocked the tunnels to hide what was there." The two Knights discussed how the excavation of the outcropping could be completed in secret. The plan was to perform this dig at night. Templar Warriors would block off the area. The hope was to dig during the night and then meet the following day to discuss the progress. Jacques found this to be very promising for the simple fact that the outcropping had never been mentioned in any previous writings. So there was finally some hope.

At midnight that very night, several Templars appeared at the outcropping. They were wearing traditional Arab work tunics. The idea was to go unnoticed. The rocks in the outcropping blocked the view of anyone passing by. Templar Guards were posted inconspicuously around the outcropping. If anyone approached the area, the guards were ordered to intercept them and redirect them. The other issue was what to do with the rocks and dirt that was removed from the dig. The builders had placed carts nearby. The carts would take the debris far away from the outcropping and spread it over a vast area. After several nights of painstaking digging, they seemingly hit a dead end. First, they had removed large boulders and then 10 feet of dirt. Then another layer of boulders.

Jacques and Michael were waiting for his dig leader to give them an update. Finally, the leader arrived and relayed the situation.

Michael asked the leader, "Is the dirt hard-packed?"

The Dig leader said, "The dirt was easily removed. It was almost powder-like."

Michael's demeanor quickly changed. He said, "The fact that the dirt was loose meant that it had been previously moved. It is often hard to tell when it was moved, but it was clear that man had worked it." He further explained that dirt that man had never moved was often tough and challenging to cut through. Next, Michael asked, "Were the boulders placed in an orderly way, or did they seem random in their placement?" The Dig Leader replied, "They were tightly packed." Finally, Michael said, "I need to see the site.

A few minutes later, the Dig Leader led Michael and Jacques to the site. They were fortunate that there was a full moon. The natural lighting was great. They began to look at the boulders. Jacques noticed that there were no air gaps between the boulders. They seemingly looked like a wall. Michael began to laugh and motion for Jacques to join him. Jacques climbed up to where Michael was standing. Michael explained, "I am sure that what we were looking at is man-made."

Everyone was very excited about this news. The Knights had been searching for six months, and finally, they had a promising lead. Michael further stated, "We have to carefully plan how we are going to penetrate the wall. If we start to deconstruct the wall in the wrong place, the entire complex could collapse, possibly hurting the workers and destroying artifacts." He continued, "We need to find the edge where there is a vertical wall. Once the vertical wall is discovered, an opening needs to be very carefully cleared."

Michael further stated, "As the opening is cleared, wood beams must be inserted to support the other boulders." This process was very slow and painstaking.

After about 30 days of clearing boulders and installing wood beams, the man-made cave was ready to be searched. Michael summoned Jacques. He arrived after a few minutes. Michael has waited for this moment for a long time. He had spent his entire adult life digging through what he believed were significant discoveries only to find out that nothing was to be found. However, he had found several Christian artifacts over twenty years, which was considered a success in the Archeology world.

Jacques and Michael both climbed through the opening and lit the lanterns they had brought with them. They immediately noticed that there was what appeared to be an Altar on one side of the room. The Altar had carvings that depicted the Nativity

Scene on one end and the Passion of Christ on the other end. Jacques stood and stared at the Alter. Then, he asked, "Why is there an Alter placed where no one could use it? What purpose did it serve?" An artisan had built it. But why.

Although this was a significant find, it did not fit into the class of a major discovery. There had to be a reason for the Altar to be installed under this outcropping. Michael confirmed that the area where they were now standing was indeed underground. The cave was carved into the rock. The walls then were covered with stones. As they were starting to leave the cave, Jacques noticed two elevated areas on the other side of the room. One higher than the other. Then it struck him. Those elevations were for kneeling. Usually, when you were kneeling, you faced what you were praying to. In this case, there was just a wall.

Then Michael stated, "That is not just a wall!" He pointed out that there was a keystone at waist level. A keystone or capstone is the wedge-shaped stone at the apex of a masonry arch at the apex of a vault. In both cases, the final piece is placed during construction and locks all the stones into position, allowing the arch or vault to bear weight. This was most likely an Alcove that had been walled in.

Michael told Jacques, "We need to remove the wall." The wall was sealed with a mud-like substance. This was most likely to keep whatever was behind it airtight to prevent decay. A Master Craftsman built the alcove and the subsequent wall, much like the Master Craftsman that were in the Knights Templar. Once again, Michael told his team, "The wall must be externally supported as it is being dismantled. Otherwise, it could collapse."

Having said that, Michael felt reasonably comfortable that since this alcove existed before it was blocked, the alcove was designed to carry the weight. It took roughly three hours to open up the Alcove. As the builders cleared the final stones, Jacques and Michael began to get their first look into the opening. It appeared that there was a large piece of wood in the Alcove.

Jacques immediately dropped to his knees. He said, "Men, I

believe that we are looking at the Cross of Jesus Christ." They all had spent significant time hearing of the Crucifixion, but it was overwhelming to look at it. You finally understood how painful this death must have been for our Lord. He died for all of our sins. Jacques's faith was always very strong, but at this point, he felt a bond with the Risen Lord that was beyond words.

While Michael and Jacques were trying to figure out the next steps, one of the workers noticed that there was also a stone box. This box was located about halfway up the Cross. Were there relics in there? The Christian Faith held in the firm belief that Christ ascended to heaven. Therefore, no body would be left behind. The workers were able to drag the box out of the Alcove. Jacques noticed that the top was loose. When the bones or relics were placed in an ossuary, it was usually very tightly sealed. This would typically slow down the effects of decay. Jacques was confident that this box was not an ossuary. He decided to open it. The heavy lid was taken off the box. Inside of it was what looked like a linen. On closer inspection, there were stains on the linen. Why was this linen hidden with the cross of Jesus Christ? The entire linen was very long. They decided to take this linen and the box back to the Temple, where they could get a better look at it. The builders removed the Box and its contents and took it back to the Temple.

After the box was removed, Jacques summoned a team of twenty warriors to the outcropping. Jacques had selected the finest warriors to guard the Cross. He decided to show them what they were guarding. All of their years of serving the Lord had meaning. They would soon get a glimpse of why they had joined the order. Jacques had them climb into the outcropping. Once they were there, he instructed them to kneel in front of the Alcove. One by one, they realized what they were looking at. They understood that hearing about the Risen Lord through the Gospels was enough to cause them to dedicate their lives to it. Now they were looking at the actual Cross. Many thought that they could still see dried blood on the Cross. The Blood of Jesus

Christ of Nazareth. Jacques instructed them that their new mission was to guard the Cross. They would travel with it if it was ever moved.

After returning to the Temple, Jacques summoned all of the Knights stationed at the Temple. He told them, "We have found the Cross of Jesus Christ. Tomorrow, in small groups, you would be allowed to pay homage." The subject then turned to security. Jacques explained that Christianity has many enemies. The Jews or Muslims would destroy the Cross if they could get their hands on it. It was decided that they would send a coded message back to the Templar Headquarters detailing the find. Jacques would ask for additional Knights to be sent to Jerusalem to help guard the Cross. It had been a long day, and the Knights were tired beyond belief. They agreed to get some rest. They would look at the linen in the morning.

Jacques could barely get any sleep. He thought to himself, "Our life's work was finally bearing fruit." The next morning, the Knights gathered in the area that was referred to as the Great Hall. They laid out many blankets so that the linen found in the Alcove would not get soiled when they spread it out. They very carefully unfolded the Linen and removed the wrinkles. The lighting was less than perfect. They needed more lanterns. Jacques instructed the Squires who were present to stand about four feet apart and hold the lanterns close to the linen without touching it. It soon became apparent what they were looking at. The face of the crucified Jesus Christ was staring back at them. In fact, his entire body, front, and back, was visible. They were confident that this was the burial cloth of Jesus Christ. Jacques needed to add this to the coded message that was traveling back to France. For many of the Knights, their lives were fulfilled. For Jacques, he still had to find and protect the Secret of Eden.

CHAPTER 16

CHILDREN OF THE FLOOD

T HE FLOODWATERS HAD receded some fifteen years earlier. The descendants of Noah and his wife Na'amah grew in number during these years. They lived in very rudimentary huts, which gave them shelter against the elements, but little else. The beasts had returned to what was left of their habitats. Survival was extremely difficult for these survivors, but they were from hardy stock. For Peleg and his brother Joktan, there was only one way. That meant hard work accompanied by prayers to the Lord Almighty. God had protected their Father, Shem, who was the eldest son of Noah, from the great flood that had stricken all of humanity. For all they knew, they were the only survivors. Therefore, it was incumbent on them to rebuild a righteous world.

One of the central tenets of this new tribe was to be fruitful. The Lord had deemed at least one of each gender of species was to survive on the Ark. This included mankind. As a man and woman came of age, they were paired together to do God's work.

The Tribal leader, who was still their Grandfather, Noah, prayed to the Lord for guidance, leading him to call a man and a woman together as man and wife. This marriage was sacred, and the bond was only broken by death. Peleg considered himself to be the most fortunate man alive. He was wed to Tytea. She was the daughter of Japheth, the third and youngest son of Noah. Tytea was fair-skinned and the most beautiful woman, any man, had ever seen. She was a very happy and optimistic person by nature. Even when a crop had failed, or a fellow tribesman became ill, she always came to aid the person who needed help with a smile on her face and an optimistic view of the future.

Peleg's younger brother, Joktan, was coming of age and soon would be paired with a woman. He had prayed to the Lord that he be granted the same favor that his brother Peleg had been given. The brothers had worked the fertile land that was adjacent to the Great River. As a result, the animals of the region had flourished. The deer had no natural predators except man. Their religion had always taught them to take what they needed from the land and no more. Any excesses were considered a sin. Every part of the beast that had been killed had to be used. The meats were for sustenance, and the hides were for clothing. This held true for everything in the tribe. If anyone was unable to feed themselves, then it was their neighbor's concern to feed them.

One of Peleg and Tytea's favorite pastimes was standing on the Great River's shores and watching the water as it flowed by. This was both peaceful and invigorating at the same time. This river represented the future for both of them. It showed the path for their tribe to grow and prosper. Man could travel great distances on this river.

One day as they stood there taking in the river's magnificence, Joktan walked up and joined them. He said, "You two often stare at this river as if it contains God himself."

Peleg said, "In many ways it does. Our future is on the water. As is our past. The three of us were raised on the water. It is part of our beings. We are the 'Children of the Flood'."

Just then, a very large person appeared behind them. They never heard him approach. It was as though he appeared from nowhere. The man said, "Do not fear. I am one of the ones that your family patriarch, Enoch, spoke of. He called us the Watchers. We have been sent from the Almighty to steer mankind on its course to salvation. Before the Almighty created the Great Flood, we were here in numbers. Our brethren lived amongst the people to educate mankind as to our ways. After a short period of time, some of our brethren turned to evil. They were enchanted by the women of this place. They gave in to temptation. This angered the Almighty and caused him to inflict the Great Flood onto the people and the wayward Watchers. Your Grandfather, Noah, is one of the righteous and was given instructions on how to save his family and the beasts of this world. You three are the offspring of the righteous. You are indeed "The Children of the Flood" and shall always be referred to as such. We have been watching you, and we have determined that you all are the Worthy ones. We are giving you the task of spreading our message and protecting a treasure that contains a secret that will explain everything. All of man's questions about the Almighty and "Why we are here" will be answered when man is ready and has followed the Almighty's rules. This secret will return mankind to the Garden of Eden and will grant access to the Tree of Knowledge once again." He continued, "I will give you a stone carving that will list these rules. You must keep it hidden from the evildoers. In addition, we have hidden the great treasure under the Great Lion that my predecessors built for mankind."

Joktan asked, "Our time here is limited to our lifetimes. So how can we protect this secret when we are dead?"

The Watcher said, "You will never die. Of course, your physical body is limited, and, of course, it will die, but your souls are eternal. You will be reborn into new bodies when the message is in danger. Your souls will be tasked with a very sacred mission. You three will be together forever. In addition to being Children of the Flood, you are the Guardians of the Secret of Eden."

The Watcher continued, "My message to you also comes with a warning. You will have an adversary. He is already present in your lives." He paused briefly, then continued, "The sons of Adam and Eve were named Cain and Abel. Out of jealous rage, Cain killed his brother Abel. God cast him out to wander the desert. He was forever scorned in the eyes of the Almighty." The Watcher continued, "As was told in Enoch's vision, God cast the fallen one, Azazel, out of heaven. Azazel will come to be known for future generations as Satan or Lucifer. Azazel adopted Cain as his disciple. Cain's children grew to be followers of Azazel. The descendants of Cain were then killed in the flood. This forced Azazel to start anew. Azazel has already corrupted a member of your family as he did with Cain."

Peleg said, "Is it Canaan? We discuss Canaan amongst ourselves. He has a very dark presence." Canaan was the son of Ham, Noah's middle son, and a cousin to Peleg, Tytea, and Joktan.

The Watcher said, "Your instincts serve you well. Someday, Canaan will be cast out by your grandfather, Noah. He will grow strong with the evil one. Dark souls will flock to him. He will be a formidable adversary for you three. His offspring will be known as the Children of Canaan or Canaanites. Canaan will be reborn as you three will be reborn. His mission will be to stop you and plant seeds of evil everywhere. He will be a very cunning enemy, but you will have the Watchers and the Almighty on your side."

✠

Just then, Jacques heard a Squire say, "Sir. Wake up. It is time for the excursion to Rome." Jacques woke up and was startled by what he had just learned. This Dream was given to him for the purpose of understanding. He needed to tell someone this story. Perhaps, he could talk to Eduard. Then it hit him. His soulmate was Tytea, and Eduard was the one who was Joktan.

CHAPTER 17

THE RESTING PLACE
OF THE CROSS

AFTER THE HISTORIC discovery of the Cross and Burial Cloth, the news was sent back to the Templar Headquarters in France. The Templar leadership began pilgrimages of traveling to Jerusalem to see and pay respect to the objects of the Lord's Passion. This occurred over many months. They traveled in groups of three or four, so they would not draw any attention to their findings. The Knights that were protecting the pilgrimage roadway were not told of the findings. It was critically important that the discoveries were kept secret. If the word got out, it would threaten the entire mission. Enemies could attack the Temple Mount in mass and destroy the findings. These findings represented the truth regarding Jesus Christ. The impression left on the Burial Cloth was unlike anything any of the Templars had ever seen. It was not a natural stain that would typically accompany a badly abused body. It was not for them to decide, but many believed that it was indeed a Miracle. The enemies would conclude that if these discoveries could be destroyed, they were never supernatural in the first place.

After the Templar leadership had completed their journeys to Jerusalem and returned to France, a meeting was held to decide what to do with the discoveries. An intense debate ensued. One side argued that the artifacts should be hidden by the Templars and not disclosed to the public. The other side argued that the discoveries belonged to the world. They said that a disclosure to the masses would help spread the word of Jesus Christ. They further argued that the Cross and Burial Cloth were not the property of any one group or entity. They belonged to all of Christianity. They decided to vote. Should the Artifacts be hidden, or should all Christians be told of the Good News? All of the Leaders voted, and the results were overwhelming. The Templars decided to make the news public.

The next question was how to make this disclosure. If they just made an announcement, the Temple Mount would be overrun with worshipers. So they decided to notify the Vatican first. Later that month, a team of emissaries was sent to Rome to meet with Pope Honorius II.

The Pope was living at the Original St. Peters Basilica in Rome. This Basilica was built on the site of the death of St. Peter. The Basilica served as a significant focal point for the Roman Empire. The original site was known as the Circus of Nero. It was the site where many Christians, including St. Peter, became Martyrs. After Constantine recognized the Church, he had the Basilica built on this Holy Site.

The fact that the Pope was now living at the Original St. Peter's Basilica was significant news because of the centuries-old wars with the Muslims and conflicting Christian followings. In fact, the fiercest battles that the Roman Catholics faced were with Eastern Byzantine Church. Battles over authority had taken place for centuries. Charlemagne had seemingly settled the authority conflict in 780 AD. After his efforts had led to peace, he was given the title of Emperor of the Roman Empire at the Basilica. After the death of Charlemagne, the peace was shattered, and conflict ensued for hundreds of years. The Popes during this period resided in various cathedrals and basilicas in France. Therefore, the fact that Pope Honorius II was living in Rome was a major statement.

Upon arrival in Rome, the Holy Father warmly greeted the Emissaries. The Lead Emissary, Lord Pierre Moussaint, announced that the Knights had been searching the Temple Mount for Christian Artifacts. He continued to tell the Pontiff about the outcropping and how the team had to dig only at night so that they would not draw any unwanted attention.

The Pope laughed and said, "I hope that you have not traveled all this way to tell me that you dug a hole in the Holy City."

Lord Moussaint made a statement that caused the Pope to immediately fall to his knees and begin to pray. He said, "Holy Father, we have found the Cross of Jesus Christ. We have also found his Burial Cloth which contains a very visible image of the Lord's Body." Then, the entire Team of Templars and the Pope's aides joined him in Prayer.

After this, the Pontiff stood up and abruptly announced that he had pressing matters to tend to. The truth was that he knew that the next discussion would be about what to do with the artifacts. The Pope needed time to think. This was not what he expected today. He said that he would like to hear all of the details over dinner in a few hours. The Templars accepted his offer. Several hours later, the entire group joined the Pontiff in a special meal to celebrate their discovery. The conversation at dinner was light-hearted, and many bottles of wine were consumed. They agreed to celebrate mass early the following day, and then they would discuss the future of the discoveries. Several of the Templars were speaking amongst themselves later that evening and had wondered if the Pope had secretly dispatched the Swiss Guard who normally protects the Vatican to Jerusalem to seize the artifacts. They commented on how there was an underlying uneasiness between the Templars and the Vatican. Unbeknownst to them, Lord Moussaint had been listening. He smiled and said to the other Templars that he had sent a team in advance to Jerusalem to warn the team of warriors who stayed behind at the Temple Mount. The Templars sat in silence for a while after this disclosure. The supposed bond between the Templars and the Vatican was becoming fragile. One speculated that the Pope probably thought that the soldiers of the Vatican were supposed to make these finds. After all, they were indeed the appointed descendants of St. Peter.

As planned, the Templars celebrated Mass with Pope Honorius II the next morning. The Pontiff himself was the Celebrant of the Mass. Afterward, they enjoyed a quick breakfast and joined the Pope in the Basilica. The Pope started by asking Lord Moussaint what he planned to do with the artifacts. Everyone noted the way this question was posed.

The Templar Leader responded, "Our journey is two-fold. The first was to tell you the good news and secondly to agree on what should happen to the artifacts." The fact that Lord Moussaint wanted an agreement with the Pope was blasphemy in the eyes of the Pontiff. The Pope felt that he was the Vicar of Christ and the decisions were his alone. Lord Moussaint went on to say that the Cross and the Burial Cloth belonged to all of Christendom. Moussaint de-escalated the tension in the room by saying that he felt that the Vatican should take possession of these artifacts, but they were for all Christians to see. He went on to say that the Cross was suffering from decay.

The air was extremely dry in the Alcove, and the wood had become very fragile. He doubted that the Cross would make the journey without suffering any damage. One thought was to distribute any broken fragments from the Cross to churches worldwide. Relics or bones of Saints were constantly touring churches throughout Europe. The small pieces of the Cross could be presented to the masses in the same manner. The bulk of the Cross would remain in hiding in the Vatican in areas where the temperature and humidity would remain consistent. Several of the Templars were scientists and had put a lot of thought into the issue. Moussaint volunteered their services to work with the Vatican to secure the final resting place for the Cross. Everyone agreed with this concept and said that the Templars would immediately begin the work. The next more pressing issue was how to transport the Cross from Jerusalem to Rome. If the church's enemies knew that if anything this important was being moved, it would be an easy target. The Templars were confident that they could fend off the bandits that were disturbing the Pilgrims who were traveling from Rome to Jerusalem. The bigger threat came from the Muslims that still had strongholds throughout the Middle East. Moussaint proposed a strategy where the Templars would have surgically placed attacks on the Muslims. This would distract them from the routes the Cross would travel on its way to Rome.

The next issue was with the Burial Cloth. The group once again decided that it belonged to all Christians. It was agreed that the Cloth would travel from church to church throughout the regions. The Templars would provide a security force of Warrior Knights to protect the Burial Cloth of Jesus Christ. The Team of Templars would remain in Rome for several weeks to finalize the plans. The Pope agreed with all that he had heard but knew once he had possession of the Cross and Burial Cloth, he and only he could decide who should know about it.

Meanwhile, back in Jerusalem, Jacques knew that the disclosure of the Cross and Burial Cloth would garner everyone's attention and keep prying eyes away from his most secret mission of finding the Secret of Eden.

CHAPTER 18

THE UNVEILING

L ORD PIERRE MOUSSAINT arrived back in Jerusalem, as did the Military Commander, Martine de Vossier. Jacques held a meeting with the two leaders to discuss the relocation of the Artifacts. Martine immediately stated that the only safe route to Rome was by sea. He described how the forces in Acre had forced the Muslim Army to the east. Therefore, his forces could protect the entire route to the seaport of Acre. From Acre, the Artifacts could be loaded on a ship and sailed across the Mediterranean Sea to the mouth of the Tiber River, where it would sail upstream to Rome and onward to the Vatican. All three leaders agreed on the strategy. It presented the most significant opportunity for success.

A few days later, Lord Moussaint began the arduous journey back to Paris to tell the Grand Master of all that had transpired, including the transport plan that had just been agreed upon. Jacques also took the opportunity to have Lord Moussaint deliver his update to the Grand Master. It was in a sealed scroll. He purposely didn't mention any of their plans by name at the Temple of Solomon. Not that he didn't trust Lord Moussaint. Jacques knew that the scroll could always fall into the wrong hands if the travel party came under attack, so he sent the message in a vague code. He said, "We will continue our mission of better understanding the Christian and Jewish communities. As we discussed in our meetings at the onset of this mission, we will also try to understand how these religious communities interact with the ancient teachings of the Old Testament." Jacques knew that the Grand Master would interpret this correctly as the following, "We will continue our search for additional Christian Artifacts and ancient Jewish Treasures. They will also keep searching for what was referred to as the Secret of Eden."

✠

The Cross and Burial Cloth began their trek to the Vatican a few months later. The caravan of carriages left the Holy City just after sunrise. The goal was to get there in two days. Extra horses were brought in case one of the horses pulling the carriages took ill. The caravan was surrounded by one hundred of the finest warriors that the Knights had in their ranks.

After the caravan had been underway for about an hour, they passed through a heavily wooded area where they were the most susceptible to an attack. Martine de Vossier was assured that no Muslims were anywhere near this area. Just then, a barrage of arrows hit the front and rear of the caravan. The Knights instinctively dismounted from the horses and formed a Phalanx. The opening salvo from the attackers had hit their target. Ten Warriors had been hit as well as six horses. The Knights were patient. They knew the enemy would soon wage an attack. After about five minutes, another barrage of arrows was fired, followed by a charge from the Muslims. This is where the Knights were at their best. The Muslims were slaughtered by return fire of arrows as they approached. The ones that made it through were quickly destroyed by the expert swordsmen that were present. The battle was over quickly. The remaining Muslims retreated into the woods and beyond.

Martine and his Captains met to assess the damage. Four Knights and six horses had been killed. In addition, sixty-five Muslims were killed in the battle. Martine decided that the fallen Knights would be taken to Acre, where they would be transported back to Paris for a proper burial. The Muslims would be left to rot as a warning going forward.

Martine sent two carriages back to Jerusalem that carried several wounded Knights and a message for Jacques. The message sent said the following, "We were attacked about an hour north of Jerusalem. The Muslims knew we were coming. There must be a leak within your operation. You must find and eliminate."

✠

After the long journey, the Artifacts arrived safely at the Vatican. The Pope developed plans to announce the finding of the Holy Artifacts at an emergency Ecumenical Council meeting that was scheduled to occur in Rome. The Council consisted of all of the Cardinals from all of Roman Catholic dioceses all over the known world. The Conference also included Ecclesiastical Dignitaries from all regions, as well as, representatives from many of the Royal Families.

He began the Conference with a Mass as every one of his predecessors had done in the past. This Council meeting was shrouded in secrecy. Many wondered what the Pope had to say. The invitation said, "Your presence is urgently requested for an emergency Ecumenical Council." The invitation went on to relay the scheduled date and that the Council was to be held at St. Peter's Basilica in Rome. This had caused many to arrange for security to accompany their Party on its journey to Rome. Many of these Travelers had turned to the Templars for safety purposes.

The Pope greeted the Council members and distinguished

guests and welcomed them to Rome. He announced that the Holy Roman church would now make its home in Rome on the very spot where St. Peter's life ended. Many thought that this could not be the reason for making us travel long distances. Where was the Pontiff heading with this? Then the Pope pointed to a remote part of the Altar and said that the Soldiers of Christ and the Temple of Solomon had made several significant discoveries. In the corner of the Altar were two separate areas that were covered with white linens with the Papal Seal on them. On the sides were places where worshipers could kneel. The Pope walked over to the first structure and summoned his assistants to remove the covering, after which he said, "Behold. You are about to see the Cross of Jesus Christ." The crowd gasped and sat in bewilderment as the Pope explained how the Templars had found the Cross. He answered many questions regarding the Cross and its safekeeping. Everyone knew what this Cross meant to the Christians, as well as the Muslim Enemies. One of the Council members proposed that as a peace offering to the Eastern Sects of Christianity, their leaders should be invited to see the Cross themselves.

After the conversation had quieted down, the Pope announced that he had additional news. He stated with great Joy the Knights had also discovered the Burial Cloth of Jesus Christ. His assistants uncovered the long and narrow structure that housed the Burial Cloth.

The Pope went on to say, "As you look at the cloth with your own eyes, you will see the results of a Miracle." He explained that somehow a very detailed image of Jesus Christ had been burned on the Cloth. The best funeral preparers in the world could not make an impression that would contain this much detail. He then motioned for them to come up in small groups and witness the Artifacts up close. Each small group came up to see these Holy Items for themselves. They all knelt and said a prayer at both stations. For many, the life and times of Jesus of Nazareth lived within the written Gospels. To see these items with what appeared to be the blood of Jesus Christ on them was overwhelming. It reminded them that their life's journey was to spread the word of Jesus Christ. Many had fallen into political battles regarding territory and other matters. They all pledged to live their lives as Jesus would have done from this point forward.

They reconvened the next day, and the overwhelming sentiment was that the Artifacts should remain in Rome. The Pope decided to announce the findings to the world. He would allow religious leaders from throughout Christianity to see the Holy Artifacts. The Knights Templar would serve as security throughout the process. After the Pilgrimages were complete, the Artifacts were to be moved to a secret location for safekeeping. This was announced to followers throughout Christianity. The Templars knew the truth. The Artifacts would remain in Rome with the Holy Father. A Sacred Archives was created in an underground set of tunnels. The Cross would find its new home there. The Shroud would be sent to cathedrals and basilicas all over Rome under the guard of the Templars.

CHAPTER 19

WESTWARD

THE MIGHTY CELTIC Warrior known as Cormac waited on the shores of Gaul for Princess Danu to join him. He had just returned from a place called Jerusalem, where he defeated his lifetime adversary, a Roman Warrior named Aurelius. He was guided both by his Dreams and his Princess Danu. The Princess and Cormac had similar Dreams that described a great Secret handed down from the dawn of man. Their Dreams also had a name for the Princess and the Warrior. They were always being referred to as the Children of the Flood. Both had inquired about a flood to one of the Celtic Elders, who was the keeper of the Celtic Traditions. He said that many cultures have told a story of a Great Flood that had covered the planet but knew little else.

Finally, Princess Danu joined him. Her Beauty was inexplicable. Here long flowing blond hair and blue eyes were a sight to behold. He told her of his conquest in the land of the Hebrews as they called themselves. He said, "As our Dreams warned us, there was an adversary that knew of our Secret. I have no idea how he knew of the secret Treasure, but he did. I took my brother Eoghan with me because, as you know, he also shares our Dreams. When I first found Aurelius, I took him into our confidence. I told him that our Seers had told us that he knows of the Secret. After much wine one night, he opened up and told us of the Treasure. I asked him, "Does anyone else know of this Treasure?"

Aurelius said, "No." Then, after a short pause, he said, "Why don't we split the Treasure between us?"

Cormac said, "Let me think about it."

"The following day, Eoghan and I set out to go and kill Aurelius. When we arrived, he was gone. This led us on a chase that led back to Rome. We ultimately found him near an ancient ruin outside of Rome. He never saw us coming. We tied him up and told him that if he was honest with us, then we would let him go." Cormac continued, "Eoghan held a knife to his throat and said, "Did you tell anyone of the Secret?"

Aurelius said, "No. If I were to tell anyone, the Treasure would surely be lost. The Treasure's power is in its secrecy. I will trade a clue of its whereabouts for my life."

Cormac said, "Then I suggest that you tell us."

Aurelius paused briefly and said, "The Secret Message that tells of the whereabouts of the Treasure is hidden behind the Keyhole."

Cormac said, "Eoghan then slit his throat. We already know of the keyhole and its location."

Danu said, "Then the Secret of Eden is once again safe and secure."

The two embraced and transitioned from Princess and Warrior back to husband and wife. They had a bond that was beyond explanation. It was as if they had been together forever.

They walked hand in hand and stared out at the magnificent view that was in front of them. The two were inexplicably drawn to the sea.

Finally, Cormac broke the silence. He said, "What next, my Princess?"

She pointed westward to what was just open sea and said, "Our future and the future of the Secret of Eden is west."

Cormac looked confused because all that he could see was open water. Danu, as always, could read Cormac's mind. She just gave him the most beautiful smile imaginable and kept walking.

✠

Jacques woke up suddenly and was startled by his Dream. He said to himself, "What does all of this mean? It is time to speak with Eduard."

CHAPTER 20

ENEMY WITHIN

THE CARRIAGES CARRYING the wounded Knights arrived back at the Temple in Jerusalem just after sunset. Jacques was summoned to the temporary medical station that was established when the Knights first arrived years ago. Several Jewish healers were already present and helping to heal the wounds. None of the injuries was life-threatening. Jacques asked one of the Knights, "What happened? Was it a complete surprise?"

The Knight said, "There is a patch of woods that we had to pass through on the way to Acre. We have been worried about this area on our trips between Jerusalem and Acre. It is very easy for assailants to hide. The interesting part of this attack is that the attackers were not seasoned Warriors. We very easily fended them off. If this had been some of the Warriors that we have encountered in the past, it could have been catastrophic."

Jacques said, "Where do you think these Muslims came from? Our scouts were certain that they were nowhere near this route."

The Knight said, "These were a combination of older men and younger boys. My guess is that they were from here in Jerusalem." He then handed Jacques the note from Martine.

Jacques said, "Thank you for your report. Hopefully, you will fully recover very soon."

Jacques found this report very troubling. He summoned his senior team to discuss this matter. He picked a place within the Temple that was out of earshot from anyone. He posted Knights that he trusted near each entrance with strict instructions not to let anyone through except the leaders.

Within ten minutes, the Senior Leaders were present. This included both Eduard and Michael. Jacques explained, "Our party transporting the Cross and Burial Cloth was attacked on the road to Acre. Our forces easily repelled the attack. Our Warrior Commanders were dumbfounded. There were no Muslim Armies anywhere near this road. One of the injured Knights said the attackers were very unseasoned. In fact, they were mainly older men and young boys. This tells us that the attack came from Jerusalem. Someone knew that we were heading on this road and pre-planned an attack. The Muslims were waiting in a patch of woods in a very dangerous part of the journey. We obviously have a security problem. I am looking to hear your thoughts on this matter."

Michael spoke first. He said, "Part of the problem is that our digs within the Temple Grounds require moving tremendous amounts of stone and rubble. So we have been hiring locals to assist. Maybe one of them overheard something."

Jacques said, "That is possible, but somehow we kept it quiet until recently. If the Muslims knew that the Cross and Burial Cloth were here. Why did they wait to attack?"

Eduard said, "We must contain our conversations to very private areas like our living quarters. Only Knights and Squires are allowed there."

Jacques said, "If you need to communicate while these locals are present, please do so in Latin. We have to assume that some of these locals speak French."

Jacques dismissed his leaders, except for Eduard. Jacques said to Eduard, "I need to find out how this transgression occurred. So I am going to send out false messages through various channels. We will then use our back channels within the city to see if any of these messages have leaked out."

Eduard said, "You don't think any of the Knights leaked out the info regarding the caravan."

"Not on purpose." Said Jacques.

"Let me know if you need my assistance with this matter." Said Eduard.

Jacques said, "Thank you, old friend." He paused momentarily, "I do have another matter to discuss with you. I would like to discuss it outside of the Temple. Perhaps tomorrow we can journey to the Old City."

Eduard said, "Sounds intriguing."

CHAPTER 21

BROTHERHOOD

J ACQUES AROSE EARLIER than usual the next morning. He had hoped that his spirit guide would guide him, but he had no such luck. He pondered whether he should come right out and ask Eduard if he was having specific Dreams or should he ask less direct questions about the Book of Enoch or the Great Flood. Jacques had no firm plan either way.

The two Knights met for breakfast after morning prayers. The conversation was mainly about the security breach. Jacques said, "Let's discuss that while we are out of the Temple."

Both Knights gave their subordinates their instructions for the day.

The two Knights began walking towards the city center. Jacques began by saying, "Our Christ Artifacts are a huge find. The Eden Artifacts could be just as large. Have you learned anything new?"

Eduard said, "Yes, we have uncovered a new symbol which is referred to as the Secret Seal of Solomon. It appears to have a keyhole on it. It brings up many questions like "When was a key-hole first invented?" and "What does it mean in this context?" If you recall, Michael found a reference to Abraham's Keyhole in Egypt."

Jacques said, "Yes, I do, and those are valid questions."

The men continued to walk in silence for several minutes when Jacques asked, "Have you ever heard the term Children of the Flood?"

Eduard smiled and said, "Is this your way of asking me if I am having Dreams about Treasures and Floods and the Lord only knows what else. Let me answer your question with a question." Eduard smiled and said, "Why is it that you always end up with the beautiful maiden?" Both men laughed. Eduard's comment had definitely removed the nervousness from the conversation.

Jacques said, "I know that we haven't talked directly about this, but what are your thoughts?"

Eduard said, "Apparently, the two of us, along with your beau-tiful maiden, were born in the time of Noah. The Watchers had caused the Great Flood, and we have been tasked with guarding the message of the Almighty for generations to come."

Jacques said, "I had a troubling Dream a few nights ago where we were both Celtic Warriors, and we had to protect the Secret from a Roman Captain. If this Roman Captain knew about it, then how many others have known about it?" He paused and continued, "It is of the utmost importance that we locate and move the Treasure to another location. We must keep this Secret to a select few within the Templars. Obviously, the Grand Master is one of them."

Eduard said, "Not only that, but I believe that the Muslims will mount a counteroffensive on the Holy City very soon. There-fore, we must redouble our efforts."

Jacques said, "Agreed." Then, he paused and said, "I would like you to meet someone."

The two men walked through the Old City's Marketplace and entered the Alchemy Tent. The older woman's daughter warmly greeted them. Jacques said, "On our last meeting, I was so overwhelmed by what your mother had told me that I forgot to ask you your name."

The young lady said, "My name is Anna. Would you like to speak with my mother?"

Jacques said, "Yes, if she has a moment. By the way, this is my friend Eduard."

"Very nice to meet you. She has done nothing but talk about you since your last meeting." Anna said.

The two Knights were led to a room in the back of the tent. Anna's mother, Mary, sat there dozing off. Finally, Anna said, "Mother, you have some visitors."

Mary opened her eyes, and a huge smile came over her face. She said, "I was so excited after our last meeting. But now, I have both living Guardians standing in front of me. What a thrill."

Jacques and Eduard were both seated at the table with Mary. Anna served them a pot of tea with cups and a plate of dates.

Jacques explained to Eduard that Mary has a special gift. She can see the spirit world. So she is probably going to tell us that my beautiful maiden is nearby."

Mary said, "She is always with you. She said to tell you that she was with you in your Dream a few days ago where you were looking west over the sea."

Jacques said, "That is absolutely remarkable."

Eduard said, "Do you have this gift with everyone?"

Mary said, "Yes. I suppose I do, but I have always been involved with the Children of the Flood."

Eduard said, "Why just the Children of the Flood."

Mary said, "I'm sorry Jacques that I didn't share it with you on our first meeting, but if you search your Dreams, you will find that there is always a Seer to help guide you on your mission. That is me, or my soul, I should say." She continued, "You asked why just the Children of the Flood? The answer is because, in a way, I am also one of them. In that lifetime, I was the wife of Noah. My name was Na'amah. I was your grandmother. When your mother was ready, I was the one that helped bring both of you into this world." Both Knights were startled. This is not something that they expected to hear. Even Anna had never heard this before.

Jacques and Eduard sat quietly, reflecting on what they had just heard. Both men sat there teary-eyed. Finally, Jacques said, "We must return to the Temple. Would the two of you like to see the Temple in the near future? I would like to invite you as our guests. We have much to discuss."

Anna said, "Yes. We would like that very much. You two are serving as the Fountain of Youth for my mother."

Jacques said, "Why don't we plan on one of the afternoons next week. I will get a message to you."

Both men hugged the women and said their goodbyes. They just had a life-altering afternoon.

CHAPTER 22

THE STAR OF DAVID

Jacques and Eduard had supper together for the next several nights. They were both shocked by what they had been told by Mary.

Eduard said, "If and when we find what we are looking for, you know that we will have to leave this Temple. The Muslim attack will come sooner or later. When we leave, we must insist that Mary and her daughter leave with us. They can move to Paris. They both know the language and will be very comfortable there."

Jacques said, "When we speak with them next, we should suggest it."

Just then Michael stepped into the supper hall. He said, "Just the two I have been looking for. There has been a breakthrough."

Both men immediately stood up and Jacques said, "Please lead us to your breakthrough."

As previously instructed, the Knights did not discuss anything while they were following Michael to the underground tunnel system.

The underground tunnels were originally meant to be passageways to the cisterns or freshwater wells for Solomon and his family. Over the years since the original Temple was built and subsequently destroyed, the Second Temple was built supposedly in the same location. That was the common belief even though there was no actual proof. Nonetheless, it was believed that many of the Hebrew Treasures were hidden somewhere within these tunnels. The Knights had been doing a thorough search for seemingly years only to come up empty handed. Then one day, they noticed something odd about the carvings of the Star of David symbols that seemed to be everywhere.

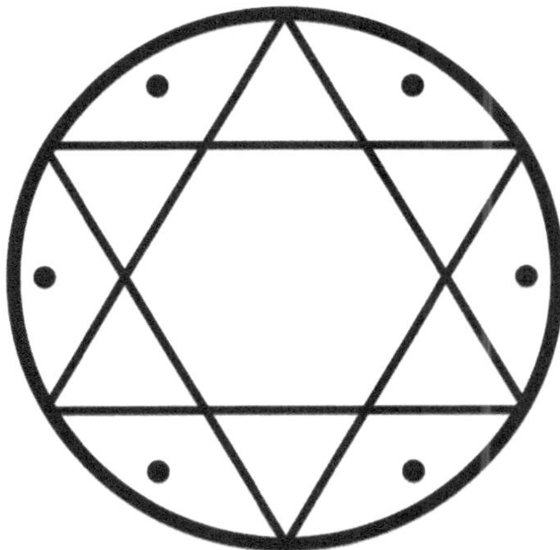

The Star Of David

Michael began telling Jacques and Eduard about the breakthrough. He said, "One of the Squires noticed that majority of the symbols were identical and had no unique features. He noticed that certain symbols had one leg of the star that was raised. The other legs were consistent with the other identical symbols. He noted the location of the symbols that had raised legs. They seemed to be leading him somewhere. Many times, the symbols with raised legs were hidden in an alcove where the lighting was poor. The symbols that have a raised leg on the Star were pointing to the next raised leg Star of David. The team ultimately was led to a star where all of the legs were raised. This had to mean something. I instructed my team to begin to look for hidden rooms and depressions within the flooring. This special symbol had to mean something."

Jacques said, "Have you found a hidden room?"

Michael said, "Yes. We have examined the neighboring walls that were adjacent to all the all-raised symbol. We would knock on the wall with a hammer. Our Team members could tell if there was a hollowness behind the wall. He continued, "Let me show you." He picked up a large hammer and hit the wall behind him with the hammer. All that could be heard was a loud thud. When he struck the wall in front of him, an echo could be heard as the sound bounced off of an interior wall that was located in the hidden space."

Eduard said, "I can see the seams on this wall. It is a block that has been fitted for this precise location."

Michael said, "Yes. The seams appeared after we were able to move the wall. I then came to get you two so that you could witness our discovery firsthand."

Jacques said, "Please proceed. We all need a significant find. It has been quite some time since we have uncovered anything of importance."

The men used pry bars and eased the block out of the way. A perfectly carved entrance was revealed. The Squires lit up some extra lanterns and handed one to Michael. He was the first to enter the opening. When he entered the cavern, he discovered seven chests full of ancient gold coins and silver pieces. Behind the chests was a hand-carved wooden box. Once again, Michael knew it was not an Ossuary because it was made of wood. Ossuaries were typically carved in stone. They opened the box, and the Golden Menorah was seen with human eyes for the first time in hundreds if not thousands of years. This was the Golden Menorah that had traveled with Moses during the Exodus from Egypt. This was the find of a lifetime.

CHAPTER 23

VISION

THE GOLDEN MENORAH was a great find that came at the perfect time. After the discovery of the Cross and Burial Cloth, expectations on Jacques team were very high. No one outside of the Archeology world understood that finds such as the Cross and the Golden Menorah were once in a lifetime finds. The fact that the Knights found these artifacts less than a year apart was sensational. The problem was that the Senior Leadership of the Templars were expecting to make these discoveries on a regular basis. This was a tall order.

Jacques sat down and very proudly wrote a message to the Grand Master that detailed the finds. He handed it to one of the Warrior Commanders and explained the importance to him. He said, "This sealed scroll is to be handed directly to the Grand Master and no one else. If you come under attack you must destroy it rather than let it fall into the enemy's hands. Please take a company of your finest Warriors and leave tomorrow morning at dawn."

✠

It had been several weeks since Jacques and Eduard had met with Mary and her daughter Anna. Eduard said, "I was thinking about Mary and her special abilities and it dawned on me that she may be able to assist us with finding the Secret of Eden. She has been part of this mission as long as the two of us have."

Jacques agreed with Eduard. He said, "That is actually a great idea. Who knows more than an ageless Seer?" He continued, "Not only is she a Seer, but she knows the Secret of Eden story forwards and backwards."

The two Knights agreed to invite Mary and Anna to the Temple the following afternoon. Their big concern was how to get the two women to the Temple. If the Muslim spy saw them entering the Templar Headquarters, then there could be trouble for the women. Eduard said, "Let's have them travel to see our Jewish Scholar friends that are working in the upper ruins of the Temple under the ruse that someone amongst the scholars is ailing and they are there with an Alchemy remedy. From there I can lead them to our safe areas."

Jacques said, "Agreed."

The following afternoon arrived and the distraction of having the women enter through the Jewish entrance worked as planned. Eduard's relationship with his Jewish friends was paying dividends. The Jewish Scholars were focused on the written word whereas the Templars were there for Archeological purposes. Eduard felt that he was betraying his Jewish friends by not sharing the news of the Golden Menorah with them. But as he reminded himself, he has sworn an oath to the Templars not the Jews.

A Squire escorted the women to a room that was reserved for high level Templar meetings. Jacques walked in with Eduard and said, "How good to see both of you. I know that we have only recently met, but I feel as if you are now part of my extended family."

Mary laughed and said, "In many lifetimes, we were family."

Jacques said, "As you already know, Eduard and I are on the great mission of guarding the Secret of Eden. We feel that we must locate it and move it. We think that there may be others who know about it and are closing in. As far as our Templar superiors are concerned, we are also here to find the Ark of the Covenant and wine goblet in which Jesus celebrated the Last Supper."

Mary said, "I can tell you with absolute certainty that the wine goblet is no longer here. It left with Mary Magdalene after the resurrection of Jesus. She took it to France where it has been hidden with her descendants. Search your thoughts, you're soul and the soul of your beautiful maiden, as you call her, have spent a lifetime in the area where Mary Magdalene lived out her life in France with her daughter Sarah."

Jacques said, "Mary, every time I see you I am more startled than our previous visit." They all laughed.

Mary continued, "I have no direct knowledge of the Ark, but the legend says that the Queen of Sheba took it with her when she returned to Africa."

Eduard said, "We have heard the same story but we still must be thorough here at the Temple. We still haven't discovered the place known as the Holy of Holies. This was said to be the resting place of the Ark."

Mary said, "Search your Dreams. Especially the ones that involve the place where Abraham offered to sacrifice his son Isaac. This place is very special for many reasons. My memory is not perfect on these matters, but I believe that secrets are held in this place."

Several Squires entered the room carrying several platters of food. Anna thanked the Knights for their generosity. Eduard said, "We should be thanking you. Your mother has brought clarity to a situation that I have wrestled with my entire life."

The Knights and their guests enjoyed the supper and casual conversation. As Jacques had guessed, the two woman were from France. Mary was born and raised in the Burgundy region.

As they finished their after-supper tea, Jacques said, "One of the other reasons we wished to speak with you today is to discuss the future. The Templars believe that Jerusalem will come under attack sooner rather than later. Once we have exhausted our searches here, the plan is to have the academic Knights move back to Paris. Neither Eduard nor I believe that you will be safe here indefinitely. We can provide you safe transportation to Paris or wherever you wish." Jacques continued, "The Muslims consider all Christians to be apostate and believe that it is their solemn duty to kill them."

Mary said, "You have given us much to consider. We came to this Holy place on a pilgrimage and fell in love with the cultures. We created our Alchemy business from nothing. We would hate to walk away."

Jacques said, "The Knights will defend the Holy City with all of its might, but I can't guarantee that there won't be bloodshed. We have already had caravans leaving the holy city attacked less than an hour's walk from here."

Mary said, "The Art of Alchemy is frowned upon in many cultures even though it was handed down from the Ancient Greeks. I consider myself a devout Christian, but I am dismayed when the Pope declares people who practice Alchemy as Heretics."

Eduard said, "As I know from my studies of history, Constantine and the Roman Emperors after him forbid anything that was a threat to their power. Alchemy is a wonderful yet powerful study that most in Rome cannot explain. Our Grand Master is a very wise man. He will not condemn something just because he cannot explain it. If we explain to him how your gifts are aiding us with our searches, he will offer you protection."

Mary said, "I do not fear for my safety, but my daughter is another story."

Jacques said to Anna, "Do you possess your Mother's skills?"

Anna said, "I am starting to see things that I couldn't before, but I have a long way to go."

Mary said, "You will find that most Seers have had a serious tragedy in their past. I saw my Parents brutally murdered by

Gypsies over the clothes they were wearing. I was able to barely escape to a relatives' house. For most of my life, I moved from Abbey to Abbey. Tragedy can open up new parts of your mind. The skill of seeing souls was with me the whole time, but I didn't quite understand what I was supposed to do with it. I kept my abilities to myself. As an adult I only began to understand my role within the Children of the Flood. The Dreams, as you both are aware, are difficult to make sense of. It has taken a lifetime to achieve the understanding that I have now. I believe that my soul's purpose was to assist the two of you at this very moment."

Eduard said, "We would love to have any guidance that you can offer. The Secret of Eden was very well hidden. Guidance from the world that we cannot see will help us find it."

The two Knights, Mary, and her Daughter, Anna, decided to meet weekly to discuss progress regarding the Treasure.

CHAPTER 24

THE SECRET SEAL
OF SOLOMON

IT HAD BEEN two months since Jacques had sent the message to the Templar Headquarters in France. Finally, he received word that the Grand Master was sending a regiment of Warriors to Jerusalem to move the Golden Menorah, as well as the gold and silver treasures found with the Menorah. A few weeks later, a team of sixty Knights arrived to transfer the treasures. The Leader of the mission was once again Martine de Vossier. Martine and Jacques enjoyed supper together and discussed how the Templars had grown dramatically more powerful over the last ten years. They both knew that the newly attained stature had much do with the findings of the Cross and Burial Cloth. Jacques said, "Once these new treasures are revealed, the fame of the Knights will grow even more dramatically."

Martine's demeanor suddenly had changed. He said, "Jacques, these discoveries will never be disclosed." Martine further explained, "The Templar Leadership feels that rumors and hearsay regarding the treasures would prove to be the source of the Templars mystique and power. Throughout history, it is a proven fact that if any nation was determined enough to overpower an enemy and steal their treasures, it was just a measure of time and money. There are many of these examples throughout history. Alexander the Great, King Xerxes I of Persia, Charlemagne, and countless Viking Kings had conquered many Kingdoms and taken their treasures. The Templars have learned from this history. Very few within the Templars would know where these treasures are hidden. My guess is that they will be moved periodically for safety purposes. Moving the treasure every so often would create enough confusion to discourage the best of the treasure hunters. The Grand Master believes that if the stories regarding treasures were a thing of folklore rather than a reality, they would be safe."

"I understand. We must choose to learn from history instead of blindly repeating its mistakes." Jacques said.

Martine stated further, "The promise of hidden treasures and secrets will be the source of the Templars' Power. Of course, if a small portion of treasure is needed to be used to pay for Templar operations, then so be it. A small portion of silver and gold would be melted and re-coined as Templar currency. No one could tell where the silver and gold had originated. These coins will prove to be the most dominant currency in Europe for hundreds of years. The Templar Banking system will flourish for a long time. No one will ever question where the Templars obtained their silver and gold."

Martine would explain that he was only instructed to transport the treasures to Acre. He would be met by another team of Templars, who would guard the treasure while it is at Acre. How long it would stay there was anyone's guess.

The conversation then moved to the Temple Mount. Jacques said, "I believe we are on the precipice of making another discovery at the Temple Mount. So, I need more time."

The truth is that Jacques's team hasn't found another Star

of David in nearly one year. Jacques was thankful that Martine didn't press him on this issue. But unfortunately, Jacques could not tell him that the only evidence that the team has is from a Dream and a Seer. Jacques knew that would be scrubbing chamber pots back in France with that kind of disclosure.

Martine listened and laughed. He said, "Do you mean to the great Jacques Courtier has only one more discovery to make?" Jacques was embarrassed. He knew that he had much success but didn't understand that he was becoming a legend back in Paris. No one knew of all of his team's failures on this mission. There would also be failures in the future.

✠

The following day there was another breakthrough. Eduard burst into Jacques's office and said, "We have found the symbol that we have been looking for. We believe that we have found the Secret Seal of Solomon."

Jacques followed Eduard to the area where the Foundation Rock was located. This was the fabled rock where Abraham was going to sacrifice his son Isaac before an angel stopped him. This was also the area where Mary had instructed Jacques and Eduard to examine their Dreams. She felt that the message that accompanies the Secret of Eden was nearby.

When the two Knights arrived at the Foundation Rock, Michael waited for them. He said, "Finally, we have something substantive to go on. One of the Squires noticed an area where dried clay had broken away from the wall. A small pile of dust was directly under the area on the floor. We very carefully broke away the remaining clay debris and saw what we believe to be the Secret Seal of Solomon."

Jacques said, "The message cannot be far away."

Michael said, "I have instructed the Squires to perform the sound tests on the nearby walls and flooring."

Eduard made a sketch of this new symbol. He said, "It clearly

Secret Seal of Solomon

contains a keyhole."

Michael looked at it and immediately recognized it as ancient Egyptian. He said, "This symbol predates the Pharaohs. Why is an ancient Egyptian symbol at the Temple of Solomon? This symbol came from a time that was thousands of years before Solomon. I have seen this symbol in an ancient book that claimed to be from the infamous Hall of Records that was mentioned by Plato. The Hall has never been found, of course. Folklore regarding the symbol states that it contains a secret that explains the existence of Mankind. It explains secrets that Mankind needs to see so that the humans don't go down the same path that previous societies have gone."

Eduard smiled and said, "Previous societies?"

Michael said, "This refers to the time of Noah and the great flood. Others believe that there have been many societies that have met the same fate as the one from Noah's time."

Eduard made eye contact with Jacques. They both smiled. Both men knew that they, along with Mary, could tell the complete story.

✠

One week later, Martine led the Army of Knights out of the Promised Land. As they approached the seaport of Acre, they were ambushed by a significant Army of Muslims. Once again, the Templars easily defeated the Muslims. Most of the best Muslim warriors had been killed during the Crusades. Two Knights and five Squires were lost in the battle. The Templars would forever remember them as God's Warriors, and they would be given a Burial befitting a Knights Templar. After the battlefield was cleared, it was time for Martine to review the details of what had happened. The only conclusion was that the Muslims knew that the Knights were coming again. The spy at the Temple Mount was still at large. Martine dispatched a messenger back to the Temple Mount to inform Jacques of the attack and forward his opinion that the attackers had prior knowledge of their voyage. Once again, the Muslims knew they were coming.

✠

Michael set out on a trip to Egypt to find further evidence of this Secret Seal. After the long journey, Michael had arranged to meet with the Egyptian elder named Maat, who was an expert on Ancient Egypt. Maat had grown very old and feeble. He barely could talk. One of his Grandsons helped translate. Michael doubted this old man would be able to be of any assistance. It was doubtful that Michael could find anyone else with these skills.

Michael showed Maat the sketch of the Secret Seal of Solomon. The old man suddenly came to life. He asked, "Where did you see this symbol?"

He thought about not telling him the truth, but figured that Maat was probably his last hope. So he told the Maat that this symbol was uncovered near Abraham's Rock in the Temple Mount in Jerusalem.

Maat went on to say, "This symbol matches the symbol that I found in a chamber underneath the Sphinx."

The story that has been passed on down through the ages is that instructions on how to understand the Secret of Eden will be with the second symbol that matches the one on the Sphinx. This was a significant breakthrough for Michael. He knew where the matching symbol was located. Maat thanked Michael as he was leaving. He said, "My life's mission has been achieved. You are on the eve of making a great discovery."

Michael said, "I will always make sure that your name is associated with this great discovery. Without your hard work, it would not have been possible."

Michael traveled back to Jerusalem. After his return, he had supper with Jacques and Eduard. Michael said, "I believe that when we find this message, it will be written in Sumerian. While I can translate some of the words, Maat could translate the entire message. Maat was one of the few people who could translate Ancient Sumerian Texts. The problem is that Maat is fast approaching his death. So we need to look for others that can translate ancient Sumerian."

✠

Jacques conducted several meetings with his Senior Leaders to discuss the issue of the spy. All were confident that the spy was not one of the Templars or their Squires. Each had sworn an oath which, if they violated, was punishable by death. Jacques had come to know all of the Templars stationed at the Temple Mount. They had nothing to gain by giving information to a sworn enemy. The next possibility was that one of the Templars had inadvertently mentioned the Templar travel party in front of one of the local workers. This was probably the more likely answer. Jacques knew that he had to double his efforts. This could not continue. If Knights are lost, their blood will be on his hands. The spy had become larger than life. This scoundrel had the Templars looking over their shoulders every time they ventured outside the Temple.

Eduard and Michael had significantly increased their efforts after Michael's trip to Egypt. Finally, after a very long day, both Men decided to get some rest. The following day the Historians woke early because they were excited to solve this mystery of the Secret Seal of Solomon. Michael walked with Eduard to the Foundation Rock, where the Templars had uncovered the Secret Seal. The two Knights stared at the symbol for what seemed like an eternity. Both finally concluded that the carvings on the symbol were not related to anything they had ever seen before.

CHAPTER 25

THE ANNUNAKI

ICHAEL AND EDUARD spent weeks studying what was known about the ancient societies. Jacques just sat and listened. He didn't have much to add to this conversation. He needed to soak up this knowledge.

When Michael had traveled back from Egypt, he brought four large chests with him. These chests contained replicas of old and sacred literature. Some of which was from Plato and some were even older. The authors of the older documents were unknown.

The men were examining everything that was in these chests. There were ancient Sumerian, Greek and Egyptian documents in these chests. They kept these chests in a place they called the map room. This was a room that was a natural cavern that could pass for a planned room. It was heavily guarded. Jacques instructed the guards, "Only the three of us are allowed in this room." The three Knights sat down in the map room to examine the writings that pertained to the Great Flood.

Michael went on to discuss the story of the Annunaki. He

said, "I think that this symbol is both very old and comes from a highly advanced society."

Michael said, "Do you know of these ancient beings?"

Eduard responded, "I only know what I have read in the Old Testament and the Book of Enoch."

Michael said, "The Annunaki were written about throughout the ages and appear in the mythological traditions of the ancient Sumerians, Akkadians, Assyrians, and Babylonians. The ancient Sumerians believed that the Annunaki were sent down from Heaven to teach mankind the wonders of the universe. The Sumerians believed that they were sons of gods while others believed that they were fallen Angels. The Bible's Old Testament Book of Numbers 13:32 speaks of the Sons of Anuk. Numbers went on to refer to them as Giants. The Hebrews referred to these beings as the Anaqiti. One can notice the similarities in their names. The Sumerians' society flourished around 4000 BC; whereas, the Hebrews were roughly 2000 years later. It was thought that many of the stories of the Sumerians were handed down to the Hebrews. One can only speculate as to what was lost in translation and what was lost or forgotten from the Sumerians. One other source of writings regarding the Annunaki was The Book of Enoch. This Book was not included by the Council of Nicea. The Book of Enoch was like many other written stories such as the Gnostic Gospels that were not considered Canon at the conclusion of the Council of Nicea."

Michael continued, "The First Chapter of the Book of Enoch was written about the Watchers. The First Chapter describes Enoch as "A just man", whose eyes were opened by God so much so that he saw a vision of the Holy One in the heavens, which the sons (The Watchers) of God showed to him, and from the sons, he heard everything, and he knew what he saw, but these things that he saw will not come to pass for this generation, but for a generation that has yet to come."

Eduard said, "This passage seems like a dire warning of some kind."

Michael said, "I believe that the Secret Seal of Solomon was related to Enoch's story. Enoch goes on to tell the story of the Watchers and details his travels to heaven and back. The Book goes to great length to discuss the prophecies that were later written by the Hebrews. It talks about how God would visit the Israelites on Mount Sinai. The basic summary is that the sinners are being noticed and they will perish. Only good and peaceful people shall live and prosper. The book also describes how the Fallen Angels had pro-created with the women of the time. The Hebrews believed that the offspring were considered Giants and called them the Annunaki. These Giants had devoured not only all of the food, but all of the birds and most of the other creatures roaming the Earth. When all of the food was gone, the Annunaki turned to mankind. They had a bloodthirst that was out of control. As the story goes, Uriel, who is a descendant of Enoch, prayed to God to destroy the Annunaki and restore order to God's children. God then instructs Uriel to meet with Noah, the great grandson of Enoch, and inform him that destruction is coming and only the righteous will survive. He went on to tell Noah that if he was truly righteous, God would speak to him directly and give him instructions on how to survive the deluge. What happens next is what we refer to as the Noah's Ark Story. Oddly enough this story made its way into the Bible in Genesis Chapters 6-9. The rest is history. Noah built the Ark and Enoch believed that the Watchers, at God's command, created the Great Flood and wiped out all of humanity except for the righteous and of all course a male and female from each species of beasts on Earth. The Book of Enoch went on to discuss the visions of Enoch and through many parables forecasted many of the future events that would affect God's chosen people."

Eduard asked, "Do you believe this story is true or is it like many old stories, it is an allegory? Do the Watchers still exist?"

Michael said, "Many times throughout history, events happen that no one can explain. Are these the works of the Watchers? Had the growth and development of mankind been guided by the Watchers? What did they think of the constant wars and killing of innocents? Was the use of slaves an affront to the guidelines of the Watchers? All of these things certainly were in conflict with the Commandments handed down from God to Moses. How do the conquests of Nations square with the Commandments? The common belief of Christians is that everyone would face a Judgement Day where they would have to atone for their sins. Somehow that explanation seems way too simple."

As they discussed earlier, Michael presented several Books that were copies of books written by Plato. One of the books was called Timaeus.

Michael said, "This is a very complex book that details many subjects. One of the subjects is creation. Plato believed that the Creator was an artisan. He instructed a subordinate God which Plato referred to as the Demiurge to create the physical earth. His theory in concept is fairly close to the other creation stories. However, Plato admits that his theory is a "Likely Story", but offers little in the way of evidence. Most of Plato's writings center on the Holistic Arts which some call the study of the soul. He believed that Man's body is merely a temporary prison for the soul. I find this subject enthralling, but I don't think it helps us understand the Secret Seal of Solomon." Jacques and Eduard made eye contact. They both knew that the study of the soul was at the center of this story.

The focus turned back to the symbol. Michael had speculated that the symbol was widely considered by Scholars to be an occult symbol. The symbol's most prominent feature was what looked like a keyhole.

Michael asked, "Is this keyhole meant to represent a key to knowledge? Was it a key to life everlasting?" The men sat quietly and speculated on the meaning of the keyhole.

Eduard finally answered. He said, "Solomon believed that he had a special power that allowed him to speak to all creatures from animals to demons. Somehow he was born with this ability, but common sense dictated that someone had to instruct

Solomon on how to use its powers. There were many items within Solomon's Kingdom that were said to have special powers. Not the least of which was the Ark of the Covenant. The Israelites would take the Ark into battle with them and the Ark would vanquish the enemies. Was this because the Ark contained the stone tablets that were carried by Moses with the instructions of Yahweh?" Neither Knight had any answers. Just more questions.

Michael said, "Many of these beliefs that were not included in the Bible were considered occult rather than from the God of Abraham. Did Solomon have access to the Watchers or any surviving Annunaki? No one knows for sure but this symbol seems to be telling Mankind of some kind of message. Is it a symbol of Hope or was it a warning for mankind to change its ways?"

Eduard surmised, "This depends on your point of view. If you are a righteous person then God will protect you from harm."

Jacques knew that Eduard, Mary, and the beautiful maiden were there at the time of Noah and knew much of the story. The problem is that their Dreams only extend back to the Great Flood and not before. They were born during the great cataclysm. They were the Children of the Flood, but had no knowledge of any previous stories.

CHAPTER 26

HIRAM ABIFF

ACQUES WOKE UP in the middle of the night. He just had an astonishing Dream. It was so astonishing that Jacques knew that he must record it or it would be lost. So he sat down and recorded the Dream. He recorded the following:

"My name is Isaac. I am an assistant to the great architect Hiram Abiff. Hiram was the Chief Architect for King Solomon. Myself and my brother Seth have worked for the great architect our entire lives. Hiram Abiff's greatest task was to build the great Temple. The Temple was built to celebrate the greatness of the almighty, Yahweh. The Temple took twenty years to complete. It was designed in accordance with Phoenician architectural designs and Hebrew Law. The Temple had many places but none more special than the room that was called the Holy of Holies. This was a room that was supposed to be where God lived. It would also be the home of the Ark of the Covenant. Everyone in the Kingdom knew about the Ark. What everyone did not know was that the room had a secret that was as powerful as the Ark. It was a sacred message. The message had been carved in stone. The message gave instructions on how to open the

vault that contained the Secret of Eden. The Secret of Eden could only be activated by the worthy. The message defined the worthy as a time period and a particular person or group of people. The people that will exist in the future time period will be peaceful and will have built a society where all men and women are equal, and all civilizations live in Peace. If the world's population could not abide by these rules, then the Watchers would destroy all of the people on Earth as they have done on many occasions. They can cause floods, earthquakes, and other seemingly natural disasters. It went on to say that there is a faraway land that has the resources and the Almighty's blessing to be the centerpiece of this civilization. Once this society was completed, the Secret of Eden would be revealed. The secret would answer all of the questions regarding the Human race and what is mankind's destiny. The secret itself was secured at another location. The other location was not revealed to anyone other than Solomon himself. It is told that Solomon identified the secret message and the Secret of Eden with his Seal.

✠

After morning prayers, Jacques met Eduard for breakfast and said, "I had a Dream about the message last night." He handed Eduard the parchment that detailed the Dream. Eduard read the notes and was astonished. Jacques said, "This Dream was very revealing, but I still don't know the exact location of the message, but I believe it was in or very near the Holy of Holies room."

Eduard asked, "Was I in the Dream?"

Michael said, "Yes. You were my brother Seth. The Dream was very short. Mary and the beautiful maiden were not part of what I saw, but I'm sure, as always, they were close by."

The Knights discussed how they felt it was essential to locate the Holy of Holies. They had to make it the focus of their efforts. They had to do this without telling Michael about the Dream.

Jacques said, "Part of our mission here is to find the Ark of the Covenant. There is ample evidence to tell us that the Ark was stored within the Holy of Holies. Michael will not question our motives."

Later that morning, Jacques called a meeting with Eduard and Michael. The meeting would take place in the map room. An hour later, the three Knights met as requested. Jacques said, "I had time to reflect on the matter of the message. We will find many answers once we locate the room known as the Holy of Holies. It was said that the Ark of the Covenant was located there. It only makes sense that Solomon would have the message of the Secret of Eden nearby. Let's conduct our searches and research to find this room."

Jacques's thoughts went back to the beautiful maiden. Was she guiding his Dreams? It seemed very coincidental that he had this Dream about Hiram Abiff at the time he needed it most.

The three Knights started to take a deep dive into finding the Holy of Holies. There were large tables there where they could lay out the maps and drawings. Eduard started the meeting by saying, "Let's review what we know about this room." Eduard continued, "Very little was known about the materials used in the Temple's construction. The Temple was destroyed by the Babylonians around the late sixth century BC. The fact that it was said to have been burned to the ground meant that the building was probably constructed from wood." The Hebrew Bible Accounts state that the Temple was plundered by the Neo-Babylonian Empire King Nebuchadnezzar II when the Babylonians attacked Jerusalem during the brief reign of Jehoiachin. A decade later, Nebuchadnezzar again besieged Jerusalem and after 30 months finally breached the city walls in 587 BCE, subsequently burning the Temple, along with most of the city."

There were precise details on the dimensions of the Holy of Holies. The Holy of Holies or Inner House, as it was sometimes referred was 20 cubits in length, breadth, and height. The Book of Exodus gives very specific details:

It was floored and wainscoted with cedar of Lebanon (1 Kings 6:16), and its walls and floor were overlaid with gold (6:20, 21, 30), amounting to 600 talents (2 Chr. 3:8) or roughly 20 metric tons. It contained two cherubim of olive-wood, each 10 cubits high (1 Kings 6:16, 20, 21, 23– 28) and each having outspread wings of 10 cubits span, so that, since they stood side by side, the wings touched the wall on either side and met in the center of the room. There was a two-leaved door between it and the Holy Place overlaid with gold (2 Chr. 4:22); also a veil of tekhelet (blue), purple, and crimson and fine linen (2 Chronicles 3:14; compare Exodus 26:33). It had no windows (1 Kings 8:12) and was considered the dwelling-place of Yahweh.

Eduard, Michael, and Jacques all agreed that this room would have burned down rather quickly if a fire was started. This led them to believe that the secret message had to be buried in the Floor. The men agreed that the next step was to locate the exact location of the Holy of Holies in the First Temple of Solomon.

CHAPTER 27

THE HOLY OF HOLIES

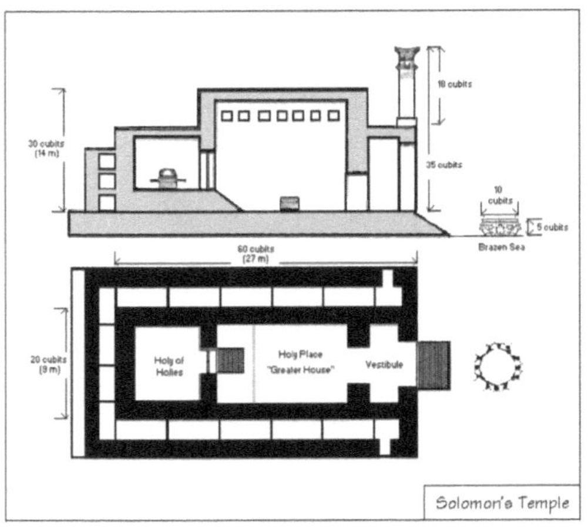

Diagram of the First Temple of Solomon

S INCE THE BIBLE recorded a very detailed set of designs of the First Temple of Solomon, it should not be difficult to locate where the Holy of Holies was within the Temple site. At least that was the Knights thought at the onset of this search. Eduard and Michael started to review the floor plan of the First Temple. They met outside of the Temple Mount for the first time in weeks. They needed to walk the grounds to look for signs of the first Temple foundation. One obvious artifact was the Western Wall. The problem is that the Western Wall was created during the construction of the Second Temple. A big problem that the Knights discussed is that other than the Old Testament; there is no proof that the First Temple ever even existed. The only written testimony regarding the First Temple had come from the Book of Exodus. While the Book of Exodus told the incredible story about the Temple, it failed to help identify its exact location. Jewish Historians have debated this issue for centuries. The common beliefs regarding the Temple come from the Talmud. The Talmud is the central text of Rabbinic Judaism and the primary source of Jewish religious law and theology. Chapter 54 of the Talmud, which is referred to as the Tractate Berakhot, states that the Holy of Holies was directly aligned with the Golden Gate, which would have placed the Holy of Holies slightly to the north of the Foundation Rock. The Golden Gate is the eastern gate of the Temple Mount. Jewish legend believed that this was the gate that welcomed God into the Temple of Solomon.

Eduard and Michael decided that this was an excellent place to start. The fact that the Golden Gate and the Foundation Rock still existed made the mission a little easier. They immediately went to the area that the Talmud had described as the location of the Holy of Holies. All that was there was an extremely hard rock floor. This floor seemed to be the original foundation of the Temple. They used hammers to check the floors for hollow cavities. None were found. Next, their attention went to the Foundation Rock. This rock was one of the most important places for Judaism, Christianity, and Islam. All of the traditions believed that this was the spot where the world began. This was the rock where God instructed Abraham to sacrifice his son Isaac. A messenger had stopped Abraham after God saw that Abraham was willing to follow God's word. The Muslims believe that the Foundation Rock is where the Prophet Mohammad left to go on his famous Night Journey.

The problem was that if the Holy of Holies was over the Foundation Rock, then the Talmud had to be mistaken. So the men decided to return to the cavern where they left all of the ancient writings.

When the Knights arrived at the map room, Jacques joined them. They updated Jacques about their thoughts regarding the Golden Gate and the Foundation Rock. Eduard gathered some ancient texts that he could not translate. He handed them to Michael to see if he could translate the messages. The texts were written in a dialect of Hebrew that Eduard had never seen before. Michael had studied the texts for hours. He struggled with the translations himself.

The Knights walked to the Foundation Rock. What clues had they missed? At the same time, Eduard continued to scour the site just adjacent to the Foundation Rock for clues. Nothing was obvious.

Eduard stared at the Rock for what seemed like hours. He was trying to picture how Abraham could sacrifice his son Isaac. What a decision that had been presented to him by God. Would God do such a thing? It seemed beyond comprehension. He also wondered, "Did the Rock always look like this or had it eroded over time. What effect did Noah's flood have on this Rock? Even though Noah came before Abraham, the Rock must have been in this same place." He spent many hours thinking about the Rock. He noticed one oddity about the Rock. It had what appeared to be a perfectly round hole in it. Some had referred to the Rock as the Pierced Rock because of this hole. Why was this hole there? It looked man-made. He tried to direct the light from his lantern down into the hole. This did not help. The hole or piercing hole was too long for the light to be effective. Finally, he decided to drop a pebble into the hole. It traveled for what seemed like a few feet then stopped. It seemed to have run into

The Foundation Rock or the Rock of Abraham

an obstruction. He then instructed his workers to fashion a long shaft out of wood. He wanted it carved out of wood from an Olive tree. The Olive tree provided the strongest and hardest wood in the region. The problem was trying to find a branch that was long enough to reach through the Rock.

The next day the workers presented Eduard with a perfectly hewn wood rod. It was very rigid, and Eduard was comfortable that it would not break off inside the Rock. Eduard took the rod to the Foundation Rock and fed it into the hole. In several spots, the rod became stuck. Eduard carefully twisted the rod and started to move again. Then suddenly he heard a sound. It was the pebble. It had reached the other side of the Foundation Rock. Eduard had expected to hit a dead end. Instead, he heard the pebble bounce off of a floor that was considerably far away from the Rock. Eduard smiled. There was an opening under the Foundation Rock. This had not been reported in any written history that he was aware of.

CHAPTER 28

THE WELL OF SOULS

ONCE AGAIN, JACQUES woke up in the middle of the night after one of his Dreams. He had kept a quill and parchment near his bed because he believed that the Dreams would be more frequent as they got closer to finding the hidden message. The beautiful maiden would see to it. He recalled the Dream as follows: *Fortunately, this Dream included the beautiful maiden. I believe that she was my wife in this Dream. She was a stunning brunette. We both dressed as if we were both Royals of some kind. Even though she was a brunette in this Dream, I knew it was her. I could smell the fragrance that I had smelled on the cliffs. There was a connection with her in all of our encounters that I could not explain. It went well beyond appearance. Our souls were connected. We were back in the time of Abraham. We were standing in the desert staring at the Foundation Rock. The Temple had not been constructed yet. The other people nearby were quite excited because tonight was the Summer Solstice. Generations of our ancestors had celebrated the solstice. Many thought that Man-kind's secrets would be revealed on this day. It was believed that the Sun would shine directly into the opening of the hole on the Foundation Stone at sunset. The whole was cut through the stone by God. If you were down in the cavern below the Foundation Stone when the Sun was setting, you would see the secret location of the sacred message that described what was called the "The Secret of Eden." The light would shine through the hole and point directly to the message's hidden location. The Locals believed that message had been hidden by Adam himself. This spot was considered the birthplace of humanity and the home of the secrets. As I stood there waiting for the Sun to set, my mother smiled at me. There was something familiar about her. Then it hit me. My mother was Mary. She smiled at me like she knew that she was part of my Dream.*

Jacques was stunned when he reread his written thoughts. His existence was extraordinary. He was part of humanity's future. He needed to tell Eduard about this most recent Dream.

Meanwhile, Jacques had many other matters to tend to. A Messenger had arrived from Templar Headquarters. The decision was made to reduce the number of Templars working at the Temple Mount. Many of the top Academics within the Templar community were working at the Temple Mount. It seems that there were other sacred sites discovered in both France and Scotland that needed to be researched. The Templars had many Warrior Knights but very few Academics. Many Junior Academics were still learning not only the ways of the Templars but the many languages of recorded history. This knowledge could only come with the test of time. The Junior Academics needed to work side-by-side with the Senior Academics so they would be Master Academics themselves one day.

✠

Eduard joined Michael and Jacques to look at the drawings, texts, and other documents regarding the First Temple of Solomon. Eduard was very excited. He started to tell us about the hole in the Foundation Rock. Eduard detailed how he forced the olive wood rod through the opening and discovered the space below.

Michael wondered, "Could this be the fabled Well of Souls?" Michael had found references, in several ancient texts, about the Well of Souls. However, most experts on the subject had declared the Well to be a thing of fiction. The flooring had been echo tested many times, and no space was detected. Michael began to summarize what was known about the Well of Souls.

Michael said, "It was believed that the Well was a natural cavern that was below the Foundation Rock. There was no known access to the Well. The Hebrews believed that the Well contained the souls of those who were waiting for Judgement Day. It was also believed to be the hiding place of the Ark of the Covenant while the Temple was under attack." He went on to say, "All of this was pure speculation because the Well of Souls has never been found. Hopefully, we will soon correct that."

Once again, the three Knights inspected the area around the Foundation Stone. They checked the site for at least 100 feet in all directions. There was no sign of an opening. Eduard began to study the Piercing Hole again. The hole went from west to east. He speculated that if they dug on the east side of the Foundation Rock, they would break through to the cavity that lies underneath. They all were concerned that if they were not careful, the entire area could collapse under the weight of the Foundation Rock. The workers began digging out a small area of hardened clay. Michael thought that it was odd that there was clay in this area. He expected the flooring to be hardened bedrock. They continued to dig for about ten inches. They cleared the balance of the clay and dirt. Eduard was looking over the worker's shoulders when something caught his eye. It appeared to be a seam. The men had to dig a wider berth to expose all of the seams.

Jacques declared, "This Stone was carved by man." By the time this stone was fully exposed, it was late in the day. The Knights decided to call it a day. Over supper, the three Knights planned what would happen the next day. Michael suggested that they bring in someday helpers to remove the stone. After the stone was removed, only Knights and Squires were going to be allowed in the area. Jacques thought to himself, "Would the Muslim adversary show his face." He reminded the Knights, "Remember to speak only Latin in the presence of the workers."

The next morning the helpers had shown up with a hoist, shovels, and pry bars. At first, pry bars were used. Then, the stone began to move. The workers continued to push the stone upward. Finally, the men were able to get a heavy rope under the stone. They tied the rope around the stone from side to side and then from end to end. The excess rope was tied to the line on the hoist. Four men then began to pull the rope that was around the hoist wheel. As the stone was lifted, a gust of stale air wafted through the entire area. The stone was removed and set aside. At that point, all of the helpers were ordered to leave the site. After the area was clear, Eduard lowered his lantern into the opening. The men were shocked by what they saw. There was a stone staircase. Michael led the men down the stairway. After sixteen steps, they finally hit the cavern floor. The Squires lit another five lanterns. The entire area was adequately lit. Near the staircase were large portions of bedrock that projected in towards the stair. The Squires called the projection to the right "the tongue." To their surprise, the floor was tiled with marble. Michael decided to have the Squires clean the cavern. The air was so heavy with dust that it was difficult to breathe.

Eduard, Michael, and Jacques decided to take a break for several hours to let the cavern air out so that it could be explored. They were very excited. Even though their mission was to find the sacred message, they had made an amazing discovery. Not since the era of the First Temple of Solomon has man laid eyes on the Well of Souls. This cavern was only mentioned in the Talmud. It was not mentioned in the Bible. What was its purpose? The cavern was always meant to be easily concealed. One of the ancient texts said the cavern was used when the Temple was under siege. We agreed that the first order of business was to locate the sacred message. After that, the entire cavern would need to be examined. There may be false doors or hidden carvings.

✠

Later that afternoon, the Knights returned to the cavern. Much of the dust had been removed. Michael immediately noticed that there were two niches carved into the walls. Michael explained that the Talmud had described the Well of Souls as having two niches. One was dedicated to David. It was the niche with a trefoil arch supported by miniature marble twisted-rope columns. The other niche is a shallower but ornately decorated prayer niche dedicated to Solomon. So far, the Talmud texts have been entirely accurate. Jacques thought to himself, "Even though these discoveries were historic, they were not part of their mission."

For the next few hours, they scoured the cavern for any clues. What they had hoped to find was the Secret Seal of Solomon. But, unfortunately, this was nowhere to be seen. It was now quite late, and then we decided to call it a day. They would reconvene again in the morning to continue the search.

The next morning Jacques and Eduard talked about Jacques' most recent Dream. Jacques said, "There obviously is a message being sent to me. Maybe from the Heavenly Father himself, but more likely they are coming from the beautiful maiden." There was an important task lying ahead for the Knights on that day. They then said their morning Prayers and enjoyed a quick breakfast of bread and various fruits.

Shortly thereafter, Eduard and Jacques met Michael and a team of Squires at the Foundation Rock. They descended the staircase. The dust had further settled. They immediately began to look at the piercing hole. Obviously, the Temple blocked the Sun. They could only speculate where the beam would hit. Jacques told Michael a slightly modified version of his thoughts. He left off any mention of his Dreams. Instead, he said, "I had a thought last night. Maybe the hole is pointing at something."

Michael instructed one of the Squires to insert the rod carved from the olive branch back into the hole from the top side of the Foundation Rock. This took a few minutes. The rod was finally inserted into the hole. It began to protrude from the other end. Eduard shouted for the Squire to stop pushing. It was difficult to place the exact spot on the adjacent wall where the beam would hit. The rod could move around. The placement could vary by four or five feet. By using a sharp stone, Michael drew a rough circle around where the sunbeam would strike. The wall appeared to be undisturbed bedrock. Eduard asked one of the Squires to light another lantern. The Squire held the lantern by the circle that Michael had drawn. There were no clear markings of any kind.

Eduard then used his hands to feel the surface. Again, the dust seemed to break free from the wall relatively easily. Finally, Eduard exclaimed, "This area has been covered over with a layer of clay. They even dyed the clay to match the same pigment of the bedrock."

The Knights knew that they were getting close. Michael instructed the Squires to very carefully scrape away the clay covering. He stressed the importance of scraping very gently. There could be a symbol under the clay. This uncovering was stirring up a dust cloud again. The Knights decided to adjourn. Eduard instructed the Squires to scrape away the clay and move the clay particles topside so that they could not become airborne again, further delaying the search.

Several hours had passed, and Eduard and Michael grew weary. Finally, Jacques told them, "The one thing that I have learned here at the Temple Mount is that we must have patience. Everything seems to take much longer here than everywhere else. Part of the problem is that we must do everything in secrecy."

Eduard said, "The work also takes significantly longer because of the dust. The Squires are no doubt struggling to both see and breathe through all of the dust."

A few minutes later, a Squire named Tobias appeared in the cavern. He explained that even though the dust was delaying them, they uncovered what appeared to be a seal. He described the seal, and the Knights agreed that it sounded like the Secret

Seal of Solomon. Michael instructed the Squire to clear the area around the Seal also. The Squire responded that it would take a while because of the dust. He concluded by saying that the Squires would work late into the night. He ventured that the dust would be settled by the following day. Michael, Eduard, and Jacques decided to reconvene the next morning.

✠

The break-in action gave Jacques time to deal with other endeavors that were going on at the Temple Mount. The rest of the digs were quickly coming to an end. Every lead had been tracked down. Sometimes they led to a find, and more often than not, they led to a dead end. Every hollow wall had been excavated. The treasures that had been discovered made the Templars wealthier than any nation in the world. Jacques knew that he would be credited with leading the entire operation. The part that no one else knew is that he had been guided by his Dreams, Mary, and, of course, the beautiful maiden. Many of the Templar leaders would credit Jacques for having great instincts, but he knew that he had special help. Jacques could only share the real truth with Eduard. In this profession, it was difficult to have long and endearing friendships. Eduard was the exception. Jacques and Eduard shared a special bond that was thousands of years old. Jacques thought about how his and Eduard's paths kept crossing. Even though Eduard had gone down the path of being a Historian, the two kept coming together. The commitment to the Knighthood was a lonely one. Their friendship made the usual solitary lifestyle of being a Knight more enjoyable.

Jacques's thoughts quickly turned to the spy that had relayed the message about the Knights transporting treasure back to France. He needed to set the trap. First, he would assign several of the Knights and their Squires to track the comings and goings of the helpers. He had noticed that the helper named Abdul seemed to keep reappearing time and time again. Nothing obvious told Jacques that Abdul was the spy, but he knew to trust his intuition. Maybe the beautiful maiden was telling him something. He noticed that Abdul seemed to be listening to the Knight's conversations. Jacques had assumed that none of the helpers spoke French. Jacques decided to make up a story about a new treasure that would be transferred over the next few days. He would make sure to speak within earshot of Abdul. Jacques wanted to catch this scoundrel red-handed. He alerted Michael and Eduard about the plan so that they could help set the trap.

The next morning Jacques met Eduard and Michael for Morning Prayers and then sat down for a meal to start the day. They soon ventured to the Foundation Rock to see how the Squires had done. They climbed down the staircase and immediately saw the Secret Seal of Solomon staring at them. This was the same seal that they had seen above ground near the Foundation Stone. Also, this is the same symbol that Michael had shown the old Egyptian man several weeks ago in Egypt. The three Knights were elated at the discovery, but what did it mean? On one side of the symbol, Eduard noticed what appeared to be a seam. Michael said, "If we keep clearing the clay, we will find a rectangular seam. This will be our sign that something is hidden behind the symbol. This scenario was identical to the hidden stone that had led to the staircase. Michael instructed the Squires to dig and expose the entire seam. The dried clay broke off in chunks this time and did not generate the dust as the earlier excavations had done. The Squires had quickly exposed the entire seam. Michael then told a Squire to get the pry bars and hoist that they had used to reveal the staircase.

After several painstaking hours, the stone began to move. Eduard told the Squires, "It is of utmost importance that you move very slowly. This stone has been here for thousands of years. This stone is, in fact, a piece of history."

The Squires very carefully inched the stone forward. Finally, they were able to get the hoist ropes around the stone. Once the ropes were secured, they could use the hoist to help ease the stone away from the wall. Eduard and Michael were discussing the Seal. Michael said, "I believe that this seal was much older than the time of Solomon's reign."

Jacques smiled at Eduard. He already knew this to be true. This stone was very likely placed there by Adam himself.

Finally, the stone was pulled away from the wall. The Squires carefully moved it away from the opening and safely set it down. Eduard then held a lantern up to the opening. He saw a rectangular stone plate roughly three feet long, two feet wide, and 2 inches thick. Michael then instructed the Squires to build a transport crate for the stone plate. The next step was very critical. From what he could see, the Tablet had carvings on it. If the Tablet was dropped or damaged, the message would be lost forever. Eduard requested that one of the Squires leave and locate the Knight named Rene. He was a Master Builder. He would construct a fixture that would not only perfectly support the Tablet but would have handles built in so that the Tablet could easily be transported. A few minutes later, Rene appeared. Rene congratulated the Knights on their find. Rene had built very steady transfer carts for all of the precious treasures. Michael showed the Tablet to Rene. Rene said, "I will have the transport ready in two to three hours." Eduard, Michael, and Jacques returned to the document room to discuss the next steps.

The Three Knights sat down to discuss the findings. Michael said, "From what I can see on the Tablet, it was inscribed with Sumerian Cuneiform." Michael further explained, "Most of my time as a Knight has been spent learning the ancient languages. Many of the findings throughout Greater Mesopotamia were written in Sumerian, which is the oldest written language ever discovered. The oldest findings were from as early as 3000 BC. As with many ancient artifacts, most finds were badly damaged by the elements and antiquity itself. One of the most difficult aspects of Sumerian was the many dialects."

Michael further suggested, "This was probably rewritten several times. As the Sumerian writing techniques improved over the centuries, they would often rewrite the messages to clarify the translation. As a result, most Sumerian writings from before 3000 BC were not translatable. He further explained that it wasn't until roughly 2100 BC during a period known as the Sumerian Renaissance that written documents could be understood by modern Historians and Archeologists."

Eduard then asked, "Michael, do you think you will be able to translate the message."

Michael responded, "I can understand certain characters, but I am not an expert. However, I have worked with several Sumerian experts at the various Archeological sites in Egypt. The old Egyptian named Maat is one of them."

Jacques said, "Since we know that the Secret of Eden is buried beneath the ancient Sphinx, we should transport the message to Giza. If we make the discovery, I'm sure that the Grand Master will want to move the message and the Secret of Eden to a safer location after."

Several hours later, Rene had appeared to announce that the transport was ready. Jacques knew that it was always accurate when Rene made such a statement. Jacques always admired how Rene would construct such things as a transport in such short order. They were always very robust. He told Rene, "The Carriage makers back in France can't hold a candle to your work."

Rene said, "I am from a long line of builders. It is in my bloodline."

Jacques, Eduard, and Michael hurried to the Well of Souls. When they arrived, they saw that the transport was at the same height as the Tablet. Rene said that the Squires would just have to slide the Tablet onto the transport. The Squires proceeded to do so very slowly. The process took approximately thirty minutes. Once that Tablet was completely removed from its resting place, the Knights agreed to have Michael try to understand the message before the Tablet was transported up the narrow staircase just in case it breaks.

Michael studied the Tablet for a few hours. Jacques looked

at the carvings and was mystified that anyone could make sense out of these carvings. Finally, he said, "This appears to the untrained eye to be just a series of straight lines that formed primitive shapes."

Eduard had brought a quill and parchment so that Michael could record the translation. Michael finally walked away from the Tablet and said, "I am sorry, but I can only translate several words and phrases from the Sumerian text." He continued, "We should stick with our plan to transport the message to Giza."

Michael wrote the phrases that he understood. His notes included the following phrases:

The Watchers
All men are created equal
Death and destruction
Stop Wars and Conquests
The Great Lion in the Land of the Great River
Secret of Eden
Key to the Secret
The Land of Plenty

The three Knights stared at these messages for seemingly hours, but it was only minutes in actuality. Eduard spoke first. He declared, "The Great Lion refers to the Sphinx of Giza in Egypt. The Sphinx was carved from limestone and had the body of a lion and the head of a human."

Obviously, Michael was very well acquainted with the Sphinx because he had spent many years in Giza. They glossed over "the Watchers." They all had discussed the Watchers at length. Even though they expected to see the term Watchers, it was still shocking to see it on this ancient carving. They understood the meanings of "All men were created equal," "Death and Destruction", and "Stop Wars and Conquests." These were basic sayings that were akin to the teachings of Jesus Christ. They were baffled by "Key to the secret."

Michael said, "There always has been a legend about the Secret of Eden. It was considered a myth by many, but those who believed in it said that it contained the answers to all of the secrets of mankind." Of course, both Jacques and Eduard already knew this.

Michael continued, "In regards to the other saying, "The Land of Plenty", this may pertain to a mysterious continent that was supposedly west of Europe, past Greenland and Iceland, and across a vast sea.

Jacques asked, "Could this be the fabled Atlantis that Plato had spoken of? We should confer with Templar Leaders back in France. Some of the elder Knights may know this "Land of Plenty.""

✠

Later that evening, Jacques and Eduard met to discuss how this discovery interacted with the Dreams that both Knights were having. Jacques said, "The Dreams have no doubt led us to this discovery. We are now in the most dangerous part of our mission. If the message falls into the wrong hands, then the Secret of Eden will be lost. I am sure that our adversaries would just destroy the message. From what I know of the Muslims, if a message came from anything other than the Quran, it is considered apostate and will be destroyed." He continued, "In the morning, I will dispatch a message to the Grand Master. Our next move must be carefully planned."

Eduard said, "Should Michael travel in advance with a written copy of the message?"

Jacques said, "I think we should only move in heavy numbers. If word has leaked out, then we should be ready for a major confrontation. Let's hear from the Grand Master first."

The two Knights discussed past encounters with strangers where the Secret of Eden was discussed. Jacques was immediately taken back to the battle with the Muslims when he was a Squire. He referred to the Muslim warrior near him on a battlefield. Jacques recalled, "With his last breath, he told me to

"Protect the Secret of Eden." I had no idea what this meant, but it was important enough for this Muslim to say it with his last breath. Who was this Muslim? Had his body been taken over by the Holy Spirit? Once again, I had more questions than answers. If this dying Muslim knew of this secret, then how many others knew? We may be walking into a trap. I can't help but wonder if they knew of the Secret that is buried underneath the Sphinx, but had no information regarding the message that was required to understand the secret. Had we just completed the task for them? Let's meet with Mary and Anna tomorrow. I will send an invitation with a Squire in the morning."

CHAPTER 29

THE FOREBODING

J ACQUES FOUND HIMSELF Dreaming of the time of Noah once again. This time he found himself, or Peleg, as he was known, much older than the first Dream of Noah. The same was true for his wife Tytea and his brother Joktan. Miraculously, Noah and his wife Na'amah were still alive. The Lord obviously had granted them favor in terms of longevity. Everyone around them had aged. They looked exactly the same.

Tytea was very ill, and Peleg was terrified that death was near. So, as they had done almost daily, they walked to the Great River. The Great Flood had spawned all kinds of new growth near the Great River. These plants were not known to be in this region before the Great Flood. There was one plant in particular that always drew Tytea to it. Its fragrance was unforgettable. It was a soft purple in color, and one sniff of the fragrance had a calming effect over Peleg and Tytea. In combination with the flowing water, the fragrance would soothe any ailment. That is why Peleg still brought Tytea to the banks of the Great River every day. He was hoping for a miracle.

Tytea turned to Peleg and said, "My days here in this lifetime are drawing to a close, but as the Watcher told us, we will be together for eternity. This fragrance will be part of my soul going forward. You will know that I am with you whenever you smell the purple flower."

✠

Jacques once again woke up startled from a Dream. First, he was saddened by the fact that Tytea was near death. Then it dawned on him. All of these people died thousands of years ago. The great news was that he periodically smelled this fragrance. He knew of it from his farming days back in France. The plant was called Lavender. He could smell it in his Dreams, and he also smelled it during his most trying times. The smell of Lavender brought Jacques a feeling of euphoria. He would seek out Lavender on his next visit to the marketplace.

✠

The first order of business was that Jacques needed to send an invitation to Mary and Anna for supper this evening. He included a question asking the women if any of the jars at their store contained Lavender. There was no doubt that Mary would understand this request.

The next item was to write a letter to the Grand Master detailing the Message and how it needed to be transported to Egypt. It would have to be heavily guarded. The letter also discussed the upcoming changes to the staff at the Temple Mount. Jacques knew that a significant number of Warriors would be leaving Jerusalem. Most of the Knights currently stationed at the Temple would travel to Egypt with the Message. Some others would remain in Jerusalem and continue their original mission of protecting the Pilgrims and serving as a Bank. Once again, he tasked his friend Martine to deliver the sealed letter. As he had done before, Jacques instructed Martine to destroy the letter rather than let it fall into the hands of the enemy.

✠

Later that afternoon, Mary and Anna arrived at the Temple. As they had done on their previous visit, they entered the Temple through the quarters of the Jewish Scribes. A Squire led them to the very private meeting room they had used at the last meeting. Jacques and Eduard joined them a few minutes later. The two Knights warmly greeted their guests. A Squire delivered a pot of tea and some fruit.

Mary spoke first. She said, "I am so happy that you discovered the fragrance with which you have become familiar. As far as your request for Lavender, yes, we do have Lavender, but it will never be as beautiful as the fragrance that you will smell when her spirit is present. However, I have brought you a gift that will hopefully bring you peace when you see it." She handed me a beautiful Egyptian silk cloth that was the color of the Lavender Flowers.

Jacques said, "You have no idea what this means to me. I will have it with me in all of my travels."

Eduard said, "Not to change the subject, but have you had a chance to think about our offer to safely transport you back to France?"

Anna said, "Yes. We still haven't made up our minds."

Mary said, "I rarely have a glimpse into the future, but I foresee a great battle taking place that involves the Templars and the Muslims. Most will think it is because of the Crusades, but it will, in actuality, be a battle for the Secret of Eden. You must succeed, or the fate of mankind will be doomed. I foresee great loss for the two of you, but I believe that the Lord Almighty will intervene on our side."

Jacques said, "I now see the truth. My chance meeting with

you was not chance at all. I believe that you are as important as Eduard and myself when it comes to protecting the Secret of Eden. I think you should join us on our mission to Egypt. You can help guide us through the worst of storms just as you helped Noah guide the Ark through the Great Flood. We will keep you far from the battle, and I will personally assign multiple seasoned guards for your protection. You are a Child of the Flood and a Guardian of the Secret of Eden just like Eduard and myself."

Mary said, "I accept your offer, but my daughter has her own path to follow."

Anna said, "Mother, please don't think for a minute that I am letting you go on this mission without me."

Mary laughed and said, "Anna, you have been a great child. I am very proud of who you have become, but I will be safe."

Anna said, "If you leave, there is nothing left for me here in Jerusalem. It is time to return to France."

Mary said, "As you wish." She paused and sipped her tea and said, "The great adversary is amongst us here in Jerusalem. He is waiting for the right moment to strike. Please do not underestimate him. Do not forget that he is a Child of Canaan and has the great demon guiding his moves." She paused briefly and said, "I feel a sense of foreboding that has come over us. The battle is near."

Jacques said, "Do you know who this enemy is?"

Mary said, "I would need to confront him and look directly into his soul. However, I believe that you already know who this person is. You must trust your instincts." She paused a moment and continued, "Having said that, I do know who he was back in the time of Noah. He was your cousin and my grandson, Canaan. He was drawn in by evil one. His descendants grew into a large and unholy tribe that was referred to as the Canaanites. Many of them were most famously destroyed in the Sodom and Gomorrah story." She paused and continued, "The most alarming part of this is what happens now. I don't mean in the next year. I'm talking about the next thousand years. For the first time since the time of Adam, the message has been unearthed, and I believe that you will also locate the Secret of Eden. These items have been just the subject of folklore and legend up until now. Please understand me. I believe that you have to relocate these great artifacts. But now, you will gain new enemies who will do anything to capture these artifacts. Dark days are upon us, but we shall prevail."

CHAPTER 30

THE PLAN

J ACQUES HAD TO turn himself away from the thoughts of the stone carving and its message to deal with the spy. He knew that the helper named Abdul was indeed the spy. He had been guided to this fact. Jacques devised a plan to make sure that Abdul was within earshot when Jacques told the Knights how the treasure would be transferred back to France via the Seaport of Haifa. Jacques had alerted the Knights of this trap that was about to be set.

Jacques summoned a Squire and instructed him to find out the whereabouts of the helper named Abdul. He explained that he had a special project and would like to have Abdul assist. The Squire hurried off to honor Jacques's request. The assumption was that Abdul was probably a Muslim and had a grievance with the Templars. The Muslims in Jerusalem were either driven out or killed during the Crusade a few years earlier. Jacques guessed that Abdul lost his family and probably his ancestral home during the Crusade. He had a grievance to settle with the Crusaders.

Jerusalem had been the source of conflict ever since King David entered the city carrying the famed Ark of the Covenant. Many nations have laid claim to the fabled city ever since. The Jews had claimed Jerusalem as their promised land, as described in the Book of Exodus. The Christians said it was their Holy Land because that's where Jesus was crucified, was buried, and rose from the dead. Roughly seven hundred years later, Mohammad had begun his journey to heaven from the Foundation Stone. The Muslims would initially claim the Dome of the Rock and the Al Aqsa Mosque as their Holiest place. Jacques knew that the conquests were far from over. The Knights could not stay there forever to keep the peace. The people of this land would have to agree on a government that satisfied all three major religions. This would be a tall order.

Nearby a team of Squires entered the Old City. This was the area where most of the helpers lived. They spoke with many of the usual helpers. Unfortunately, no one seemed to know where Abdul was. After several hours of searching, they returned to the Temple Mount with several of the usual helpers. They brought them into the Temple under the guise that they had work for them to complete. The lead Squire told Jacques the news that they had not located Abdul, but they had brought in several helpers that usually were seen with Abdul.

Jacques met the Squires in the Great Hall. They had the helpers waiting there also. He asked them as a group, "Where is Abdul?" No one spoke up. The group of helpers had a leader named Mahmed, who usually negotiated their daily rates, which did not usually come in the way of coin, but they were generally paid with food and grains that would support their families. Jacques summoned Mahmed to walk with him.

At first, Jacques offered double the usual daily rate of food and grains. Mahmed hesitated but said, "I don't know anything." Jacques knew from the way that he carried himself throughout the conversation that Mahmed knew something. Jacques then pulled out a gold coin that he had been saving for the right moment. Jacques thought to himself that if this doesn't work, then, Mahmed truly doesn't know the whereabouts of Abdul. Upon seeing the gold coin, Mahmed's eyes lit up. This was enough gold to feed his family for months. He could also buy some livestock so that his family could have its own sustenance going forward. Mahmed agreed to speak. Jacques summoned a Squire who could translate the conversation. Jacques wanted to clearly understand what Mahmed had to say. Once the translator was there, Jacques asked, "Mahmed, this gold coin is yours if you tell me Abdul is."

Mahmed replied, "Abdul had left with a group of Muslims who had been hiding out in the Old City. They left one day earlier for Egypt." Jacques's blood began to boil. He knew that he had waited too long to confront Abdul. Jacques thought to himself, "This will not happen again." He then handed the gold coin to Mahmed and headed back to meet with the other Knights to tell them of Abdul's departure.

Jacques informed Eduard and Michael that Abdul had left for Egypt. The three Knights knew that danger now awaited them in Egypt.

"The Tablet has not yet been translated. So Abdul didn't know what he was looking for." Eduard said.

Jacques said, "This is more about the attack on the Knights than any treasure. Remember, the Quran forbids Muslims from worshiping any false gods. They were only to bring praise to Allah and his Prophet Mohammad."

Jacques knew that it was critical to travel with a large army of Knights. The Muslims would have their experienced warriors waiting in Egypt for the Knights. Jacques knew it was time to bring his old friend Martine de Vossier into the plan. Martine had defeated the Muslims many times and was an expert on the Muslims' tactics. Jacques sent a message via a Squire to summons Martine back to Jerusalem.

Jacques also prepared a coded message for the Grand Master. He had to convey that the Knights were on the verge of finding one of the most important discoveries ever. Perhaps the Grand Master himself would like to be there for the discovery. Also, there was another reason. Many of the Squires had performed admirably at the Temple. It was time for many of the Squires to be knighted. Jacques knew that the number of Knights needed to be increased. They were fighting battles on many fronts. The Knights were being spread thin. He dispatched a team to travel to the Templar Headquarters in France with a coded message.

✠

Martine de Vossier arrived at the Temple Mount several weeks later. He joined Eduard, Michael, and Jacques for Afternoon Prayers and supper. Martine praised the Knights for all of our work and discoveries at the Temple Mount. He said, "I know that it is not your goal, but you are becoming famous within the ranks of the Knights." The Knights shrugged it off, stating that this mission at the Temple Mount is their duty.

Jacques informed Martine of the stone carving and its significance. He said, "Nothing is as important as finding the Cross of Jesus Christ, but we believe that this find comes in a close second. We are not sure what the Muslims know. Since the dawn of man, the stone and the treasure that lies underneath the Sphinx have been the subject of folklore. Since the Muslims will consider this treasure to be an insult to Islam, they will be intent on foiling our mission and destroying our treasure. Just the chance to kill an infidel will be enough to call all Muslims to battle."

Martine said, "I have spent much time in Egypt. If we are to be successful, we must rule the Nile. We must secure a port near Giza where we can load the treasure and quickly escape. This battle will be different than any we have fought. Usually, our fights are about conquering lands and keeping them secure. This will be about seizing something special and returning via the Great River." He continued, "I think we should send a large contingent of Knights to secure a port and then have a flotilla of ships secure the surrounding Nile River area. This operation will take weeks to deploy. We should have the Grand Master buy-in before we put any plans in place."

✠

Roughly a month had passed since Martine and Jacques had discussed the Egyptian plans. Finally, the Team of Squires that had been sent to France had returned to the Temple Mount. Jacques gathered Martine, Eduard, and Michael to share the message. The return message was from the Founder and Grand Master of the Templars, Hugues de Payens.

Jacques broke the Seal of the Grand Master and began to read the document. It said, "I congratulate you on your discovery. The discoveries of the Cross and Burial Cloth of their Lord Jesus Christ had transformed the Knights and the Holy Roman church to their rightful place as the seat of power for the entire world. The new treasure discoveries, even though they are held in secret, have sealed the Templars as the wealthiest organization in the world." Jacques continued to read the Grand Master's message. He said, "The mission of the Knights is not about wealth, but is about spreading the word of Jesus Christ. The treasures allowed them to spread the message from a position of power. This is very important going forward because the Muslim Armies in the East are gaining in strength. Even though the Templars do not represent a Nation-state, they represent the ideology of Jesus Christ." Jacques summarized the rest of the message by stating that the Grand Master is on his way to the Temple Mount. He wishes to preside over the granting of the Title of Knighthood on the deserving Squires. The Grand Master deems it a great honor. He also said that he looked forward to celebrating our success in person.

Jacques set down the letter with a big smile and said, "I think we need to clean the place up." They all shared a laugh.

✠

Several weeks later, a large contingent of Knights arrived with Grand Master of the Knights Templars, Hugues de Payens. He was also accompanied by several Templar Council Members and a handful of Knights who were also Historians. Eduard, Michael, Martine, and Jacques were waiting as the Grand Master dismounted his horse. Their White Tunics had never looked so clean. They proudly represented the Templars with their exploits and their decorum. The Grand Master greeted each of his hosts with a hug and a hearty congratulations. Then, the entire contingent ventured into the makeshift Chapel at the site where Jesus was crucified.

The Knights celebrated mass and retired into the Great Hall. Jacques thought to himself, "In all of the years that I have been stationed at the Temple Mount, I have never hosted a dinner in the Great Hall. The Leadership of the Knights Templar was here to celebrate our great success. We must prepare the Great Hall accordingly."

The celebratory dinner went as planned. One of the Knights who probably had too much wine stated, "They still haven't found the Holy Grail." Everyone laughed. The Grand Master had a special smirk on his face like he knew something that no one else in the room knew. Jacques and Eduard knew why.

Jacques discussed the Dreams regarding the Holy Grail later with Eduard when they were alone. He said, "In the two Dreams that concerned the Grail, my beautiful guide was there for both. Just thinking about her allows me to smell her fragrance. In the first Dream, a French Royal family known as the Merovingians was in possession of the Holy Grail. They passed in down through the generations. They claimed a direct ancestry to Mary of Magdalene. Mary had taken the Grail when she left Jerusalem after Jesus was crucified and rose from the dead. In my second Dream, I saw Mary hide the Grail in her belongings before she set out to cross the Mediterranean Sea on her way to France."

Both Eduard and Jacques had learned Mary of Magdalene was the Matriarch of the Merovingians. The Templars had a very close relationship with the Merovingians. Even though they were no longer in power, it was rumored that before he founded the Knights Templar, Hugues de Payens was married into the Merovingian family. This was never discussed. They all had taken a vow of Chastity. This was in direct conflict with that vow even though the marriage was before the founding of the Knights Templar. Anyways, the Grail was in safekeeping for now. The Templar way was to be very secretive about their findings and treasures. Secrecy helped to create the Templar's illusion of immense power.

The evening went on for several more hours. The tales of greatness became more extensive as the wine stores were being emptied. At the conclusion of the evening, Jacques thanked the Grand Master and the Knights that accompanied him for making the Journey. Next, Jacques suggested that the group meet for Morning Prayers, and then he would give the group a tour of the Temple Mount and summarize how and where the artifacts and treasures were found. Everyone agreed and parted for the night.

The next morning the group met for Morning Prayers as planned. Then they went on the tour of the tunnels below the Temple Mount and the Well of Souls. The historians marveled at the surroundings. They claimed that Eduard and Michael acted as though God was guiding them. Next, the Grand Master requested that Martine and Jacques meet with the Templar Leadership. Jacques suggested, "Let's meet in our Map Room to discuss the Egyptian plan. It is secure."

After everyone was seated in the Map Room, Jacques explained the situation with Abdul. He admitted that the Muslim Spy had successfully worked his way into our search teams. But, he said, "While Abdul was aware that something special was being transported to Egypt, he didn't know what the stone carving was or what its message meant."

The Grand Master interrupted Jacques by saying, "The fact

that the Muslims were lying in wait for them was actually a blessing. The Knights would get to face the Muslims in battle instead of the small skirmishes that they had become accustomed to." The Grand Master went on to say, "Martine will lead the major force on horseback to secure the Giza port. A fleet of ships from Acre will sail to Giza and secure the Nile. The second smaller team of accomplished warriors led by myself will sail in with the stone and a contingent of Pilgrims a few days behind the ships from Acre. Anything short of success will be a failure."

CHAPTER 31

THE JOURNEY TO GIZA

ODAY WAS THE day that Jacques and Eduard would introduce Mary and Anna to the Grand Master. The two Knights were waiting in the usual room to meet with Mary and Anna. One of the Squires escorted the two women to the room. They exchanged warm greetings as always. Jacques started the conversation by stating, "Our forces will be escorting the stone carving to Giza by ship in a few days. The fleet will sail across the Mediterranean Sea and then enter the Nile River, where it will sail to Giza. Eduard and I will be on this ship, and we would like you to join us."

Anna said, "Will we be getting off of the ship in Egypt? This probably will be our only chance to see the Pyramids."

Eduard said, "If we feel that it is safe. You will be amongst many who have made the pilgrimage to Jerusalem. So please blend in with them."

Jacques said, "Having said that, we would like you to meet one of the Egyptian elders. He is the one who will translate the message on the stone. I think you will find him intriguing."

Mary said, "I am not worried about Anna and myself. I am worried about the two of you. Your adversary is already there waiting for you. He must be lured away from the Sphinx for there to be success."

Jacques said, "We will come up with a diversion that makes it appear that we are working elsewhere." He continued, "The other matter at hand is that we want you to meet our Grand Master, Hugues de Payens."

Mary said, "Believe it or not. I knew him as a child. We were from the same village." Everyone was astounded. Mary laughed and said, "You must remember. We are all on a mission. Even you're Grand Master."

Then Hugues de Payens entered the room. He stopped and stared at Mary for what seemed like an eternity. Finally, a smile came across his face. He said, "Mary?"

She said, "Yes, Hugues, it is me."

The two old friends took a few minutes to catch up. The Grand Master said to the rest of us, "Mary and I were childhood friends. Mary was very special. The last time I saw her, she told me that I would be somewhere very special and our paths would cross again. That was over forty years ago."

Jacques said, "Mary is indeed very special. She was a very important member of the team here in Jerusalem. We would not have found the stone without her. We feel that she also can help us find the Secret of Eden. She has extensive knowledge of the Secret."

The Grand Master said, "I have never forgotten Mary. I am not the least bit shocked about what you just told me."

Jacques said, "We would like her to travel to Egypt with us and then back to Paris with you."

The Grand Master said, "Very well. Mary, you and your daughter, are welcome to travel with the Knights. You will be our guests. The Knights will protect you with their lives."

The Grand Master looked at Jacques and said, "Every time

I think you are complete with your update for me, you bring to light something even more amazing than your last update." Everyone smiled.

✠

Later that afternoon, the Grand Master led the ceremony that promoted the Squires to Knights. Everyone congratulated the newly knighted. Everyone was very happy for the former Squires, but there wasn't much time to celebrate. One negative result that occurred is now there was a severe shortage of Squires. The Grand Master recognized this and instructed the Knights that they would have to assume the tasks that were usually performed by the Squires. When this mission was completed, Hugues de Payens would enlist many new Squires into the knighthood. Many young men had expressed interest in becoming a knight. The Knights had grown immensely over the last few years. Prospective Squires would be standing in line back in France.

The Grand Master and Martine finalized the plans of the venture to Egypt. The other Knights were reminded that Hugues de Payens was a decorated warrior before founding the Knights Templar. He relished in the opportunity to fight on behalf of the order that he had founded. Both the Grand Master and Martine realized that they would probably be attacked as they reached Giza. Which side of the Nile would the attack come from was the question. It was critical that they set up a secure harbor so that their forces and supplies could unload. They also had to be able to quickly escape with the treasure when required. This mission was not their typical overwhelm and conquer like most of their conquests resulted in. This was to be a quick extraction followed by a quick escape. The Muslim Commanders would be baffled by this tactic. Jacques thought to himself, "Abdul was not a Commander, but he knew what the Templar's mission was. I wonder if he has similar Dreams."

Several hundred Knights left Jerusalem on horseback on day

one of the mission. They were led by Martine. Their orders were to travel to Giza and arrive from the west. The last leg of their journey involved crossing the desert. They were to secure the port first. Their mission was probably the most difficult. Next, a fleet of ten ships would sail out of Acre. Their mission was to secure the Nile. The last contingent would include four ships. One of the four would be Hugues de Payens Command Ship. The Message Stone would be on this ship. It was accompanied by Jacques, Eduard, Michael, Mary, and Anna. These ships would depart from the port city of Haifa.

✠

Three weeks later, the Command ship arrived in Giza. The various ship captains met with the Grand Master upon his arrival. A fact of war is that nothing ever went entirely according to plan. Jacques joined the Captains meeting. The Grand Master was told the disturbing news. The Knights on horseback, led by Martine, never arrived. This meant that there were no horses or carts available for transport. The Knights would have to barter with the locals for supplies. This was a complication that bothered the Grand Master. He knew that any great army is only as good as its supply chain. The mission was not off to a good start.

✠

One positive note was that the village that the Egyptian Elder Maat lived in was a short walk from the Nile. Michael and Eduard convinced Jacques that they could go ashore dressed as locals and convince Maat to travel to the ship where he could translate the message. Jacques received permission for the mission to find Maat from the Grand Master with the requirement that six warriors would also accompany them.

CHAPTER 32

THE TRANSLATION

ACQUES LED THE team on one of the lifeboats to the shore. Jacques said, "The art of the battle requires one to rely greatly on his training. Nothing would ever go as planned. Warriors needed to be able to adjust their plans on a minute's notice. They were dressed in typical peasant Egyptian garb. After making landfall, they headed to the village where Maat lived. Thirty minutes later, they arrived in Maat's village. They proceeded to Maat's hut. They were greeted by a younger man. Michael asked, "May we see Maat."

The young man replied, "I am very sorry, but Maat died several weeks ago." Michael was very dismayed.

Michael asked the young man, "Is there anyone here in this village that had previously worked with Maat?"

The young man said, "I am not sure. Maat was my Grandfather."

Michael said, "I am very sorry for your loss. Your Grandfather was an extraordinary man and a great Archeologist."

Michael then handed the young man a hand sketch of the

secret Seal of Solomon and asked him if this symbol meant anything to him. The young man replied, "No. I will ask around to see if there is anyone here that worked with my Grandfather." He departed and went to talk to some men who were sitting nearby. Michael said to Jacques and Eduard, "There were always helpers from this village on our digs. Someone surely knows of the Seal."

Several minutes later, the young man returned with a middle-aged man. Michael immediately recognized the man. He was involved in many of the digs. He introduced himself to the man.

The man responded, "I am well aware of who you are." He went on to say, "You are one of the men that take our treasures from Giza and sell them for a profit. You did not share any of your profits with Maat. He died without anything. One of his lifelong dreams was to leave his sons with something of value. Instead, you left him with nothing."

Michael immediately recognized that this was about gold. The question that needed to be answered was did this man have any information that would lead to the location of the Secret Seal of Solomon. So he showed the man the symbol.

The man said, "I have never seen this symbol." While his words said no, his body said yes. Michael had studied the non-verbal language that all men and women speak with. He didn't have the patience to banter back and forth with this man. Instead, Michael said, "I will get directly to the point. I will give you two gold coins now, three when you show us the symbol, and then five after locating anything that may be hidden near the symbol. This is for Maat. He and his family deserved to be compensated for all he had contributed over the years."

Jacques thought to himself, "This is more currency than this man could make in ten years. He could build a major farm with this much gold."

The man said, "We have a deal."

Michael said, "How can we be sure that you know where the symbol is hidden?"

The man replied, "My name is Hamid. Maat was my father.

I was with my father when he found the symbol. After we made the discovery, we looked extensively for months for a hidden chamber but found nothing."

Michael responded, "I have the best Egyptologists with me. If there is anything to be found, we will find it." Michael continued, "We found the ancient Message Stone at the Temple in Jerusalem. We believe that it contains clues regarding the hidden chamber at the Sphinx. The problem is that the message is written in ancient Sumerian. Is there anyone here who can translate the Sumerian Text?"

Hamid said, "One of my father's associates is an expert in the Sumerian culture and translating their language. His name is Mufti. He went on to say that Mufti was an older man with minimal needs but would like to leave a dowry for his children. You must also be willing to compensate Mufti." Michael agreed.

Michael said, "You both must be willing to travel to our ship, which is anchored very close to here." Michael continued, "There are many Muslim warriors that would kill you for even talking to us. We will escort you back to our ship after nightfall."

Michael added, "I worked very well together with your father. He knew that for us, it was about the quest for knowledge, not about selling treasure. My intent was never to take advantage of your father. As a Knight, I have sworn a vow of poverty myself. However, my needs are taken care of by the Templars. I fully understand that you have needs, and we will gladly compensate you for your services."

Hamid responded, "Thank you. My father had the utmost respect for you. He was a great Archeologist, but not a very good businessman." An hour later, darkness began to fall on the Giza plain. The Templar party, including Hamid, Hamid's three sons, and Mufti, set out for the Templar Command Ship.

CHAPTER 33

THE DESERT

A FEW HOURS LATER, Jacques's landing team arrived back on the Command ship. Introductions were made, and the Egyptians were led to the lower compartment that contained the Message. Mufti's eyes lit up when he saw the stone. Even though he spent his life studying the Sumerian culture, he had only seen a few actual pieces of Sumerian artifacts. After a few minutes, Mary and Anna were led to the same room. They were introduced to Mufti and Hamid. Mufti was immediately taken back by Mary. He said, "When I first saw the two Knights (pointing at Jacques and Eduard), I knew they were special, but I didn't know why. Now that I see you with them I understand. You three are the Children of the Flood. It was thought only to be folklore, but now I realize the stories are true with you three standing right in front of me. To take it one step further, you have found the ancient message that was hidden by Adam. This indeed is a wonderful day."

Mary said, "Yes. It is true. I immediately recognized that you are a very old soul who has been on a mission to get answers. We are very close. You are asked to be a part of our mission and help us understand what the stone is trying to tell us." She paused momentarily and looked around the room, and finally said, "The lifetime work of Maat and Mufti is coming to a glorious conclusion. The treasure known as The Secret of Eden is about to be unearthed."

✠

The next morning, several Templar Scouts arrived at the banks of the Nile. They were part of Martine's horseback brigade. They made their way to the lifeboats that had been brought ashore by the Templar security forces. The lead scout told the Knights guarding the lifeboats, "We have a very important message for the Grand Master. We must see him at once."

The guard responded, "We can take you to the Command ship, but we must return to this shore immediately after we drop you off. Our orders are to wait here for our landing party to return. They are trying to trade for horses and carts in the village."

The Scout said, "Very well. We will leave our horses here with your men."

The guards rowed them to the Command ship, where they quickly boarded. The scout said to the guards on the ship, "We have a very important message for the Grand Master."

The guard walked off and returned several minutes later. He said, "Please follow me." He led them to the Grand Master's Quarters that was serving as the Command Center."

The Scouts said, "Greetings and salutations, Grand Master. I have a sealed message from my Commander that is only to be read by you." He handed the sealed scroll to the Grand Master. He opened it and read it to himself. It said, "*Grand Master – we have been significantly delayed by an impassible sand storm that has encompassed the entire desert. We have lost the better part of a week. We are now back underway. We should arrive on the night of the full moon.*

That is my first reason for this message. The more important reason is that our scouts have located a Muslim encampment to the south that is roughly a thousand men strong and a second encampment to the north of five hundred men. I think they were also slowed by the sand storm. I believe that we are walking into a trap. We will be vastly outnumbered. We are moving as fast as we can to meet you. Your faithful Commander, Martine de Vossier.

CHAPTER 34

THE MESSAGE

L ATER THAT SAME afternoon, Jacques, Michael, and Eduard entered the Grand Master's Quarters to share the great news. Jacques greeted the Grand Master and said, "The Egyptian Elder has successfully translated the Tablet."

The Grand Master asked, "What does it say?"

Michael said, "Many things but the one item that jumped out to Mufti was that there was a warning for humanity to correct its ways. We were expecting this, but we were surprised by some of the remaining sentences. It referenced the Great Flood of Noah. It set out a set of rules for humanity to live by. It also mentioned a great land to the West that would be the centerpiece of humanity's future." Michael looked at his notes and continued, "Mysteriously, it did not contain any direct clues regarding any treasures. Instead, it had what appeared to be vague references. It made mention of the matching seal under the Lion of the Desert but little else. It referenced how the Great Falcon and the Lion of the Desert were in a great stare down on the longest day, much like the Secret of Eden had stared at Ra. Here is the translation. Let's see if you interpret any differently." Michael unrolled the papyrus that contained the translation and handed it to the Grand Master. It read as follows:

We are the Watchers. We have been here since the dawn of humanity. We came at the direction of the Almighty Creator. We have instructed many generations of humankind of the Creator's will. None have followed our direction. We have the ability to create Earthquakes, Great Storms, and Great Floods. We have punished the unworthy with death and Destruction. We will continue our quest until Humankind abides by the Creator's will. The Creator's will was already handed down to the one you call Moses. Somehow several vital aspects were neglected to be recorded. The Creator also will send his Son to deliver the message. Humanity has made strides but still falls short of the Creator's expectations. The Creator's wishes are the following:

All Humankind are created equal and will be treated equally

All Wars will cease. Humankind will not kill his brothers and Sisters.

All Humankind will follow the laws handed to Moses.

Humankind can only honor the Creator by following his rules.

Humankind will share its resources equally.

The Great land to the West will be the home of the righteous and the foundation of the Creator's Promises. This will be the Land of Plenty.

The Seal of Solomon is the keeper of the Secret of Eden. The Seal stares at the Secret of Eden as the Great Lion in the Land of the Great River stares at the Great Falcon as he is going to rest on the longest day.

When Humankind has successfully mastered the Creator's will, only then will the Secret of Eden be revealed.

The men sat and stared in silence. The Grand Master finally spoke up. He said, "This document has been updated. It mentions Moses and Jesus Christ." He wondered out loud, "Are these

Watchers walking amongst us? Are they visible? Do they look like humans?" The Knights had more questions than answers.

Eduard then stated, "It sounds like even if we do find this treasure, we may not understand it or be able to do anything with it."

The Grand Master interrupted and said, "We must find this secret and move it to a more secure location. A small group of Knights and their descendants will be the only ones to know about the Secret of Eden. This treasure must never fall into the wrong hands. This includes the Church in Rome and all of the Kings around the World." Michael and Eduard were shocked that the Grand Master did not want to share this with the Pope. The Grand Master reminded them, "The Power of the Knights Templar is in the secrets that they hold."

The message of the Stone caused the men to be confounded by its words. Michael said, "I believe that I understand the message regarding the Seal." Michael continued, "The Egyptians and many cultures before them always depicted the Sun God Ra as a Falcon. The Great Lion is obviously the Sphinx. The longest day refers to the summer solstice. The Falcon going to rest refers to the sunset."

Eduard had also specialized in astronomy as a student. He said, "If we figure out the angle between the Great Sphinx and the Sun at sunset on the Summer Solstice. We will then have our answer."

Michael said, "If we can find the seal, then we can transpose the angle onto the opposing wall. This will be the resting spot of the Secret of Eden."

Jacques said, "Fortunately, we know where the seal is. Hamid was with his father, Maat, when he discovered the Secret Seal of Solomon underneath the Sphinx."

The Grand Master said, "Can't we just tear down the opposing wall."

Michael said, "Ancient documents tell of great calamities that befall the unworthy that try to unearth the Secret of Eden.

Therefore, we must be very careful in our excavations. I believe that the treasure is protected by traps. The other reason is that the wall may be supporting the entire structure. We must be cautious to support the wall with wood beams as we dig. Otherwise, a collapse may occur, and all will be lost."

The Grand Master summoned the only Astronomer that had made the journey. He also was an Archeologist. He had been studying the Egyptians for years. The Knight's name was Jean-Pierre Trudeau. He was given the task of identifying the angle of the Sun at the summer solstice and thought about it for a few minutes.

Jean-Pierre said, "There is an ancient depiction of the summer solstice in the Temple of Menkaure. This Temple was famous because it was the Tomb of Queen Khentkaus. It showed the entire region with the three Pyramids and the Sphinx that supposedly depicted the Summer Solstice. I made a sketch of it." He said, "I have it stored in my crate in my quarters. Let me retrieve it."

Eduard said, "If we can extrapolate the angle between the Sphinx and the Sun from this sketch, then we will have something to go on." If the depiction was accurate, the Knights would get their answer.

Jean-Pierre returned several minutes later. He had a sketch. Michael looked at the sketch and said, "The sunbeam is at roughly a thirty three degree angle."

CHAPTER 35

THE DECISION

ACQUES, MICHAEL, AND Eduard met with Hamid and Mufti the next morning. The goal was to determine where the Secret Seal of Solomon was located. How precisely could they pinpoint its location?

Hamid said, "Much of the Sphinx is buried under years of sandstorms and traumatic weather events. While we were digging under the head of the Sphinx, the cave that they had cleared suddenly collapsed. After we cleared the debris, we realized that a previously unseen tunnel had appeared. This time, we installed wood beams to thwart another collapse. We then entered the tunnel and traveled down a long narrow corridor, and discovered a large cavern. The cavern appeared empty. After further inspection, we discovered the symbol. We had never had seen the symbol before. My father had sketched the symbol. We briefly searched for hidden caverns or hollow walls. Then, we decided to leave the cavern undisturbed. The plan was to come back with the proper tools. My father was committed to researching the symbol, and maybe one day, they would return with some answers. We exited through the tunnel and buried the opening but noted the exact location where we had dug. I am sad to say that we never returned. My father said that we are not part of the worthy. I never fully understood this statement." He removed a piece of Papyrus from his satchel and handed it to Michael. It showed a crude map of where the tunnel opening would be found.

✠

The Grand Master was battling several issues. Not the least of which was the Knight's escape. The reports that the Scouts had delivered were very troubling. The Knights expected conflict, but not to this scale. The Knights were outnumbered threefold. The Knights that were coming on horseback needed to be accounted for in the escape plan. The Grand Master dispatched a team to secure another five ships so that the horseback Knights and their horses could escape. The Dust storms were way too fierce this year to escape by land. The Knights would be trapped. The Nile was the only possible escape for all of the Knights.

The other major issue troubling the Grand Master was the Treasure itself. Should the Knights attempt a daring extraction knowing full well that the Muslim Armies were bearing down on Giza from two directions? Could the Knights return at a later date to extract the Treasure? He knew that it would be a long time before the Muslim Armies left Giza. For that matter, they might never leave.

The Grand Master thought about this situation for most of the morning. Then he summoned Jacques, Michael, and Eduard to his quarters. They arrived a few minutes later. The Grand Master stated, "I have a major decision to make. It seems that a major sand storm delayed our ground forces to the west of here. During the delay, the Scouts discovered two large Muslim Army encampments within a day's march from here to the northwest and southwest. I can only surmise that they knew we were coming. If I was their Commander, I would let our ground forces through to the outskirts of Giza and then attack. Our ground forces would be slaughtered. My only option is to have all of our ship-bound forces go onto land and create a perimeter around Giza. The village is the closest to our current position. The Sphinx is on the outskirts, just to the west of the village. The Great Pyramids are to the west of the Sphinx. Therefore, our forces would need to be slightly west of the Pyramids. Even though we are outnumbered, we will have a chance to hold off the Muslims at least temporarily while our ground forces join us. We will then have an organized retreat to the ships on the Nile. This will all take place over the next two days. Those two days will be your only opportunity to find and seize the Treasure. I suggest that you make the most of it."

Jacques said, "We will mobilize immediately. I would like to use the Knights that were with us today on our journey to the village."

The Grand Master said, "As you wish."

CHAPTER 36

THE GREAT SPHINX OF GIZA

THE NEXT DAY Jacques, Eduard, and Michael arrived at the Great Sphinx. Jacques stared at the great Lion and thought to himself, "This is even more extraordinary than I imagined. There is no way that man could have constructed such a monument." Michael helped a team of Squires set up a tent that would appear to be living quarters for the Archeological workers right over the spot that Hamid had located as the spot of the tunnel opening. The tent intended to hide the excavation that was taking place. They would begin digging that evening. Michael had hired several more helpers from Mufti and Hamid's village. There would be a considerable amount of sand to relocate. The sand they were moving would be transported far away so that no attention would be drawn to their dig. After the sun had set, the Squires and the hired helpers began to dig where Hamid had directed them. They were about eight feet down when one of the Squires struck wood. They continued to dig around the wood until a tunnel opening appeared in front of them. Michael climbed down the ladder. He assessed the tunnel. He noted that the wood beams were suffering from wear. They would need to secure some new wood beams to secure the tunnel further. Hamid's helpers were instructed to bring some wood beams from Giza. The beams were installed over the next few hours.

At sunrise, Jacques mounted one of the horses and rode up to a nearby hilltop. He could see a vast distance west into the desert from the hilltop. Jacques saw Muslim armies advancing towards Giza from the northeast and southeast. Further to the west, he could see a large contingent of Knights making their way to Giza on horseback. Nearer to Giza, he could see the Knights setting up a perimeter just west of the Pyramids. These forces couldn't see each other as Jacques could see them. An epic battle would soon take place. Jacques immediately rode back to the Sphinx. He entered the tent and told Michael and Eduard what he saw. He said, "We have two or three hours at the most. We must move faster."

Eduard and Michael returned to the task at hand. The tunnel under the Sphinx was not completely clean and secure. The cavern at the end of the tunnel reminded the men of the cavern under the Foundation Stone back at the Temple Mount. Both caverns were natural and were being used to hide a secret so powerful that it could shake the planet to its core. That is where the similarities ended. Once the lanterns were all lit, they looked around and found nothing but an empty cavern. They focused on the western wall. They figured that if it followed the layout from above where the Lion is looking west. The Seal should be on the side where the sun was entering, and then across the room at roughly thirty three degrees lower, they would find the secret vault. They went over the entire wall, looking for loose clay. Nothing was immediately found. Then, Eduard looked down and noticed a small pile of clay dust. He went from ceiling to floor above this dust pile, looking for an imperfection. Eduard held a lantern high up on the wall, and there it was. The Secret Seal of Solomon. It was covered with dust that had fallen from above. He called Michael over and informed him that he had found the Secret Seal.

Jacques said, "There is no time for celebration. The battle has started. Our brother Knights have set a ring of fire that the Muslims will have to cross. Arrows are flying everywhere."

Eduard's attention then turned to the opposite wall. Michael went over with a lantern. He began to do the knock test on the opposite wall. The wall seemed like solid Bedrock. Near the floor, he noticed a rough surface. This was different from the rest of the wall. Eduard grabbed a trowel and began to scrape what looked like chunks of dried clay. He started to notice rocks under the layer of clay. The rocks were perfectly selected so that the fit was perfect. No mortar was necessary. Michael had seen several other sites over the years where perfectly fitted rocks had formed a wall. Much like the alcove where the Cross of Jesus Christ was found. The rocks in total went to a level that was about four feet above the ground. Michael noticed that the rocks were perfectly cut in straight lines. He had never seen rocks that were cut so perfectly.

Michael said, "These rocks were not cut by any artisans that I have seen. The Watchers must have cut them."

Eduard instructed the Squires to get some tools and break down the wall into pieces. Eduard and Michael returned to the tent. They wanted to get some fresh air for a minute. They were both anxious for the Squires to get the wall removal done. Both men had a drink of water from a canteen. The musty taste of clay dust felt like it was everywhere. They could now hear the battle. The clash of sword against sword was unmistakable. They ran down the tunnel to see if the wall had been removed. It was halfway down. Eduard jumped in and began ripping the rocks away. A few minutes later, the opening was exposed.

One of the Squires lit a lantern and entered the cavity. His face was full of shock. Michael said, "What do you see?"

The Squire said, "I am not sure. I have never seen anything like it."

Michael said, "Let's get a few of the Squires in there and see if you can pull it out." So the Squires lifted the box and carried it out into the open. It was a shiny silver rectangular box-like container that had what looked like a keyhole perfectly cut into its top. It was made of a metal that these men had never seen before. There was no lid. It was just solid all the way around."

Hamid said, "Is this the Secret of Eden?"

Michael said, "Yes. This is the treasure of all treasures. Someday, when mankind has become worthy, the Secret will open up and provide all the answers to the universe. It will answer the questions that humanity has pondered since the time of Adam and Eve."

Jacques suddenly could smell the Fragrance. It was his greatest moment, and her spirit was with him.

Eduard ordered the Squires to carry the box out of the tunnel and load it on a cart.

Michael said, "Hamid, you, your sons, and Mufti are welcome to go with us."

Hamid said, "This is our home. We do not want to leave here. But, if the Muslims ask us what we are doing, we will tell them the truth we are part of an Archeological dig team that is exploring underneath the Sphinx."

Michael said, "Thank you from the bottom of my heart. I'm sure your father, Maat, is very proud of you." He then handed Hamid a satchel that contained at least three times the gold coins he had promised.

Meanwhile, Eduard and Jacques were waiting up top outside the tent. The Squires had just loaded the silver box onto the carriage. Eduard covered it with blankets. Michael came topside and jumped on the carriage. Jacques decided that he would help clear the way for the carriage. The battle was now in front of them. Eduard remained back, giving the workers instructions to cover up the cavern and to bury all of the holes that were dug.

After he was done giving instructions. He realized that he had waited too long.

Meanwhile, Jacques had a sword in each hand. He was cutting down Muslims right and left. Arrows were flying just over his head. He could hear them as they sped right by his ears. The Fragrance was still with him. Jacques believed that she was somehow protecting him. They were now approaching the Nile. He could see the carriage directly ahead come to a stop. Michael was ordering the Squires to load the silver box onto the lifeboat. They did so, and the boat immediately left the shore. Jacques could see that Michael had been hit. The boat was heading directly for the Command ship. It was finally out of the range of the arrows. Michael was slumped over in his seat, but he was still moving.

Jacques experienced great happiness, which was followed by a great sadness. Why was he so sad? Perhaps Michael would survive. Jacques had just delivered the Secret of Eden to safety. It was his life's mission. Then it struck him, Eduard. Jacques could sense that Eduard had passed. He circled back towards the Sphinx. He came across Eduard lying on the ground.

Jacques jumped off of his horse and looked at Eduard's face. He was dead. He threw Eduard's body over the front of the horse and then jumped on and rode towards the Nile. The Last of the lifeboats were just leaving. He screamed for them to wait. They had formed a Phalanx which protected them from the arrows. This gave Jacques enough time to carry Eduard's body to the lifeboat. Jacques looked out to the Command Ship and saw the silver box being loaded onto the ship. They had succeeded in protecting the Secret of Eden. He then climbed in the boat, and they began to move. Jacques looked back at the shore and saw pure evil. It was Abdul. He was standing there laughing. Just then, as if ordered by the Almighty himself, an arrow went right into Abdul's eye. Jacques experienced a sense of relief. His relief was too soon, however. Just then, out of the corner of his eye, he saw an archer release an arrow. It hit him in the chest. The Squires around him were trying to stop the bleeding.

A few minutes later, Jacques was lifted onto the ship. He knew that there was no hope.

He just laid there looking up at the stars. Then, his mind began to drift. He started to see images of himself, his soulmate, and Eduard in past life settings. Suddenly, he could smell the Fragrance once again. Only this time, he could see her. She was the most beautiful woman that he had ever seen. She was soon joined by Eduard. She reached out her hand and said, "Come join us." Jacques's spirit then left his body and joined his soulmate and Eduard. Suddenly, Jacques became aware like never before. He had accomplished the task that his soul had set out on for this lifetime.

The three Guardians of the Secret of Eden drifted up the Nile River. They drifted past the Command Ship, where Jacques spotted Mary standing on the bow, looking up at him with a big smile on her face. She was happy. Once again, the Children of the Flood were reunited.

THE END OF THE BOOK ONE

THE KNIGHTS TEMPLAR DREAM

CHAPTER 37

<h1 style="text-align:center">BOOK TWO FOREWORD</h1>

<h1 style="text-align:center">APRIL 10, 1858</h1>

NATE AND HIS sister, Jane, sat dumbfounded after they read the written story of the Knights Templar and the Secret Treasure that was based on Nate's Dreams.

Nate said, "When you read this story in its totality it tells the tale of a group of people that were the offspring of Noah. So why am I dreaming of this?"

Jane said, "I don't have any answers for you."

Over the next several months, Nate and Jane started reviewing the notes from the second set of Dreams. These Dreams took place in 14th Century Scotland. They had a very odd similarity to them. Nate wondered to himself, "Were they related to the Knights Templar Dreams? The characters in this set of Dreams had a familiarity to them. It wasn't just that it involved the Secret of Eden once again. It was the people. They spoke a different language. They were not Knights or Priests. They lived in a different country, and they were not at war with anyone at the current moment. Yet they were similar. They were just regular Scottish people that worked for the local Clan Lord. But somehow, they were seemingly the same people as the characters in the Templars story. How could this be?"

Jane was compelled to do some basic research on the Scottish people and the Clan system. She discovered that it was very complicated. One Clan would be loyal to the Scottish King, and the neighboring Clan would be sympathetic to the British King. It was making an already complex story about a treasure even more complicated. Before the Dreams could be written, Jane thought that both she and Nate needed to fully understand the culture that they were writing about. She wanted to fill in the gaps related to the Clans and the surrounding governments.

The story continued to be centered on the Treasure that the Knights Templar had found at the Temple Mount and the Sphinx of Giza. The story continues several hundred years later with a set of Dreams centered around the 14th Century Scottish Noble and, of course, the Treasure.

Jane and Nate started their research by speaking to an organization called the library of Michigan. This library was founded in 1828 and consisted of a caravan of horse-drawn carriages. Unfortunately, it was pretty limited on books regarding Scotland. Several books had an overview of Scotland's History, but not much more. They were both dismayed. This was a daunting task. Then Jane saw the Spire of Sainte Anne's. This was the church where their brother Nick married his longtime girlfriend, Ella. It was the Basilica of Sainte Annes de Detroit. The Basilica was operated by French Priests but had a Scottish Curator. The following day they traveled to Sainte Annes. They were greeted by one of the younger Priests, Father Louis Toussaint.

Jane told Father Toussaint of the dilemma. She said, "Yesterday, I saw the spire from a distance, and it reminded me of the fact that the Basilica's Curator, Mrs. McGill, spoke of her days in Scotland. She had told us how she had emigrated from Scotland to America when she was sixteen. I wonder if she could help us with our research. Is she available?"

Father Toussaint said, "She went to pick up some supplies for the free meal program. She should be back within the hour. I am very confident that she has a large collection of Scottish History Books. She is always dreaming of her homeland. I am sure that she would love to help you."

While Nate and Jane waited, they were admiring the Gothic Construction. This old church was founded in 1701. Jane read a document that detailed how father Gabriel Richard had expanded the Basilica in 1796.

About thirty minutes later, Mrs. Agatha McGill walked into the church. She was carrying supplies that were needed in the kitchen. Father Toussaint helped her with the goods and informed her that she had visitors waiting for her. She walked over and immediately recognized us from the wedding. She said, "How good to see you again. We have spoken many times here about your brother's wedding to his bonnie Bride."

Mrs. McGill has been a widow for the last 15 years. She and her late husband John McGill had five children, and now she has eighteen grandchildren. She spoke of them glowingly. She told Jane that she hoped Jane would have as much joy with her family as she did. Jane said, "Thank you for your kind words. My brother Nate and I are doing some research on Scotland. We both thought, who would be a better person to ask than Mrs. McGill?" Her eyes lit up. Jane continued, "We are looking for background information on the Scottish Clan System and were very interested in the Time Frame of 1350-1400 AD."

Mrs. McGill said, "That was a very eventful time in the history of Scotland. Much of the folklore and songs that all Scots know are from that time." She continued, "That period in Scotland's History was very tumultuous. This was the era of Scottish Civil Wars which caused King Edward of England to step in.

His assistance was welcomed until everyone realized that he was looking to make all of the Scots subjects of the English Crown. This gave rise to heroes like William Wallace and Robert the Bruce. They saved Scotland. This is a subject of great pride for all Scots."

Mrs. McGill asked, "Is there any particular Clan you are interested in?"

Jane said, "Yes, we are very interested in the Clan Sinclair."

She said, "Every Scot knows of the Sinclairs. They were considered Royals too many. They were from the Village of Rosslyn." She went on to say, "You are in luck. I have several old books that detail the various Scottish Clans throughout the ages. They should have some information about the Sinclairs." She led Nate and Jane to the Rectory in the back of the Basilica. She said that she would be back momentarily with the Books.

She returned a few minutes later with a stack of books. Some books detailed the entire history of Scotland. They spent several hours going through the volumes of information. Finally, Jane found an old manuscript that described what a Clan was and how it fit in with the Sovereign or the Royals. The Royal family of Scotland recognized a Clan as a landowner who had special rights over its Septs. The Septs were the common people who lived on the Clan's land. For the most part, these people were not a relative of the Clan's leader, who was known as the Earl or the Lorde. The Earl was deeded the land. He was allowed to rule as he wished. Many Clans had their own rules to manage how the Septs lived their lives. The Clan protected the land and all of its inhabitants from other Clans or Foreign Invaders. The Earl usually lived in a castle that always had a village nearby that was part of the Clan. The Earl would charge a tax that was very rarely paid with currency but was usually paid with livestock or something else of value. Often a Sept could further his standing by offering a daughter to be married to one of the Earl's sons or grandsons. The Earl would make sure that the village had all of the services that the Septs would need, such as

Blacksmiths, Apothecary, Church, Trading Post, Fur Trading depots, and Clothiers.

The more prominent Clans were granted a Coat of Arms from the Royals. Some of the Clans were seen as favorites of the Royals. Being considered a favorite by the Royals usually meant that you sold out another Clan, or at least it was perceived that way, this always created conflict. The Clans were often battling each other, which often led to bloodshed and death. The Clans were built on two basic principles. First, the Earls had the authority to protect their land and Septs. Any dispute with another Clan required the two Earls to meet and find an acceptable accommodation. When an Earl died, his Clanship would transfer down to his eldest son. The Earl also had the option to go outside of his family if he was without an heir. Many times, this would result in conflict. The second rule was that the Earl and the entire Clan owed allegiance to the Royals.

The Coat of Arms was very important to the Clan. They had it displayed proudly all over their territory. The men usually wore kilts that also showed the Coat of Arms. It was important to display your loyalty. Some Clans were considered Highlanders, and others that were considered Lowlanders. The Highlanders were always held in higher regard because they were much more rugged and lived in harsher environments. Most of the trading, such as cattle and other livestock, happened in the Lowlands areas.

The Clans each had their own Folklore that usually came from Scottish and Irish Legends. Most of the Clans were established by Land Grants from whichever Royal was in charge at that particular moment. The Clan system was supposed to bring order to the entire Kingdom but rarely did so. The Clans lived on the honor system. This was passed down from the age of the various Knights Groups such as the Knights Templar. The concept of Chivalry and Honor was supposed to be the basis for cooperation between the Clans.

Many of the newer Scottish legends involve the Knights Templar. On October 13, 1307, the infamous Order of the Poor Fellow

Soldiers of Christ and the Temple of Solomon, otherwise known as the Knights Templar, was disbanded by King Phillip IV of France. He was working in conjunction with Pope Clement V. They secretly ordered that all of the Knights were to be arrested during the night. After their arrest, many were imprisoned and tortured. The charge was heresy. Most were tortured until they confessed. After they confessed, they were put to death. Most were burned at the stake. The Grand Master of the Knights, Jacques de Maloy, was tortured and burned at the stake. Before his death, he was said to have issued a curse onto the Heads of both King Phillip IV and Pope Clement V. He said that both would be dead within a year. Pope Clement died only a month later, and King Philip died in a hunting accident before the end of the year.

The mystery of the Knights Templar continued even after the death of Jacques de Maloy. Several years later, during the interrogation of the Knight, Jean de Châlons, by a French Court, the Knight claimed that he had heard that the Preceptor of the French Templars, Gérard de Villiers, had been warned in advance of King Phillip IV's decree. He said that De Villiers had escaped with fifty Knights and eighteen ships, including the fabled Treasure of the Knights Templar. It is believed that the Knights had escaped with the Treasure and had set sail to Scotland. When they arrived in Scotland, they were welcomed by the King of the Scots, Robert the Bruce. The Templars and their legends assimilated into Scottish culture. Several new orders, such as the Order of the Lodge, were formed over the years. The Templar history and Treasure were believed to be passed down through a Clan closely connected with the King. This Clan was known as the Sinclairs.

The Sinclairs arrived in Scotland from Normandy in the 11th Century. In Normandy, they were known as St. Clair or Saint Clair. St. Clair was originally the place where they lived in Normandy. The Sinclairs aided William the Conqueror with his invasion of England. Also, William of Saint-Clair provided a service to the King by accompanying Saint Margaret to Scotland in 1068. Many wars were going on at this time. The roads were treacherous, especially for a member of a Royal family. In return, the King gave him the title of Baron of Rosslyn. The Sinclairs ruled the region surrounding Rosslyn for hundreds of years. The Clan remained fiercely loyal to King Robert the Bruce during his reign from 1306 to 1329. There was also a connection between the Knights Templar and the Sinclairs that had lasted since their days in France. Very few people knew this. Robert the Bruce was one of them. It seems that the Founder of the Knights Templar, Hugues de Payens, was married to the sister of the Duke of Champaine, Henri de St. Clair. During the Pinnacle of their power, the Knights Templar and the Sinclairs had a very strong but secretive bond. As previously mentioned in the final days of the Knights, Grand Master Jacques de Molay had his loyalists in the French Government spy on King Phillip IV. Once the Grand Master heard of the French King's plans to disband and arrest the Knights, he instructed his leaders to move the Treasure to Scotland. Under cover of darkness, the Treasure was moved from its secret location at the castle of Gisors in France to Rosslyn, Scotland, via the port of La Rochelle. The Treasure was placed in the hands of the Sinclairs with the guarantee of protection from King Robert the Bruce. In 1358, upon his father's death, William Sinclair, Henry Sinclair I was granted the title of Baron of Rosslyn and Earl of Orkney.

✠

After Nate and Jane had completed the background study of the Sinclairs, Nate said, "This helps me understand the Dreams. I wish that I had learned this before having any of these Dreams. Then, the whole story would have made more sense."

Jane said, "I am sure it would have helped." She paused then continued, "I am not sure why, but this whole study of the Clan Sinclair has brought up thoughts that I had as a young girl. Am I possibly part of this story?" By the day, it was becoming more apparent that Jane's fears were proving to be true.

BOOK TWO

The Clan Sinclair

CHAPTER 38

May 15, 1385
Village of Rosslyn, Scotland

I T WAS A somber spring day as the villagers walked up to the casket to say their final goodbye to an extraordinary woman. Her name was Clara MacIntyre. They had already paid their respects to her husband, Ian, and her sons, Gavin and Francis. The boys were 7 and 5 respectively and probably didn't fully understand what it meant to lose their mother.

Several months ago, a group of Religious Leaders from Rosslyn traveled to London for a Council of the Bishops. After a two-week stay, they traveled back to Rosslyn. Unfortunately, they were unaware that their horses were transferring fleas carrying the Black Plague. Many had believed that the Black Plague ended back around 1350. But as Ian tragically discovered, there were still periodic flare-ups. The Black Plague took Clara and fifty other Villagers from Rosslyn.

Clara was unlike anyone else in the village. Everyone had known her since she was a wee lass. She was not only bonnie, but she had a spark that made everyone feel good whenever they were around her. Even back in their childhood days, Ian and his closest friend Angus were always with Clara. The three of them were inseparable.

Some said that Clara had special abilities. She could see into the spirit world. She rarely talked about it because she had been advised to keep her mystical capabilities to herself. The Church had a powerful influence in 14th century Scotland. Whenever they couldn't explain something, they simply declared it to be heresy.

Clara had spent considerable time with a middle-aged woman named Agatha. You could say that Agatha was Clara's mentor. Agatha taught her how to recognize things only the two of them could see. Clara referred to Agatha as a Seer. Clara would always say, "The more time I spend with Agatha reminds me of how much more I need to learn. The lessons always led into something new that I have never considered before."

Agatha tried to console Ian at the cemetery, but no words could soothe his pain. Finally, she said, "I hope you understand that Clara is a very special soul. As a matter of fact, she is standing next to you right now." Just then, Ian smelled the lavender flowers that Clara loved, even though there were no lavender flowers anywhere nearby.

Ian asked Agatha, "Can you smell the lavender fragrance?"

She said, "That is not from the flowers. You are smelling Clara's essence. Whenever you smell that fragrance, she will be nearby."

Ian said, "I know I am very distraught, but Clara said some very curious words to me with her final breaths. She said, "Please do not grieve. I am only passing from the physical world to the spiritual world. You and I, as well as Angus and Agatha, have been together forever. We are guardians of a great secret. Your life's mission lies ahead of you. Never forget that. As always, I will be at your side as you achieve wonderful deeds for all of humanity. As you will learn, we are Children of the Flood."

Agatha smiled, "You will understand this over time. Everything Clara said is true. You are a special soul. You will learn through your Dreams."

Ian said, "I don't have the gifts that you and Clara have. How can I learn this?"

Agatha said, "Just open your mind. You already have the knowledge. Now you need to learn how to access it and use it."

Even though this day was tragic, Ian would always consider this day to be the day that he came alive. His life would take a fantastic turn on this day.

CHAPTER 39

TOISEACH

IT HAD BEEN thirteen years since the Lord had taken Clara. Ian's sons Gavin and Francis had grown into fine young men. They were at the point in their lives when it was time for them to choose their careers. Gavin had chosen the path of an Academic. He was most interested in history. Ian had secured Gavin a position with Malcolm McBride. Malcolm was the Village Elder who managed the Clan's documents and historical artifacts. He was also a lifetime mentor to Ian.

Ian's other son, Francis, had chosen to be a Warrior for the Clan. This was a broad title that included being part of a team of like-minded men who protected the Clan and its lands but also were skilled sailors. Even though Rosslyn was at least a day's ride from the sea, the Clan Sinclair was mainly known for its sea-related activities.

Ian had much in the way of help when it came to raising the lads. His closest friend Angus and his wife Abigail were unable to have children of their own. Hence, they participated in helping Ian raise his sons. Gavin and Francis referred to them as Uncle Angus and Auntie Abigail.

Both Ian and Angus started working for the Earl, Henry Sinclair, at a very young age. They both began as stable hands, which usually means that they were cleaning out the pens and feeding the livestock. Both Ian and Angus worked very hard, which caught the attention of the Earl. They both worked their way up the ladder within the Clan. Ian began to take an interest in the financial and academic pursuits within the Clan, whereas Angus headed down the path of being a builder and a warrior. He excelled at both.

During the winter of 1398, the top aide to the Earl, Conner McGill, took ill and died. Both Ian and Angus were in line to replace Conner as the Toiseach for the Clan. This was the person who advised the Earl on all Clan decisions. The Toiseach was second in command of the entire Clan. The Earl recognized that he had two exceptionally talented leaders with Ian and Angus. He came up with a unique solution. He selected both of them for the position of Toiseach. The Earl recognized that these two men worked well together, and choosing one over the other might have caused a conflict. They each would be responsible for matters that they were a fit for. Ian was in charge of the treasury, all academic interests, and historical matters. Angus was the Sergeant at Arms. He was in charge of the Clan's Militia and the shipping activities of the Clan. What the Earl didn't know was that these two men had a far deeper connection than he ever realized. These two souls have been together since the time of the Great Flood.

It was a beautiful autumn day in Rosslyn. Ian and Angus were meeting with the Village Elders to discuss the upcoming St. Andrew's Day Celebration. Even though the big day was a few months away, quite a bit of planning was required. The St. Andrew's Day celebration was held on November 30 every year since the reign of Malcolm III over one hundred and fifty years ago. Saint Andrew was the disciple in the New Testament who introduced his brother, the Apostle Peter, to Jesus of Nazareth. The Scots used their allegiance to St. Andrew in an appeal to the Pope in the Declaration of Arbroath for his protection against the English Kings. Ever since then, St. Andrew's Day has been a National Day of Celebration for the Kingdom of Scotland. The day includes a Mass to pray to St. Andrew for his continued protection. After the Mass, it was time for the Highlander Games. These games featured many feats of strength combined with the mass consumption of ale and wine. Members from the Clan would arrive in Rosslyn from a vast area that the Earl governed. They would arrive days in advance with the hope of staying on the grounds of Rosslyn Castle. This was also the one day of the year when all of the Septs would have access to the Earl to request some type of aid from the Clan. It was also the day when you could confront another clan member for a grievance in the presence of the Earl. The Earl would then pass judgment on the situation. After all of the requests were made, and grievances were settled, the entire Clan would celebrate with a feast. This was usually a roast of the Earl's finest oxen and barrels of his finest ale and wine. Dinner was always followed by music and dancing.

This year's St. Andrew's Day planning would be placed on hold, at least temporarily. The Earl had a larger task for Ian and Angus. The Earl had summoned the two men to a private meeting at the Castle. Ian knew what this meeting concerned. He had been dreading it for some time. The Earl had arrived at a decision regarding the Treasure. For most of the Clan, the Treasure was just a legend. After all, no one had actually seen it, with the possible exception of the Earl himself. None of the other Clan members knew that Angus, Ian, and Clara had been involved with this Treasure in numerous previous lives.

Since the death of Clara, Ian has discovered that he has special skills that include communicating with the spirit world. Clara came to him in his Dreams. He has dreamt about great joys as well as horrible losses. The Dreams always involved the Treasure and the Great Secret that accompanied it. Angus and Ian both had these Dreams, but they rarely discussed them. There was non-verbal communication between these two men. They also had a similar relationship with Agatha. She was like a mother to both of them. Ian resisted the urge to ask Agatha about the Treasure. He often recounted how, after Clara's wake, Agatha had said that she, Ian, Clara, and Angus were Children of the Flood. Ian wasn't sure what the connection between the Treasure and the Great Flood was, but he knew that he would understand it someday. He had vague images within his Dreams that involved the Great Flood. Recently, his Dreams were increasingly about the Treasure. Some of the Dreams involved great battles. Others involved peaceful times with Clara. No matter which Dream Ian had, he could be certain that the Treasure was always nearby. Now, in his wake world, plans were being made that involved moving the actual Treasure. His life had a purpose.

CHAPTER 40

KING HAAKON V OF NORWAY

THE PREVIOUS SUMMER, Angus and Ian were asked to join the Earl on his trip to meet with King Haakon V of Norway. King Haakon V had become King after his Father's death, King Haakon IV, in 1380 AD. The Kingdom had moved its Capital many times over the centuries but was now located in Oslo. Henry Sinclair had a very good relationship with the Kingdom of Norway. In fact, the Norwegian King had given him the title of the Earl of Orkney. The Orkney Islands were a territory off of the coast of Norway. Henry had led an army of Scots to defeat the Norse Warlords led by the descendants of Harald Fairhair. This disagreement between the Kings of Norway and the Norse Warlords had gone on for decades. Henry had won a decisive victory in this battle, and in return, he became the Earl of the Orkneys and Shetland Islands of Norway. It was not common for anyone to be an Earl in two different Kingdoms. Henry tried to see the King of Norway at least once a year. This visit would be a little different because Henry wanted to make a request of the King. Henry wanted to ask for safe passage for himself and his crew to Vinland, which was the land west of Greenland that is usually referred to as the New World.

The famous Viking Leif Eriksson had discovered Vinland around 1000 AD. The land was given the name Vinland because grapes grew naturally there. These grapes supposedly yielded a very fine wine. The Vikings had explored this new territory all the way down to the Great River, which led to vast inland fresh-water lakes. The Vikings were shocked by the vastness of Vin-land. They had sent fishing vessels further south with the expec-tation of finding the Southern boundary of Vinland. The south-ern end of Vinland remained a mystery to the Vikings. The few ships that traveled south had reported that the shores were the home of vicious savages. This always caused them to turn back.

The Earl needed to get a decree from King Haakon V that allowed him to sail through waters near the lands where there were known Norwegian settlements. Otherwise, the Earl and his fleet could be open for attack from renegade Vikings. He was confident that he would be granted the safe passage, but he was worried that the King would push him regarding the reason for this voyage. The Earl would try to sell the journey as being one of purely exploration. Ian knew, however, that this voyage was about moving the Treasure of the Knights Templar to what the ancients referred to as the Land of Plenty.

The voyage to Oslo started on a warm July morning. The Earl's ships set sail with two ships under the command of the Earl. The two ships were the newest in the Earl's fleet. They were acquired in a trade with a Viking shipbuilder in the ancient port of Agdenes. Angus traded jewels and gold coins for the ships. One of the ships was built as a warship and was referred to as a Langskip, and the other was a merchant ship which was called a Knörr. The Earl brought the Merchant Ship, the Knorr, to send the message to any Pirates nearby that he was on a peaceful mis-sion. The Earl brought the Warship, the Langskip, to send a mes-sage that he was ready for any attack they could muster. Both ships flew under the flag of the Sinclairs. The white sail with the Red Cross was very prominent and could be seen from great distances. Everyone in the Nordic waterways knew what that meant. The people on these ships were connected to the Royalty of both Scotland and Norway.

The Earl, Angus, and Ian were on the lead ship with the gifts for King Haakon V. The gifts consisted of a finely crafted sword with King Haakon's Family Coat of Arms carved into the blade, a small chest of jewels, and two barrels of the Earl's finest wine. The second ship consisted of ten of the Earl's finest warriors who were guarding two Viking outlaws that had escaped from Norway into Scotland. The two were accused of killing a member of King Haakon's extended family. The King would be pleased to finally dole out justice to the two.

The trip usually took five or six days to complete. Ian dreaded making these journeys because he usually found himself vomiting for the first few days. Angus, as always, had no sympathy for his old friend. The Earl seemed to find the entire matter amusing. Ian began to get his sea legs by the end of the second day.

After breakfast on the third day, the Earl summoned Angus and Ian to his cabin. He wanted to discuss the upcoming meeting with King Haakon. He was worried about Haakon asking too many questions about the upcoming trip to Vinland. Several months earlier, the Earl had an idea. He explained, "When the Knights Templar made their escape from France, they had, in addition to the Treasure, several old maps that dated back to the Phoenicians and the Ancient Greeks. The originals have been kept with the Treasure." Henry's Father, William Sinclair, had made copies of the originals. Henry gave Ian instructions to create a fake map that looked like the original but did not include the location of the future home of the Treasure. Next, Henry instructed Angus and Ian to memorize the fake map. He had no doubt that Haakon would ask to see the map and probably would have many questions. Therefore, they needed to be prepared for all possibilities.

Late on the fourth day, the crew began to see the Coast of Norway. By the following day, Angus was navigating the ships up the Akerselva River on the approach to Oslo. The Royal Port came into view, and soon they were pulling into the docks. The Royal Sentries were waiting for them. They gathered up their belongings and the gifts for King Haakon and proceeded onto the land. The second ship did the same. The guards escorted the prisoners and handed them over to the Sentries. The Sentries guided the Earl's party to a carriage that would transport the Scots to the Royal Castle.

Shortly thereafter, they arrived at the Castle. They were taken to what they called the Great Hall. The room was filled with dignitaries, scholars, and several Warriors. King Haakon greeted Henry with a smile and a hug. The two men were friends as children and often were paired together during their Warrior Training when they were in their teens.

Haakon stated, "The Crown always welcomes Henry Sinclair after what he had accomplished for Norway in the battle for the Orkney and Shetland Islands."

The Earl presented the King with the gifts. The King greatly admired the sword. The King said, "This will be mounted above the fireplace in the Great Hall.

The Earl then announced, "We have captured the escaped murderers you have sought and brought them to you for Justice."

Haakon smiled and said, "Henry, you are my oldest and dearest friend. Welcome to my Kingdom, and please make yourselves comfortable." Haakon told one of his aides to tap one of the barrels of ale. Everyone in the room was given a mug of ale. Haakon and Henry began toasting each other and their long friendship. Most foreigners were not given this type of welcome. The Norwegians were Vikings, after all. They usually didn't accept outsiders. They all sat down for a Royal Feast of pheasant and duck. Henry, Angus, and Ian sat at the Royal Table. Henry and Haakon shared stories of conquest and victories from the glory days. Their families were always close.

Haakon finally broke the ice and said, "Henry, you requested an audience with me. What did you travel all of this way for?"

The Earl told Haakon of their plans to travel to Vinland. He
asked Ian for the doctored map. The Earl explained that they
had found this ancient map and wished to explore to see if the
lands that the ancients spoke of were real. He went on to say that
they wished to take harbor at one or more of the Norwegian
settlements that were along the way in Greenland, Iceland, and
Vinland if the situations called for it. The Earl said, "Of course,
if any gold or silver is discovered, we would share the haul with
your Kingdom."

The King understood what Henry was asking. He said, "I will
confer with my elders tomorrow and give you an answer." Haakon further stated, "Our settlements in the New World are home
to many former Viking Warlords. I cannot guarantee you a safe
passage. You must be prepared for battle." He paused momentarily and said, "If I grant you passage, someday I may call on you to
clear these new lands of the Warlords as you did in the Orkneys
and Shetlands."

As many Viking celebrations had gone on over the ages,
there were usually challenges to fight and other games such as
ax throwing to entertain the drunken natives. As in many other
Kingdoms, there are many adversaries to the King. This Kingdom was no different. Today's adversary was a Viking named
Oleg. After the dinner was complete, he made himself known to
Angus and Ian. Both of the Scots were stunned. Ian thought to
himself, "There is something very familiar about this man. He is
from the Dreams. There is always an adversary. In some Dreams,
he was a Muslim. In others, he was an Egyptian Guard. Even
though he never looked the same in appearance. The soul was
the same. He was the face of pure evil. This Viking who went by
the name of Oleg was the adversary. We will see him again. That
is for sure." Ian could tell by the look on Angus's face that he also
could sense their enemy. Oleg challenged Angus to a fight. Ian
stepped in and said, "We are guests in King Haakon's home. We

are not here to fight."

Oleg said, "I do not trust the Scots and especially not Henry Sinclair."

Angus and Ian walked away before trouble had a chance to fester. They joined the Earl, departed the Great Hall, and made their way to their designated sleeping quarters.

When they were out of earshot of the Vikings, the Earl explained, "There are many warring factions within the Kingdom of Norway. The peace amongst the many tribes is very fragile." He continued, "Even if we are granted passage by King Haakon, we must be at the ready to be attacked by any one of the splintered Viking Groups. Having said that, the Right of Passage should be meaningful in peaceful settlements. They will not cross the King."

The next morning the King held court. King Haakon greeted the Earl and said, "I invite you to hear any opinions on why I should not grant you passage." The Scots sat there and listened to many who agreed with the passage. The common viewpoint was that Norway and Scotland share a common enemy, the English. They felt that Henry was an Earl for Scotland and Norway and would always be loyal to King Haakon. The dissenting opinion was from Oleg. He stated, "The Vikings had discovered Vinland, and allowing a Scot to travel there would eventually lead to conflict. Our brothers in the New World will never let a Scot pass through their waters." The Earl knew that there was a much larger reason that Oleg objected. He guessed that Oleg was part of the losing faction in the battle of the Orkneys. Oleg's resistance was personal.

Haakon finally spoke. He said, "I have come to a decision. I will allow only the travelers from Clan Sinclair safe passage. Henry, or one of his leaders, will travel back and report to me regarding what he has discovered."

Henry agreed, and the two men shared a toast. The Scots spent the rest of the day in Oslo. Ian met with the Elders from Haakon's staff. They were curious about the map and inquired as to what the Earl and his loyalists hoped to find. Ian told them how the Ancient Phoenicians and Greeks spoke of gold, silver, and other metals such as copper and lead were readily available in Vinland. After Ian had answered all of the Elder's questions, he asked them about Oleg. Ian asked, "Why did this Oleg have so much anger directed at our party?"

One of the Elders said, "Oleg is a direct descendant of Harald Fairhair. Henry Sinclair's forces killed Oleg's Father and several family members in the battle of the Ornkeys." Their answer was very clear and foreboding.

Ian asked, "Why is he allowed in the Royal Circle? I would think him to be a threat to the King. After all, wasn't it Haakon's Father who ordered the attack on the Ornkeys?"

One of the Elders said, "The answer is that after the war was over, Oleg was given no choice, so he swore an oath of loyalty to Haakon V. He had not, however, sworn an oath to any Scots." For Oleg, that battle had never ended. At that point, Ian knew that they had not seen the last of their adversary. The next day they began their journey back to Rosslyn.

CHAPTER 41

THE ARK

T HE FORTY DAYS of rain had just started several days back. All of the animals and Noah's family were now aboard the Ark. As always, Peleg and his cousin Tytea sat together on the deck that included the animals that they had been accustomed to, such as sheep, cattle, goats, and horses. They comforted each other through the sensation that they felt as the Ark began to float. The fear was crippling. The Almighty had promised their grandfather Noah protection if he followed the instructions. However, their faith in their grandfather's story and the stories as told of their ancestor Enoch were being tested. Both Peleg and Tytea were only eight years old. Nothing like this flood had ever happened before. How long would it last? How long would they be afloat? Was the Ark capable of handling such a trip? Thankfully, they had each other. Their bond was well beyond that of an eight-year old's. Their grandmother, Na'amah, had told them that they were both very young souls, and she could foresee that they were destined to spend eternity together.

This was beyond their comprehension.

After the forty days of rain had ended, the Ark had stabilized, and for the first time, the excessive rocking had stopped. They were now just floating. Noah had gathered his family together to discuss the future. He said, "The Lord Almighty has finally stopped the rains. Everything as you once knew it is gone. We have to start anew to build a righteous society that will live by the rules that the Lord has handed down through the Watchers. Hard days will be ahead. I have no idea how long the flood water will take to subside. We must continue to feed the animals and clean out their stalls as we have done thus far. I invite all of you to go topside and take in the heavenly view."

As everyone was heading topside, Na'amah said to Peleg and Tytea, "Your Grandfather would like to have a word with both of you."

Noah walked up to the children and said, "You two, as well as young Joktan, are the chosen ones. You have been chosen to protect the message and the Secret of Eden. This Secret was handed to our forefather Adam. The message contains instructions for all of humanity to follow. The society that was just vanquished refused to follow the rules. We are now starting anew. The message has been carved into a stone that you must hide and protect. The Secret of Eden resides under the Great Lion as it always has. When humanity has proven itself worthy, the secret will reveal itself. The secret will bring back the Tree of Knowledge that was torn away from Adam and Eve generations ago. The great reveal will take thousands of years. Of course, your bodies will die, but your souls will be eternal. Your mission will continue until the people are deemed worthy, and the secret is revealed. Only then will you join the Almighty in heaven. Now go topside and understand that the magnificence you will see is the Almighty himself. You will always be drawn to this vision. It will bring you solace and fortitude in your most troubling times."

Peleg and Tytea walked up the ladder that would allow them to see daylight for the first time in months. When Peleg opened the hatch, the two were overwhelmed by the blue skies and the bright sunshine. They walked to the side of the Ark and were astonished by the scene in front of them. There was water in every direction. The water contained every shade of blue imaginable. It was indeed infinite and breathtaking in its beauty. Now Peleg and Tytea understood what their grandfather meant when he said, "You will see the Almighty."

✠

Just then, Ian was awakened by his son Francis. He said, "Father, wake up. You have overslept. Today is St. Andrew's Day. You have much to do today." Ian sat there in amazement. Finally, the great mystery of his existence had been explained. Everything that he had seen in his Dreams finally made sense.

CHAPTER 42

St. Andrew's Day

AN QUICKLY DRESSED and mounted his horse for the ride into Rosslyn Village. As had every other St. Andrew's Day, the day started with a mass in the small church in the village. Ian arrived and quickly made his way to the second row, as was the previous Toiseachs' custom. Angus, Abigail, Gavin, and Francis waited for Ian to be seated. The Earl, his wife, Countess Jean Haliburton Sinclair, and their children were in the first row. Ian thought to himself as he looked around the church, "I learned more from the Dream that I had the previous night than most of these people have learned in a lifetime."

Ian turned around to see who else was seated nearby. Malcolm and Agatha were two rows behind him. Ian made eye contact with Agatha, and she gave him a smile that said, "I know about your Dream." This bewildered Ian. He thought, "How can Agatha know of his Dreams?" Seemingly, she knows the entire story of the Guardians of the Secret of Eden. It was like she was waiting for Ian and Angus to get caught up. Ian then glanced over at Angus. Ian thought, "Did he know any of this?" Angus and Ian barely discussed anything that was supernatural. Instead, they often discussed the Treasure because they knew someday they would be tasked with moving it. Ian thought, "What a glorious coincidence that both Angus and I would be the ones that see the Treasure. No other Scots would be given that opportunity. Obviously, this was not a coincidence."

Ian thought back to the Dream. He instantly recognized that Tytea was Clara in this lifetime and Joktan was Angus. The person that knew the most was Agatha. She was Na'amah in Noah's lifetime. He thought it remarkable that all of these souls came together in each lifetime to guard the Secret.

After the mass had concluded, it was time for the St. Andrews Day celebration to begin. Everyone was dressed for the big day. All of the men wore their finest plaid green Kilts, and the women wore their newest ankle-length tartan skirts, along with a color-coordinated blouse and vest. A tartan earasaid, sash, or tonnag (smaller shawl) was also worn. They usually were pinned with a brooch or sometimes with a clan badge or other family or cultural motif. Ian walked with Angus and Abigail to the Highlander Games, where Gavin and Francis joined them. It brought back fresh memories for Ian of being at the games with Clara. Both of their sons were just wee lads. Now, they were both grown men. They were both old enough to start their own families. Clara would have been so proud of both of the boys. Gavin was twenty-two years old. He would soon marry his long-time sweetheart, Mary. As with many in the village of Rosslyn, they have known their spouses for a long time. Their Wedding day was scheduled for the following spring. The Earl insisted on hosting the wedding at the Castle. The fact that Clara would not be there to see her eldest son be wed was heartbreaking. Francis had just turned nineteen. He was more interested in participating in the Highlander Games than anything else today. He was a mountain of a man. They all had several glasses of ale while they watched Francis perform the log roll. The log roll involved balancing yourself on a floating log while your opponent was trying to join you on the same log. Francis won all five of his contests and was named the top Log Roller in all of Rosslyn. This earned him the right to wear a bright blue vest for the rest of the day. Ian thought, "It is great to have all of us together."

Next, it was time for Angus and Ian to make their way to the Castle for the once a year event where the Septs could make a request of the Clan or file a grievance against another Sept. This year was a little different, the Earl had requested that Ian and Angus arrive early. He had a special announcement for the two of them. Ian knew what this probably meant. The Earl was about to set the plan of moving the Treasure into motion. The two friends rode to Rosslyn Castle as they had done many times. The splendor and architecture of the Castle never seemed to amaze either of the two men. It was overwhelming to think that they both had risen to be at the top of such a powerful Clan.

As they approached the Main Gate, they were greeted by the Sentry at the Gate. He said, "The Earl has been expecting you. Please follow me." Angus and Ian laughed. They had been playing in this Castle since they were wee lads. Both men knew the Castle far better than this Sentry. They thought that they should be guiding him. They were led to the anteroom next to the sleeping quarters of the Earl. The Countess first greeted them. She tended to their children, Young Henry II, John, William, Elizabeth, and Marjory. Henry II was the next in line to the Earl. Behind her, the Earl sat at his large mahogany desk. He greeted them warmly and offered them a cup filled with wine.

Ian jokingly said, "Are we starting the Celebration early?"

The Earl responded, "After this meeting, you may wish to have a few more cups."

The Earl started by saying, "Scotland is undergoing a major change. Since the death of Robert the Bruce, the Kingdom of Scotland has been on a long downward spiral. When Robert the Bruce died, the heir to the throne was his son David II. The problem was that David was only seven when his father died."

Henry laughed about having a seven-Year-old King who, incidentally, was married to an eight-year-old. He pointed out that the Royals had appointed very competent managers of the Kingdom until David was old enough to effectively reign over it himself. He continued, "When David II died unexpectedly in 1371. His half-nephew Robert II took the reins until his recent death in 1390. This ended the Reign of the Bruce's."

He paused to refill his wine glass and then continued, "The Bruce's always offered protection for the Sinclairs because of the ties to the Knights Templar. Robert the Bruce was aware of the Treasure but decided, because of dueling factions within the Scottish Hierarchy, not to tell any of his descendants about the Treasure. The biggest threat has always been from the French. On Friday the 13th of October 1307, the French attempted to destroy the Templars and secure the Treasure for themselves. Robert the Bruce and his successors had always served as a deterrent to a French attack. When the reign of the Bruce's ended, the Stewarts stepped in. The House of Stewart became the Monarch of Scotland and England. It was unclear if the Stewarts would stop the French from attacking Rosslyn. There is no bond between the Stewarts and the Clan Sinclair. I fear that if any one of the Stewarts found out about the Treasure, they surely would have laid claim to it merely for the fact that it lies on Scottish soil."

After a few cups of wine, Henry declared, "I have decided that it is time to move the Treasure. We will move it to the New World, The Land of Plenty, as the Templars called it. This did not come as a shock to Angus and Ian. They knew that this was the reason for our trip the previous year to Oslo. Henry went on to say, "The trip will be very dangerous. Not only because of the uncharted waters, but because of the natives that we would no doubt encounter." Both Ian and Angus could tell that he was holding something back.

Ian asked him, "What is troubling you?"

He hesitated for a moment and then finally said, "I'm going to ask one of you to stay in the New World to lead a force that protects the Treasure." Neither Ian nor Angus had thought of this possibility before today.

The Earl went on to say, "I will need one of you to stay and guard the Treasure while the other needs to return to Scotland and tell the story and new location of the Treasure to a very select few so that the Secret can be passed down through the ages. Then, upon my death, the one who comes back will inform my heir of the Treasure."

The Earl continued, "I would like to stay in the New World. The problem is that if an Earl disappears, many will come to search for him." This would definitely be the case.

The Earl went on to say, "Also, we need to slip the Treasure out of Scotland without anyone noticing us. This will have to be very carefully planned."

Ian asked, "What about our Families?"

The Earl paused for a moment and said, "They are welcome to join the party, but would be expected to play a role in the New World."

The Castle of Rosslyn

Henry then detailed the timing. He said, "The plan is to start the journey next spring." He then asked Ian and Angus to speak to their families and give him our decision over the course of the next few weeks. He stressed the importance of not mentioning the Treasure to even their families. He suggested that they tell them that the have been asked to take on this mission by the Royal Highness, James Stewart himself. They would find out about the Treasure soon enough.

The Earl had given both men much to think about. However, they needed to put this off to the side because now it was time to perform their duties as the Toiseach for the Clan.

The Septs began to form into a line on the Castle grounds. The Septs would have their annual chance to meet with the Earl. Ian and Angus were required to be at the side of the Earl during this entire process. Angus took it upon himself to make sure that he and Ian had a full glass of ale during the entire process. He gave a servant the assignment of filling their steins every few minutes. This could go on for hours. The ale helped to make it bearable. The Earl granted every request that made sense. If the Sept had requested land, then a trade of some kind was in order. Some of the requests came in the form of asking for a break in taxes for this year. The Earl required that there be an adequate reason for a break. Most blamed the drought that occurred in Scotland that year. Many came to the Earl to express a grievance. The grievances usually involved livestock. One Sept would accuse the other of stealing several of his goats. The reply usually was that they were payment for supplies that had been borrowed and never repaid. The last Sept in line finally had finished his request, and it was time for the Feast.

The servants at the Castle had been preparing the oxen all day. The smells began to permeate the entire grounds. Everyone was seated. Some of the Septs had to sit outside because there simply wasn't enough room. Everyone was served a bountiful portion of oxen, as well as roasted potatoes. Of course, no food was consumed before the Bishop from the Village had said the blessing. There were multiple urns filled with ale at every table.

The food was wonderful, and the Earl was in an especially joyful mood. When Ian asked him why he responded, "The incredible burden that had placed upon my shoulders would soon be over." Ian knew that he was referring to the Treasure. He always felt that there was a threat. Whether it was the English or the French did not matter. He had many sleepless nights because of worrying about the Treasure. Nevertheless, he was happy to move it to a largely uninhabited place.

As the dinner was being finished, the Clan members were being serenaded by a musician that was playing a new instrument that was only known to Scotland. The instrument was called the Bagpipes. The music was very enchanting. Ian thought, "I would like to learn how to play the Bagpipes. Maybe I would take a set of Bagpipes with me on the journey." The Bagpipes eventually gave way to the violins, harps, and various other stringed instruments that had been present at the Clan's celebrations for as long as Ian could remember. The tables were cleared for dancing. The Earl and Countess were the first to join the dance floor. Then it was time for Angus and Abigail, and then it was Ian's turn. He was escorted out onto the dance floor by Gavin's Fiance Mary. He was surprised. The last person that he had danced with was Clara. This was a very memorable night. In another room, all of the young children sat around the fireplace and were told old Gaelic Tales of adventure. This night more than any other, defined the culture of the Clan Sinclair. The Feast went into the wee hours of the night. Ian took in every moment, knowing that possibly it would be his last St. Andrew's Day celebration in Rosslyn.

At the end of the night, Ian told his sons that he loved them both very much and how their mother would have been very proud of the men that they had become. He also told them that he would like to meet with them the following evening. He had a matter to discuss with them. So he requested that they meet him at his home for supper.

CHAPTER 43

THE DECISION

AN WOKE UP the next morning feeling like he had so many times on the morning after the St. Andrews Celebration, like a herd of bulls had trounced him. He was sipping on his tea and pondering his future. The easy decision would be to tell the Earl no and live with the consequences. That would solve many problems. He would not have to tell his sons that he may never see them again. This would have been the easy way out. However, a burning flame within him always told him that he was here for a reason. He knew that his soul's mission was with the Treasure and the Secret of Eden. He knew that Angus must have been going through a similar struggle.

The two men had a bond that could not be explained. Angus's decision was, however, more complicated. He had a wife to consider. Ian knew that if Clara were still alive, he would never consider leaving without her. One thing was certain, Abigail would never agree to let Angus go on such a dangerous mission without her. The truth was that none of the team could guarantee that they would be back. Ian had to think about how he would present this to Gavin and Francis. Gavin was just about ready to start his new life with his soon-to-be wife, Mary. They would soon be wed and start a family of their own. On the other hand, Francis had no one if Ian had left. Without telling his sons everything, Ian had to figure out a way to explain the mission. No matter the consequences, Ian could not mention the Treasure. This decision would be the toughest of Ian's life.

Later that morning, Ian exited his quarters. Both Ian and Angus lived on the Castle grounds, but not in the Castle itself. Both men had grown very accustomed to living on the grounds of the Castle. Even though neither of the men would ever be the Earl, living on the grounds of the Castle offered many of the same benefits. All of their food was prepared by the Earl's staff. Their clothing was always laundered by the staff. Their horses were fed and cared for in the Clan's stable. The same servants that tended to the needs of the Earl also tended to Ian and Angus's needs.

The Earl and the Countess were waiting for Ian in the Main Dining Room. The conversation started lite, but within minutes the conversation changed to the mission. The Countess said she feared for the Clan if Henry did not return. She further stated, "Young Henry is old enough, but does not have the life experience yet to become an effective Earl." She continued, "He would need to be surrounded by experienced advisors. With all of you going on the mission, who would serve as the advisors?"

Henry said, "My Dear, who can be a better advisor to the young Earl than you? You have been my sounding board for decades." He then smiled and said, "On many occasions, I had arrived at a decision only to have it reversed shortly thereafter by the Countess." He further stated to the Countess, "No one knows this Clan better than you." She did not offer a countering opinion. Instead, she said that she would need help.

She said, "Ian, with you joining Henry on this sacred mission, who should I lean on?"

Ian thought about it for several minutes and finally said, "My older son Gavin has been at my side throughout the years. He has been with me when many important decisions were being made by the Earl. Five years ago, when we decided to extend our southern boundary, he spent many nights with me discussing both sides of the issue. He understood the complexity of the other Clans. One wrong move could have caused the other Clans to unite against us. His opinion was a conservative one. Many younger leaders would have sided with those who wanted conquest. Gavin, however, sided with caution. He is the main reason I counseled you not to extend our boundary. With the subsequent upheaval the following year of several of the Clans, we ended up adding their territories to the Clan Sinclair anyways."

The Earl then joked, "You mean that I could have had your son counseling me this whole time? I could have saved the Clan a substantial wage." They all laughed. The conversation then returned to the lighter fare of discussing the previous night's feast.

✠

Later that afternoon, Ian was tending to some of the decrees that had been agreed upon by the Earl yesterday when he heard a knock on his door. He opened the door to see that Angus and Abigail were standing there. They both had a very serious look on their face.

Angus said, "May we join you for a few minutes?" Ian showed them in and offered them some tea. They all sat down, and Angus started by saying that he had talked to Abigail about the forthcoming trip.

He started to tell Ian about her response when she interrupted him, saying, "Ian MacIntyre, don't you think for a minute that I am agreeing for my Angus to go on this journey without me. Angus is my life. Whether the journey goes well or not is inconsequential. The fact that I will be with Angus is all that matters."

Ian said, "I understand. However, you two should make your case to the Earl at once."

She went on to say, "The Earl doesn't shit without getting your opinion first." All of them laughed.

"I will do what I can." Ian said.

Angus finally said, "I will only agree to go if Abigail is at my side." The two then parted, and my attention turned to my own family.

✠

As planned, Gavin and Francis arrived at Ian's quarters for supper. At first, the conversation was very light. They both had stories from the previous evening. Everyone was laughing and enjoying the memories.

Finally, Gavin broke the ice. He said, "Father, you seem very bothered. What is troubling you?"

Ian said, "The Earl has asked me to possibly make a one-way trip to the west." Ian told them that he couldn't tell them the real nature of the journey, but he did say that the survival of the Clan and possibly Scotland depended on it. He told them he would like to promise to make it back, but he could not guarantee it.

Francis responded first. He said, "Father, I don't have any ties here in Rosslyn other than you and Gavin." He continued, "I would like to join you on this mission. Many men my age get to go to battle for what they believe in. I have had no such experience. I can handle myself with a sword, and I am considered a master marksman with the bow. I can be an asset to your mission."

Ian said, "I would like you to take a few days to consider this. Then, if at the end of the two days you still want to be a part of the team, I will make a recommendation to the Earl."

Then the focus turned to Gavin. He said, "Father, I am about to be wed. So the timing of this mission is less than good."

Ian said, "Son, there is a different mission for you. The Countess is very concerned about the Clan's future with Henry, Angus, and myself being on a faraway journey. I have recommended you to become Senior Advisor to the Countess and Henry II. I believe that you have the proper disposition and countenance for this position. This would allow you and your young bride to move into my quarters on the Castle grounds and have the good fortune of having servants help you with your family's more mundane tasks so that you can focus on the business of the Clan. Your wife, Mary, would be able to focus on raising your children." Ian paused for a moment and continued, "I believe in fate and destiny. I believe with all of my heart that this is your destiny."

The discussion pursued for another hour or so. Gavin was horrified that he may never see his Father or Francis again. Ian told his sons, "The Vikings have visited the place where we are going for centuries. Some of us will be staying for security purposes. The plan is for the Earl and either Angus or myself to return to Rosslyn."

Gavin then asked, "Will I be allowed to visit you and Francis at some point?"

Ian responded, "This will be for the Earl to decide, but I believe that there will be many future trips to where we are going. I am sure that if it makes sense for the Clan to travel, you will be allowed to do so. We will be able to send word to you periodically as ships travel back and forth."

Gavin said, "The opportunity sounds great, but I will need to discuss this with Mary." They agreed to have a decision for the Earl within two days. Ian firmly believes that Francis recognized that this is his destiny as well.

The most important person that Ian felt was needed on the mission would probably be the toughest sell to the Earl. That was Agatha. She understood the Treasure and its message better than anyone. So Ian said to himself, "I need to convince the Earl of the need to have Agatha on the mission, but first, I probably need to convince Agatha herself."

CHAPTER 44

THE PLAN

EVERY DAY THE Earl would meet with each of his Toiseachs. Ian's consultation was after breakfast, and Angus was after lunch. First, Ian had breakfast with the Earl. The conversation was purposely kept light due to the fact that the Earl's children were there. After the breakfast was over, the Earl and Ian moved to the anteroom, which was a much more private setting. The Earl asked, "Have you come to a decision yet?.

Ian responded, "I intend to go, but I had given Gavin until tomorrow to deliver his decision. To be perfectly honest, my younger son, Francis, would like to join us. He has proven himself in the warrior training. He now needs real experience. So I would be delighted if you would consent to let him join the mission."

The Earl said, "The mission could be very dangerous. I cannot guarantee his safety."

"We both fully understand the risk." Ian said.

The Earl said, "I have no issues with him going."

Ian said, "Thank you, sir. As for Gavin, he just wanted to tell his fiancé of the opportunity. I am certain that he will accept. Only a fool would say no. I think that the fact he deliberates on every decision is one of his best traits. You will never see him make a rash decision."

The discussion quickly turned to the mission itself. The Earl had been looking at the maps and notes of the Ancient Phoenicians and Greeks that were in the Clan's library. The maps detailed a specific area on the coast of Vinland. The Earl said, "Unfortunately, they do not tell you how to get there. The mission is complicated because of prevailing winds and currents. One wrong move, and you will be directed straight out to sea. The bottom line, as of right now, is that we need to depend on the King Haakon to guide us to the area shown in the ancient maps."

Ian said, "I'm sure these maps came to us from Malcolm. He is the Clan's best authority on history and ancient civilizations. I will wager that he has a vast wealth of knowledge on this subject."

The Earl said, "Very well. Consult with him and see if he has relevant knowledge. But, as always, do not tell him about the nature of the true mission."

The Earl said, "Recently, one of the former top aides for Robert the Bruce sent me a sealed letter that provided me one of the most exciting leads on finding Vinland. He said that there was a fisherman who had not been seen for twenty years, but suddenly reappeared in the Ornkeys. Apparently, he had been shipwrecked at the very place in which we intend to travel." He paused and sipped his tea. He continued, "The fisherman's name is Antonio. I sent out messages that I would like to meet this Antonio. Perhaps Antonio would join us on the mission. Therefore, I am going to instruct Angus this afternoon to travel to the Ornkeys and find this Antonio. He could be our guide."

The Earl said, "The document also refers to a place known as the Holy Well that could be found at the end of the Gold River. Supposedly, previous explorers thought this place was exceptional. It also discussed a tribe of natives that were called the Mi'kmaq. They guard the Holy Well." The Earl continued, "None of these leads are very solid. Over the next several months, you need to vet all the clues and theories. I don't want to venture out into an ocean without firm guidance."

"Understood." Ian said.

Then the Earl showed Ian a document found in France at the Templar Site in Gisors. It detailed a previous mission to Vinland that followed the Star they called Deneb. It is said that if this Star were followed, it would lead you to the New World.

Ian said, "I will also ask Malcolm about this star."

✠

Later that evening, Angus stopped by Ian's quarters for a visit. He brought a flask of Mead with him. Either he was coming to tell Ian that he decided not to join the mission, or was this for celebratory purposes to toast the upcoming voyage. The latter was true. He and Abigail would be joining the mission.

Angus said, "Someday, you and I will discuss our common past. There was no way that I could live with myself if I didn't join you. I was only concerned about Abigail. She is excited about the journey, but her biggest concern is her mother, Maggie. As you know, Abigail's father had passed before we were married. Abigail is Maggie's only child, so if she left, her mother would be by herself. Maggie is a well-known seamstress in Rosslyn. The Earl had fully understood the situation. The Countess was also present when we spoke and offered an accommodation. Maggie would take on the role of seamstress for the Countess. She would live at the Castle, and all of her needs would be taken care of. Furthermore, if a settlement were developed in the New World, Maggie would be granted passage."

The two men celebrated the good news. Their mission that had started generations ago would continue.

Ian said, "That is wonderful news." He continued, "I am sure that Gavin and his wife would accept the offer to become a Senior Advisor to the Countess. It was an opportunity of a lifetime."

A few minutes later, a courier arrived to notify Ian that Francis, Gavin, Angus, Abigail, and Maggie were required to dine with the Earl and the Countess the following evening. They would like to discuss the upcoming mission and the arrangements that had been agreed upon. As soon as the courier left, Gavin entered. He had a broad smile on his face.

Ian said, "Am I speaking with the New Adviser to the Earl?"

He said, "Aye, it is true." The three of them shared a toast to their new adventures.

From Ian's perspective, everything had fallen into place except Agatha. He needed to figure out a way to convince the Earl to include her on the mission. Today, an opportunity presented itself.

Malcolm and Agatha had met later in life. Both were widowed. They had married several years earlier in a very small and private ceremony in which Ian served as Malcolm's witness.

The fact that Malcolm was the leading authority in the Clan on Ancient Civilizations, and Agatha was the leading authority on the Treasure would make it easier when it came time to convince the Earl. So the first task was to convince them to agree to the journey. Then, Ian had to convince the Earl without telling him the true nature of Angus, Agatha, and himself.

This caused Ian to reach for the pitcher of Mead. His life's mission was like a tree with many branches. He had to cultivate each one perfectly. This branch would be the most difficult. The next morning Ian would visit with Agatha and Malcolm.

CHAPTER 45

THE DECREE OF THE LAIRD OF ROSSLYN

THE NEXT EVENING, Ian arrived first in the dining hall at the Castle. He was followed by Angus and Abigail and then Ian's sons and his future daughter-in-law, Mary. Abigail's mother, Maggie, was also in attendance. Everyone made small talk while they waited for the Earl and the Countess. The door finally opened, and in walked Henry Sinclair, Countess Jean Sinclair, and Henry's heir Henry Sinclair II. The Earl was finely dressed in his best Kilt. The Countess was in her new gown. Young Henry was also dressed in a kilt that matched his Father's. Henry informed everyone present that he was recording all of the changes and new assignments in the form of a Decree. An aide then entered the room and unrolled a parchment. It read the following:

I, Henry Sinclair, Baron of Rosslyn, and Earl of Orkney, decrees the following:

I, Henry, will lead the mission to the New World.

In my absence, Henry II will assume the duties of Earl until I return from my journey.

Jean, Countess of Rosslyn, and wife to Henry Sinclair, will advise Henry II on all Clan matters and will provide consent to the reigning Earl.

Ian MacIntyre will assume the Senior Advisory Role to Henry Sinclair on the New World mission.

Angus Moore will assume the Senior Advisory Role to Henry Sinclair on the New World mission.

Gavin MacIntyre will assume the Senior Advisory Role for the Countess and Henry II.

Francis MacIntyre will assume Security Role on the New World mission.

Abigail MacIntyre will assume the role of shipmate on the New World mission.

Maggie Curran will assume the role of Seamstress to the Countess.

The reading of the decree ended with Henry congratulating everyone on their new assignments. He went on to say that this mission was critical to the future success of the Clan and the survival of Scotland. He said that he would meet with Angus and Ian daily to start the mission plan. Gavin would meet with the Countess and Henry II daily to discuss Clan matters. Gavin could immediately assume his living quarters on the castle grounds. After their wedding, Mary could join him. And last but not least, Maggie could assume her living quarters on the Castle grounds. She would start her new role as Seamstress for the Countess immediately. This concluded the decree and announcements. They all sat down and enjoyed a fine dinner of Pheasant and Potatoes. After the dinner plates were cleared, everyone enjoyed a celebratory glass or two of wine. Everyone was giddy with excitement and spent the balance of the evening discussing everyone's new role. On the next day, the real mission would begin.

CHAPTER 46

AGATHA AND MALCOLM

THE FOLLOWING DAY, Ian went to the Clan Library because he knew that Malcolm would most certainly be there. Malcolm was very particular about his daily routine. Ian knew that unless Malcolm had taken ill, he would be sitting at his desk at the Library.

As the door opened, Malcolm rose to warmly greet his favorite student. Ian said, "It is always so good to see you. I am here with the hope of speaking to both you and Agatha."

Malcolm said, "Agatha is currently at home. That nuisance who calls himself a Priest keeps bothering her every time he sees her. He is asking questions that lead us to believe that he thinks Agatha is a witch."

Ian said, "Would you like me to have the Earl speak with him?"

"No. That could only make matters worse. She is staying at home for the most part. She prefers it that way anyway." Malcolm said.

Ian said, "Agatha is closer to God than anyone that I have ever met. This Priest is just not smart enough to understand her."

Malcolm said, "I agree wholeheartedly." Then, he briefly paused and said, "Why don't you join us for supper this evening? Agatha and I would be thrilled to have you over to our home. You know she thinks of you as her grandson."

"That would be lovely. I will arrive at six o'clock if that works." Ian said.

Malcolm said, "Perfect."

As Ian was walking back through the Village, he thought to himself, "She thinks of me as her grandson because I was her grandson. At least in the time of Noah."

✠

At precisely six o'clock, Ian arrived at Malcolm and Agatha's home. He came with a fresh loaf of bread from the Earl's kitchen, as well as a jug of the Earl's finest wine. As always, Agatha was always so excited to see Ian. She said, "It's so good to see you. I can see that you have many heavy matters weighing you down. Hopefully, this evening will give you peace."

Ian said, "There is nothing that gives me more peace than to be with you. I need to speak with you regarding my soul."

Agatha replied, "Ian. I know why you want to speak with me. However, if you are concerned with Malcolm hearing anything that you might say, please understand that Malcolm is not only my husband, but he is my best friend. He knows everything about our past lives, the Ark, and of the Secret of Eden."

Malcolm, "Trust me, Lad, if I was to tell anyone of this story. They would think that I had gone mad. Or even better, they would have that feeble-minded Priest here to exorcise the demons from within me." Everyone laughed and took their seats.

Agatha served supper, which consisted of oxen and potatoes. The supper conversation was kept very light. Agatha wanted to hear about Gavin and Mary's wedding plans. She was so excited.

Agatha said, "I hope you know that Clara will be there as well." Then as if on cue, Ian could smell the Lavender Flowers. They were always Clara's favorite. Ian and Clara's home always had a batch of Lavender growing in the yard, which was no small feat given the cool climate in Scotland.

Ian said, "I Dream of her often. However, I have noticed that the Dreams are more prevalent when I have an important matter in front of me."

"Aye. That is her best way to communicate with you. Maybe someday you will learn how to speak with her more directly as I have learned." Agatha said.

Ian said, "Now to the matter which I need to speak to both of you. First of all, I am sure that both of you will keep this matter confidential." He paused for a moment and said, "The Earl has decided that Scotland is no longer a safe place for the Treasure. He wants to move it to a place called Vinland."

Malcolm said, "Many ancient societies refer to this place the Earl calls Vinland as the New World. The prophecies are endless."

Ian said, "Malcolm, given the fact that you are an expert on the ancient societies and Agatha, you are an expert on the Secret of Eden and its Treasure, I believe that both of you should accompany our team when we set sail next spring."

Agatha said, "I knew this day would come. I know what my role is in this story, but please understand that I will not go anywhere unless I am with Malcolm."

Ian said, "I would never think of asking one of you but not the other. But, first, we must convince the Earl that both of you are necessary for success." Then, after a brief pause, Ian asked, "Should we just tell him the truth?"

Agatha said, "Aye. We should tell him everything. I assume that he doesn't know what he possesses with the Secret of Eden. He is placing his life and the future of his Clan in danger. He deserves to know the truth. When he fully understands everything, he will understand why Malcolm and I are necessary."

Ian finally said, "I will set up a meeting with the Earl and the both of you. We will explain the entire story. I think Angus should be there as well."

Ian said his goodbyes and thanked them for supper. He knew that he had a task that needed to be completed before the meeting with the Earl. He needed to meet with Angus.

CHAPTER 47

THE TALE

THE FOLLOWING MORNING, Ian woke up and prepared himself for the day. He had been avoiding this day for a long time. Today he would talk about the Secret of Eden with Angus. For some reason, he felt apprehensive about this discussion. He was not sure why.

An hour later, he had his morning meeting with the Earl. They discussed the Clan matters first. Winter was upon them. There were always items that needed to be repaired. Also, the Earl was concerned with the Septs that didn't have homes. He wanted to ensure that adequate shelter and provisions were available to these Septs. Ian assured the Earl that the Septs would be cared for by the village leaders.

After all of the daily Clan matters were discussed, Ian said, "I have another matter that I would like to discuss with you. It involves Malcolm and his wife, Agatha."

The Earl said, "I know where this discussion is headed. Unfortunately, they are both too old to take on our voyage. Can't they be useful here in Rosslyn instead?"

"Sir, when you hear the entire story, you will think otherwise. Would you be available to meet with them this evening?"

"Can't you just tell me? I have the ultimate respect for Malcolm and his wife, but I do not wish to discuss the Treasure with them." The Earl said.

Ian said, "I promise you that when you hear the story in its entirety, you will have much more clarity on the mission. You will not regret it."

The Earl said, "Very well. Invite them for dinner this evening."

"Also, this involves Angus as well. I will also invite him."

The Earl said, "I rarely enter a meeting without knowing what will be discussed. In fact, I usually try to have the upper hand somehow. But, Ian, this is not one of those times."

Ian smiled and said, "You will not be disappointed."

✠

Ian immediately rode to the Library to inform Malcolm of this evening's plans.

Malcolm said, "We will be there. I do believe that we were all placed here for this very reason."

"It would seem that way," Ian said.

✠

Ian then made his way back to the Castle to find Angus. One of the workers told Ian that Angus was out near the river where an old bridge was about to collapse. Ian rode out there where he found Angus knee-deep in the frigid water, trying to install a new support.

Ian smiled and said, "Did I catch you at a bad time?"

"No, you arrived at a perfect time. Now please remove your shoes and join me in the river before this bridge collapses on top of me." Angus said.

Ian jumped from his horse and joined his old friend in the river. Ian said, "You know that you are not going to die this way. You and I have to protect a certain Treasure as we have done over thousands of years."

Angus said, "I wondered when we were going to have this discussion. The Dreams are beginning to drive me crazy."

Ian said, "Well, old friend, I believe that our moment for this lifetime is upon us. Are you aware of how Agatha plays into this story?"

Angus replied, "Other than being our grandmother back in the time of Noah and being a relevant person in our lives ever since, I have no idea what you are talking about." Both men laughed.

Ian said, "Malcolm, Agatha, you, and I have all been summoned to the Earl's Dining Room this evening."

"The good news is that with all of the dinner meetings, Abigail has barely had to cook. I will tell her to go visit with her mother this evening." Angus said.

The two men finished repairing the bridge and headed back to the Castle grounds.

✠

Since there had been so many dinners at the Castle recently, everyone knew to be there precisely at six o'clock. Everyone was seated when the Earl and the Countess entered the dining room. The Earl welcomed everyone to the Castle then added, "Ian tells me that this evening will be remarkable."

Angus added, "That is putting it lightly." Everyone laughed, especially the ones who already knew the story. After that, the Dinner conversation consisted mainly of small talk about the village and how the winter was slowly creeping in.

After dinner was concluded, the Countess wished everyone a good night and departed the dining hall. The Earl then said, "Let's retire to my anteroom. It offers much more privacy."

Everyone was seated. The Earl had added a few chairs so that everyone could be seated in comfort.

Ian said, "Let's have Agatha sit directly across from the Earl since she will be the one telling the tale."

The Earl said, "I have been waiting like a young child all day. Please, Agatha, tell me this tale."

Agatha said, "Well, as with any great tale, this one must start at the beginning. It begins with a Seer that went by the name of Enoch. You may have heard of him in the Old Testament. He was the great grandfather of Noah. Emperor Constantine purposely saw to it that the Book of Enoch was left out of the Bible. His story managed to survive through the ages, though. Enoch had written that he had communicated with the ones that he referred to as the Watchers. They were sent by the Almighty. The Watchers had given Enoch a set of rules for man to follow. The Watchers said, "If the laws of the Almighty are not followed, then a cataclysm will wipe out all of mankind. Needless to say, mankind did not follow the rules. In the time leading up to the cataclysm, the Watchers reached out to Noah and instructed him to build the Ark." She paused briefly and said, "I am sure you know what happened next. After the waters subsided, the Watchers once again reached out to humanity. This time they spoke to several of the descendants of Noah. They instructed Noah's wife Na'amah and her grandchildren, Peleg and Joktan, who were brothers, and their female cousin Tytea that they would now be responsible for guarding the message and also a Treasure which they called the Secret of Eden. They would forever be known as "The Children of the Flood." They would guard the Secret of Eden throughout the ages until the Almighty declared that humanity was indeed worthy of learning the Secret."

Agatha paused for this to sink in. Then, she asked the Earl, "Are you familiar with the term reincarnation?"

The Earl said, "Of course, I have heard of it but have not pursued it because the Church considers it blasphemy."

Agatha said, "The Church is a topic for another day, but

suffice it to say, it is real. Other religions such as Buddhism consider being reborn as a central tenant of their faith. Anyways, the Children of the Flood were reborn whenever the Secret of Eden was in Jeopardy. In the twelfth century, the two grandsons were the Knights Templar leaders that discovered the message underneath Solomon's Temple. That led them to find the Treasure underneath the Great Sphinx in Egypt. Unfortunately, their success in that lifetime was short-lived because the adversary who appears in every lifetime had managed to kill both of them while the Treasure was being transported out of Egypt. These same two were once again Knights Templars earlier in this century. They were the ones who secretly transported the Treasure to Scotland as the Knights were being arrested and tortured. The Treasure was then handed to your ancestor, Henry St. Clair. I believe that you know the rest of the story of the Treasure."

The Earl said, "That is quite a tale."

Ian responded, "You haven't heard the most intriguing part of the story yet."

The Earl said, "Then please continue."

Agatha paused and then said, "The Children of the Flood are here once again to protect the Treasure. In fact, three of them are with you this evening."

The Earl was startled. He looked around the room with a look of confusion on his face.

Agatha said, "In Noah's time, I was his wife, Na'amah. Ian was the elder grandson Peleg, Angus was the younger grandson Joktan, and Ian's late wife Clara was Tytea."

The Earl looked at Ian and Angus and said, "Is this true?"

Both men nodded aye.

Agatha said, "That is the core of the story. Of course, there is much more to tell, but you should first let this sink in. We haven't even gone into some of the most harrowing parts of the tale, such as how the message was originally hidden or how Clara's previous incarnation was as a Cathar Priestess who gave her life to protect the secret."

Ian had not heard this before. He was startled. He would meet with Agatha at a later time to discuss this.

Ian finally gathered his wits and said, "Agatha has great knowledge of the Treasure, and it's his history. Therefore, I believe that she should travel and stay with the Treasure. Malcolm is the authority on the antiquities, as well as the native cultures in the west."

Malcolm finally spoke. He said, "Sir, one thing that I have learned about these primitive cultures is that they believe in the supernatural. Every village seems to have a healer who has special gifts. I believe that these healers will instantly recognize that Agatha has a similar gift. She could be a great help to you concerning traveling peacefully throughout their villages."

The Earl said, "This mission could be not only dangerous but grueling. You are both older than me. Do you think you can weather the unknown?"

Agatha said, "My spirit has weathered the unimaginable. This mission will be no different. Also, one thing about being old is that you have done many things. In addition to being a healer, I am used to cooking for large groups, and I am a well-practiced seamstress."

The Earl said, "Welcome to the mission."

After Malcolm and Agatha left, the Earl, Ian, and Angus drank mead until the wee hours of the morning. The Earl was utterly shocked and happy by what he had heard.

The Earl said, "Agatha mentioned an adversary. Should I assume that this person will appear at some point in the future?"

Angus said, "He has already made himself known. He is the one we met in Oslo who goes by the name of Oleg. It seems that you battled his father and brothers in the Ornkeys. In each lifetime, he has a different mission. In this lifetime, his mission is vengeance for his family. We assume that he knows nothing of the Treasure." Angus sipped his drink and continued, "Oleg is like us in that he will be reborn. He is known as a Child of Canaan. His mission is to plant seeds of evil wherever he goes. In this lifetime, he has also taken on the mission of vengeance."

The Earl said, "Never forget. He is a Viking. If he discovers that we have a Treasure, then he will double his efforts."

The Earl closed the night by saying, "I thought that I played a significant role because I am in possession of the Treasure. Now I understand that we are all part of a much larger scheme that is biblical. The survival of mankind depends on our success."

CHAPTER 48

THE FISHERMAN

Several weeks passed with everyone settling into their new roles. There was plenty of work to be done. Angus was given the directive to secure new ships. They had to be robust and hold a substantial cargo with a host of sailors. Angus set out with Francis to the shipyards at the seaports. They were looking for ships already built because the trip was scheduled to commence the following spring. However, they were also on a separate mission. They were searching for the fisherman who had been lost for so many years. This fisherman had claimed that he spent many of those years in a place that he called Estotiland. The Earl wished to meet with him to discuss the upcoming venture.

After a month had gone by, Angus and Francis had returned to Rosslyn. He recalled the entire journey for the Earl and Ian. The trip back to Rosslyn had taken several days. Abigail was very happy to have Angus back. Everyone got cleaned up and then worked their way to the Castle where the Earl was patiently waiting.

Angus said, "The first stop was the Orkney Islands. We were confident that we could find the ships that we were looking for in the Ornkeys. Most of the master shipbuilders reside there." He went on to say, "The locals were pleased to supply ships to the Clan Sinclair because the Sinclair's had freed them from the grips of the Nordic Warlords. Also, the Orkney Islands were where the lost fisherman had reappeared. After several days of visiting shipyards, we secured the ships, but we could not locate the lost fisherman. The locals believed that he had headed back out to sea on a new fishing expedition."

Angus paused momentarily to bring forward the ship ownership paperwork. Then, he continued, "We had finalized all of the arrangements to purchase seven vessels. They are square sail rigged ships that were built to sail across vast bodies of water. They have deep hulls with heavy keels to keep the ships upright even in the roughest seas. They each have a large cargo hull and are equipped with an adequate galley with living quarters of up to sixty people. As with most large sailing vessels, the Captain's cabin is aft and is large enough to have a dining room, separate sleeping quarters, private head, and cabinets for charts."

The seven ships needed to carry enough food supplies for a one-year mission, building supplies for building temporary quarters upon arrival, large amounts of weaponry, and a minimal amount of livestock. Roughly half of the men hired for the mission had to be experienced sailors. The other half were combination builders and farmers. All had to be able to handle the weaponry.

The subject then turned to the fisherman. Angus said, "We spent our last evening in a small fishing village in a protected harbor on the east end of the Orkney Islands. The following morning we were scheduled to board a courier vessel to take us back to the mainland. The next morning as we were waiting for the courier, we heard on knock on the door. We both reached for our swords because there are still Vikings milling about these Islands. I cautiously opened the door. A smallish man stood there.

I said, "Who are you?" The man said with an Italian accent, "I am Antonio. I am the one you seek." Angus continued, "I explained that the Earl, Henry Sinclair, would like him to speak with him in Rosslyn. I offered to pay him handsomely for the trip. Antonio agreed, and I instructed him to get his belongings. Shortly after that, we boarded the courier ship and headed back to the mainland. We then made the trip back here to Rosslyn as fast as possible."

Angus then escorted Antonio into the Earl's anteroom. The Earl very warmly greeted the fisherman. He even carried on a short conversation in Italian with Antonio. Angus mentioned that Antonio also speaks Latin. It probably saved his life. Antonio nodded that this was true. Then, the Earl asked, "Antonio, please tell me the entire story from what port you departed from through your arrival back in the Orkneys."

The Earl poured Antonio a glass of his premier wine. Antonio proceeded to detail a fantastic tale of adventure that included things usually included in a fairy tale. He said, "There were beautiful women, natural springs with pure water flowing from them, and natives that had a clear understanding of the stars." He continued, "The leader of the natives is an Englishman who had a vast library of books written in Latin. This man told stories of ancient Greeks and Phoenicians that had traveled throughout this new land and had found major scores of gold, silver, and copper. This man goes by the name of Goosecap."

Antonio's demeanor suddenly changed when he spoke of the other neighboring tribes. He said, "The other native tribes are vicious and will kill strangers on sight. They are cannibals who treat human meat like it is a delicacy. They had killed all seven of the other Fishermen that were with me. I managed to escape before they were captured."

Ian asked the man, "What was it like to be lost for twenty-plus years?"

Antonio said, "I wasn't lost. I was in a land where food was plentiful, and the water was pure. At first, I was treated very poorly by the natives. However, everything changed when they discovered that I spoke Latin." Antonio detailed how he liked the place so much that he turned down many opportunities to travel back to a Viking Settlement. Finally, he decided to head back to Scotland after he was again lost at sea. He was saved by a Viking fisherman who helped him make his way back to Scotland. However, he missed the place he had called home for twenty years.

The Earl asked Antonio, "Could you find the place again?"

Antonio responded, "Yes."

The Earl then offered Antonio employment. He told him that he would be handsomely paid and all of his needs would be provided for. Antonio smiled and said he was ready to return to Estotiland. The Earl asked Antonio, "Do you have a map or something else to guide us."

Antonio responded that he didn't need a map. He went on to say, "It is simple, just follow the Great Swan. It will lead you to Arcadia." When Ian heard this, he nearly fainted. He broke out in a cold sweat.

For the remainder of the meeting with Antonio, Ian sat quietly, trying to pay attention. His mind was elsewhere. He was desperately trying to recall the details of his Swan Dreams. The Swan Dreams started shortly after Clara died. The Dreams always started with the fragrance. As always, Ian knew that the fragrance meant that Clara was there. The Dreams were a combination of him seeing Swans floating in the water and also staring at an image of a large swan in the nighttime sky. What did it all mean? Was Clara trying to tell him something from the other side? All of the other Dreams were about past lifetimes. This one was seemingly about the future. Many of the Dreams also included an image of a Cross in the Sky. Could the Cross and the Swan be related? He needed to speak with Malcolm to see if he had any understanding of the Great Swan or the Cross.

At the end of the meeting with Antonio, the Earl asked Ian, "You look like you had seen a ghost when Antonio mentioned the Great Swan. Is everything all right?"

Ian replied, "I have been having a recurring Dream since Clara passed where I am on the open sea and was being instructed to "Follow the Great Swan."

CHAPTER 49

ANSWERS

THE FOLLOWING MORNING, Ian woke up with more questions than he had the previous day. The disclosures have added another level of questions that left Ian with very few people with which to turn. Of course, the most obvious person to turn to is Agatha. But, first, Ian needed to understand the historical context and time frames in which the revelations originally took place. For this, he would turn to Malcolm.

After his daily meeting with the Earl, Ian traveled to the library again. As usual, Malcolm was sitting at his desk. He warmly greeted Ian and offered him some tea. Ian said, "Tea sounds perfect right now. I have some news that I would like to share with you." He paused briefly and continued, "The Earl has been inquiring with his friends who were aides to the Bruce's about the New World. At first, he had not heard anything, but recently he received a letter that described a fisherman who had been lost at sea for twenty years. This fisherman, whose name is Antonio, finally made his way back to Scotland and told a tale of living in the New World amongst the natives. The Earl believes that the place where Antonio lived is also a possible destination for the Treasure. Angus located this fisherman and brought him to Rosslyn. The Earl has hired him to guide us back to this place."

Malcolm said, "That's great news. Does he have a map?"

Ian responded, "No. He just said to follow the Great Swan, and it will lead you to Arcadia."

"Does he believe that he was living in the fabled Arcadia?" Malcolm asked.

Ian said, "Antonio certainly believes he has been there. However, the part that caught my attention is that I have had numerous Dreams about a Great Swan which sometimes included a Cross in the sky."

Malcolm smiled and said, "The Fisherman was talking about the constellation called Cygnus. It was called the Great Swan by the ancients. Modern Astronomers call it the Northern Cross."

Ian said, "I have heard of the Northern Cross, but I have never noticed it in the sky."

Malcolm said, "As far as Arcadia is concerned, it is an ancient Greek term representing the New Atlantis. It has been the intended destination of many explorers, but none had found it. So instead, there are tales of journeys made by Ancient Greeks and Phoenicians to a New World where gold and silver were abundant, and the land was perfect for starting a Utopian society."

Ian said, "I believe that Clara once again is guiding my Dreams. It finally makes sense. The stars will guide us to the New World."

Malcolm said, "You should discuss this with Agatha. I will be heading home shortly. You can join me if you like."

Ian said, "I was going to try to see Agatha today as well. I have numerous questions for her."

✠

Agatha greeted Ian and Malcolm and showed them to the dining table. She had enough food for Ian as if she already knew he was coming.

Ian said, "It is utterly impossible to surprise you."

Agatha said, "I am just happy to have you at our home once again."

She served tea with fresh bread and a fruit plate.

Ian said, "I believe that Clara is guiding my Dreams once again. For some time now, I have had many Dreams about swans. Now a lost fisherman shows up and tells us to follow the Great Swan, which Malcolm tells me is a well-known constellation in the night sky."

"She would rather be here with you in the living, but this is the next best thing. She can see things that most people cannot see." Agatha said.

Ian said, "What I really wanted to speak with you about is Clara's previous incarnation being a Cathar Priestess. I have no recollection of this. Weren't we always together."

Agatha said, "You don't have any recollection because you were not alive when she went through her greatest trauma. A very evil man had killed both you and Angus's incarnations. He is the same spirit that will try to stop our venture to the New World. So do not underestimate him."

"Please tell me the story," Ian asked.

Agatha paused for a minute and went on, "Ian, you may find this difficult to hear, but during the 13th century, the Pope was on a rampage to kill anyone who differed from the message that had come from the Church. You were killed shortly after your marriage in one of the raids on the Cathar Villages. The Cathars were a threat to the Pope. While the Cathars believed in Jesus Christ and the Trinity of God, they had other beliefs such as the belief in reincarnation that were contrary to the Church's message. They also believed that women could rise to the level of Priesthood. Pope Innocent III ordered one of his armies to wipe out the Cathars. He ordered that every man, woman, and child was to be struck down. In fact, when one of his leaders was asked which of the Villagers were the Cathars? The Leader's response was to kill them all. The Lord will figure out which ones were Cathars and which ones weren't. This Pope and his henchmen were pure evil. To think that this man, who ironically called himself Innocent, was supposed to be the Vicar of the Church and be walking in the footsteps of Jesus Christ is an abomination. His path to power is for another day, but to refer to him as Satan would be putting it lightly. His men killed your entire family." Agatha paused to collect herself. This memory was very overwhelming for her.

After a few minutes, she continued, "Miraculously, Helena, which was Clara's name in that lifetime, escaped to northern France to the town of Gisor. She had become a Priestess. She went there because of the secret, which is the same secret that we are discussing in this lifetime. Her mission was to protect the secret. She was the only Guardian of the Secret of Eden left at that point. The adversary in that lifetime was a man known as Simon de Montfort. He was the leader that killed all of the Cathars, including your loved ones. When he was a younger soldier, he killed you in cold blood. As the leader, he became aware that Helena knew a secret. Simon de Montfort had learned that the secret promised riches beyond anything he could imagine. He captured, tortured, and finally killed Helena. However, she never gave up the secret." After Agatha paused to collect herself, she continued, "Helena managed to get word to the Templars that the Treasure was in jeopardy. As a result, the Templars moved the Treasure once again."

Ian said, "That is horrible. It pains me that she had to go through this." But then, he paused and continued, "Obviously, this also pains you. Were you alive in this lifetime?"

Agatha said, "Aye. I was Helena's young aide. I was the one who alerted the Templars."

CHAPTER 50

THE THREAT

A S THE MONTHS went by leading up to the mission launch date, the activity both in Rosslyn and the port of Edinburgh had ramped up. The Earl hired his old friend Captain Joshua McQuinn, who had served with the Earl in the Orkneys to manage the ships and security at the port. Captain McQuinn was as seasoned of a warrior as you would ever find. He led the Earl's ships to victory against the Norse. However, just the sight of his flagship would cause the most hardened of Vikings to retreat.

Ian and Angus visited the port so that they could report back to the Earl regarding the ships' readiness. Angus said to Captain McQuinn, "The problem with the port is that seven ships being loaded and prepared was a hard thing to conceal. Anyone who visits the port will know that something major was underway."

There were rumors of several Viking ships visiting during the previous night. It was as if they were probing the defenses of the ships. A handful of the Vikings were reported to have left their ships and walked into the Village of Edinburgh. Captain McQuinn had searched high and low but found nothing. This caused great concern for Captain McQuinn. The Earl was scheduled to visit the following week. The port was not secure, and the Earl could be in danger. Ian decided to send a message back to the Earl. The courier's instructions were to deliver the message and return at once with any message from the Earl.

A week had passed, and the courier had not returned. Both Ian and Angus had feared the worse. So, finally, they decided that they must make the trip to Rosslyn themselves. Captain McQuinn selected ten of his best men for security. The party left just after sunrise on the very next morning. They were about halfway back to Rosslyn when Ian noticed that four or five hawks were circling.

Ian said, "Let's stop and investigate."

The men drew their swords and had their shields at the ready in their other hand. As they approached, they could begin to notice that unmistakable smell of rotting flesh. They finally arrived only to find the corpse of the young courier. He had been badly beaten or tortured before finally having his throat slit.

Angus said, "This was not a random robbery. Average thieves do not take the time to torture their victims. Whoever did this was looking for information."

One of the warriors noticed blood all over a nearby boulder. The courier had been tortured on the boulder. There were letters written in blood on the side of the boulder. On closer inspection, the letters spelled out the word "VEGVISIR."

✠

The following day, Ian and Angus arrived back at the Castle. The Earl was in his anteroom looking at the manifests for the mission. Ian and Angus walked and greeted the Earl. Ian said, "We have news that can't wait."

The Earl said, "What is it."

Ian said, "Several nights ago, a handful of Viking Ships entered the port during the night. An unknown number of Vikings left their ships and ventured into Edinburgh. We sent a courier to warn you. The courier had strict instructions to return to the port after delivering the sealed message to you. He never returned. Captain McQuinn sent a team of warriors with us to come to Rosslyn to warn you. Yesterday, we found the young courier's badly beaten and tortured corpse. He somehow was able to leave us a message. With his blood, he wrote the word "VEGVISIR.""

The Earl said, "We must assume that he intends to attack the Castle."

Angus said, "I thought the same thing, so when I returned, I summoned our Commanders and ordered them to assemble their forces and surround the Castle. They have instructions to sound their horns if the Vikings are spotted."

The Earl said, "Very good."

Ian said, "Sir, you said "He intends to attack"?"

The Earl said, "This is no doubt that brute Oleg. All of the elders in his family wear a medal around their neck with a symbol and the word VEGVISIR. It is supposed to protect them while they are at sea or in battle."

Ian said, "We need to set a trap for Oleg."

CHAPTER 51

FOLLOW THE GREAT SWAN

THE FOLLOWING DAY the Earl called a meeting of the Clan's warriors. This would take hours just to get the word out. Many of them lived at the far reaches of the Clan's territory. The purpose was to warn everyone that Vikings had landed and were looking for retribution against the Earl and the Clan Sinclair. The meeting is to take place this evening at the castle. Each commander was given the instructions to summon the nearby warriors and warn them that Vikings were in our midst before they traveled to Rosslyn. They were ordered to stop anyone who wasn't in the Clan Sinclair.

✠

Meanwhile, the Earl insisted that the team continue preparing for the trip to the New World. Ian met with the Earl for their usual morning meeting. After they went through their usual rundown of preparations for the journey, the Earl discussed his many concerns about the voyage. He said, "I looked in the Stone Barn yesterday. I am concerned that we don't have enough ships. I will discuss this with Angus later today, but just looking at the crates in the barn, it would seem that we may have a problem."

Ian replied, "We have to bring provisions for an entire year. We have no idea whether or not we can safely hunt in the New World. So we are planning for the worst case."

The Earl said, "We must be able to hunt and fish, or we will not survive. It will be upon me to negotiate with the natives. We should speak with Antonio and see what we should take with us for bartering." The Earl summoned one of his sentries and asked him to locate Antonio and bring him to the Earl.

Several minutes later, Antonio arrived and was seated across from the Earl. The Earl said, "We are discussing the natives near the Gold River. First, my understanding is they are Mi'kmaq. Are there any other tribes nearby?"

Antonio said, "No. Many years ago, the tribes fought, and the territories were settled. As a result, we will encounter only Mi'kmaq."

"What should be brought for gifts and trade?" The Earl asked.

Antonio said, "Metal pots and pans, steel axes, and weapons." Then, he paused and continued, "Seeds and small ships are also essential to the Mi'kmaq."

Ian said, "I would advise holding the weapons for last. Let's make sure that we have a good working agreement before we arm them." The Earl nodded.

The Earl asked, "Antonio, you described a place where there is what the natives referred to as a Holy Well where the water is pure and endless."

Antonio said, "It is a two-day walk through heavy woods to get there. The place is magnificent. The Holy Well is on land that is on a clearing that overlooks a lake."

"Do the Mi'kmaq consider this land sacred?" The Earl asked.

Antonio replied, "It is not part of the Mi'kmaq culture. It is said that many generations ago, darker-skinned men came by ship and briefly settled in this area. They are the ones that built the Holy Well. They considered it Holy, not the Mi'kmaq. Eventually, these dark-skinned men moved on." Antonio continued, "The water is very pure and naturally flows up from the ground. The dark-skinned men had never seen anything like this where they come from. It was very special for them."

Ian said, "It sounds to me that this is a natural spring. We have them throughout Scotland, but there are places such as the areas surrounding the Mediterranean Sea where there are no such springs." Ian continued, "A spring is a naturally occurring flow of water through cracks in the bedrock that is significantly below the surface. The water goes through many beds of smaller rocks, which serve as a filter that purifies the water. The water is also generally very cold, which helps to keep it pure."

The Earl said to Antonio, "You previously stated that this area is significantly upriver and uphill from the Ocean."

Antonio responded, "They have small mountains in this land. The Gold River flows the heaviest after the snow has melted."

The Earl thanked Antonio for his input, and the Sentry escorted Antonio out of the Earl's quarters.

The Earl said, "We need to prepare for a trip to carry all of the materials and the treasure uphill and a great distance inland. This will require oxen and carts."

Ian said, "We can build the carts there, but obviously, we must take the oxen."

The Earl said, "Aye. We need to take a good look at all that we must bring. We may need another ship or two." He paused briefly, then continued, "Another thing that I have been thinking about is marking the way for our descendants. I'm sure that the land all looks the same from the water. So I plan to plant a certain species of trees that would serve as markers for the Gold River. These trees are native to Africa. They grew very tall and are very robust. Once they are fully grown, they will be perfect markers for the entrance to the Gold River. I have acquired fifty saplings that I plan to bring on the mission."

The subject then turned to Malcolm. Ian explained to the Earl how he was shocked when Antonio used the term, "Follow the Great Swan." Ian explained how he has had Dreams of Swans and has heard that exact phrase ever since Clara passed. The Earl was not shocked. He said, "After what I heard several nights ago, nothing will surprise me."

Ian said, "When I told this to Malcolm, he simply responded that explorers have been following the Great Swan or the constellation Cygnus for generations."

The Earl said, "There are many stories and legends on the high seas. Figuring out which ones are real is the difficult part.

Just then, a Sentry appeared and said, "Malcolm McBride and his wife Agatha are here to speak with Ian. They seem troubled."

The Earl said, "Show them in."

A few minutes later, Malcolm and Agatha were shown to the Earl's anteroom. The Earl welcomed them both and said, "The Sentry tells us that you both were distraught. What troubles you?"

Malcolm said, "Thank you, sir. We don't mean to trouble you, but we have a few things that we need to share."

The Earl said, "You are part of my inner circle now. Do not fear upsetting me. Your wife has knowledge that I will never have. So please proceed."

Malcolm said, "First of all, Agatha prepares food for the downtrodden and homeless every day. This morning while serving an elderly woman of Norwegian descent, the woman said, "Last night several Vikings walked through Rosslyn Village. She knew that they were Vikings once she heard them speak. There is no doubt once you hear their dialect."

"How many of them were there?" The Earl asked.

Agatha responded, "Three."

The room was quiet for several minutes when the Earl finally spoke. He said, "Thank you for reporting this news. We are making arrangements to have our Clan warriors move into this area to protect the Clan. We lost a young warrior to these scoundrels several days back. I would like both of you to travel back to your home and gather what you need for several days. I would like both of you to stay at the castle as my guests until this situation is dealt with."

Agatha said, "I still need to feed the homeless."

The Earl said, "Of course, we will still take care of our most vulnerable. Now you will have several skilled warriors escort you when you need to provide meals." He paused, then said, "After I learned of your past lives, I now know that keeping you safe is critical for the future of the Clan."

Malcolm said, "Thank you, sir."

The Earl said, "Malcolm, I would like to take advantage of having you stay here at the castle. Since I was a wee lad, you have spoken of Mystics and Ancient Mysteries. It is no longer a legend. It is now a reality for all of us."

Malcolm laughed and said, "Finally, someone is saying, "That crazy old man is not crazy after all." Everyone laughed. Malcolm continued, "I would also like to stop off at the library. I have several old documents that pertain to great explorations to the New World."

Agatha suddenly turned very somber. She finally said, "There is another matter. I rarely get a look into the future, but last night was one of those occasions. I saw many Vikings, probably twenty or so, hiding near a bridge. They are lying in wait for the Earl's carriage to travel through. When the carriage arrives, they surround it and wait for their leader to come and kill the Earl. Their leader is the one who wears the medal that says "VEGVISIR.""

CHAPTER 52

THE WEDDING

NOAH HAD DECIDED that it was time for Peleg and Tytea to be married. Both were now twelve years old, and it was their time to be united in the eyes of the Almighty. So Noah summoned both of them and their parents to his tent.

After everyone arrived, Noah said, "You are the eldest of the Children of the Flood and have been chosen to be paired in the eyes of God so that you may carry out the sacred duty of producing the next generation. For years to come, your offspring shall work these holy lands in the Almighty's name. There will be no mattan or gifts for your parents, and no mohar or dowry, as there has been in the past. For these two, there will be something far more everlasting. Peleg and Tytea's souls will be united forever in the mission of protecting the message of the Almighty that has been handed down to us by the Watchers."

Noah then recited the sacred teachings handed down by Adam and his wife Eve. Finally, Peleg and Tytea recited their vows to one another. Everyone present knew that these vows were eternal, especially in the case of these two souls. That evening, Noah's family gathered together to celebrate this sacred union. It was a very joyful night. Noah had fulfilled one of his most important tasks. This task sealed the covenant between himself and the Watchers. The future generations will always have these two souls present to protect and defend the most sacred message from God. Noah knew that he would add a third soul to this covenant when the time was right. The soul of his wife Na'amah would also always be there to teach and support the Children of the Flood. Noah's mission was almost complete.

At the end of the celebration, Peleg looked at his bride. She was the most beautiful woman that he had ever seen. She had one of the purple flowers in her hair, and her smile etched a special place within his soul. He looked into the eyes of his wife and saw pure bliss as though he was looking into the kingdom of heaven itself. He knew that he was indeed blessed for all of the days to come....

✠

Just then, a rooster crowed and woke Ian out of his special Dream. He knew that he had this Dream at this time because today is to be the day that his son Gavin is to be wed to his betrothed, Mary.

✠

As Ian made his way into the Castle for his morning meeting with the Earl, he recounted his discussions earlier in the week regarding Gavin and Mary's wedding.

Ian had said to the Earl, "In light of the revelations regarding Oleg and the threats to the Clan Sinclair, maybe we should postpone the celebration until after this matter resolves itself. Gavin can take Mary to the church and have a very small ceremony."

The Earl said, "Nonsense if we postpone the wedding, this heathen wins. I will not grant him the satisfaction. I have all the security in place to thwart any attack that this Viking could muster. So we will have the grandest celebration that the Clan has ever seen."

Any thoughts of having a low-key wedding had just ended. Also, the preparations for the trip to the New World would have to be put aside temporarily. Today is to be about the wedding of Ian's eldest child. Even though Ian understood that Clara would be there spiritually, it breaks his heart that she won't be there standing at his side.

Agatha helped Ian with the decorations for the celebration. She had secretly grown a large patch of Lavender flowers for this day. The flowers were transplanted into pots that adorned the entire courtyard of the castle. The fragrance was everywhere. Ian couldn't distinguish between the actual flowers and Clara's essence. Either way, it didn't matter. The fragrance gave Ian great comfort. The courtyard was so beautiful that the Earl joked, "I may have to leave you here to be my gardener when we set out." Everyone laughed. Angus was present at the time. He just smiled at Ian. He knew that Clara was indeed there guiding Ian's every move.

Last evening, the Earl and the Countess had a special dinner for Ian and his family, which of course, included Angus, Abigail, Malcolm, and Agatha. The Earl toasted Gavin and his lovely bride-to-be. He stated, "Gavin Is quickly becoming a fine aide. He has a bright future in front of him." The Earl also told Mary, "Don't forget that behind every successful man, a strong woman is telling him that he is wrong." Everyone laughed.

The Countess said, "I second that toast." This drew an even louder roar from those in attendance. She went on to say that it was lovely to have them both living at the castle even though I knew that Mary wasn't living there quite yet.

After dinner, the women all retired to their quarters, leaving the men to share stories of conquest and glory. Some were actually true. They also shared a large amount of wine. Ian was able to have a private moment with both of his sons

Ian said, "I have been thinking about your mother quite often. She would be so proud of how you both turned out. I assure you that she was watching over you every day."

Francis then asked me, "How can you be so sure?"

Ian said, "I will tell you someday, but not today." It was time to call it a night, and Ian thanked the Earl for his generosity.

The Earl responded, "I would not have it any other way. Both Angus and you are like sons to me."

✠

The following day, Ian was enjoying his breakfast with the Earl. Ian finally excused himself. There was much to be done today. His next stop was the seamstress room at the castle. Abigail's mother, Maggie, had been very busy. She had made a new kilt for the Earl, Gavin, Francis, and Ian. They were made from the finest wool fabrics using the patterns that represented the Clan Sinclair.

For herself and Abigail, Maggie made light blue dresses with shawls made from the same fabric as the kilts. For the Countess, she made an elegant dress made from the same shade of green that was in the Earl's kilt. Last but not least she made a beautiful white dress for the bride, Mary. Clara would have been in tears if she had seen the beautiful attire to be worn by the wedding party.

Later that afternoon, the guests started arriving. Most were old family friends, as well as dignitaries from the Clan. Malcolm and Agatha were the first to arrive. They were seated where the groom's grandparents usually sit. Then, the rest of the guests were seated, and the ceremony was about to begin.

Shortly after that, the Reverend McGee made his way down the Chapel aisle and up to the Altar. The Chapel only held around twenty people. Just family were to witness the actual ceremony. The rest waited eagerly outside. After exchanging vows and rings, the groom kissed his bride, and everyone cheered loudly. The newly married couple led the procession out of the Chapel, where they were greeted their guests. The entire wedding was then seated and served a spectacular feast of Pheasant and Roasted Potatoes. Dinner was followed by a pair of bagpipe players serenading the guests with many of Scotland's favorite folk songs. This gave way to traditional Scottish music with violins, guitars, and flutes. Many danced the night away.

Everyone enjoyed the night. They tried to block out what would happen in a few days. The Earl was going to travel to Edinburgh to inspect the ships. At least, that is what he told the Countess. However, the real mission was to confront Oleg.

CHAPTER 53

EDINBURGH

IAN SAT AND watched as the Earl's Carriage approached the bridge over the Water of Leith River. This river has brought life to the ancient settlers of Scotland for generations. The river has provided a natural seaport and harbor of refuge for explorers from the time of the ancient Phoenicians up to today's seafarers. Travelers from Rosslyn needed to cross the Water of Leith River to access the Village of Edinburgh.

Ian thought of the preparation that led up to today. There were countless meetings at the castle, as well as the loading of armaments that were destined for the Clan's newly purchased ships.

Angus and the Earl had discussed what type of weapons the Norse or Vikings, as the Earl referred to them, would use. The consensus was that Oleg would only have bows and swords. The Vikings traditionally preferred hand-to-hand combat.

After this Viking incursion was dealt with, Ian knew that there were countless crates that contained food, grains, seeds, apothecary supplies, livestock, and weapons that had to be transported to the ships. However, this task could not be completed until the road and Water of Leith River Bridge were secure.

Angus detailed what supplies would go with each ship. The supplies would be split evenly amongst the seven ships. If a ship was lost, the surviving ships could carry on. The manifest was developed according to skills. The manifests would then be given to the Countess.

Most of the warriors would be on two of the ships. If the fleet were attacked, these two ships would go on a full attack against the marauders. The other ships had a handful of warriors scattered amongst them. Each ship had to be prepared for an attack by Oleg if he was not dealt with on this fateful day. Angus included fire arrows in the manifest. Fire arrows were standard long arrows with cloth wrapped around the arrowhead that would be dipped in oil and set ablaze. Orders were to launch the fire arrows if any shipped approached. The Earl's flagship, which would have the Treasure aboard, was to be protected at all costs.

Ian's thoughts returned to the present as the Carriage approached the bridge. Would Agatha's vision be correct, or was this all a false alarm? That question will be answered very soon.

The Earl's Carriage was ornately decorated even though it was fit for battle. The driver's seat was contained within a metal frame that could withstand a barrage of arrows. The driver could pull down a cover for further protection. The side of the Carriage displayed the Coat of Arms for the Clan Sinclair. For anyone who saw the Carriage, there would be no doubt that either the Earl or his family was on-board.

A message had been spread throughout the Port of Edinburgh that the Earl of the Sinclair Clan, Henry Sinclair, would be inspecting his new ships during the following week. The inspection day had finally arrived.

As the Carriage reached the mid-point of the crossing, Vikings that had been hidden suddenly appeared from the woods on either side of the bridge. There were roughly twenty Vikings in total. The leader ordered the Carriage to stop, which it did. The driver pulled down the cover and locked it in place.

The Viking leader yelled, "Driver, down from your seat, or we will burn the carriage with you in it."

The Driver responded, "I am just a Sept. I mean you no harm."

The Viking leader looked at the Carriage. He could not see inside because the shades were drawn. He yelled, "Henry Sinclair, open the door at once, and we will spare your driver's life."

There was no response. The Viking leader repeated his demand.

The leader finally instructed his men to break down the door.

One of the Vikings reached for the door and said, "It is not locked."

The leader said, "Then open it up."

The door was then opened, and the look on the Viking leader's face was pure shock. The cabin contained the corpses of the three Vikings that had been sent out to probe Rosslyn. He had walked into a trap. Just then, a barrage of arrows came from the nearby woods. This was followed by roughly one hundred clansmen charging the Carriage with swords drawn. They made quick work of the outnumbered Vikings.

Ian stood next to the Earl and Angus on a hilltop nearby. The trap had worked perfectly. Agatha's vision was correct.

The Earl looked at a hilltop on the far side of the river. Oleg stood there watching his men get massacred. He soon disappeared.

Captain McQuinn gave the order for his men to chase Oleg. He said, "He is not to make it back to his ship."

A chase ensued. Oleg and several of his men raced on horseback to the shore on the north side of the port. They were considerably ahead of Captain McQuinn's men. Oleg continued to race to a lifeboat that was just beyond the surf. Oleg reached the lifeboat and climbed aboard. His men quickly rowed out to sea. From a hidden cove further up the shore, a large ship could be seen heading south. This was Oleg's ship.

The Earl, Ian, and Angus finally caught up to Captain Mc-Quinn. The Captain said, "Do you want me to send ships after them?"

The Earl said, "No. We don't know how many ships he has with him. We will fight him on our terms at some point in the future. This will not be the last time we encounter this Oleg."

Ian's thoughts suddenly recounted his Dreams where great battles had taken place against this adversary. This battle would be no different. The Earl had won this battle, but many more would follow.

CHAPTER 54

THE FINAL DAY

T WAS MAY 1st, and preparations for the trip were complete. The final manifests were given to the Countess. If the mission was never heard from again, the Countess would know who and what items were on the journey. The future heirs of the Earl would at least have some account of what happened. The Earl also provided the Countess with a summary of the ports that were scheduled to be visited on the mission. If any search party were sent to find out what had happened, at least they would have a starting point.

The only items that weren't already loaded onto the ships were personal items such as clothing and small keepsakes. Malcolm had also packed a large crate with maps and ancient documents that would accompany the Treasure.

Several days earlier, Ian and Angus had a meeting with the Earl at the castle. At this meeting, the Earl finally discussed the Treasure. He said, "It is contained in eight or nine very heavy chests. We need the heavy work carts to be used for the transfer, as well as a handful of trusted warriors."

Ian and Angus shared a private conversation later that day. Angus said, "The Earl doesn't need to tell us how heavy the Treasure is. I think the two of us have lifted each chest on multiple occasions. At least that is what I see in my Dreams."

Ian said, "You are correct. Usually, we find ourselves dodging arrows or swords while we are moving it." Both men laughed.

The discussion then turned to their futures. Would one or both of them stay in the New World?

Ian said, "I suggest that we both bring what is near and dear to us, as well as all of our clothing. We should both plan as if we were not coming home. After all, we could be shipwrecked and unable to return home."

Angus then said, "I will be traveling with my wife. She is everything to me. Therefore, I think that I should be the one to stay permanently." He went on to say, "You have a son, daughter-in-law, and future grand bairns back here. You should make every effort to return. Unfortunately, it will be unlikely that they will be able to travel and visit with you. It pains me to think that you could never see Gavin and Mary again."

Ian thanked him and said, "This is a decision for the Earl."

Ian was very torn on this issue of whether to return or not. Rosslyn was his home. It was where he and Clara raised their two sons. The wedding had brought these thoughts to the forefront. He wanted to see his future grand bairns grow up. Then his thoughts turned to Francis. He is such an adventurous spirit. It would not surprise Ian if Francis decided to stay in Vinland and keep exploring. Ian would have to deal with these emotions later. There was much work to be done.

Later that evening, Angus and Ian dined with the Earl. After dinner was concluded, the Earl asked both men to adjourn to the anteroom. The three of them were seated, and the Earl poured three cups of wine. He made sure that no one was within earshot of the anteroom. He had instructed all of the servants to stay out of that part of the castle.

The Earl asked Angus for an update on the final preparations.

Angus replied, "The ships are loaded with everything except for personal effects and, of course, the Treasure. Everyone going on the mission other than the ones hand-picked to move the Treasure will board a carriage just after sunrise for the trip to the port. I have told the hand-picked team to be ready about two hours before sundown the following day."

The Earl began by saying, "Very well. Everything is in order." He paused to sip his wine and continued, "This is a momentous day for the Clan Sinclair. As both of you know, the Clan is in possession of the Treasure of the Knights Templar. It was brought to our Clan because of our family ties to the Templars based in France. In fact, one of my ancestors was married to Hugues de Payens, the Founder of the Templars. This, of course, was before he founded the Templars because the Templars were not allowed to marry."

The Earl continued, "I apologize to both of you for keeping you in the dark regarding the Treasure. I did this for your safety. I will give you more details once we are out to sea."

Angus said, "Before we part company, I have a request." He continued, "I discussed the matter with Ian, and I believe that I, along with my wife, should be the ones to stay in the New World. I have no family left here in Rosslyn. Ian has a son and a new daughter-in-law."

The Earl responded, "I understand your point. Let me consider this."

They finished their wine, and then Angus left first. He said that he needed to get home to Abigail. They were preparing all of their possessions for the journey. Ian then parted by saying, "I will not keep you. I know this is the last evening with your family. I wish to spend this evening with my son and daughter-in-law."

The Earl said, "The glory begins tomorrow."

Ian then departed and headed to Gavin's home.

CHAPTER 55

THE TREASURE

IAN WOKE UP the next morning and finished his packing. He was able to fit everything into one crate. Inside this crate, he had a smaller box that contained letters and other keepsakes that were reminders of Clara. The keepsakes were for Francis. Gavin already had many of Clara's possessions such as fine china and her artwork. Over the last few months, with the help of Agatha, Ian had learned how to connect with Clara almost anytime he wished.

After Ian completed his packing, Francis walked in. Ian said, "Are you packed."

Francis pointed to the small box in the corner and said, "That is all I have." Ian laughed and said, "The Earl will be happy. He thinks that we already have too much."

Ian spent the rest of the evening with Gavin, Mary, and Francis. It was tear-filled night. Ian told Gavin, "Angus will most likely be the one to stay in the New World. I will return with the Earl in approximately one year." This helped to reduce the heartache.

✠

Ian woke up shortly before sunrise. There was much to do. All of the people going on the mission gathered near the gates of the castle. They were saying their heart-filled goodbyes to their loved ones.

The Earl joined the group and was shaking hands with all of the well-wishers. He was looking for Malcolm. Finally he spotted Malcolm and Agatha as they were loading their crates onto the carts.

The Earl said, "Malcolm and Agatha, welcome to the journey. I am going to send the initial sailing instructions with you. Please find Captain McQuinn when you arrive in the port. Please tell him that we will be heading to Eystribyggð, Greenland. This port is on the very southern tip of Greenland. Ask the Captain to consult his charts. Also, as we have discussed, please have Antonio ready just in case we need his input. He will be most valuable as we arrive in the area near the Gold River. I am suggesting a more northern route because the waters are typically calmer there."

Malcolm said, "Thank you Sir for this great honor. Also, for the trip to Greenland, especially when you have long summer days, the best form of navigation is the Viking method of using a Sun Stone. This stone allows you to know where the sun is even when it is cloudy or foggy. I have them for this very occasion."

The Earl said, "I have heard of the stones. I will welcome any help that we can get. It's a very large ocean out there."

Nearby, Gavin and Mary were saying their goodbyes to Francis. Francis promised his brother, "I will be back." Somehow Ian knew this to be true.

Everyone finished boarding the carts and then the caravan began its day long trip to the Port of Edinburgh.

✠

The Earl, Angus, and Ian made their way into the castle for a brief meeting. The Earl said, "We will leave this afternoon shortly before sunset for our journey to retrieve the treasure. Angus have you assembled everything we need for lifting the chests?"

Angus said, "Aye. I have pry bars, and two winches as you have instructed."

The Earl urged everyone to get some rest. He said, "It may be some time before you can rest easy again."

✠

Unfortunately, Ian was unable to get any rest. He spent the afternoon trying to go over all of the details of the journey. He finally dosed off after a few hours. When he woke it was time to meet at the gates. When he arrived, he was met by Gavin and Mary.

Ian said, "When I see you next, I plan on being a Grand Sire."

Gavin said, "We will try not to let you down."

Ian had an ominous feeling that he would never return, but he tried his best to hide it. No one knew when they would see each other again. Gavin knew that Francis was an adventurer. This was his life's mission.

Ian then gave Gavin a long hug. They finally parted with both having tears running down their faces.

Angus was busy making sure that the team had everything that it needed to retrieve the treasure. Abigail had left with the morning caravan.

Ian then witnessed a very heartfelt moment with the Earl and his family.

The Countess said, "We knew this day would come. You are on a mission to save the world. Please don't let us down." The Earl then hugged the Countess and his children and everyone climbed aboard the transport. The warriors all rode on horseback. The Earl took the reins of the transport. He was the only one that knew where they were going.

✠

The sun had not completely set quite yet and the Earl took the carts about a mile out of the Village. They were near the Old Cemetery. They sat and waited for the darkness to be complete. The Earl then led the team into the cemetery and went all the way to the very back where his great great grandfather, Henry of Saint-Clair had been laid to rest. Henry of Saint-Clair had been the first in the family to immigrate to Scotland in 1160.

The cemetery was very overgrown with foliage. Virtually no one visited this cemetery because there was a newer one very close to the village. As they approached the back of the cemetery, a small mausoleum came into view. Once they drew closer, they could see the name Saint-Clair over the doorway of the mausoleum. Everyone dismounted and made their way to the mausoleum. Henry removed a very old key from his satchel and opened the door. Everyone entered and then lit a few lanterns. A tomb came into view. It had very intricate carvings on it that included an effigy of Henry of Saint-Clair. Henry went to the header of the tomb and removed a keystone near the floor. He did the same near the footer. He then instructed everyone to push the footer forward. The Tomb slowly moved. After a few minutes, an opening became visible. After the entrance to the underground chamber was uncovered, a lantern was placed over the opening. A staircase came into view. It only had four large steps. The Earl was the first one down the stairs. He summoned several of his guards to go down into the vault with him. A winch was set up over the opening.

The Earl and his assistants began to tie ropes around the various chests. They began to lift them one by one. Ian thought to himself, "I have seen all of these before in my Dreams."

Ian looked over at Angus who smiled as if to say, "This all looks very familiar."

As each chest was removed it was loaded onto the transport outside. They had removed ten chests. Ian knew that there was still one very important chest to be removed. Ian then spotted the large silver container with no opening or lid. This container has haunted his Dreams since he was a wee lad. It had a large keyhole etched into its cover. Ian knew that once again he was looking at the Secret of Eden. Guarding this secret is the mission of his soul. Ian looked closely at the box. It was made of a shiny metal that was like nothing that anyone in the 14th century Scotland had ever seen before.

The Earl saw to it that the vault was returned to the condition that they found it in. Everyone exited the mausoleum and the Earl locked the door. The carts slowly made their way out of the cemetery and joined the road that led to Edinburgh. Angus knew this road like the back of his hand. The Earl had instructed everyone to stop for no one. Roughly eight hours later the team arrived in the Port of Edinburgh.

CHAPTER 56

BON VOYAGE

THE TEAM ARRIVED at the Port of Edinburgh just before sunrise. They quickly loaded the treasure onto the Earl's flagship. As pre-planned, once they had confirmed the Earl's arrival, the six other ships pulled out of their slips and would wait for the Earl's flagship outside of the Harbor. After securing the treasure, the Earl's ship immediately shoved off and headed off to sea.

After roughly a day, the coast of Scotland became smaller and smaller until it was finally gone. Ian knew that this would be the last time that he would see his homeland. Ian was taken back to the Dream of the Celtic Chieftain Cormac, where he and his wife Danu stared at the sea as she said, "Our future and the future of the Secret of Eden is west." Ian looked west, realizing that all of his future lives would be in the fabled land to the west. He had a feeling of exhilaration.

Several days had gone by. Then, one morning, Ian witnessed the most beautiful sunrise. He stood near the bow admiring the tremendous blue ocean in all directions. It wasn't just the blue color. It was the shades of everything from turquoise to a very dark blue right next to the ship. The ocean represented greatness that was beyond words. Its power and majesty were indeed a look into the Almighty, as Noah had said so many generations ago. Ian felt that on some level, he was meant to be a mariner. He always knew that at some point, he and Angus would be the ones to move the treasure west.

The previous evening, Ian heard Malcolm say, "If the ships can stay on course and have adequate wind, the trip to Greenland would take roughly two weeks." Two weeks seemed like a long time to Ian.

✠

After four days at sea, Ian finally felt that he had his sea legs and was ready to spend time below deck. He wandered down the steps and could immediately smell the food that Agatha was preparing for supper. It was a stew made from the oxen. After this meal, the only meat that the crew would have will be the dried and salted oxen strips. The door to the Earl's cabin was open, and Ian decided to step in and say hello and ask him if he needed anything.

The Earl replied, "I would like to dine with you, Angus, Malcolm, and Agatha this evening. It is time that you learned what we are carrying."

Ian said, "Thank you for the invitation. I will inform the others."

✠

Everyone was seated for supper when the Earl stated, "Thank you all for coming. I wish to discuss our stop in Greenland and, as promised, I would like to discuss our sacred cargo."

They shared a few bottles of wine. Ian passed on the wine. He didn't want to push his luck with nausea. The supper conversation centered on winds and currents. It wasn't easy to gauge our progress thus far. The good news was that the winds were favorable. Henry did say, "The winds and seas can change on a minute's notice, so please keep your wits about you."

After the plates were cleared, the Earl brought several boxes and some documents to the table. He started by saying, "As you probably already have surmised were are in possession of many chests full of gold and silver. Many of the pieces are coins, and many are Jewels." The Earl continued, "We also have several significant religious artifacts." This statement caught Ian off guard. He only knew of one artifact.

The Earl had Angus assist him with lifting one of the chests onto the table. The Earl then opened it and said, "Here is the Golden Menorah. It is solid gold and was used by Moses as he led the Hebrews on their Exodus from Egypt."

Malcolm explained its significance by stating that this is written about in the Old Testament. He said, "It always sat near the Ark of the Covenant in what was referred to as the Holy of Holies in Solomon's Temple." Both Angus and Ian looked at each other when they heard the term Holy of Holies. Memories of the days as Knight Templars flooded Ian's mind.

The discussion then turned to an ornate box that the Earl had placed on the table. He reached into his satchel, removed an equally ornate key, and unlocked the box. When he opened the box, everyone was stunned by what they saw. The Earl said, "This, my friends, is the chalice that was used at the Last Supper by Jesus Christ when he performed the Sacrament of Communion. Some refer to it as the Holy Grail." Everyone was stunned.

Much current folklore included stories that said that the Templars had taken possession of this sacred artifact during their days at the Temple Mount. However, both Ian and Angus knew that this was not the case.

The Earl stated, "This did not come from the Templars." He continued, "This has been in my family for generations."

Malcolm asked, "Your family has had this in their possession?"

The Earl responded, "Aye. My family comes from the French noble line referred to as the Merovingians. They were the Kings of the Francs back to the year 509. However, the family legend passed down through the ages is that we were descendants of Mary Magdalene. There is no factual basis for this legend. However, somehow my ancestors came to possess this chalice. It is unclear how that happened."

Agatha said, "Ian and Angus, search your Dreams. You will know that this is indeed the chalice that Mary Magdalene took with her when she escaped Jerusalem."

The Earl said, "Agatha, your visions coupled with the fact there is a long history of documented miracles while in the presence of this chalice have made many of my ancestors' believers. The news of these miracles has made its way to the Vatican. For years, the Vatican's legions have been trying to take this from my family. That is why I want to secure it in a safe place in the New World."

The Earl went on to say, "If we are successful in our mission, the Holy Grail will be hidden forever or at least until the day that we wish to bring it to light."

Malcolm was quiet for a while but finally said, "I think I need another glass of wine. Maybe two." They all broke out in laughter.

Agatha then said, "We haven't discussed the largest secret of them all."

Malcolm said, "It is hard to believe that we have something grander than the Holy Grail and the Golden Menorah, but we all know this to be true."

The Earl said, "Aye, first I must disclose the message that goes with the Secret of Eden." He then brought forward a document written in French and had been subsequently converted to English.

The Earl said, "Before I reveal the document, I must tell you the story of how the Templars came into the possession of this artifact. Angus and Ian, please correct me if I get any details wrong." Everyone laughed. He continued, "The Templars were searching for treasure and religious Artifacts in the tunnels underneath the Temple Mount for years. Finally, they reported that they were guided by a series of markings that they called the "Secret Seal of Solomon." They finally found a message that described the Secret of Eden that lies underneath the Foundation Stone, which is from the Old Testament story of Abraham and his son. The message led them on a quest to the Great Sphinx in Giza Egypt." Angus and Ian looked at each other once again. So far, the Earl had been very accurate.

The Earl continued, "Amidst an epic battle with a Muslim Army, the Templars had unearthed this silver box. When you look at it, you will see that it has no openings and is very heavy. The Templars transported the strange box, the carvings, and all of the treasure to the Port of Acre and then on to Gisor castle in France, where it sat for almost two hundred years. On October 13, 1307, the French King arrested what he thought was all of the Knights. After extensive searching and the torturing of many Knights, the King was surprised to find no treasure. Several Templars had advanced warning of the forthcoming arrests and snuck all of the treasures and artifacts out of France and gave them to my great-great grandfather Henry for safekeeping. They have sat beneath the mausoleum that we entered several nights ago ever since. Now I will show you the translated document that explains the Silver Box." He pulled out a scroll and unrolled it. It read the following:

We are the Watchers. We have been here since the dawn of Humanity. We came at the direction of the Almighty Creator. We have instructed many generations of Humankind of the Creators will. None have followed our direction. We have the ability to create Earthquakes, Great Storms, and Great Floods. We have punished the unworthy with death and Destruction. We will continue our quest until Humankind abides by the Creator's will.

The Creator's will was already handed down to the one you call Moses. Somehow several key aspects were neglected to be recorded. The Creator also will send his Son to deliver the message. Humanity has made strides but still falls short of the Creator's expectations. The Creator's wishes are the following:

All Humankind is created equal and will be treated equally

All Wars will Cease. Humankind will not kill his brothers and Sisters.

All Humankind will follow the laws handed to Moses.

Humankind can only honor the Creator by following his rules.

Humankind will share its resources equally.

The Great land to the West will be the home of the righteous and the foundation of the Creator's Promises. This will be the Land of Plenty.

The Seal of Solomon is the keeper of the Secret of Eden. The Seal stares at the Secret of Eden as the Great Lion in the Land of the Great River stares at the Great Falcon as he is going to rest on the longest day.

When Humankind has successfully mastered the Creator's will, only then will the Secret of Eden be revealed.

Everyone read the document and sat in shock.

Malcolm said, "This explains why we are traveling to the New World. You believe that Vinland is the Land of Plenty that they speak of. Our goal is to not only secure all of the Treasures but to start the society that will be the foundation of world equality and fairness."

The Earl answered, "Aye, my family has been protecting the secret for generations. You all need to digest what you have just learned. The new society that is to be founded on this new land will happen in the years to come. Our mission is to move the Secret of Eden there and make sure that it is adequately protected."

Angus jokingly said, "That's it?" Everyone laughed and departed the Earl's stateroom.

The Earl said, "Malcolm, please make a list of everything that we are taking to the New World. Our ancestors will need to understand what we are about to hide." He paused and continued, "Angus, please show Malcolm the silver box."

— 266 —

CHAPTER 57

THE FOLLOWERS

THE FOLLOWING MORNING Angus and Ian were standing at the bow discussing what they had heard and seen the previous night. Angus was still trying to get his mind around his feelings regarding the visions he had of the treasure.

Ian said, "There are some things that we may never fully understand. It's like someone is trying to deliver a message to us. We must be willing to receive it."

Angus said, "I will speak with Agatha when I feel the time is right. I need time to collect my thoughts on the subject."

It was a very clear morning. All of the previous days had a light fog that did not hinder the journey, but would not allow the crew to see very far. However, the winds had changed, and the fog was gone. As Angus turned aft, he saw the masts of at least four sailing vessels on the horizon. They were a great distance away, but seemed to be following the same heading that the Earl's fleet was on. Ian said, "I will notify the Earl that we are being followed."

Moments later, the Earl came topside and could see the vessels. They were just above the horizon. He could not make out their sails quite yet.

Several hours had passed, and the ships were slightly closer. The Earl could finally see their sails. They were black. The Earl then climbed up to the Crow's nest for a better view. He had a small scope with him. He sat up in the Crow's Nest for at least twenty minutes.

When he finally came down, he said, "Those look like the ships that I battled in the Orkneys. They are warships. The only reason a Captain would use black flags is that they are difficult to see at night. Most of their attacks occur at night. We will have to confront them if they come any closer."

The Earl said, "Let's see if they gain on us. I don't believe that they will engage us on the open sea. It would probably be suicide for them. Notify me if they make any gains on us."

Ian thought to himself, "Oleg doesn't want to kill us by firing a cannon and sinking our ship. For Oleg, death must be much more personal. The long-standing Viking way of hand-to-hand battle would be the only way. He is just following us, so he will know where we are when he finally has the chance to attack."

CHAPTER 58

THE DOVE

P ELEG AND TYTEA were always at Noah's side when it was the day that he would release one of the doves. Noah would do this once every seven days. The rains had stopped several months ago. He did this because he knew that if the dove returned, it would mean that there was no land anywhere in sight. The dove would not land in the water. If the dove failed to return, or better yet, the dove returned with small sticks in its beak, then land was nearby. The first task for the dove would be to build a new nest.

Several days later, Peleg and Tytea watched as the dove landed back on the Ark. It had a beak full of sticks. They ran to tell their grandfather, Noah, the news.

It was day twenty-two. Everyone was becoming restless. They had witnessed wind-less days, monsoon-like storms, and rough seas.

They were ready to see land.

Malcolm was able to track the Stars on clear nights. He showed Ian how the outermost stars in the Big Dipper, Merak and Dubhe, line up directly with the North Star, which is in the North Sky. Malcolm called the North Star Polaris. He said that every time he was able to see Polaris, he could tell that the ships were still on a West-Northwest Heading.

The Earl was confident that they would see Greenland soon. The part that he was concerned with was how far north the current had taken them. The air was getting more frigid, which was giving the Earl concern. Everyone except the lookouts went to sleep earlier than usual that night. The waves were manageable, and the pure exhaustion kicked in.

As the Sun rose the following day, Ian was in his very small sleeping quarters thinking about Clara. "How would she have done on this trip? Of course, she would have gone on the mission because she wanted to be with Francis and me, but I think the whole experience would have turned her into a land lover." Ian laughed to himself.

He finally decided it was time to get up. He helped himself to some tea in the galley and made his way topside. As was his morning ritual, he stood on the bow and admired the sheer beauty before him. Then, out of the corner of his eye, he noticed something moving. It was a seagull. This could only mean one thing. Land was near. His mind drifted back to his Dream of Noah and the dove. Just then, he was brought back to the present because one of the sailors yelled "Land Ho." At roughly eleven o'clock, you could see a speck of land. If this were indeed Greenland, it would take several more hours for the great landmass to appear.

The Earl called Angus, Ian, and Malcolm to discuss their next steps. After everyone arrived in the Earl's stateroom, the subject of the meeting was what to expect with King Haakon's representative in Eystribyggð.

The Earl started by saying, "As we approach Eystribyggð, I want everyone to pay attention to the people with whom we come in contact. We are guests of King Haakon, and I expect to be treated respectfully. I want to pay tribute to the leader of the settlement with bags of seed and several barrels of our mead."

Malcolm asked, "Surely this leader will know that you are the Earl of Ornkey? So technically, you are Norwegian royalty."

The Earl responded, "Aye. This is true, but please don't forget that there may be Vikings that we fought against in the Ornkeys present here. I would like to pay our tribute, spend the night, trade for some fish and vegetables, and then head back out to sea."

Angus asked, "The four black sailed ships are still behind us. Can't we assume that they may attack while we are in the harbor?"

The Earl said, "It would be an act of treason for Oleg to attack while on Norwegian territory. But I will instruct Captain McQuinn to have his men at battle stations the entire time we are in the port. I want this ship to be the furthest ship out on the docks. No strangers will be allowed to board."

By the time the meeting was finished, the land was in full view. The Earl changed course to a southwest tack. He thought they would arrive at the Port of Eystribyggð within one day. The Crew then began to hide the treasure under the feedstock.

CHAPTER 59

EYSTRIBYGGÐ

O N DAY 23, the Earl's fleet finally arrived at the Port of Eystribyggð. The Earl had moved his Flag to one of the other
ships. He did this because he needed to pull into a slip.
He did not want the ship carrying the Treasure to be easily
boarded. He moved his best warriors onto the treasure ship so
that the Treasure could be easily guarded. Angus, Abigail, Malcolm, Agatha, and Ian rowed into shore on a smaller boat that
was provided by the Port.

The settlement was much larger than Ian expected. Supposedly there were four thousand full-time settlers. It was seemingly many more. It had all of the features of any Norwegian Village. There were Christian churches, central meeting rooms, a
makeshift castle for traveling Royals such as King Haakon, and
numerous housing developments that all had grass roofs. The
landscape was mountainous but did not have any trees. Ian immediately thought to himself, "The wood for shipbuilding must
be coming from elsewhere, possibly Vinland." There was a large

shipyard where at least four large sailing ships could be dry-docked at any one time. Ian wondered, "How good can the hunting be without any trees for cover." Greenland seemed like a barren wasteland.

As the Earl's landing party approached the Royal Quarters, King Haakon's representative walked out to greet them. He said, "Welcome. I am Bjorn. I am the Governor of this settlement. My cousin King Haakon V told me to expect you." He continued, "Earl Henry Sinclair, everyone knows of you in these parts. Your reputation is legendary."

The Earl responded, "Your cousin is a great King and has been a friend to the Clan Sinclair for as long as I can remember." The Governor directed them into his quarters, where there was a large gathering hall. Every one of the Earl's party was seated at the head table.

The Governor was the first to speak. He said, "On behalf of the Kingdom of Norway, I welcome you to Greenland. I warmly extend a greeting to you and your entire party from King Haakon V."

The Earl responded, "Governor, I thank you for your hospitality." The Earl went on to introduce all of his party to the Governor. The two leaders continued to exchange pleasantries.

The Governor said, "The message that I received from the King stated that you will be passing through on your way to Vinland."

The Earl said, "Aye, as I explained to his Royal Highness. We possess an ancient map created by Phoenicians explorers that details a land where gold and silver are plenty. The King granted us passage. In return, I have promised to share anything of value that we discover."

They dined on a meal that consisted of cod and some greens that the Scots had never seen before. Considering that they had not eaten anything new in weeks, this meal tasted great. The Governor held court for several hours after dinner. The settlers were coming to him with both requests and grievances. This reminded Ian of the Clan's St. Andrews Day Festival.

Malcolm found this an odd place to find Vikings despite what the Governor said about this settlement. He said, "This was once a Viking settlement. I find it very odd. There is nothing to plunder anywhere near this place. Why were they here? It is just a vast wasteland. I don't think the Vikings will stay here forever unless it becomes a major stopover on the way to the New World. However, very few had heard of Vinland. For most that had heard of it, Vinland was just another fable much in the way that Atlantis was to the Greeks."

Ian said, "What if the lost city of Atlantis was on Vinland?"

Malcolm said, "It is a possibility. Others have asked the very same question."

While they were finishing their meal, a very odd man walked over to the Earl's table. The Governor introduced him as Frode, the healer. It turns out that Frode was the leader of a group of healers to care for the four thousand settlers. Frode's skills included the ability to speak with the Viking gods.

He looked directly at Agatha and said, "You are a healer. I could sense your presence as you stepped off of your ship. When you have some time, I would like to speak with you."

Agatha looked at the Earl, who nodded affirmatively then said, "My name is Agatha. Aye, I have certain skills that I was born with and many others that I have acquired over a long lifetime. I do serve as a healer, but my form of healing is spiritual. Nevertheless, I will meet with you perhaps tomorrow morning. I will bring Malcolm with me. While he doesn't necessarily speak with the spirit world, he is a master of ancient history and the spiritual beliefs of Ancient Greece and Egypt. I find the spiritual world is closely tied to these ancient societies."

Frode responded, "Agatha, I too am a spiritual healer. I believe that there is only one kind of healing. I tell my apprentices, "Heal the Spirit, and the physical problems take care of themselves."

Frode continued, "Although I consider myself a master

healer, I have yet to conquer the process of aging. My time is fast approaching, and there is nothing I can do to stop it."

Agatha then said, "Frode, aging is a natural way. To interrupt it is to go against the Creator's Will."

She then looked at Malcolm and said, "Enjoy every day with the same quest for knowledge that you had as a young man. Enjoy the little things that each new day offers. But, most importantly, enjoy the company that you hold dear."

Frode laughed and said, "I feel better already." He then told Agatha that he would reach out to her tomorrow morning to schedule some time.

The Governor said, "Your healer will be highly respected by the natives. They are a highly spiritual people and will recognize Agatha's gift immediately."

After supper was completed, a group of Vikings entered the hall. They were led by Oleg. They sat down at a nearby table. Oleg said to the Governor, "You let Henry Sinclair sit at your table. Do you know what he has done to our people?"

The Earl said, "Your people? Your people have killed and plundered other Norwegians for years. I was asked by the King of Norway's father, King Haakon IV, to rid the Ornkeys of the outlaws. The outlaws were your people."

The Governor finally spoke. He said, "Oleg. You have sworn an oath of allegiance to our King. The Earl of Ornkeys is here as a guest of our King. Your behavior could be considered treason."

Oleg said, "I have done nothing other than talk. I will respect the King's wishes while I am on Norwegian soil." Ian recognized the veiled threat.

The party had become very quiet. The Governor said, "Everyone, please resume what you are doing. There is nothing to see here."

The Earl's party made small talk amongst themselves for the rest of the evening. Then, when it was time to leave the hall, the Earl walked over to talk to the Governor privately. Angus and Ian began walking to the door. Suddenly, Oleg stepped in front of them. The VEGVISIR Medal was staring Ian right in the face. He said, "You two are not Norwegian Royalty. You are just lowly Scots. Why should I let you pass?"

Angus had consumed a considerable amount of mead. He wasn't going to take being called lowly by this beast. He said, "Because you are unlucky. Just as your kinsmen were unlucky on that bridge."

This caused Oleg's face to turn red. It was like looking at the devil himself.

Ian said, "Oleg. Don't you know who we are? Search your Dreams. You have been our adversary for generations."

This seemed to calm Oleg down. He said, "Aye. As I have always seen you in my Dreams, we will do battle at the appropriate time and place." He then stepped out of their way.

✠

The Earl's party made their way back to the ships. Ian stood on the bow, trying to recall the evening's conversations. He had looked into the eyes of his soul's enemy. Oleg may not completely understand his soul's journey, but he certainly feels that he is destined to avenge the death of his father and brothers.

Just then, Ian looked over to the nearby break wall. The full moon had just appeared from behind the clouds. The moonlight caused him to see the silhouette of Oleg. The two men just stared at each other for several minutes. All of the scenes of battle from the Dreams rushed into Ian's thoughts. Destiny was leading these two souls into battle once again. Ian finally walked below deck.

CHAPTER 60

MARCO AND PIETRO ZENO

HE FOLLOWING MORNING, Ian went topside as he has done so many other mornings. On the previous evening, when Ian had his stare down with Oleg, he noticed the additional ships in the harbor. At least four of them were Oleg's ships. This morning, they were gone. There was no sign of any ships out on the horizon in any direction.

The Earl soon joined Ian. Ian asked, "Oleg's ships left early this morning?"

The Earl responded, "Aye. They left last night soon after we arrived back at the ship." He continued, "I had a sentry climb up to the crow's nest to see if we could get their heading. These ships left in total darkness. There were no lanterns lit on any of the ships. They were soon lost in the darkness. Oleg did not want us to know which direction in which they were heading."

"I assume that this is troubling," Ian asked.

"Aye." The Earl said. "We will no doubt see him in the future."

✠

The plan was to be back out on the sea before sundown. The Earl called a meeting with Angus, Ian, and Malcolm. After they arrived, he said, "While you two (looking at Ian and Angus) were having your discussion with Oleg, the Governor told me of two brothers who are currently here in this settlement. These brothers have traveled back and forth to Vinland many times. The Governor thought that we should at least speak with them before we depart. Evidently, they understand all of the native tribes up and down the coast of Vinland. So let's reconvene after we speak with them. The Governor believes that we should take them with us."

Malcolm said, "We have many unknowns from this point forward. So it can't hurt to speak with them."

The Earl said, "Obviously, we tell them that we are simply on a mission of exploration."

Malcolm said, "Also. Agatha is supposed to meet with the Healer, Frode, this morning. She is focusing on blocking her thoughts regarding the treasure and the Secret of Eden, but sometimes that is easier said than done."

✠

Later the morning, the Earl, Angus, and Ian met with the Governor at the royal quarters. The Governor introduced the guides Marco and Pietro Zeno to the Earl and his aides. He said, "The brothers are of Italian descent, but have spent most of their lives exploring the Oceans. They are seasoned travelers to the New World." The Earl sat near them. He asked them to describe their many missions.

Marco responded first, "We have set sail on a course west of here on many occasions. We have encountered many islands and a large mainland with a great river. There are several different tribes of natives in these lands. Most will kill everyone in your party on sight. They don't like outsiders, no matter whether you are religious missionaries or conquerors. We have learned the hard way. Many of our crewmates have been killed over the years. Over the last ten years or so, we have come to an agreement with these tribes. On one of the trips, we showed up with a large force. Instead of fighting, we asked for their leader. We told them that we are not there to fight. We are not looking to start a settlement. We only wish to hunt and fish these lands. We offer a trade of sailing ships for furs. Once they understood our goals, they opened up to us. We established the same arrangement with the other tribes."

The Earl said, "We have a fisherman named Antonio with us. He claims that he has lived in the New World for a long period of time."

Both of the brothers smiled. Pietro said, "We thought that Antonio had perished at the hands of the Mi'kmaq."

The Earl stated, "Antonio lived with the Mi'kmaq for nearly twenty years and was very happy. He eventually made his way back to Scotland."

The brothers were curious about how he managed to survive.

The Earl said, "Ask him yourself. He is with us. He is helping to find a place in the land of the Mi'kmaq that is called the Gold River."

Marco responded, "We know of this place. There is an island nearby that travelers have used for centuries to land their ships. This island helps with keeping your ships concealed from the Mi'kmaq. It is far enough from the mainland so that they can't see your activities. The Mi'kmaq believe that the island is possessed by spirits. Some believe that ancient Phoenicians had traveled there. Some believe that many treasures have been buried there. Nonetheless, the Mi'kmaqs will not bother you when you are on that island."

The Earl said, "Antonio speaks of a European man being the leader of the Mi'kmaq. He stated that he had a library of books written in Latin."

Both brothers stated that they stayed away from the Mi'kmaq. They are the one tribe that has not been approached for a trading agreement.

Pietro said, "This may be the proper time for such an agreement." Pietro then asked the Earl, "What is your purpose for this mission?"

The Earl responded, "We are simply on a mission of exploration. We have heard about this Gold River, as well as a very special well that flows the purest of water. We wish to see this with our own eyes."

The Earl then invited the brothers to make the journey with his team. He said, "I would like to hire you to be our guide into the New World. I assume that you have your own ship?"

Marco said, "Yes."

Both parties agreed on a fee of ten pounds sterling. The Earl said, "I will pay you half now and the other half when we arrive at the place with the Gold River."

The brothers agreed and shook hands with the Earl. They then rushed off to prepare for a quick departure.

✠

Afterward, Ian joined Malcolm and Agatha for their meeting with Frode. They met at Frode's Alchemy store. It was a small structure with jars everywhere full of various plants, powders, and liquids.

Frode said, "Welcome to my store."

Agatha said, "Thank you. I can see that you have collected many items. Obviously, they must not have been native to Greenland?"

"No, not much of anything grows here. I travel back to Norway once every summer for new supplies." Frode said.

Malcolm said, "Are any of your offerings from Vinland?"

Frode replied, "Aye. I have grape seedlings. The grapes are a wild plant there. I'm sure that is why the people that went there before us named it Vinland."

Malcolm said, "Some call it the land of plenty. Some consider it a Utopia."

Frode said, "I have never been there. Very few from our settlement have been there. The ones that have made the crossing only have gone to the former Viking settlement of L'Anse aux Meadows. No one that I know has ventured further other than the Zeno Brothers."

Malcolm said, "Why do you call it a former Viking Settlement? Isn't this place a Norwegian Settlement?"

Frode replied, "Because this place is supposed to be governed by Norwegian law. From what I have heard, this place is much more akin to yesterday's Viking establishments. Please be careful." He paused and continued, "Agatha, I can tell that you are a very old soul. You have seen much."

Agatha said, "Aye. I have seen much indeed. This adventure to Vinland excites me very much. It is completely new to my soul. I hope to create new memories there."

Frode said, "I sense that you have been close to the seeds of power in your past."

Agatha laughed and said, "Aye, but I was usually on the wrong side of the power. So I have tried to be on the side of the everyday man who is poor in possessions but rich in spirit."

Frode said, "Well, it has been very good to meet with both of you. If you find anything unique or interesting in terms of Alchemy, please send me a jar or two."

Agatha said, "We will be sure to send you anything that we find that is not native to our European homeland."

After Agatha and Malcolm arrived back at the ship, Agatha said, "He was searching my thoughts for our true mission. I think I successfully hid my thoughts, but we should not meet with him again. He has excellent skills."

✠

Around midday, the Earl summoned Ian, Angus, and Malcolm once again. Once they arrived, he said, "As you know, I have hired the Zeno Brothers to be our guides. Antonio knows how to get to the place we call the Gold River, but he doesn't know the tribes along the way. The Zenos' should help us communicate along the way if we need to make a stop." He continued, "I would only like to speak in generalities with them. They are never to be aboard my flagship, and they are not ever to know of the treasures. Once we find the Land of the Holy Well, as discussed by Antonio, we will send the guides back to Greenland. We need to consider everyone who is not part of the group that traveled together from Scotland as possible enemies. We are to treat them with respect, but be careful what you say around these guides. After we pull out of the harbor, I will return my flag to the ship housing the treasures."

Malcolm said, "I want to make you aware that we met with the healer, Frode, today. He was trying to read Agatha's thoughts about our mission. We don't think he was successful, but nothing is sure in her realm. So we need to fend off any further attempts by Frode to meet with Agatha."

The Earl said, "Should anyone ask for her, I will say that she has taken ill. With that news, let us make an earlier departure than we planned."

✠

Roughly an hour later, the Earl's fleet began to pull out. The dock line had just been released when Frode appeared with several men who appeared to be healers as well as a few security people. Ian said to them, "I'm sorry, but the Earl has ordered us to depart."

The Earl said to Malcolm, "Did they honestly think that I was going to allow them to take Agatha into custody?"

CHAPTER 61

ONWARD TO THE NEW WORLD

T HE EARL'S FLEET had left Greenland two days ago and once again found themselves in the open sea where there was nothing but an endless ocean ahead of them. They were heading on a southwest course to a settlement called L'Anse aux Meadows. This is the fabled landing spot of the famous Viking Explorer Leif Eriksson. Many believed that the tales of Leif Eriksson were simply fairy tales. Detractors wanted you to think that he had merely landed on an unexplored area in Iceland.

Nevertheless, the Vikings had developed this settlement, and it became home to about 150-200 Settlers. It had certain advantages over the settlements in Greenland. According to the Zeno brothers, it was known to have caribou, wolf, fox, bear, lynx, marten, all types of birds and fish, seals, whales, and walrus. L'Anse aux Meadows was an attractive place to travel to for many Vikings, but the problem was that the seas were very treacherous. Many ships set sail from Greenland to L'Anse aux Meadows and never arrived. The Crossing was very difficult. The trip from Greenland went against the current. The current wanted to force your ship east. If you went too Far East, the seas were much rougher. The Zeno brothers understood this and plotted a course that would encounter land far north of L'Anse aux Meadows. You would then sail down the coast until you safely arrived at the port. The Zeno brothers had lost many comrades over the decades because of this current. The lessons learned were very costly.

The trip was scheduled to take 12-14 days. As if the sea wasn't dangerous enough, the land could prove to be even more deadly. There were native tribes along the northern islands that were not part of any trade agreement. If your ship was severely damaged, you had to abandon it and join the crew of another vessel. Most voyages usually had at least four ships with them. Often only two or fewer ships would survive the journey.

The Zeno brothers had warned everyone that they should only plan on spending minimal time at L'Anse aux Meadows. Norse Warlords currently ruled it. These Warlords have been co-operating to a degree with King Haakon. However, they were so far out of the King's grasp that they could run L'Anse aux Meadows like it was their own Kingdom. The Earl worried that even if they safely passed through L'Anse aux Meadows, they would not keep quiet regarding the Earl's journey. He knew that they would be sold out if Oleg came this way searching for them. So the Earl set a plan that would have him and his flagship and four other ships travel past the settlement at night. The Zeno brothers said there was a safe harbor roughly 20 miles up the Coast. The Zeno brothers insisted that at least one or two ships needed to stop and pay tribute. If no tribute were paid, it would be a sign of disrespect, and there would be trouble. So a plan was put into place where the Zeno brothers would enter the port and pay tribute with grains and several barrels of mead. They would concoct the story that they were leading a Ramada of ships for exploration purposes in the New World. The Earl would go as far as having the Zenos show the Norse the decree from the King.

They would also inform the Norse that the mission was secret and, if any secrets were divulged, would be an act of war against the Kingdom of Norway.

On day 12, they saw land. Ian wondered, "Is this the Land of Plenty that the Watchers had promised. This moment could be historic if the mission didn't need to be so confidential." Ian felt that everything was going too smooth.

As they approached the land, Ian looked over and spotted Francis on one of the other ships. He was trimming a sail. Ian asked the Earl, "Is that ship to our starboard one of the ships that would enter the port of L'Anse aux Meadows."

The Earl answered, "Aye."

Ian had a very bad feeling about this day. So he asked Clara to protect their son.

Ian yelled to Francis, "I can ask the Earl to have you transferred to my ship."

Francis responded, "I am happy where I am. I have worked my way up to First Mate."

Ian was proud but at the same time afraid. Francis had never been involved in an actual conflict. He trained for years as a warrior, but he was hot-headed. Ian told Frances, "When you go ashore, keep quiet and let the Zenos' do the talking and don't tell them that you are from the Clan Sinclair."

Francis said, "Don't worry about me. I can handle myself."

Ian probably could have forced his will on Francis, but that would not be right either. Francis was trying to stand on his own two feet. He no longer needed his father to watch out for him.

Ian said, "Alright. Just be careful."

CHAPTER 62

L'ANSE AUX MEADOWS

O N THE EVENING of the 14th day, since the Earl's fleet left Greenland, they came within several hours of the port of L'Anse aux Meadows. As planned, the Earl's flagship waited until complete darkness had occurred before it passed the port. They were roughly two miles offshore. Between the great distance and the darkness, they were confident that they had not seen. After they passed the port, Angus noted that there was a fishing boat to their starboard side. After the Earl's ships passed them, they noticed that they began to row towards shore. This was not a good sign. The Earl had no way of notifying his two ships that were heading towards the port. The Earl made a quick decision. He could not trust the fishermen. They came about and headed directly towards the port. The Earl knew that he would have to deal with the consequences no matter what they were.

Meanwhile, the two ships from the Earl's fleet entered the L'Anse aux Meadows port and were waived into the slips. The first to step on shore was Captain Joshua McQuinn. He was a seasoned warrior and could speak through any difficult situation with courage and strength. Many of the warriors remained on their ships. A party of twenty went ashore. They were greeted by a group of 40 Vikings who all had their swords drawn. The Leader had red hair and a beard. He introduced himself as Eric III. He claimed that he was a descendant of the famous Viking Explorer Eric the Red. He abruptly asked Captain McQuinn, "What is the nature of your mission?"

The Captain said, "We are on an exploration mission on behalf of King Haakon."

Eric said, "King who?" All of his party laughed.

Eric then said, "We don't recognize any false Kings here."

The Captain said, "We mean no insult. We had heard of this settlement and stopped to pay tribute."

Eric said, "What do you offer?"

The Captain said, "We offer grains, seeds, and several barrels of mead."

Eric then said, "We will also require your ships." At that instant, the Captain noticed that the Earl's flagship had just entered the harbor.

✠

The Earl was thankful that he decided to change plans and head into the port. He could see that the settlers had their swords drawn and were taking an aggressive stance. He ordered all warriors to prepare for battle. He also ordered the warriors to prepare the Long Bows for the Fire Arrows. He could see Captain McQuinn in the middle of the Group. The two had been in so many battles together. The Earl knew that he needed to take them by storm. Captain McQuinn would be ready to strike quick when Henry's arrows were launched. The settlers would undoubtedly threaten to kill the Captain and his landing party. The Earl knew that the only option was to overwhelm them with force. He was well aware that he would probably lose some men.

Just then, the Earl noticed Oleg walking out of a nearby hut. The Earl hadn't had a chance to survey the other ships in the harbor. He would have noticed the four ships he had just encountered in Greenland. He was close enough to hear Oleg give the order to close off the mouth of the harbor. This would involve having Oleg's ships physically block the harbor entrance. No ships would be allowed to enter or leave.

The Earl instructed his warriors, "Take aim and fire at those ships moving towards the harbor entrance."

The archers' immediately hit their targets. Three of the ships soon became engulfed in flames. They all stopped short of the harbor entrance. All of the Vikings on these three ships were now jumping into the frigid water.

Eric's men soon took aim at Captain McQuinn and his landing party.

The Earl commanded his archers to aim at all of the buildings.

He yelled to Eric, "Stop, or I will burn down your village."

Oleg yelled, "Henry Sinclair. This is between you and me. Surrender, and I will set your men free."

The Earl yelled, "Oleg. The problem with you and your kinsmen is that you don't understand when a battle is lost. I will spare this village if you stand down."

Just then, Oleg swung his sword and cut down two of Captain McQuinn's men. This caused the Earl to give the order to launch the fire arrows. The structures near the shoreline had grass roofs. The Arrows fired and hit their targets. At the same instant, McQuinn's men drew their swords and attacked the settlers without mercy.

Ian could see that Francis was one of the men on shore. He was in a sword fight with one of the settlers. His enemy was swinging his sword wildly. Frances had been trained for this very situation. He let the man swing wildly; then, as soon as the man's sword passed by Francis's mid-section, he swung at the man's midsection and hit. The man dropped to his knees, and Francis finished the man off by plunging his sword through the man's heart. While he was doing this, he failed to notice the man coming from behind. Francis saw him and moved at the last second, but the man's blade hit his leg. Francis went down quickly. Captain McQuinn was nearby and flew through the air while swinging at the man's head. His sword cut through the man's neck and removed his head. Francis was in shock. Ian thought that he was dead for sure. The Captain helped him up and told him to try to make it back to the ship.

The settlers that were not instantly killed were retreating. Erik was among them. He decided that he would get his revenge another day. His mission right now was to contain the fires.

Back on the flagship, the Earl stood and watched the mayhem. He knew that Captain McQuinn would go on the offensive as soon as the arrows started to fly. The Earl's goals were twofold. First, to protect his fleet, and second, to send a message to anyone who thinks about attacking the Clan Sinclair.

Henry jumped onto the pier and walked toward Eric III. He looked Eric in the eye and said, "We came in peace on behalf of King Haakon. Your men didn't need to die, and your buildings didn't need to burn."

Eric said, "Haakon has turned his back on the ways of the Viking."

Oleg yelled from across the harbor, "Henry Sinclair. I will follow you to the ends of the earth. I will avenge my family and those that you killed today."

The Earl's attention suddenly went back to Eric. He said, "You made a grave mistake today. You listened to a man who is on a suicide mission." He paused then continued, "Your ways are done. The Vikings have transitioned into a people that are fierce warriors, but only when provoked. The sooner you learn this, the better. Please understand that I could kill all of you, but what would that accomplish."

Eric replied, "A true Viking would have killed us for honor's sake."

Henry replied, "I am a Scot." Henry then returned to his flagship and ordered his forces back to their ships. He then yelled for everyone to hear, "We came in Peace. Your Leader-led you down a path to a very bad place. But, it did not have to end this way."

Out of the smoke, Ian saw Francis as he was helped back to the Earl's ship. Ian jumped onto the pier to help him. He had suffered a severe leg injury in the battle. Others helped Ian carry Francis aboard the flagship. Ian took off his shirt and tied it around the wound to stop the bleeding. They transferred him below deck, where Agatha was waiting. She looked at the wound and feared that Francis might lose his leg. Francis was terrified and in extreme pain.

Agatha said, "Let's try to stop the bleeding first. We will deal with the leg later." All of the ships were headed back out to sea. So far, the New World looked a lot like the Old World.

Agatha was able to stop the bleeding. Ian spoke with Agatha. She said, "He has lost a lot of blood. I was able to stop the bleeding and sew the wound." She continued, "The best course right now is sleep and many fluids. He can have some wine for the pain, but not too much. He needs to drink a steady stream of water. He may not lose the leg, but would never be the same. The sword that cut him had cut right through muscle tissue. He would probably need crutches for the rest of his life."

Ian thanked her for everything that she had done. She then said something that shocked Ian, "I see your son changing his life course now. He will grow to be the one who perpetuates the Secret of Eden. His life's mission will be to guard its message and pass on its location to the chosen few." Ian immediately thought of Clara. She would have been heartbroken to watch her son almost die in battle. Francis would have to change his ways. He was a warrior no more.

CHAPTER 63

UNEXPLORED WATERS

THE EARL'S FLEET set sail out of the port of L'Anse aux Meadows as quickly as possible. They headed on a western then southern heading as advised by the Zeno brothers. They described a course that would have them follow the island's coastline that was the home to L'Anse aux Meadows. At the end of this island, there would be another open expanse of water that would take several days to cross. In addition, there was a series of smaller uninhabitable islands if you needed emergency refuge.

The Earl said, "Can the natives be worse than the supposed friends at L'Anse aux Meadows?"

Ian said, "Let's hope not."

The Earl had lost four of his warriors. He said, "We will find a safe landing tomorrow and give the warriors a proper Christian Burial."

Ian checked on Francis, and he seemed to be resting. The risk of infection was his worst enemy right now. If infection set in, he would lose the leg. There was nothing further that Ian could do, so he decided to get some rest. He thanked Agatha for everything that she had done.

Somewhere during the night, the Earl had Antonio transferred to his flagship. He would need to guide the ships to the Gold River.

The Earl asked Antonio, "Is there a safe harbor for the burial of our dead?"

Antonio said, "We should come upon a small island before we are back in open waters." He told the Earl that the safest place was one of the smaller islands. Most were completely uninhabited. He also said that they should probably make landfall at night.

As daybreak was upon them, Ian could see land at their port side. It seemed to go on forever. Antonio knew of a protected harbor near the end of this island where there was a narrow strip of land that led to an uninhabited peninsula. He had been there before when his ship had suffered damage on a crossing some twenty years ago. He said that the waters were very deep right offshore in this harbor. Our ships could provide protection from anyone attempting to come across the small strip of land. He said it would probably be another day before they reached this protected harbor. They were sailing into a strong headwind which caused the ships to tack back and forth. It seemed as though they were making very little progress. At least the seas were relatively calm.

Later that morning, after everyone had completed breakfast, Ian checked again with Francis. Agatha was there with him. She said, "He has taken on a small fever overnight. This is the body's way of fighting off infection."

They went topside, and she said, "I fear for the worst with his leg. If the infection worsens, I will have to remove it."

Ian said, "What does that mean for his overall chances of survival?"

She said, "The prospects are good because I will sear the

resulting wound and provide some excess skin to wrap around the nub." She went on to say that she assisted healers during the many battles that had plagued Scotland over the years.

Ian said, "At least he will survive. Francis is very resourceful. He will take on a new life's mission, and no doubt prosper."

✠

The next afternoon the Earl saw the protected harbor that Antonio had spoken of. The Earl summoned all of his leaders. This included Captain McQuinn. He detailed the plan to send a team ashore led by Captain McQuinn to find and prepare a proper burial spot befitting their fallen comrades. Then a second team led by the Earl would accompany the makeshift caskets to their final resting spots. He then detailed how the other ships were to protect the landing parties. He explained that the water was deep enough to get right up to shore, but wanted the ships to set anchor far enough out to be safe but close enough to provide cover should the natives' attack.

Later that afternoon, the first landing party went ashore with pickaxes and shovels. The Captain would signal the Earl when the graves were dug and ready for burial. About two hours after landing, the signal came from Captain McQuinn. He used a section of a mirror to shine a light towards the Earl's flagship. The Earl's lifeboats were then loaded with the caskets and enough warriors to row the Earl and the fallen warriors to shore. After a few minutes, the lifeboats arrived at the beach, and the warriors were buried. The Earl led those present in a short prayer service. Fortunately, it was a full moon, and the visibility was excellent. It was at that moment Ian noticed movement on the shoreline. The natives came out of the woods with spears and bow and arrows. Our ships began firing warning arrows at them with the longbows. The attack on our landing team was imminent. Our teams were just exiting the woods. They saw the natives and began to run towards the lifeboats. They quickly boarded the lifeboats and began rowing towards our ships. It was then that Ian noticed that several of the natives were European. He recognized one in particular. It was Oleg. Ian thought, "Where is his ship? Where is his crew?"

The landing teams safely returned to their vessels, and they immediately set sail. Once Ian saw the Earl, he immediately told him, "Oleg and several other Europeans were amongst the natives attacking you."

He looked concerned but said, "We must press on. I will have to confront Oleg in the future, but for now, let's focus our attention on getting to the Gold River."

CHAPTER 64

THE GOLD RIVER

T HAS BEEN six days since the Earl's fleet had buried their warriors and had a brief encounter with Oleg. They have been sailing with the coastline to the starboard side for several days. Ian was speaking with the Earl when Antonio arrived and was very excited. He said, "After that next point of land we should turn west. We will enter into a large bay. The Gold River enters into this bay at its deepest point. We should make the landing at a nearby island. This island will prove to not only be safe harbor, but will keep us out of sight from the Mi'kmaqs. I will need to go inland to speak with the Mi'kmaq Leaders and locate Goosecap."

The Earl asked, "Remind me again. Who is Goosecap?"

Antonio said, "He is the European explorer who the natives revere as a God. I will set up a meeting with Goosecap where I will introduce you and the rest of our leaders."

In light of what they heard from Antonio, the Earl ordered everyone to be ready for anything which includes battle. He went on to say, "We need these natives to accept us. We need to offer to teach them our ways of fishing and growing food. We must assure them that we come in peace. We also need to stay alert. Oleg will no doubt appear at some point."

✠

They took down the sails from all of their ships as they neared the island that marked the Gold River. They quietly rowed near the east side of the island. As they approached the island, Angus commented that the island was a perfect place to set up a small ship repair facility. He pointed out that as they came closer that it appeared that there were actually two islands. Angus stated, "It is currently high tide. When the tide comes out in the morning it will look as though this is one island. We can set up a dry dock at low tide for both protecting and repairing our ships. We would need to build up a rock flooring so that we can work on the ships. Otherwise, the area will be a large mud bowl. Vikings have engaged in this practice for centuries."

They loaded four lifeboats to make landfall. Ian insisted that the landing party include Malcolm and Agatha.

Stepping onto this land felt like a very special moment for Ian. Possibly one of the momentous occasions in the history of mankind. Almost as if she was reading his thoughts, Agatha said, "Many souls have stepped foot onto this island. From the explorers from Atlantis, the Phoenicians, to the Vikings. Many souls are present on this island. Some good some bad."

Malcolm said, "Many believe that the Phoenicians traveled to this vast land many times because they discovered great copper quarries. This is thought to have fueled the Bronze Age roughly 3000 years ago. This area may have been a stopover point for them."

Ian also wondered what stories this land held. He doesn't remember it in any of his Dreams. When it was nearly nightfall, several warriors rowed Antonio over to the mainland where he would set out on foot to meet with the Mi'kmaqs.

✠

Meanwhile, the infection in Francis's leg had gotten worse. Unfortunately, the leg would have to be removed below the knee. Malcolm gave him much wine to ease the pain. Also, Agatha gave him a concoction of tea with special herbs that had put Francis fast asleep. Malcolm gathered some warriors to hold him down. Ian told Agatha, "Please get this over quickly."

She said, "It won't take long." She continued, "As I told you shortly after this happened that he has a bright future ahead of him. This loss of a limb will change his future forever. He will be revered as a Great Man."

Ian suddenly could smell the lavender flowers. This could only mean that Clara was there for her son's darkest moment. This was too much for a parent to bear.

Agatha then pulled out the saw and very quickly cut the leg off. Francis screamed in pain. Agatha then seared the wound. She left the tourniquet in place for roughly thirty minutes. Agatha fed Francis many more cups of wine and tea. Ian told Francis, "I am very proud of you and I am certain that you will take on your future with even more gusto than you have in the past. You are a true warrior."

Agatha said, "He needs to rest for three or four days. I will keep an eye on the wound." Ian thanked her for saving his son's life.

✠

The next day, the Earl's warriors began to set up temporary shelter on the island. This involved several large tents. Most of the people would stay on the ship for now. Angus instructed several builders that were on the mission to unload the carts and start locating some large rocks. He was planning on creating a working surface during low tides so that he could dry dock at least three of the ships at the same time. Once they were in dry dock, the hulls could be cleaned of algae and be repaired if necessary.

Later that afternoon, Antonio signaled the lookout that he was ready to return to the island. Roughly an hour later, Antonio entered the Earl's tent. He said, "The Mi'kmaqs were not happy to hear of our arrival. They insisted that we leave at once or they will attack."

Antonio continued, "I insisted that we come in peace and our goal is not to settle. They were steadfast in their opposition. It was then that the great Goosecap entered their village. He was just as I remembered. He reminded me of the Nobility that I have seen in London or Paris. The Mi'kmaqs bowed down to him as if he were a God. He welcomed me and said, "Antonio, you have returned. I thought for sure that you were lost at Sea." I explained how I had made my way back to Scotland where I met you, the Earl of Rosslyn. I went on to say that I have served as a guide for you and that we had arrived in this area the previous day." He said, "The Earl is here?" I said, "Yes." He wanted to know what your intentions were. I said, "The Earl comes in peace. He does not come as an invader. He wishes to meet with you to discuss his mission. He said, "Tell the Earl that I will meet with him tomorrow. Tell him not to bring any warriors or the Mi'kmaq will attack.""

Antonio continued, "I told Goosecap that you will come with a small party of Scholars and Leaders."

Goosecap asked "Scholars?"

Antonio said, "Yes. Their mission is one of learning, not conquest. I set up the meeting for the clearing just north of the mouth of the Gold River at noon."

The Earl thanked Antonio and said, "Job well done. We shall meet with this Goosecap tomorrow as scheduled."

Antonio left the tent and then the Earl said to Ian, "I would like to meet with you and Angus after supper this evening to discuss our strategy. Please notify Malcolm. Oh, and tell him to bring Agatha. I think she soon will become a very important asset for us."

Ian said, "Aye sir." Ian thought to himself as he exited the

Earl's tent, "He will soon learn that Agatha has already proven to be invaluable."

After supper, the group met in the Earl's stateroom. The Earl started by recanting what Antonio had said earlier. Everyone had several hours to think about it. Angus spoke first, "What are our intentions here. We haven't discussed that in detail. I think we all understand that the main mission is to secure the treasure here so that no one will find it unless they are very carefully guided to it."

The Earl said, "As of right now, our mission is open-ended." He went on to say, "It all depends on how discretely we can hide the treasure. We will need to have it found intact when the time is right."

Ian said, "Let's see what kind of chap this Goosecap fellow is before we make any firm plans. As we have discussed before, we will need to leave a trusted member or members of our party here to keep an eye on the treasure." Everyone agreed. They decided to convene a meeting again tomorrow after they meet with Goosecap.

✠

Now that the Earl's fleet had safely arrived at the island, it was time to justly pay the Zeno Brothers for delivering on their promise. The Earl explained as he handed Pietro as small satchel filled with gold coins, "Thank you for your service. You are free to go. Rather than further agitate the Mi'kmaq, I would prefer that you set sail in the morning. We will start our research here shortly. Some of my team may stay through the winter and then return to Scotland next summer." He continued, "I would prefer that you keep the news of our expedition quiet. The natives have accepted us because they believe that we will be here short term."

Pietro said, "Thank you Henry Sinclair. Please let us know if we can be of service in the future." The men all shook hands and parted ways. The Zeno Brothers made more from this journey than they had over the previous two years.

CHAPTER 65

GOOSECAP

ANCIENT MI'KMAQ LEGEND

N THE BEGINNING, the Kji-Niskam (Creator) handed down a set of rules to live by. He sent his Puoinaq (Angels) to guide mankind on these rules. Mankind was given the gift of free-will to decide whether or not to live a righteous life or not. If mankind chose the path of the righteous and chose to live in peace then the Kji-Niskam would have a great reward for his people. If they chose the opposite then they would face destruc-tion. This was proven ages ago when the rains and floods nearly wiped out all life. Only those who chose to live by the Kji-Ni-skam's rules survived. The path of mankind was made more dif-ficult because one of the Puoinaq turned evil. He would very easily draw certain men to his path. Even though the number of evil-doers is small, they always wreaked havoc on the righteous. They start wars based on lies. They cause untold destruction for reasons that make their war chests richer. They will cause wars that will force tribes from all over the world to take sides. Many take the evil side without really understanding its aims. There will be a few chosen ones that will repeatedly live a righteous life. After their death they will be born again to propagate the wishes of the Puoinaq. They guard the Kji-Niskam's secret. They will be the ones that finally deliver mankind to the just and rightful side of the Kji-Niskam. As everything in nature is in balance, so to, the evil-doers will have a few that will battle with the chosen ones. Like the chosen ones, they will be born again to carry out the evil-doers wishes. Victory will only be decided after the epic final battle with the evil-doers. If the chosen ones are successful, then all of the secrets of the stars will be revealed.

-Translated from Tli'suti (language of the Mi'kmaq) to English by Sir James Glouchester of London – 1380 A.D.

✠

The next morning Ian woke to the sounds of Francis screaming as Agatha was redressing the wound. Agatha was attempting to pull the skin over the nub. This was quite painful, but she assured Francis that it will heal faster this way. Angus had instructed one of the builders to construct a set of crutches for Francis. Ian told them to make them for someone his size. After all, Francis and Ian were almost the same height. Ian sat down for breakfast with Angus and Abigail. He asked Abigail, "How do you like this location so far?"

She said, "I have only had a chance to walk the island thus far. We were looking for wild berries and such. To answer your question. I think it is beautiful. I just hope the natives will accept us." She went on to say, "As long as I am with Angus, I will be happy." Angus kissed her on the cheek. It made Ian think of Clara. He wondered, "Was Clara one of the spirits possessing this island that Agatha had referred to yesterday?"

Just then Agatha walked by. She wished to go ashore and walk the island. Ian said, "I will go with you."

Agatha said, "I must do this alone. There is great conflict amongst the spirits on this island. I must help resolve this."

Ian said, "I will stay behind you at a great distance. Remember, we still have not spoken to the natives yet."

Agatha said, "Very well. I know that your heart is in the right place."

Ian rowed Agatha and himself to shore. Once on shore, Agatha lit a stalk of white sage. She said, "This helps cleanse and bring order to the spirits that it touches."

Ian watched as Agatha walked nearly the entire island. At times she almost seemed to be arguing with someone. Finally, she returned to the lifeboat. She had a smile on her face. She said, "I explained who we are and what our purpose is here. It took some convincing, but we will now be accepted and welcomed by the spirits. A peace has come over them."

✠

Later that morning the Earl, Angus, Ian, Malcolm, Agatha, and Antonio loaded into two lifeboats. The Earl chose only to bring swords. He did not want to appear as an aggressor. They loaded into the lifeboats on the western shore of the island and made their way over to the mainland. It was an unusually hot day for this particular climate. They could see the clearing where the meeting was to take place. Someone had gone to the trouble of setting up a canopy so that they could at least meet in the shade. They pulled the lifeboats ashore and made their way to the canopy. Then all of a sudden several natives appeared. One was the Chief. He wore a red, white, and yellow headdress made of many feathers. The Earl smiled and nodded at them. There was no reaction.

Finally, the Earl said, "Goosecap?" The Chief smiled and looked to the nearby trees where an English Gentleman was standing.

After several seconds, Malcolm shouted, "Glouchester?" The Gentlemen looked at each other and smiled. He then walked over and shook hands with Malcolm. Malcolm then said, "Earl Henry Sinclair of Rosslyn and the Orkneys meet Sir James Glouchester of London."

The Earl said, "You two know each other?"

Malcolm said, "Aye. We studied Archeology and History together when we were lads." Malcolm then looked at Sir James and said, "The last I heard you were lost in a shipwreck off the coast of Scotland."

Sir James said, "That was the story that I put out. I was chasing down leads on the fabled Arcadia. I made sure that my family knew that I was safe, but I kept venturing west. I was following ancient cuneiform carvings that described the new Garden of Eden which Plato referred to as Arcadia."

Sir James then asked the Earl, "What brings your fleet to this part of the New World."

The Earl responded, "The same thing that brought you here. Arcadia." He went on to say that our mission is simply exploratory and we don't plan on settling. He further said, "We may leave a handful here so that they can continue our research." The Earl went on to introduce the rest of us to Sir James. Antonio needed no introduction.

Sir James said, "As I told Antonio yesterday, we all thought he was dead." Antonio replied "Yes, God was not ready to call me yet." The introductions continued.

When Sir James came to Agatha, he paused and said, "You are a healer. I have picked up several skills over the years and I clearly recognize your aura."

Agatha smiled, "Sir, you are a very old soul. Your spirit has been involved in many critical world events."

Sir James responded, "I would like to think so, but sometimes I'm unsure whether I am dreaming of the past or I have a very active imagination." Everyone laughed.

Malcolm then interjected "Why Goosecap?"

Sir James responded, "It was one of those translation errors that stuck."

Malcolm asked, "Do you now prefer Goosecap or Sir James?"

He said, "It depends who we are with. The Mi'kmaq only know me as Goosecap. To the rest of the world, I prefer James."

The group sat down mainly on the ground. The Earl and Sir James had the only two chairs. The Earl started first by telling Sir James of his past travels and how he was an Earl for both Scotland and Norway. He said that he has many friends, but also some enemies. He explained the encounters that they had with Oleg and the unfriendly welcome in L'Anse aux Meadows.

Sir James interjected, "Some Vikings are unwilling to give up their old ways."

The Earl went on to say, "Unfortunately, I expect this beast Oleg to appear here at some point. This is why we have traveled with so many ships. We are ready to take on all comers." The Earl continued, "Please tell the Mi'kmaq that we come in peace. We have many offerings for them and can show them some new ways to catch fish and grow food."

Sir James said, "The Mi'kmaq will take time. They have seen explorers come and go. Some, like many of the Vikings, come to do harm. Others are simply on an educational excursion. Having said that I do have a suggestion. I would like to introduce your healer to the Mi'kmaqs. My guess is that she will be revered by the Mi'kmaq."

The Earl turned to Agatha and asked if she was ready to meet the Mi'kmaq.

She said, "Yes. But I would like Malcolm to go with me."

Sir James said, "Also, I think it would be a good idea to send Antonio with us. They are always happy to see him. He has many friends here."

The time together would give Malcolm and Sir James a chance to catch up. The Earl asked Ian to join Malcolm, Agatha, and Antonio. The rest would return to the island. The Earl said, "Sir James, I would love to have you as our guest for dinner tomorrow." Sir James agreed.

As Ian walked to the Mi'kmaq village, he couldn't help but

wonder how fate plays into all of our decisions. First, Angus and Ian have been connected since they were young boys. Next Ian suggested that Malcolm and Agatha join the mission. Then, they arrive at this remote island and Malcolm finds his long lost friend, Sir James. Then, Agatha is ushered off to meet the Mi'kmaqs where she most likely will help us stay here peacefully. Is this fate? Then a thought came to Ian and he said to himself, "Clara, is this you're doing?"

Agatha turned around and said, "Of course it is." Both Ian and Agatha laughed.

CHAPTER 66

THE MI'KMAQ

THE CHIEF LED the group back to his village. Before entering the large teepee that was his home. He stopped and spoke in very clear English, "My name is Waabakwa. I welcome you to my home."

The group entered the Chief's home. Agatha immediately made eye contact with the tribe's healer. They walked over and embraced each other. Both women had tears streaming down their faces. Obviously, they knew each other. The healer for the tribe spoke first. The Chief translated, he said, "First, please meet my mother, Megis. She is our healer. She says that she and the one you call Agatha have been together in many lifetimes." He then paused and listened. He continued, "She said that Agatha is a very special healer. Our tribe is very fortunate to have her in our presence." He paused again while his mother continued to speak in her native tongue. He was shocked by what she said next. He looked at his mother with surprise. She nodded, which told him to proceed. He said, "My mother says that you are the ones that we talk about in our oldest prophecy. You have come here to make a necessary step according to the will of Kji-Niskam."

The others present who were members of the Chief's family were also shocked. The story in the ancient legend was generations old, if not thousands of years old. Chief Waabakwa's people have been chosen to be part of the heavenly task.

The Chief said to his old friend, "Goosecap. How can the Mi'kmaq help with this mission?"

Goosecap responded, "I am just learning of this just as you are learning of it. Give me time to understand everything. The one certain thing is that the evil-doers that we discuss in your prophecy may be on their way here. Earl Henry Sinclair is prepared to defend against an attack from the sea. I would suggest that you prepare your warriors for an attack from the land. I believe that you and I are about to become part of the legend."

Megis then spoke to her son. He translated and said, "My mother knew something extraordinary was going to happen today. For the first time in our lifetime, the spirits on the Island where you are staying are at peace. My mother says that Agatha is the one to thank for this."

Agatha then said goodbye to her old friend. She said, "In the coming days, I would like to spend more time with you. If that is alright." Chief Waabakwa translated.

Megis smiled and responded in her language. The Chief translated, "She says, "Of course. She would like that very much."

CHAPTER 67

BACK AT THE ISLAND

WHEN MALCOLM, AGATHA, Ian, and Antonio arrived back on the island, it could be seen that Angus's men were making significant progress with the stone flooring for the low tide area. They were splitting the large stones so that there was a flat side that would face up. Other workers were setting up temporary shelters onshore. At a minimum the fleet would be there for sixth months, but most likely a year. Others were out in the lifeboats setting nets for fish. Everyone was very sick of eating the dried oxen. Approximately ten hunters were exploring the island looking for deer, wild turkey, and various kinds of other fowl. One thing was sure, the team will be eating very well here while on this island. The team noticed while they were on the mainland that the Gold River flowed with what appeared to be spring water. It was very cold and very clear. Before they parted company with Sir James they asked for permission to send some forces back to secure some water for drinking and cooking. Antonio would be assigned the mission. Everyone knew him and therefore there was an inherent trust with the Mi'kmaqs that would not be afforded to anyone else. Sir James replied, "Take as much as you wish."

The Earl knew that Abigail loved gardening so he placed her in charge of planting the Canopy Oaks. He explained that these oaks would grow twice as tall as any other tree on the island. These oaks would eventually serve as a marker for the Gold River. After all, these islands all looked very much alike from the water. The goal was to hide the treasure adequately, but not to make it so well hidden that even the worthy couldn't ever find it.

Later that afternoon, the hunting party returned with one buck and two does. That would be enough food to last weeks. I'm sure a significant amount of the venison would be dried so that it could be eaten weeks if not months later.

The fisherman came in shortly thereafter. They had netted roughly 50 Striped Bass. These were very good fish that could be cooked very easily over a campfire. Between the venison and the fresh fish, the team would have the makings for a delicious supper when Sir James was scheduled to join them the next evening.

The Earl summoned everyone that met with the Mi'kmaq to his tent. He also requested Angus. Moments later, everyone arrived.

The Earl asked, "How did it go with the Mi'kmaq?"

Malcolm replied, "Shockingly good. The Mi'kmaq healer knew Agatha in previous lives. Their meeting was more of a reunion than anything else. Evidently, the Mi'kmaq have a similar legend regarding the Secret of Eden. The healer recognized that Agatha was a living component of the prophecy. This caught everyone off guard."

The Earl said, "They know about the Secret of Eden?"

Malcolm said, "They only know their prophecy. They sensed that the prophecy has brought us to their shores."

Agatha elaborated, " The Mi'kmaq are a very spiritual people. I was able to read the healer, Megis's, thoughts. The Mi'kmaq have been here for thousands of years. Their people originally came by boat from a faraway place. I believe that they may be descendants of the Phoenicians. I believe Sir James knows the answer. I need to spend more time with Megis to learn about the Mi'kmaq. One thing is certain, their culture is very important to them." Agatha paused briefly then continued, "Conquerors have tried many times to take this land. Several times it has led to great bloodshed. The Spirits of the fallen still dwell on this island. It seems that this island is where they bury their dead. I spoke with spirits earlier today. They understand our mission."

Finally, the Earl asked Agatha, "Do you think this place is where we should be hiding the Secret of Eden."

She responded, "If the Mi'kmaq truly knew what we had in our possession and fully understood its spiritual significance they would guard it with their dying breath. However, it cannot be a place of annual visits by treasure seekers and the like. I believe that the entire matter needs to be presented in the proper context to the Mi'kmaq. I think that I can be that messenger."

The Earl said, "Let me consider this. I want to say a special thank you to Agatha. You have been an amazing addition to this expedition. I believe that we have all been placed here for a special purpose. It's very hard to explain, but I believe all of you understand that we have been brought to this moment in time for a very special reason."

✠

They all parted company and agreed to reconvene in the Earl's stateroom for supper.

Later that evening they all dined in the Earl's stateroom. They enjoyed several bottles of wine. Everyone was a little giddy. Ever since they left Rosslyn they have been on a whirlwind trip.

Finally, the Earl said, "It's time we get down to business. I would like everyone's thoughts on Sir James. Can we trust him? What motivates him? Is there a benefit in telling him of the secret?"

Angus spoke first, "No matter whether we tell him or not, we must guard the treasure even after it is hidden. As we have discussed, the treasure and the secret should be hidden inland. We have spoken of the place called the Holy Well. I think we should travel there and survey it. Does it offer the natural protection that we need?"

Ian chimed in, "I agree. Can we sneak this treasure by both the Mi'kmaq and Sir James? The answer is probably not. I think Malcolm should answer this since he has known the Good Sir the longest."

Malcolm responded, "I knew this man a long time ago. I believe that he is interested in discovery rather than riches. Having said that I believe that any man would be tested with the knowledge that the Holy Grail of Jesus is nearby, as well as, the Golden Menorah. I believe that we should disclose the secret, but not the religious artifacts. At least not yet."

The Earl then looked at Agatha and asked, "Have you looked into this man's spirit?"

She responded, "Yes. He is a very spiritual man who is guided by science. I believe that protecting the secret would turn into a lifelong mission for him."

The Earl then said, "It is decided. We will introduce Sir James to the Secret of Eden tomorrow when he visits for supper."

After the meeting was adjourned Ian asked for a few minutes with the Earl. He wanted to speak with him regarding Francis. Ian told the Earl everything that Agatha had predicted for Francis's future. "She said that he will become the keeper of this secret and will be the one who carries it forward for generations to come." Ian said.

The Earl responded, "I have no issues with the selection of Francis to articulate the message. Let's start including him in the discussions."

Ian said, "Do I have your permission to start discussing this with him?"

He said, "Aye, but make sure to include Malcolm. There will

be certain Secret Societies that we will want to deliver this message to. We will never give it to them directly. We must have a very detailed plan. Francis will have to live in a world where people speak in codes and very few will understand how to interpret the codes. It will actually be very exciting for him."

CHAPTER 68

THE MESSENGER

THE FOLLOWING MORNING Ian joined Agatha for another walk around the island. Agatha said, "Today is much different than yesterday. The spirits are at peace. They are happy to see us."

Ian asked, "Do they want something from us?"

She said, "At first, they wanted us to leave. Now they want us to spend time with them and share the energy from our living souls."

Ian said, "Christianity teaches us that souls go to heaven. So why are these souls still here?"

She said, "Your soul is very old. The same question could be asked of you." She paused and continued, "For a soul to go to Heaven, it must complete its tasks."

"After we hide this Treasure, will my soul's mission be complete?" Ian asked.

Agatha responded, "Heavens no. Your task will not be complete until all of the tasks listed by the Watchers have been finished and the Secret of Eden is revealed."

Then Ian asked a selfish question, "Will I be with Clara again?"

She laughed and said, "Of course. I foresee that you will be together in the living many times before your mission has ended."

Suddenly Ian could smell the fragrance. Ian knew that Clara was there. Agatha went on to say, "Clara is your soulmate. In the next life, both of you may meet each other as young children, or you may not meet her until you are old, but yes, you and Clara have always been together and will always be together." She continued, "Clara is also very excited about Francis's future. She is the one who has been telling me what life has in store for him."

They walked quietly for a few minutes. Finally, Ian spoke. He said, "Do the spirits here on this island want us to complete our mission?"

She said, "Aye. Now that they understand that our overall mission is for all people to be treated with equality and kindness, they are at peace. They said that if unworthy people show up searching for the secret on this island, they will make their stay miserable."

Ian said, "I believe that we call that a haunting." Ian paused for a few minutes and said, "It would be better if everyone that is looking for the secret and is unworthy thinks that the secret is here on this island. Meanwhile, it will be elsewhere where only the worthy will know of its location."

Ian and Agatha concluded their walk in silence.

All of the Treasure was transferred to Captain McQuinn's Ship during that day. Everything except the Secret of Eden, which remained on the Earl's Flagship. Everyone prepared for the meeting. Malcolm requested that he has some time with Sir James after the meeting. He wanted to show him his private library. Sir James had already offered to reciprocate.

Everyone was ordered to clean up their areas, and the ship was to have all of the hatches open so that the ship could be aired out. The Earl inspected the ship. The only one to be given some slack was Francis. Ian spent some time with Francis that afternoon to discuss his new assignment. He sat down at Francis's bedside. Ian could already tell that Francis was in better spirits.

Francis said, "Before we speak about my new assignment, I would like to talk to you about Mom. The night before Gavin's Wedding, while I realized you had way too much to drink, you spoke of speaking to Mom. Do you speak with her?"

Ian replied, "Aye. I do. As a matter of fact, I spoke with her today. I should clarify. It is difficult to speak directly with her. Agatha can make it much easier."

Francis then said, "At first, I wasn't going to say anything because I thought you would think I'd gone crazy, but during the amputation, I could swear that Mom was right next to me holding my hand and telling me that everything was going to be alright. I thought it was all the wine you had given me, but then I thought back to our conversation on the eve of Gavin's Wedding."

Ian said, "After all that I have been through the last few years, I would never tell anyone that they are crazy."

The subject then moved to his new assignment as the Messenger. Ian told him that after he sails back to Scotland, he will be introduced to several high-ranking members of society who are also members of a Secret Organization. You have to always remember to never speak of this mission or this place with anyone. You will only be communicating via secret codes and messages. Just remember, if anyone wants to speak with you on this matter, you are to say, "I have no idea what you are talking about." You will have a high-ranking job with either the Clan Sinclair or a Royal family. From the very beginning, you should create a succession plan where you will have a successor that you will somehow pass the knowledge to in the event of your demise. This location must remain secret until the right people come along.

Francis then asked, "How will I know who the right people are?"

Ian said, "Well, you now know what the treasure is and what the secret is. The right people will start a nation here in the

New World. They will be righteous and capable of starting a new country. My guess is that it will not happen in your lifetime. The Secret will be passed on for maybe two or three hundred years from now. As of right now, very few people even know of the New World. It will take time for people to settle here and leaders to step forward. Your successors will have to present the secret to the right people."

Francis asked, "What about the treasure?"

Ian said, "The Silver and Gold will probably be used to finance a new nation. The artifacts will represent power. Just the rumor of them will give a government power." Ian continued, "That is enough for one day. Angus has rigged a chair where you can sit with us and have your leg elevated at the same time. Please get yourself ready. If you need any help getting dressed, just let me know. Angus and I will come and get you when Sir James is almost here."

CHAPTER 69

SIR JAMES GLOUCHESTER

A S THE AFTERNOON wore on, several of the cooks were preparing the meal. The Earl wanted all of the men to share in the bounty that he was about to enjoy. Abigail led all of the cooks on the seven ships. The venison was being prepared over a fire pit onshore. A second fire pit would be used for the Striped Bass. The fish didn't take nearly as long to cook so it would wait until the last minute for grilling. The meal would also include roasted potatoes and of course wine from the Earl's personal collection. The smells from the roasting venison began to waft through the entire island. The table in the Earl's stateroom had been set for the occasion. The whole scene brought back fond memories of celebrations at Rosslyn Castle.

As the sun began its downward motion that afternoon, the Earl received word that Sir James has boarded the lifeboat and is on his way. This put many things in motion. The Earl was handling this the same way that an event at the castle would have been handled. Angus and Ian very carefully moved Francis into the stateroom. It caused him great pain. They gave him his own pitcher of the strong mead that the had acquired in Greenland. Ian told Francis to just listen this evening. He had much to learn.

Shortly thereafter, the Earl and Malcolm welcomed Sir James ashore. The three men strode through the island with Sir James detailing its history and what it has meant to the Mi'kmaqs. He said, "The Mi'kmaqs have legends that go back thousands of years. As the story goes, Phoenicians had landed on this very spot. There was infighting amongst their leaders. The argument was over whether or not they should further explore the southern coastline of this new land. They had already filled their hulls with copper ore. Their mission was to secure copper, not to explore. This led to the bloodshed that resulted in ten Phoenicians being killed. The side that wished to go home with copper ore prevailed. The bodies of the fallen were buried on this island. The ships then departed for the Mediterranean Sea and their homeland. A party of thirty opted to stay and guard the gravesites. They grew into the Mi'kmaq Nation."

The party boarded the Earl's flagship where Angus and Ian welcomed them. The Earl gave Sir James a tour of the vessel. Sir James stated, "This ship is Viking in nature. I always found them to be best shipbuilders in all of Europe."

The Earl agreed, "Their craftsmanship usually involves carving large trees into hulls rather than using hewn boards. They prove to be much more seaworthy." He went on to say, "We are in the process of building a small repair yard where we can get the ships out of the water and clean their hulls. High seas are no match for the damage caused by the growths that can permeate the wood hulls."

Everyone finally adjourned to the stateroom where Francis patiently waited. Before they arrived he was able to get himself to the private head that was in the stateroom. This was a major victory for Francis. He motioned to Ian to refill his pitcher of mead. Unbeknownst to him, Ian substituted the weaker mead this time. Everyone was seated. The only one who hadn't met Sir James yet was Francis.

The Earl made the introduction and told the story of the battle which cost Francis his leg. Sir James complimented Francis for his courage and said, "That battle is not why you will be remembered. What you do from this point forward will be your heritage." Francis thanked him for the kind words and promised that he will lead a righteous and worthwhile life.

It was then that Ian asked Sir James to tell his story and how he achieved the status of knighthood. The Earl decided earlier in the day that Ian would be the one to ask this question. He didn't want it coming from Malcolm, who already knew the answers.

Sir James responded, "I earned my status the old fashioned way, I was born with it." Everyone laughed. He continued, "It seems that I am a direct descendant of Alfred the Great. For those of you that don't know of Alfred, I will give you a brief refresher. Alfred became the King of Wessex at the age of 23. His brothers had been Kings before him. The reigns of his brothers were all very non-consequential. Alfred was the one King that was able to unite the neighboring Kingdoms of Wessex, Mercia, Essex, Surrey, Northumbria, East Anglia, Kent, and Sussex. One of the things that he was known for is that he promoted having the offspring of his own noble families marry offspring from noble families of other Kingdoms. He was married to a woman named Ealhswith who was the daughter of a Mercian Nobleman. He felt that this would help form a very strong bond that would eventually unify the Kingdoms. The Kingdoms were already bonded when it came to defending their collective lands from constant attacks by the Vikings. They fought many battles against the invaders. They lost many at first, but Alfred always learned from his losses. Many times he was actually on the battlefield himself. He could see what tactics worked and what didn't. He eventually began to have successes against the Vikings. One tactic that goes unheralded is that he introduced Christianity to the Vikings. For the Vikings, their culture was based upon conquering and stealing treasures from others. They believed that their gods instructed them to do so. Once some were converted to Christianity the situation became more civilized. Alfred eventually struck a deal with the Vikings that would give them land in exchange for peace. The land that he gave up was inconsequential for his purposes."

Sir James continued, "The thing that catches my attention most regarding Alfred was his efforts to promote education. Alfred once said, "We have an abundance of Religious Canon written in Latin in our possession, but sadly there is no one that can translate it." Education was his passion. He pronounced that every young man who is not currently employed must attend school so that they can at least read and write in English. If one wishes to be a Man of God he will provide those classes in Latin. He established a full-time academy for the children of Noble Families where they would learn religion, art, and philosophy. This also included the children of nobles from other Kingdoms. These children went on to inter-marry and carry the important tradition of education forward. Over time this would help to unify the Kingdoms into one Kingdom. Many of the other Kingdoms had been weakened by the constant barrage from the Vikings. They eventually pledged their loyalties to Alfred and the Anglo-Saxon Nation was born. This nation went forward to be known as England. Alfred's Lineage was known as the House of Wessex. His Successors at the House of Wessex ruled for several hundred years. The reigns of England have changed hands several times. The House of Denmark and the House of Normandy have taken the throne at various times. Since I began to explore the New World, I have divorced myself from these allegiances, but I still proudly consider myself a descendant of Alfred the Great and a Member of the House of Wessex."

Sir James said, "I have some basic knowledge of the Clan Sinclair, but could you please inform me of your clan."

The Earl stated, "My ancestors were from the Normandy region of France. The original name was Sainte Claire because that was the village that they were from. The family lore states that we were from a long line of Merovingian Nobles who were supposedly descendants of Mary of Magdalene. Supposedly she traveled the Mediterranean after the death of Jesus Christ. The story tells how she spent her remaining days in France. Her offspring were instantly given nobility status and the rest is history. Unfortunately, there is no written proof of any of this. The question that always comes up is, "Who was the father of the offspring." As you can imagine this concept has caused an uproar in Rome. The Popes have labeled Mary of Magdalene as a prostitute. Even though there is no mention of this in any of the Gospels. The Pope figured that this would taint any story of offspring. I believe that someone knows the answer. Anyways, my family migrated to Scotland and assisted William the Conqueror in the battle to free Scotland from the British grips. My family was aligned with the Bruce's when they were in power. Now that the power has transferred to the House of Stewart we are sadly figuring out our place in the fragile Kingdom."

The dinner was served and enjoyed. The Cooks had outdone themselves. The group was served pie as a dessert that was made from blueberries found on the island. This, of course, was served with wine and mead depending on what everyone preferred. After the dessert was cleared, it was time for the big moment of the evening.

Ian interjected. He said, "Yesterday, when we met with the Chief and his mother, they mentioned a legend where the mother, Megis, believes that we are the ones sent by the Almighty to carry out his task. Could you please explain this legend?"

Sir James said, "Yes. This statement that was made by Megis caused a stir throughout the Mi'kmaq community. That particular legend is what caused me to stay here many years ago. It is very similar to a Phoenician legend. It basically states that God has sent angels down with a set of rules. If mankind follows the rules, the great secrets of the universe will be revealed. If mankind does not follow the rules then a great catastrophe will befall on them. The rules are contained within a message that will be protected by a chosen few. These chosen ones will live and die a normal life but will be reborn again to perpetuate the mission." He pause and sipped his wine and then continued, "Megis thinks that the chosen ones are within your party."

There was silence for a moment. Then the Earl then looked at Sir James with a stern face and said, "We have not told you the real purpose of our mission here in the New World. Not to be too dramatic, we are on a mission to save mankind. But first I need you to swear an oath to keep what I am about to tell you in confidence. You will be allowed to research the subject all you want, but it must be kept confidential."

Sir James responded, "I cannot do that if it goes against the British Throne."

The Earl responded, "This is a worldwide secret that will not affect any nation or Clans per se." He paused then said, "I cannot predict what will happen hundreds of years into the future, but for our lifetimes the British Monarchy will not be affected."

Sir James then said, "You have my pledge of secrecy and hopefully I can be a productive addition to the endeavor." Sir James went on to say, "Malcolm, I should have known you were up to something." Everyone laughed. They decided to take a break for a moment. They adjourned for ten minutes to refresh themselves.

They all returned several minutes later. Sir James said, "Malcolm, you old sage, what is this big secret that you are teasing with?"

Malcolm finally laid it all out for him. He said, "No doubt in your studies of Ancient Societies you have heard of the term Watchers."

Sir James said, "Of course. Nearly every society has ancient stories leading back to the Watchers."

Malcolm continued, "Well our story starts with the Knights Templar and their exploration under the First Temple of Solomon. It seems that they had discovered a symbol that they called the Secret Seal of Solomon. It is not to be confused with the Star of David which is usually attached to the early Hebrews. There were ancient cuneiform writings that spoke of a secret that has been around since the dawn of Humanity. Anyways, the Templars made many discoveries under the Temple in their ten year search. It seems that underneath the Holy of Holies, which was acclaimed in the Old Testament to have housed the Ark of the Covenant, a chamber was discovered. After a careful search was performed a stone carving was unearthed in this chamber that had a message for Humanity." Malcolm then unrolled a scroll in which the following message was written:

We are the Watchers. We have been here since the dawn of Humanity. We came at the direction of the Almighty Creator. We have instructed many generations of Humankind of the Creators will. None have followed our direction. We have the ability to create Earthquakes, Great Storms, and Great Floods. We have punished the unworthy with death and Destruction. We will continue our quest until Humankind abides by the Creator's will. The Creator's will was already handed down to the one you call Moses. Somehow several key aspects were neglected to be recorded. The Creator also will send his Son to deliver the message. Humanity has made strides but still falls short of the Creator's expectations. The Creator's wishes are the following:

All Humankind is created equal and will be treated equally

All Wars will Cease. Humankind will not kill his brothers and Sisters.

All Humankind will follow the laws handed to Moses.

Humankind can only honor the Creator by following his rules.

Humankind will share its resources equally.

The Great land to the West will be the home of the righteous and the foundation of the Creator's Promises. This will be the Land of Plenty.

The Seal of Solomon is the keeper of the secret of Eden. The Seal stares at the Secret of Eden as the Great Lion in the Land of the Great River stares at the Great Falcon as he is going to rest on the longest day.

When Humankind has successfully mastered the Creator's will, only then will the Secret of Eden be revealed.

Everyone remained silent which gave Sir James several minutes to digest the message.

Sir James then said, "This is extraordinary. We must find the secret. This could be the culmination of all of mankind's discoveries." The room fell silent.

After a long pause Sir James said, "Malcolm, have you found the Secret of Eden?"

Malcolm responded, "I didn't find it, but I know where it is."

Sir James asked, "Well, where is it?"

Malcolm said, "I believe you tripped over on your way to relieve yourself a few minutes ago." Everyone laughed.

At the moment Angus and Ian went outside the stateroom and picked up the secret box. They set it down in front of Sir James. He stared at it with wonderment.

Sir James finally said, "I don't see an opening, how does it open and what is this metal that was used to construct it? Also, I'm sure that this keyhole has significance."

Malcolm said, "We don't know on all accounts. You now know as much as we do about the Secret of Eden." Malcolm further pointed out that the team has the actual carved stone which contained the message.

The Earl went on to say that his family has been the custodian of the secret since the Templars were arrested and brutally murdered by the French King in 1307. The Earl continued, "The question for me and my family, is what do we do with it? We felt that it was no longer safe in Scotland so we decided to bring it to the New World. As you can see, it speaks of a land to the west which it calls the Land of Plenty. We believe that the New World is indeed this land. Our intention is to hide it here and only inform the ones that we deem worthy of its location. This place where we sit has been mentioned in various scrolls as a special place. What are your thoughts?"

Sir James paused and said, "We must hide it quickly. The Viking remnants still sail these waters."

Malcolm said, "Yes that is our intention." He paused briefly and said, "There is one other matter. I will let Agatha explain this to you."

Sir James said, "There is more?" Everyone laughed.

Agatha then spoke. She said, "In the time of Noah, after the waters had receded, the Watchers spoke to several of Noah's grandchildren. They were chosen to be the future Guardians of the Secret of Eden. They will live normal lives, die, and then be reborn whenever the treasure is in jeopardy. They are to be known as the Children of the Flood. Megis was correct. They are with this expedition. Actually, two of them are sitting with you right now." Agatha paused briefly then continued, "Ian was Noah's grandson Peleg. His late wife and soulmate, Clara, was known as Tytea. Angus was another grandson. His name was Joktan. I myself was Na'amah. The wife of Noah. I am with them in each lifetime to serve as their guide."

Sir James sat in stunned silence. He finally spoke, He said, "This is extraordinary. When I first landed here, I had dreams that told me that this land was special. The person in my dream said that something spectacular would take place here someday. So I decided to stay."

The Earl summarized the night by saying, "Sir James, we gave you much to think about this evening. I suggest that we all sleep on what we've learned this evening. It is late, you are welcome to stay aboard my ship this evening. I will have several of my guards' escort you back to the mainland in the morning."

Then Malcolm said, "I plan on taking in some air topside if anyone would like to join me."

Sir James said, "Yes. I could use some fresh air myself."

No one noticed Francis. He had a smile on his face. He now understood the truth about his parents. His mother had only died in the flesh. His feelings that she was somehow with him were true. This gave him great comfort.

CHAPTER 70

THE MORNING AFTER

THE NEXT MORNING Ian woke up later than usual. Last night was not only a late night, but a stressful one as well. They had taken a relative stranger into their trust. Ian sat in silence as he enjoyed his morning tea. He was just taking in the pure beauty of this pristine setting.

Ian's silence was broken as he noticed Francis working his way up the ladder. The fact that he has progressed so far was truly a miracle. He was taking this on with great courage. Ian wanted to help him but he knew that was the last thing Francis wanted. However, Ian did offer to get him tea and something to eat which Francis graciously accepted. They made small talk for several minutes about last evening's festivities. Soon thereafter, Malcolm joined them.

Francis stated, "If I am to be one of the keepers of the secret, I feel that I must learn its complete histories along with the history of the Knights Templar. What I currently know of the Knights sounds like something from a Fairy Tale rather than a group of warriors that they probably were."

Malcolm replied, "Sir James and I could give you a great start. When you return to Scotland, we can direct you on where to turn for further studies. I agree you should know this subject from front to back. Do you have an interest in history?"

Francis said, "Aye. However, most of my knowledge is confined to Scotland and the Clans and of course the teachings of the church."

Malcolm replied, "What you may find out is that what you have been taught in both your schooling and your religious training is that certain norms were to be followed. As you go through your future education you will find that many of these norms were created to control people's behavior rather than supply them with the truth. The church is very uncomfortable with science and anything that is counter to their message. A great example is Agatha. She is a devout Christian, but has certain skills that even the top scholars in Rome can't explain. When they can't explain something they just consider it to be heresy which can result in jailing or worse. She has had to keep her skills to herself and a few others in which I am fortunate to be one of. I am very happy that she is here with me. I feared for her safety back in Rosslyn. That small-minded priest would probably insist that she is arrested at some point. With the Earl being gone, I see the church overstepping its bounds and declaring Agatha a criminal. I knew that if she came on this mission, she could be her natural self which would be an asset to the overall mission."

Malcolm paused for a minute and then continued, "There are great men of science that have kept their discoveries under wraps. They don't want to be labeled as a heretic. At a minimum, the heresy charge will inhibit their ability to travel and work freely. They do record their findings to parchment where someday they will be accepted and heralded. This impediment has led to the creation of many secret societies. Human nature drives men to explore and to question everything. In today's era, advances in knowledge are usually confined to the secret libraries and vaults that contain untold discoveries. I wonder how this Secret of Eden would be received by the powers in Rome. My guess is they may try to destroy it. It would threaten their power like nothing else that has come along. They at first would try to destroy it, but they would soon discover that it cannot be destroyed. They would probably hide it where it would never be found. We are also hiding it, but you will be the guide for those who are deemed worthy."

Frances asked, "How will I know who is worthy and who is not?"

Malcolm responded, "That will be up to the Earl and most likely his successors. We should include the Earl in this discussion. We will ask him that very question."

After a few minutes, Francis decided to go below deck to have Agatha look at his wound and then get cleaned up for the day. Everyone had the urge to help Francis, but knew better. It took him a few minutes to navigate the ladder. His upper body would have to gain strength because he would often have to lift his entire body weight. After Francis painstaking accomplished descending the ladder, the Earl made his way up to join us. Ian volunteered to go get a pot of tea. Everyone seemed like they needed a little extra this morning. Last night had been an enlightening evening, but tiring at the same time. When Ian returned, Angus had joined the group.

The Earl said, "Today, we must begin to plan not only the treasure's hiding spot, but also since many of us will be here for a year or more we must plan our housing."

Ian interjected, "I believe the Mi'kmaq will not want us to stay on this island for long. It is sacred to them and their traditions."

The Earl said, "I would like to speak with the Mi'kmaq Chief about using the natural harbor as a dry dock for ship storage and repair. One usually has to look far and wide for a harbor that changes so perfectly from low to high tide."

Malcolm said, "I briefly spoke with Sir James on this topic. He detailed how great storms can pass through during late summer which are strong enough to change the shape of the island. He understands the urge to use this as a repair yard, but cautions against using it as a long term solution. He even stated that the Mi'kmaq will see a storm coming as a sign that their gods are angry at us for desecrating their sacred grounds."

The Earl then said, "I will task Captain McQuinn with looking for more protected areas. Ideally, he can find an area with a deep water entrance that has a similar look at low tide. For now, let's use our present location for our repair purposes."

The Earl went on to say, "Sir James and I agree that we have an urgent need to hide our artifacts. I decided to tell him that I also wish to hide the treasures that my family has collected over the last three or four hundred years. I told him that I no longer trust the Royals in Scotland. I am placing it here for safekeeping. I did not go into detail about what the treasure consists of but what I told him is the truth, at least a version of it. Make sure that all containers are secured and locked before we begin transporting it. We agreed to meet after our lunch meal today. We will meet at the clearing near the mouth of the Gold River again. I would like all of you to be present for this meeting. Malcolm, I would like to have Agatha there as well."

Ian commented, "I would like to have Francis attend. I will navigate one of the lifeboats from here around the end of the island and on to the meeting place."

The Earl replied, "Very well."

CHAPTER 71

THE SIGHTING

F RANCIS FINISHED HIS midday meal, and it was time to make the journey to the meeting site. Since he was not ready to walk across the island just yet, he was helped into a lifeboat which would travel around the north end of the island and on to the meeting. Several warriors did all of the rowing. Francis said to his father, "It is nice to be off of the ship even though it is only for a short while."

Ian replied, "Soon, you will be able to leave anytime you wish." By the time the lifeboat made it to the Gold River, everyone had already arrived.

Francis said, "I must be able to walk across the island like everyone else. The path we took caused us to waste time."

Ian said, "In due time, Francis. Your recovery has been nothing short of miraculous." They exited the lifeboat and joined the others. Malcolm had been thoughtful enough to bring extra chairs for Francis and Agatha. Francis thanked him for the kind act.

The Earl started by stating, "Thank you to everyone for making last evening's festivities a success, but also for attending our meeting this afternoon. The first item that I would like to discuss is the place known as the Holy Well. Sir James, what is your knowledge of this place? Is it real? How far? Does it offer seclusion?"

Sir James paused and collected his thoughts before he said, "I have been there several times. The well is not a well that was dug in the traditional sense. It is a holding area for a nearby natural spring. The Mi'kmaq think it is special because the spring water makes for excellent drinking water. The oddity for me is that a stone structure was constructed around this well. The Mi'kmaq say that it was not them. It could have been another tribe or other visitors from Europe. I have been looking for other signs of European exploration, but I have found nothing. I think that if the Vikings had ventured inland that far the Mi'kmaq would have known about it."

Sir James paused and continued, "I cannot be sure if anyone has gone to the Holy Well from a different direction. Please remember that this land is a peninsula. There is water on most of the other side of this Peninsula. I have repeatedly asked the Mi'kmaq Chief if anything in their history describes visitors coming from inland. He said no. He even went as far as asking his fellow Chiefs around the region if they have had any visitors. The answer was just the Vikings. In general, the Vikings never had an interest in this place because there was no gold and silver to plunder. They have shown a mild interest in the Gold River but soon found out that the river's naming was not appropriate. So this supposed Holy Well remains a mystery. The place is, however, ideal for building a small fortress. It is elevated and has a beautiful view over a nearby lake. It is surrounded by dense woods. The Mi'kmaq have cleared a trail that begins north of here that allows access to the Holy Well."

The Earl asked, "Can the river be navigated by a small vessel or barge?"

Sir James said, "No. The river contains many rapids and

several waterfalls. The fact that it is difficult to get to makes it even more attractive. The water flows down from the natural springs in the Holy Well area. Other than the mystery stone well construction, I think that this would be an ideal spot not only to hide something but to build a small homestead that could serve as a guardian's perch. It is a two-day journey from here. I advise you to travel there to see it for yourself." Everyone agreed that the Earl would have to select a party to go to the Holy Well and then make a concerted decision.

Just as the meeting was concluding, the Mi'kmaq Chief and several of his warriors burst from the trees. They spoke in their language to Sir James. He seemed troubled by what he was hearing.

Finally, Sir James said, "The Chief has informed me that while several of the Mi'kmaq were hunting a day's hike north of here, they saw two ships with black sails heading this way. They knew that in previous times this meant trouble for the Mi'kmaq. The hunters were confident that these ships were not part of the group that Goosecap had introduced to their Chief and Elders. They decided that they would have to get the message back to the Village as quickly as possible. So they began running."

Just then, two ships with black sails rounded the point and were heading into the bay.

The Earl said, "Fortunately, the current and wind are working against them. So we will have time to deploy our ships." The Earl always carried a horn with him that was fashioned from a Bull oxen's horns. When used properly, the sound would carry for a great distance. One horn blast meant the Earl would like to deliver a message – pull along the port side. Two blasts meant rough seas ahead – lower your sails. Three blows – meant prepare for battle – attack imminent. The Earl blew the horn three times, then waited thirty seconds, then three blasts again, then another thirty seconds and another round of three blows. The Earl then ordered everyone into the lifeboats. He felt that they were all safer near our ships and weapons. He asked Sir James,

"Would you like to join us?"

Sir James said, "No. My place is here with Mi'kmaq. This is our home that we are protecting." Everyone loaded into the lifeboats and began making their way back to the island.

Angus and Ian both told Francis that they would help him cross the island. Angus said, "There is much more time in the future for you to show your determination. Today we must hurry back to the ships." Francis seemed to understand.

CHAPTER 72

THE CHASE

APTAIN MCQUINN HAD heard the horn. By the time the Earl's landing party reached the island, four of the Earl's Ships set their sails and were underway. The Earl's ships had a clear advantage. Both the wind and the currents were at their back. Soon enough, the black sails spotted the white sails with the red crosses and turned in the opposite direction. Captain McQuinn was closing the gap quickly.

After the battle that had taken place at L'Anse aux Meadows, the Earl had a meeting with Captain McQuinn in which he issued the orders that if he came into conflict with any adversaries that, he was to sink the ships. He didn't want to give anyone the option of returning to L'Anse aux Meadows or Greenland for reinforcements. That meant he was allowed to take prisoners and leave the dying. Once in the water, it would be very difficult for anyone to survive the frigid waters of the North Atlantic.

Captain McQuinn was in the lead vessel. He instructed his Lieutenants to have the longbows ready for action. They would arm the arrows with flame. This would be devastating for the enemy. In most cases, the enemy's efforts would turn to fire suppression instead of the battle that was about to overwhelm them. The Captain and the Earl had been in many battles together over the years. The Captain was a Scottish Highlander. Even though he came from one of the smaller and weaker clans, he was still a Highlander. This meant that he was always prepared for a fight. He learned to sail as a young boy. He knew that he wanted to live his life on the seas. That's where he felt most at home. He knew that sea battles were the future. As exploration expanded west, he knew there would always be a need for a warrior who knew how to command a ship.

The Captain's allegiance was always to the Earl. As a young man, he met the Earl on one of the campaigns against the English. They were reunited during the battles for the Orkney Islands. The Earl and King Haakon had a castle built in the Orkneys that became known as the Kirkway castle. This was more of a fortress than a castle. It was right at the edge of the sea and had four very tall towers so that lookouts could see what seemed like all the way to Norway.

The Earl stationed the Captain at Kirkway and was given the title of Protector of the Orkneys. This was a prestigious title during times of conflict. There were numerous Norse Warlords that wanted to live by the old Viking ways. Captain McQuinn was constantly sending ships to cut off the Norse Ships. He always had the advantage. From the Towers, Captain McQuinn could almost see the entire set of Orkney Islands. His patrols regularly visited the parts that he couldn't see. There were several major battles that drew the attention of the Earl. The Earl would often lead the forces into these battles. Some Captains would be upset by their Senior Commanders taking all of the glory, but not Captain McQuinn. He knew the Earl would always give his Officers credits for victories. He learned much from the Earl. It seemed that the Earl was a natural-born War Commander.

Over the last five years, the battles were all but gone. The

Norse Warlords had either been killed or had moved on to another part of the world. This thought always gave the Earl trepidations as he ventured to the west. He now knows that many of them ended up in Vinland at L'Anse aux Meadows. The Earl explained to Ian and Angus, "Those Vikings that we just defeated at L'Anse aux Meadows will come after us. Their honor has been tarnished. Oleg's people were simply living the life of Vikings as the gods expected them to. I have taken away Oleg's chance to go to Valhalla and drink at the table with the past fallen warriors." The Earl continued, "There is something different about Oleg. He could have asked for reinforcements at L'Anse aux Meadows, but it doesn't appear that he has. Oleg's mission is not about plunder. It is about vengeance and honor."

✠

The Earl's ships closed very quickly on the slower black sails. As they came into range, Captain McQuinn gave the order to launch the long arrows. He knew that the Vikings didn't have anything with the range of the long arrows. The Scots under the command of Henry Sinclair may not have invented the long arrow, but they certainly perfected its range and accuracy. No one could beat them while on the seas.

The arrows hit their marks. Soon both ships were set ablaze, and the crew was fleeing into the frigid North Atlantic water. Captain McQuinn launched his lifeboats and pulled the surviving Vikings to safety.

✠

Back at the island, Angus and Ian made sure that Francis was safe. There were makeshift chairs at the beach near the Earl's flagship. They left Francis, Malcolm, and Agatha there and went to check in with the Earl. They climbed aboard the Earl's flagship and found him looking off into the distance with a scope.

He was staring at the two flumes of smoke to the north.

Ian said, "I would wager that Captain McQuinn made short work of the two enemy vessels."

✠

Angus and Ian patiently waited for any sight of the White Sails with the Red Cross. They knew that the return trip would take longer because of the wind direction and current. Finally, after about an hour, all four ships rounded the point. They all cheered. Everyone expressed relief except the Earl. His instincts were never wrong. The Earl waited for the ships to get close enough to send a boarding party. Captain McQuinn signaled the Earl that he had eight prisoners. All four of the ships began setting their anchors. The Earl, Angus, and Ian manned a lifeboat and headed to the Captain's Ship. Upon arrival, they climbed up the ladder and were greeted by the Captain.

The Captain said, "We have eight Prisoners. All of the others aboard the ships perished. However, that scoundrel Oleg was nowhere to be found. I have not spoken to the prisoners yet. I waited for you to be present. I suggest that we separate them before questioning and see if their stories match."

The Captain continued, "There is no reason to celebrate. I fear that Oleg had already gone ashore." This caused alarm for everyone present. They all knew that Oleg would have the element of surprise in his favor if he had gone ashore. In addition, he would have many places to hide.

Aboard the ships, the prisoners were given blankets to warm themselves. Captain McQuinn knew that they would force these prisoners to talk. The Earl said to the Captain, "Let's let the prisoners get warm. Also, feed them and give them water to drink. After that, we shall interrogate them."

CHAPTER 73

THE PRISONERS

THE EARL SAID, "The prisoners are dried off and their bellies are full. It is time for them to talk."

Angus said, "At least we are reducing Oleg's numbers."

The Earl agreed but said, "This just hastens the need to hide the treasure. If this attack was about conquest, Oleg would have come with more ships and men. They could have put up a much better battle. This fight that we had today was a mere charade to hide his real intentions. His fight is more personal than anything else. He knows that he has no chance to defeat us with just two ships. This was just a scheme to get our forces out to sea. The thing that protects us is the fact that we are on this island. We have longbows positioned on all sides of the island. I believe that his strategy is to go very unconventional. If I had to venture a guess, I would say that he wasn't even aboard either of those ships. He is on land with only the Lord knows how many forces. We must meet with the Mi'kmaqs. They are probably angry that we have brought this battle to their shores."

Meanwhile, onshore, Ian rejoined his son. He heard Francis ask Agatha, "Does your vision tell you how this battle will end?"

She said, "I don't get direct answers on future matters. I get overall feelings. I sense that we will have success, but there will be costs. I cannot tell what the cost will be, but I sense suffering. The reason I don't have clarity is that these men must still fight this battle. These warriors have freewill that can be unpredictable. The fights can go either way, but I do feel comfortable that we have proven warriors on our side. They have faced many battles and have learned from each one. There is nothing more powerful than an experienced warrior. Many times they understand that the best option is to stand down and live to fight another day. This is not one of those days. We have something in our possession that can alter the History of Mankind."

Francis asked, "I still don't understand who this secret came from?"

Agatha said, "It came from the creator by the hands of the ones who Enoch called the Watchers."

Malcolm joined the conversation, "Francis, societies all over the world have one thing in common. They all speak of beings that oversee us. In the early days, some believe that these Watchers even interacted with the humans. The story goes that the Creator was very dismayed over this and struck them down. The Sumerians, Akkadians, Assyrians, and Babylonians all have stories about the ones that they call the Annunaki. The Chinese culture believes they are descendants of the Huaxia tribe of the Yellow Emperor. Many believe that the Yellow Emperor was Annunaki. The Bible speaks of the Sons of Anuk in the Noah story. Some equate the Annunaki with the story of the fallen angels in the Bible. The Egyptians have built numerous structures that are to honor the gods who some believe were the Annunaki. Some believe that the Annunaki helped them build these structures on the banks of the Nile. When you first lay your eyes on these great structures in Giza, you soon realize that man was not capable of this architectural feat. You immediately wonder, "Who helped them?""

Malcolm went on to say, "Many equate the Greek gods with the Annunaki. There are many parallels. My thoughts are that the Watchers are the ones who had not fallen. The Annunaki were the fallen who had not followed the Creator's wishes. The most important thing for you Francis, is that you make the most of your time here with Sir James and myself. Once you leave, you will probably not be returning. We will teach you all that we can, but your education must be completed in the learning centers of London, Paris, and Rome."

Back on the ship holding the prisoners the Earl prepared for the questioning. Each man was brought topside one at a time and questioned. The Earl gave each of them the same opportunity. He stated, "This is your fortunate day. You will be given a choice. Tell all that you know of Oleg and live or remain quiet and die. Should you choose to become helpful you will be treated humanely and possibly will become part of our workforce."

All of them chose to live. It seems that they were simply mercenaries. They were living day to day and Oleg presented a means to fill their bellies and have shelter. They all said that Oleg and eight of his longtime associates had gone ashore a day's sail to the north. They all said that Oleg seemed obsessed with someone named Sinclair. They described how they pulled up to the point at night several days ago and could see the Earl's ships. It was a full moon and they could clearly see the encampment. Oleg ordered them north where he and the eight men embarked on their landward journey. They were not privy to Oleg's plans, but they believed that he was planning a sneak attack. The object was not only to kill Sinclair, but those close to him.

CHAPTER 74

SECURITY

AN STOOD ON the shore of the mainland with Clara. The clouds were black as the impending storm gathered its strength. Clara had a look of despair on her face. Ian looked down the beach and saw a man in traditional Arab dress walking towards him. His instincts told him that this man was Canaan.

As the man drew closer, the image changed. He was now the Egyptian guard who persecuted the Hebrews during the time of the Exodus. Ian looked at Clara. She now took the look of his Hebrew wife in that lifetime.

As he looked forward, the man had drew closer. He was now the Roman who went by the name of Aurelius. Clara took the form of the Celtic Princess named Danu. She had beautiful flowing blond hair. As with each lifetime, she was stunningly beautiful.

Ian looked forward again. The man was now the Muslim Warrior named Abdul. He just smiled at Ian as if he knew something that Ian didn't know.

As he drew closer, he changed into the Pope's henchman, Simon de Montfort. Clara became the Priestess Helena. Dread began to overtake Ian's spirit.

Now the man was only a few feet away. He was now Oleg. He could feel that something was pulling Clara away from him. Ian screamed, "Don't harm her. She is innocent in all of this." Then she was gone.

All of a sudden, Ian could smell the foulest stench that one could imagine. He could feel the breath that was pure evil. He finally looked forward. Satan was just a few inches from his face. Ian could see boils that were oozing puss all over the face. The eyes were bright red and were looking right through Ian's soul.

Satan said, "Join me and I will spare your soulmate."

Just then Agatha was shaking him. She was saying. "Come out of this vision. Clara is fine. I am sure of it."

This Dream was the most realistic Dream that Ian had ever had. He needed to get out of his bed and go on with his day. Nothing good would come from just lying there dwelling on the horrific vision that he just had. Just then, he could smell the lavender flowers. He knew that Clara was safe.

✠

Meanwhile a new day was upon the team. Much had changed since the previous morning. Ian was staring at the shoreline of the mainland. He thought to himself, "Somewhere on this land, Oleg is preparing for his attack."

The Earl had ordered the eight men to be locked up separately. Two prisoners would reside on each of Captain McQuinn's ships. He didn't want them to be able to talk to each other. All of the leaders were ordered back to the Earl's flagship. This included Captain McQuinn and the four Captains of each ship.

Once all of the leaders were on the flagship, the Earl began by saying, "You all have performed admirably. However, Oleg went ashore with eight of his loyal men several days ago. I fully expect them to attack us over the next few days. These attacks will consist of two or three of our men being the victims of a surprise attack. Therefore, we must post men on the ships and the island. During the days we will need to have men onshore to protect our workers. Also, we will soon be conducting a mission that is a two day's hike inland. Our security personnel cannot be everywhere so we must be vigilant. I will speak with the Mi'kmaq. We will need all of us to be on the lookout for Oleg and his men. We will review and update our plan daily. Please instruct the men in your command as to what we are up against. Any questions?" No one spoke up.

The Earl then said, "You are dismissed."

Later that afternoon, the Earl, Angus, Malcolm, Agatha, and Ian made their way to the mainland to meet with Sir James. Upon arrival, Sir James inquired about the attack. The Earl gave him the update and advised Sir James that he believed that Oleg was onshore and is a danger to us all.

The Earl said, "We need the Mi'kmaq to assist us if we are to move the secret to the Holy Well. We can have guards escort us to and from, but I believe that we need more. If the Mi'kmaq could post guards at the trailheads then we will be able to flush Oleg out." He went on to say, "We must move quickly to hide the secret. We must draw Oleg out into the open. This will be difficult. I believe that he is a seasoned warrior. In the meantime, I would like to travel to the Holy Well site so that we can begin to construct a plan."

Sir James asked Malcolm and Agatha to join him as he set out for the Mi'kmaq Village. The Earl sent word back to Captain McQuinn to send ten warriors to escort our team to the Mi'kmaq Village.

The task regarding the Mi'kmaq keeps getting larger by the minute. Sir James's request must play on the idea of the Mi'kmaq survival. He must convince them that the Mi'kmaq have been chosen to be guardians of a message from the Creator.

After the warriors arrived to serve as the escorts. The team walked quietly through the woods. Their thoughts were consumed with the upcoming encounter with the Mi'kmaq Chief. Ian could sense that Oleg was nearby. He thought to himself, "After last night's Dream, anything is possible. There were many forces in play that he could not begin to understand."

Upon arrival, Sir James gave the Chief an update regarding the battle between the ships yesterday. He explained the Earl's request to post guards at the trail heads. The Chief accepted the Earl's request. His warriors would be posted immediately.

✠

Meanwhile, back at the island, Captain McQuinn had summoned all of his Lieutenants. He told them, "Our enemy has gone ashore and an attack is imminent. There are only a total of nine of them so I expect their attacks to be small and targeted. I want guards to be posted every two hundred feet on the island. A large attack of a ship on this island is highly unlikely, but a small attack via a canoe is not. This enemy whether they know it or not is on a suicide mission. Their leader, Oleg, has revenge on his mind. It seems that his father and brothers were killed in one of our skirmishes in the Orkneys. I will pass out these horns. Once again, when on land one blow means attack imminent. When you are on guard or sentry duty you must have the horn with you at all times. If you hear a horn blow, proceed to the sound of the horn and be ready for battle with swords drawn. We will guard this island day and night. Some of you will be asked to go to the mainland with a landing party. Otherwise, you are confined to this island and your ships."

CHAPTER 75

THE TREE OF LIFE

L ATER THAT AFTERNOON, the Earl invited Sir James to join the team for supper. While having their meal, the Earl said to Sir James, "I will not hold you against your will, but I believe that you should reside here on my flagship until this entire matter with Oleg is resolved. The fact that you know what we possess makes you a risk. Oleg would do whatever he needed to do in order to make you talk." Sir James put up an argument, but he knew that the Earl was right. The agreement that they came to was that the Earl would send several warriors with him every morning to travel to his home and also to get an update to the Mi'kmaq Chief.

Sir James and Malcolm decided to make the most of their evenings together. They agreed that they would use this time to work with Francis.

After supper was concluded, the team met for their usual round table discussion. This included Francis. They told him that if he was to be the messenger, he had to know the history of the secret better than anyone.

It was time to develop a strategy regarding the future message that Francis would take back to Scotland. Malcolm said, "This secret that we are about to place into its next resting place would cause a ruckus like the world has never seen before if it became public. Furthermore, there would be certain people that would consider its message a threat."

Sir James said, "Let me guess, you are talking about the Church in Rome."

Malcolm said, "Aye, anything that is perceived as a threat, is declared to be heresy. Their power reaches everywhere. At least in Europe, that is. When this part of the world is discovered and populated, I hope the new explorers have the foresight to allow people to have differing opinions." He paused briefly and said, "The study of alchemy is forbidden in most of Europe because the Church is afraid that it will cause people to stray from their message."

Sir James then said, "Malcolm, do you have any books that show the Kabbalah's Tree of life?"

Malcolm went to his quarters and returned with a leather-bound book that looked ancient. He explained to Francis, "This Book is a study of the Ancient Hebrews. It shows many symbols and artwork from the period pre-dating David and his son Solomon."

Sir James added, "Many ancient mystics communicated by using artwork. Many seemingly benign paintings contained messages. Only a trained eye could ascertain what these messages were trying to convey. In Ancient times, written language was only known by a select few. There were so many languages and dialects that artwork became the preferred method of getting one's point across." Sir James opened to a page that depicted what he called the Tree of Life.

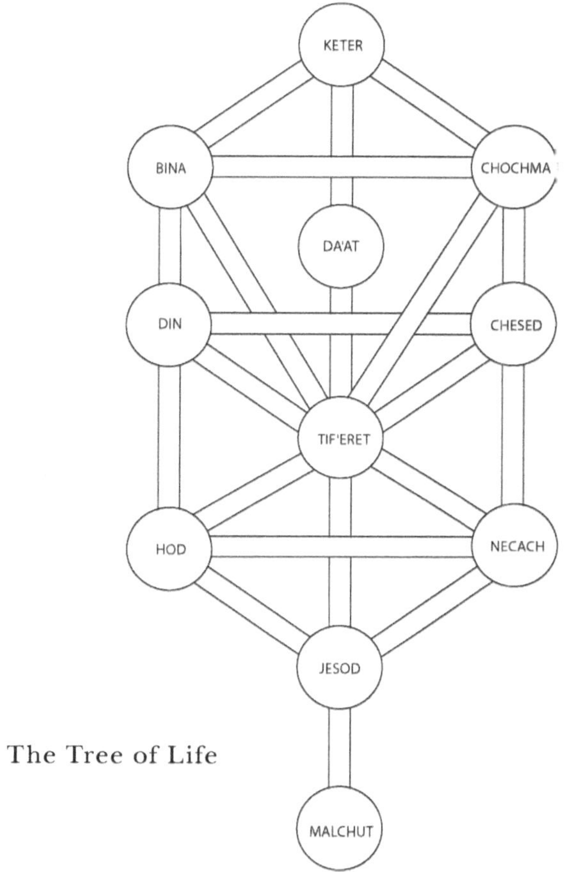

The Tree of Life

CROWN ('KETER'):
the Creator Himself.

WISDOM ('CHOCHMA'):
Divine reality/revelation; the power of
Wisdom.

INFINITE SHARING (Da'at):
all sefirot exist in their perfected state of
infinite sharing.

UNDERSTANDING ('BINA'):
repentance/reason; the power of Love.

MERCY ('CHESED'):
grace/intention to emulate God; the power
of vision.

STRENGTH ('DIN'):
judgment/determination; the power of
Intention.

BEAUTY ('TIFERET'):
symmetry/compassion; the power of
Creativity.

VICTORY ('NECACH'):
contemplation/initiative/persistence; the
power of the Eternal Now.

SPLENDOR ('HOD'):
surrender/sincerity/steadfastness; the power
of Observation.

JESOD ('FOUNDATION'):
remembering/knowing; the power of
Manifesting.

KINGDOM ('MALCHUT'):
physical presence/vision and illusion; the
power of Healing.

Sir James said, "We are showing you the Tree of Life because
it seems to run parallel with the message of the Secret of Eden."
Malcolm further stated, "The Tree of Life is at the foundation

of all civilization. It was first depicted in art by the Assyrians in the 9th Century B.C. It is the summary of man's relationship with the Creator. It is at the foundation of the world's three major religions; Judaism, Christianity, and Islam. Man has always strived to be at one with the Creator. This Tree is a map of how to get there. Many refer to it as mysticism which means oneness with God. Others have given it a more sinister meaning, but you have now been given its true meaning. There are special people such as Agatha that are blessed with the gift of mysticism. These people are born with a higher level of consciousness and understanding than the rest of us. Others can learn how to access it through focused meditation and prayer. Agatha's ability to communicate with the spirit world is an inherent ability that we all have, but are unaware of how to access it."

Malcolm said, "I could talk about the Tree of Life for weeks if you let me, but if you would like to learn more, please ask. After all, you have two leading authorities on this subject and another who lives within this Tree of Life every day (looking at Agatha)." Agatha smiled.

Malcolm continued, "Sir James and I have had numerous discussions on the fact that we need to continue to relay the message about the Secret of Eden through Art and Symbology. Just in the way, the ancient Jewish Leaders in Solomon's time hid the secret behind the Secret Seal of Solomon. We are recommending to the Earl that we do the same. We have chosen the Tree of life because it will always be recognized by Historians and Philosophers everywhere. The Message of the Secret of Eden needs to literally and figuratively be contained within the Tree of Life."

Sir James added, "Francis, it is paramount that you understand not only the Tree of Life but all other historical artwork. The artwork from the past is full of messages. You just have to know how to read them. You will need to convey the message about the secret to the worthy through codes and artwork. This will mean that you will need to commission certain artists to hide your messages within their work. This will not be easy, but we will help you surround yourself with like-minded artisans who spend their lives relaying messages through art. I strongly suggest that you further your education as fast as possible."

Malcolm said, "The structure where we intend to hide the secret will take months to build. However, we should meet daily to further your knowledge and understanding while the structure is being finished. By the time the structure is complete, you will have a much better understanding of the symbolism involved."

Malcolm then looked at Angus and said, "This hiding place must be armed with traps should the unworthy get that far. These traps should be so lethal that everyone who witnesses this fury will abandon their mission."

Ian could not help but feel a strong sense of pride at this point. The future of humanity will rest on the shoulders of his son. But, Ian thought, "What Francis doesn't understand yet is that his mother will be guiding him also. It will seem like intuition to him, but I know it will be guidance from her. It almost seems like fate has chosen my family and me to play an important role in humanity's survival."

Sir James went on, "We are proposing that the structure at the site of the Holy Well is built from stone that is in the shape of the Tree of life. Once the walls are complete and we can work in seclusion, we will build an underground vault underneath one of the Tree of Life symbols. We will have to choose the one that is the most appropriate. The one that jumps out to me is Mercy. The definition of Mercy ("Grace/intention to emulate God") is the closest to the overall message of the secret. Francis, you would then very discretely use the term Mercy in future messages to the worthy. If they are truly worthy, they will understand the message and be led to the hidden secret. You must also include clues that lead them to this island and the Holy Well. As we have said, this should be done through artwork. There is already plenty of clues that will lead people here. After all, hidden messages and stories led us here. The promise of this place being Arcadia is enough to make people come here."

Francis asked, "Arcadia, what is that?"

Sir James replied, "Arcadia is a phrase that came from Ancient Greece. It depicts a utopia similar to the Garden of Eden as depicted in the Book of Genesis. So there is an irony that we are hiding the Secret of Eden in Arcadia."

CHAPTER 76

THE HOLY WELL

THE NEXT MORNING, the team traveling to the Holy Well site woke early so that they could get an early start. Angus and Ian were standing topside finishing their morning meal. Ian had asked Agatha to join them. They had a matter that they wished to discuss with her. A few minutes later, Agatha joined then.

Ian said, "Angus and I have been meaning to speak with you."

Agatha interrupted him by saying, "You wish to tell me that you are now able to read each other's thoughts." They all laughed at the irony of what she had just said. She continued, "I learned that I had this capability when I first met Malcolm. It would make him crazy. Having said that, I limit my outreach, if that is what you call it, to the Children of the Flood. Before she passed on, Clara had learned how to do this. You, Angus, and Clara were all born with this ability. You had to learn how to understand it first. You two probably have had times when you could finish each other's sentences. You probably didn't think much of it at the time, but you were actually communicating on a much higher level. You need to keep practicing this skill. You will both become much stronger when you finally face Oleg."

Angus asked, "Does Oleg have this skill?"

"Not that I am aware of. It usually requires face to face conversations to get in stride with someone's thoughts. Thankfully, I have not spoken with this man yet."

Ian thanked her. Once again, her presence has had a calming effect on these two men.

✠

A few minutes later, the Earl, Angus, Ian, and ten warriors set out on the journey to the Holy Well. The builder Tomas also joined them. He would survey the land and develop a plan to build a small fortress on this land. Tomas had built many churches and cathedrals back in Scotland. This task would be less difficult than most of the structures that he had previously built.

Their first stop would be the Mi'kmaq Village where they would meet their guides. Sir James had described it as a two-day walk. The Earl told the team, "We are going to try to make it in one day. We cannot be certain where Oleg is so I would like to keep moving. We are at our most vulnerable when we rest. My understanding is that the area of the Holy Well has a large clearing. It will be much easier to defend ourselves in a clearing."

A few minutes later, they were joined by two Mi'kmaq guides. They knew the best routes to get there as quickly as possible. Angus and Ian were walking in lockstep with the Earl. They discussed the art of messaging. The Earl said, "My family has discussed building a chapel in Rosslyn to not only honor our family's deceased, but to also honor the Knights Templar. I think our messaging should be hidden there. I will hire artisans from all over Europe to create the artwork. Our message will be cleverly displayed there. Francis must be very thoughtful on how he displays our clues."

The Earl continued, "I'm not sure when we can build this chapel. I must first return to Scotland and assess the political situation with the Stewarts and the French. These are troubling times for Scotland. The Clan system is being tested every day."

Angus said, "I don't understand? The Clan Sinclair is stronger than ever. You are very close to the seat of power in both Scotland and Norway."

The Earl replied, "Aye. That is true for now, but I don't trust the Stewarts. Their motives are focused on the perceived treasure that they think we possess. I want them to believe that the treasure is still in Scotland. I will play a game with them where I give them false hopes periodically. My big concern is after I'm gone. Will my Son have the wherewithal to keep the Clan together? Will he have the perseverance to press forward? Only time will tell. Ian, I am counting on Francis making the proper decisions. Our legacy can only be as strong as my son and Francis make it. I do feel relieved that we have moved this secret and our Blessed Artifacts out of Scotland. Our power will be held in secret codes and hidden artwork."

Ian said, "The message must be in many places. If the cathedral suffers a fire, all will be lost. Francis must be diligent in placing the message with the proper people and only displayed in the proper places."

The group had been moving at a very quick pace for most of the day. As they came closer to the Holy Well, they found themselves very close to the Gold River. The water here was even more refreshing than the water they have been drinking from the Gold River where it entered the Bay. They all were very thirsty.

As they sat and took a break, Ian had the ominous feeling that they were being watched. He surveyed the area, but found nothing. He concluded that it was probably nothing other than his imagination run amok. He found himself being especially nervous ever since the recent Dream. The heat of the day was beginning to finally wane. The warriors had taken a handful of rabbits and squirrels on the way. The group was confident that they would eat rather well this evening. The dried oxen strips would have to wait for another day. The last hour consisted of uphill terrain which was very tiring. Finally, they reached a clearing and the Mi'kmaq informed them that they had arrived. The view was breathtaking. The clearing overlooked a beautiful lake off in the distance. Ian's thoughts went to the fact that some of the party would call this home. There was an abundance of fresh water, game for hunting, and breathtaking scenery. What an appropriate place to hide the Secret of Eden. Ian couldn't imagine that the original Garden of Eden was as beautiful as this.

Upon surveying the grounds, Angus immediately noticed the stone well. He said, "It is definitely man made." On further inspection they confirmed what Sir James had told them, it is not a true well. It was a holding vessel for a natural spring.

Ian said, "This natural spring site will be a perfect place for a homestead. There is an unlimited supply of clean drinking water."

Angus said, "Many times, natural springs are part of cave or tunnel system. The water flow may have been so heavy at one time that it cleared out a tunnel. The water is flowing from the west. In the morning we will try to find its source. We may find a cave as well."

The Earl was trying to figure out how old the man-made stone well structure was. He said, "It is very well constructed. Judging from the growth around it and the disheveled appearance, it may be hundreds of years old."

The Earl wondered out loud, "The Famous Viking Explorer Leif Eriksson may have sent his explorers through here more than three hundred years ago. They may have seen this spot and thought, as we have, that this would be a great place for a homestead. Something caused them to leave. It was unlikely that rough winters would have chased them away. They were Vikings after all. It may have been too desolate for even the Vikings. They usually like to live in a larger community. We may never know. At some point, Malcolm and Agatha will be here. We may find out that this place is the home to spirits just like the island is." Everyone laughed.

They all feasted on the rabbit and squirrel that the Mi'kmaq hunters had provided. The warriors and the Mi'kmaq hunters took turns standing guard around the clearing.

The following morning they woke up to the smell of tea. Ian had brought Agatha's special brew. He said, "I have always felt that a day that doesn't start with tea is not worth starting." The others made fun of him, but were soon standing in line for the tea when it was ready. The view was even more remarkable as the sun was rising over the lake.

Angus said, "Abigail will love this place. She is a farmer by nature. She will prosper here."

Ian said, "I believe that you are going to get your wish. I think the Earl is going to want me to go back with him and Francis after we complete our task. If I had to guess I would say that Malcolm, Agatha, Abigail, and you will probably stay here. I'm sure that he will leave some of his warriors as well."

After a quick breakfast, they began to survey the area. Angus headed west looking for a cave or the sound of flowing water. They searched for several hours and were about ready to call off the search when one of the warriors came running to the Earl. The Earl said, "He thinks he found something. It's actually to the north in a ravine."

Everyone rushed over to the ravine. There was an opening that a person could barely fit into. The Earl ordered the builder Tomas to check it out. Tomas asked one of his aides to go back to the camp and get a lantern.

Ian said, "I hope this isn't a bear's den that our friend Tomas is about to crawl into."

The Earl said, "I have not seen any bear tracks around here. He should go armed with a knife just in case."

The aide returned moments later. Tomas started working his way into the tunnel. He finally came back out of the opening and said, "As I proceeded forward I could hear flowing water. At the top of one of the walls, I could see a gap. I was able to climb up. I couldn't see anything yet so I positioned a lantern. What I was able to see was amazing. There was a large expanse that was thirty to forty feet wide and had several natural tunnels leading from it. One seemed to head in the direction of our camp. Unfortunately, I couldn't proceed any further. There is a large boulder blocking the entrance. The large stone didn't appear to be holding anything up. Given the proper amount of force, the stone could be moved far enough to allow passage."

The Earl asked Tomas, "What tools have you brought with you that are capable of moving this boulder?"

Tomas replied, "We have several pry bars, shovels, and picks. By using the pry bars we should be able to move the stone."

The Earl said, "Let's take a quick water break and then return with the tools. We will have Tomas and several of the warriors enter the cave and attempt to move the boulder. If they are successful we will trade places with the warriors and examine the cavern. We must stand guard outside this cave opening. Oleg could appear at any time."

CHAPTER 77

THE CAVERN

WHILE THEY WERE waiting for Tomas to return with their tools, the Earl, Angus, and Ian were discussing how they would like to use this cave. The Earl said, "Since we are building a small castle here. I would like to have a secret access to the cave from within the castle. The entrance that we are exploring today should be only used as an escape exit. We need to create a way that the large boulder that we are trying to move could pivot to create an opening only from the inside. If the castle came under attack then the inhabitants would have an exit that is out of sight from the would-be attackers."

The Earl continued, "The secret access must be completely hidden from view and would require some knowledge to gain access. Angus, you have no doubt seen the secret access that my grandfather built into Rosslyn castle?"

Angus said, "Aye, I recently performed a repair on the moving wall. Those type of features usually have a locking mechanism that when released, allow the door to swing in one or both directions. The weight of the wall is carried by the shaft and wheel arrangement. The shaft is solid steel and can absorb the weight of the wall and the wheel is easily turned so that access can be allowed. I believe that I have what I need back on one of the ships to achieve this. Fortunately, we brought our drilling tools on this mission. For this entrance in the cave, we should be able to use the boulder that is already in place. Inside the castle, however, we will have to create a false wall that has a secret release that is hidden on a nearby bookshelf or some other inconspicuous place."

The Earl then moved onto the treasure vault. He said, "For the vault, as Malcolm and Sir James have said, we should have several false clues that lead to the demise of the unworthy treasure hunter. If they move a false device, then hidden spears or something similar would spring from a hidden crevice. We will leave the proper symbols for the worthy. Whoever is accessing this treasure has to know the proper symbols to access the vault."

Angus said, "Let's see what we are working with inside the cave and then come up with a plan."

Tomas and his aide appeared with their tools and several extra lanterns. First, they needed to expand the opening. After the work was complete, the builders would return the entrance to the condition that it was in when the team found it. Tomas was the first to enter the cave opening. He continued to move several boulders out of the way. By the time he was done, anyone could almost walk upright into the entrance.

Angus entered and examined the large boulder. He said, "If we can lay the boulder on its side, we should be able to install the pivot wheel that we discussed." For now, the boulder would lay on its side away from the newly created walkway. Tomas entered and placed lanterns at various spots so everyone could see what they were walking into. The cave was magnificent. It had stalactites that possibly had never seen light. There were three natural tunnels leading out of the main cavern. Ian noticed the walls had ancient drawings on them. Someone had been here before.

The drawings looked at least a thousand years old.

Ian said, "Malcolm and Sir James will need to see these."

The Earl said, "Aye. However, they will be unable to tell anyone of their findings. We need to see if there are any other entrances that these ancient cave artists may have used to gain access." They continued to search. They started with the tunnel to their left first. After about a hundred feet it appeared to end. No access was visible. They retraced their steps and went to the tunnel on the right. A similar dead end was found. As they walked into the middle tunnel they could hear water flowing above their heads. There were several spots along the walls where water was coming down the walls.

Angus said, "If we are to use this tunnel we will have to support the ceiling. During the spring season, after a large run-off from a heavy winter, water could break through this ceiling. All would be lost at that point." The Earl nodded in agreement. They continued to walk for seemingly two hundred feet when they noticed the bottom of a man-made structure.

Angus said, "I believe that we are looking at the underside of the well. It is supported by this bedrock wall from underneath. I believe that cave artists may have entered the cave from this direction in ages past." Next to it, there were several small natural caverns.

The Earl asked Angus, "Could this area be fashioned into a vault?"

Angus said, "Aye. We would need to construct some walls from the nearby bedrock but given the proper amount of time, the task could be completed with a movable wall for access, as well as, some traps for the unworthy."

Before they knew it the day was almost gone. It had been a very productive day. They were all exhausted. They had a late supper and then all went to sleep. The guards stood watch and the night was uneventful other than a brief rain.

In the morning they sipped on tea and chewed on dried oxen strips. The Earl reviewed the tasks for the day. He said, "First of all let's get an overall measurement of the clearing. Malcolm was very clear that we needed the castle to be proportionally correct. So let's sketch the clearing and we will design the layout back at the ship. Second, let's survey the area for building materials such as strong trees like oak, and third, we need to find boulders and smaller rocks for the walls. We don't need to move them today, but we need to understand what is readily available when we start the construction."

Ian asked, "How are we going to move the boulders around. Are we going to bring the oxen from the ships here?"

Angus said, "Aye. We will use the oxen. We also will have to construct rolling platforms for the larger boulders. I'm more concerned with the lack of hardwoods, I don't see any of the hardwoods that I am accustomed to back in Scotland. We will have to cut down a few of the trees here to see what we have to work with."

The Earl had the entire group meet after breakfast. He told everyone about the tasks for the day. The plan was to head back to the island tomorrow. He said, "Today, you will all be given tasks that involve gathering information regarding building materials such as wood and stone. Please be specific with what you find."

Everyone split up into groups. Angus and Ian worked together in surveying the clearing. The clearing was 230 feet long and 140 feet wide. The Holy Well was closer to the eastern edge of the clearing. The goal is to have the well to be inside the castle walls. Angus thought it was feasible. The well would most likely be near the main gate. The other concern was that there would be an adequate area for a large garden. The garden would have to have proper exposure to the Sun. The growing season was similar to that of Scotland. Abigail had made sure that she included enough jars for canning. Having enough food to make it through winter was critical to their survival.

The rest of the men returned in groups later that afternoon. The Earl led one of the teams that had found a significant quarry of rocks and boulders down near the lake. Tomas had cut down several trees that consisted of a very hard wood that he called Ash. Angus had never seen these types of trees before. There was also an ample supply of Maple and Birch. They enjoyed our final night there.

Angus commented, "Most importantly, I must learn how to make our own mead."

Ian said, "I'm sure Malcolm has a recipe somewhere in that mountain of scrolls that he brought with him." They both laughed.

Ian said, "I believe that this climate will also be adequate for growing grapes. You can make your own wine." They added several logs to the fire and went off to bed. Tomorrow would surely be another grueling day as they make our way back to the island. At least going this way was mostly downhill.

As the night went on, Ian had a growing feeling of unease. Not only were they being watched , but it was as if Satan himself was scheming against the team. He barely was able to sleep that night. He kept walking from sentry to sentry trying to sight anything that moved or was out of place. This proved very difficult on this particular evening because there was heavy cloud cover. There was no moon to be seen anywhere. For most of the night, he stood still in complete darkness. The sun rising at dawn was indeed a welcome sight.

CHAPTER 78

BUILDING A CASTLE

I T HAD BEEN a month since the construction project began. A group of thirty men had traveled to the Holy Well site with their tools and the oxen. Angus was in charge of the project. Abigail was with him. She was responsible for feeding all of the men. She was counting on some of the men going on hunts.

✠

Meanwhile, back at the island, Ian was having breakfast with Agatha. Ian said, "For some reason, I feel a sense of sadness today."

Agatha said, "I am sensing the same thing." Ian understood that it probably had meaning when both he and Agatha were feeling something.

Later that morning, the Earl, Malcolm, Sir James, and Ian discussed the castle and, more specifically, the vault. Malcolm suggested, "The treasure should be hidden behind a false wall that has a hidden Secret Seal of Solomon on the wall. The entire wall would have a layer of clay paste that would hide the seal."

Malcolm said, "We should have a false symbol on the opposite wall that would confuse any unwanted treasure hunters. I think the Star of David would be appropriate. The message that Francis would carry forward would give a clue that states, "The treasure is in opposition to the Star or something to that effect." He continued, "If the messaging is properly carried out, anyone who first found the island and then followed the clues to the Holy Well and then gained access to the cave underneath and then also understood to look for the secret Seal must certainly be worthy."

One of the warriors interrupted their conversation. He said, "A Mi'kmaq messenger has arrived with a note. The guard handed the Earl the letter that the Mi'kmaq messenger had given him. The Earl read the note. He said that this note was from Angus. It reads, "Our efforts had been going very well until today. Two men set out to hunt and never returned. I sent out a team of four warriors to look for them. Later that day, they returned with the bodies of the two men. Their throats had been slit. The entire group is distraught. A proper Christian Funeral was conducted, and the men were laid to rest in a beautiful spot overlooking the lake. I ordered the men to travel outside the compound in groups of no less than six. Please send some additional warriors for security. I believe that this was the work of Oleg."

They all sat quietly. The Earl finally said, "For this mission to be successful, we must hunt down and kill Oleg."

Sir James said, "I propose that we speak with the Mi'kmaq. They have several very experienced trackers. By tracking their travels, we should be able to locate them eventually."

The Earl agreed and stated, "It is time for us to go on the offensive." In the meantime, the Earl dispatched ten more warriors to the Holy Well site.

CHAPTER 79

AUTUMN

T HIRTY DAYS HAD passed without incident. The reports were that the castle walls were now complete, and the castle's structure was near completion. The builders were racing against time. The leaves on the trees were beginning to change, which meant that winter was not far behind. The plan was to have all ships in dry dock on the island before winter began. A small security force would remain on the island to protect the ships even though it was doubtful that anyone would attack from the frigid sea. The rest would travel inland to hunker down at the newly built castle for the winter. Everyone had a job to do. The builders needed to at least get the roof completed. Hopefully, the fireplaces and chimneys will be functional. The hunters and gatherers would supply enough meat and vegetation for the entire group to survive. Angus figured that they had roughly thirty days until the first snowfall.

One morning, Ian had a bizarre breakfast encounter with Agatha. She seemed troubled. It seemed as though she had been communicating with Clara. However, she would not tell Ian what was shared. Ian said, "How am I supposed to help fix whatever it is if you won't tell me what the problem is."

She said, "Somethings must not be told." This infuriated Ian.

Ian said, "If the encampment is in danger, I must inform the Earl."

She said, "This only involves you." This sent a shiver down Ian's spine.

Ian said, "I have been safely tucked away on the Earl's flagship since I returned from the Holy Well site thirty days ago. How is any mishap going to threaten me?" She said nothing in return.

Ian's focus went back to the mission. Which tasks were most important? His thoughts then drifted to Francis. He thought to himself, "He still is not adequately prepared for his future tasks. In many ways, he is the most important member of the party. I will discuss Francis's situation with Malcolm. How can we better prepare Francis for his future? The immediate thought is that Malcolm and Sir James will have the entire winter season up at the castle to educate him."

Later that afternoon, Ian discussed the matter with Malcolm. Malcolm said, "Since I will be moving there permanently, I will be taking my entire library with me. Therefore, we will have ample time before he departs next spring."

This helped ease Ian's fears, but Agatha's unclear warning was still bothering him. He felt that he should be spending as much time with his son as possible. He thought, "Not because of the message, but strictly because he is my son. We have not spent enough time together. It's not because I didn't want to, but he was always at school or training to be a warrior. He has grown to be a man in a blink of an eye. But, he is not just any man. He will be carrying forward the message that could save all humanity."

Ian had an overwhelming sense of pride in both of his sons. Clara would be so proud. Suddenly Ian could smell the fragrance.

Ian decided to walk topside for some air. He walked up to the bow where Agatha was standing. She turned and gave him a hug. Obviously, she knew what had just happened.

CHAPTER 80

FATE

WINTER WAS ABOUT to arrive in the New World. Ian saw very little difference between the winters in Scotland and the New World. It was getting especially cold on the island. Ian hoped that the castle would be a little warmer because it was off of the water. The castle was complete enough to live in. Shutters were covering all of the windows. The shutters for the windows were airtight once they were closed. Tomas was a true artisan. With all of the fireplaces going, the castle would be much more comfortable than the ship. The doors were heavy maple and reminded Ian of the doors back at Rosslyn castle.

The team transferred the Treasure to the castle several days ago. Ian had the honor of accompanying the Treasure to its resting place as he has done so many times in his previous lives. No one knew how long it would stay there. It could be several years or several hundred years. Once they arrived at the castle, Ian helped Angus wrestle the heavy containers down through the cave entrance. The secret entrance from the castle would be a winter project. The Earl had ordered Captain McQuinn and his best warriors to stay at the castle and guard the Treasure while the Earl made the final journey to the island for the year. The builders stayed and continued building the interior. They had accomplished much over a very short time. The Earl, Angus, and Ian returned to the island with ten warriors. The trip was uneventful. The next trip back to the castle would be the final journey until next spring. Those moving to the castle would gather up all of their belongings and be ready the next morning.

The Earl's team arrived back at the island early that evening. They decided to have a feast with the last of the dried oxen strips. There was plenty of local venison for the warriors that would stay and guard the ships. There was also enough to feed the prisoners. The ships would have all of their stoves going. This would help the ships stay warm enough during the frigid days to come.

The dried oxen tasted great as long as it was consumed with a large quantity of mead or wine. Several of the hunters had found a beehive that had a large amount of honey. Once they finished battling the bees for the honey, they were able to bring it back to the ship. Honey is the main ingredient in mead. The other was water. As luck would have it, the hunters had an abundance of the purest water they had ever tasted. So they made a few large batches of mead. They had gotten creative by adding blueberries and cranberries for extra flavor. The berries help disguise the fact that the mead was more potent than usual. Ian discovered this the hard way on his last night on the flagship. Everyone sat around and sang old Scottish songs and toasted the journey.

As the night wore on, Ian had a chance to spend some time with Francis. They discussed how Ian had learned to communicate with Clara. He explained the essence of the lavender flowers. Ian said, "As you move forward on your mission, you must be open to the supernatural. Please be aware as you begin to understand the supernatural; you must keep these thoughts to yourself. There are still many in Scotland and most of Europe that would be threatened by these thoughts." Ian continued, "Take in as much as you can from Malcolm and Sir James this winter. It is doubtful that you will find anyone in Scotland who knows more the ancient secrets than these two."

Ian stated further, "I like the Earl's thoughts on building a chapel in Rosslyn where the secrets can be hidden in plain sight. Your education over this winter will show you how artwork and symbols are used to convey messages. You can assist the Sinclair's with this task. Codices and other ciphers also are used to protect secrets. One must know the cipher to unlock the secrets. You will meet others in secret places and within secret societies. I know that your leg injury saddens you, but it has opened a new door that you would have never had access to if it wasn't for your leg wound."

Francis said, "Don't forget, you will also be there to guide me."

Ian said, "Aye." Ian then had the feeling of impending doom once again. It wasn't like there was anything that told him that he would be harmed, but he just saw blankness. This was the first time that he felt so empty.

Their conversation then moved on to Gavin and Mary. Were they parents yet? Ian said, "Probably too quick for that." Both Ian and Francis discussed how much they miss their family back in Rosslyn.

The mead was starting to get the best of Ian, and he decided that it was time to call it a night. He went to say good night to Malcolm and Agatha. Malcolm was feeling no pain. He was leading the others in song. Ian sat next to Agatha. She seemed to be suffering from melancholy again. He asked her, "Agatha, what's wrong?"

She responded, "Nothing is wrong. Unfortunately, life sometimes giveth and sometimes taketh."

Ian said, "I feel Clara's presence regularly now. She gives me peace. I sense that she is very proud of what we are accomplishing. The future that is in front of Francis is astonishing. I'm sure that she is very proud."

Ian continued, "Agatha, you are on a momentous journey

with the man that you love; you are obviously in a very spiritual place with the Mi'kmaq, and you are assisting with the survival of humanity. Why are you so sad?" I could see a tear running down her face.

She said, "Thank you for coming into my life. You have been a great friend." I thought of this conversation all night. Was Agatha dying? I certainly hope not. Malcolm needs her as much as she needs him.

✠

The next morning everyone was moving very slowly. The Earl was not having any of it. He was barking out commands just after sunrise. The good thing was that all of the traveler's possessions were already loaded into the lifeboats and ready for the journey. Ian helped Francis into the lifeboat. He was moving around very well, but the terrain on the island and the mainland was pretty treacherous. Francis would ride on the oxen-led cart with Malcolm, Agatha, Sir James, and Ian. Angus had fashioned a wooden leg and a cane for him at the castle. He would have much greater maneuverability once properly fitted for the new leg.

They arrived on the mainland shortly thereafter. Angus and the Earl walked ahead of the carts with several warriors. The ominous feeling that they were being watched returned to Ian again. Ian's senses were on high alert. He yelled to the Earl, but no one heard him. Instantly, Ian began to think of Clara again. This time he could smell the lavender fragrance stronger than all previous encounters. Ian thought, "Why now?" Suddenly the cart came to a complete stop. Malcolm pulled back on the reins to stop the oxen. Something was wrong with the wheels on the right side. Ian jumped off of the cart. He was shocked to discover that a wood rod had been inserted into the spokes of the wheel. By the time Ian heard the rustling in the trees, Oleg's men had surrounded them. Ian yelled for the Earl again, but it was too late. Two of the Earl's warriors tried to fight back but were quickly cut down. The element of surprise had worked to perfection. Ian tried to fight, but one of Oleg's men jumped onto the cart and held a knife to Agatha's throat.

The Earl and Angus were one hundred feet ahead of the cart when they heard Ian yell. Ian watched as they ran back to the scene where Oleg had taken many hostages. One of Oleg's men then grabbed Ian and held a knife to his throat.

Oleg then yelled, "Henry Sinclair, this fight is between you and me. Drop your weapons and surrender, and I will let everyone else go." Oleg continued, "Do not make me wait. I will start killing these members of your party one at a time."

Ian noticed movement out of the corner of his eye. The Mi'kmaq Warriors were in the woods. Then, suddenly, Oleg noticed them as well."

The Earl yelled, "You are vastly outnumbered. If any harm comes to any one of my people, I will kill all of you."

Oleg yelled back, "Henry Sinclair, I came here to kill you or be killed. It does not matter."

The Earl responded, "All of you that came with Oleg, did you come here to die as well?"

There was silence. What happened next was surreal. Ian and Angus had perfected their communications without speaking a word. Ian sent the message that said, "Angus, when I give you the signal, have the archers fire their arrows and attack. I have a knife in a holster tied to my leg under my kilt." Angus gave Ian a nod that said, "Message received." The next scene happened very fast. Through his newly acquired skill, Ian could hear Angus whispering to the Earl, "Don't ask me how, but Ian and I can communicate without speaking. He is going to give the signal, and then we are to attack."

The Earl nodded.

Oleg said, "You try anything, and all of these people will die. I will see to it personally."

Just then, Ian counted down to Angus, "Three, two, one... attack."

Everything happened so fast. Ian managed to grab his knife from its holster and stabbed the man holding him hostage. The Earl threw an ax that hit Oleg squarely in the chest. Arrows were flying from the woods. All of Oleg's men had been hit. Ian tried to escape the scene but tripped over one of Oleg's fallen men. This gave Oleg a chance to lunge at Ian. His sword pierced Ian's midsection. Oleg's soon-to-be, lifeless body, then fell on top of Ian. He could feel the warm sensation of Oleg's blood hitting his skin. Ian was staring directly at the VEGVISIR Medal. This was an image that would be engrained on his soul. Angus ran and pulled Oleg off of Ian. Ian had been stabbed just below the heart. Ian was losing blood quickly. Agatha immediately came to his aid. Ian said, "Is this why you were so somber last night."

She had tears running down her face. She said, "Aye. I didn't know how, but I thought we would be attacked today. I didn't have anything to tell the Earl, so I kept quiet. I will never forgive myself."

Ian said, "You can just make it up to me in the next life." Agatha laughed through her tears. Then Francis made his way over. He was sobbing uncontrollably. Ian said, "Son, I have succeeded on my mission for this life. The Treasure is safe. You will become a true hero on this mission. So go forth and tell the message to the worthy. Your mother and I will be at your side the whole time."

Just then, Ian noticed that Clara was standing next to him. She looked beautiful. She said with the most welcoming smile, "Come join me. You have completed this life's mission. We have many more missions awaiting us."

After several minutes Ian began to slip away. He started to see Knights. They were definitely Templars. They had the white robes with the red crosses that Ian had seen depicted. Suddenly, he was one of them. He looked over at Oleg. Oleg had now turned into Abdul.

Then the scene shifted. Ian and Clara were hovering over the box that he and Angus had just moved. The Secret of Eden was safe. Clara was smiling at Ian. Everything was now crystal clear. The mission of this lifetime was now complete. He looked over, and Clara was still there. She said, "I always have been and always will be at your side."

— 373 —

THIS ENDS BOOK TWO

THE CLAN SINCLAIR DREAMS

EPILOGUE

MEANWHILE BACK IN 1858

NATE FINISHED READING the Stories of Jacques Courtier and Ian MacIntyre and was both shocked and relieved at the same time. These crazy Dreams that he has been having finally made some sense. In many ways, he was a witness to events that were not in any history books. The thoughts of treasure and secrets were every boy's dream. However, this was way beyond any boy's imagination. The details that Nate had remembered from his Dreams were not just cursory. Nate remembered conversations that had taken place 700 years before he was born. Everything that happened during those times was not recorded in the written word. They simply became part of the folklore. The problem with folklore is that it gets exaggerated or altered over time. The stories were told in the way that whoever was telling the tale, wished it to be. Nate wondered how many stories that historians consider facts, are actually true. Fortunately for the stories of his Dreams, Nate seemingly was a witness.

Nate told his sister Jane, "Since I recorded my Dreams and

you turned them into a story, I no longer have Dreams of Jacques Courtier or Ian MacIntyre. It is as though the Dreams were forcing me to write down these stories. Now my Dreams seem to be centered on our Great Grandfather Jeremiah."

The stack of notes that Nate recorded about their great grandfather told a story that was just as astonishing as the Knights Templar and Henry Sinclair stories. The difference was that these Dreams were about a relative. These Dreams seem to suggest that Jeremiah was one of the Founding Fathers. History books had no mention of Jeremiah Briggs. Why was that? Nate and Jane knew how their great grandfather came to the Colonies with nothing other than the shirt on his back and the promise of opportunity. He managed a Milltown in upstate New York. How was he connected to the Founding Fathers?

Nate's thoughts suddenly went to the Treasure and the Secret of Eden. Were they real? Did he have enough information to locate them? Were they still there? Maybe the Dreams involving Jeremiah would help answer these questions. Jane was more concerned about the message of the Secret of Eden. She said, "Did our society meet the expectations of the Watchers? In many ways, the Constitution of the United States of America righted the wrongs that had been ongoing in other parts of the world. There was no royalty. Every man had the opportunity to be great if he worked hard enough."

Then a very dark thought hit Nate. He said, "Obviously, slavery does not comply with the rules of the Watchers. Is a great flood or earthquake about to come down on us?" Slavery has always been an affront to not only to Nate's parents, but many others in Michigan. It was wrong when looked at through the lens of the Bible. It was wrong when looked at through the lens of the U.S. Constitution, and it was certainly wrong in the eyes of the Watchers. Maybe abolishing slavery was to be Nate's mission. Maybe the Dreams were just a messenger from above telling him to be part of the solution. If he was to believe his Dreams, then it was apparent that Slavery had to be stopped at all costs. This would give Nate much to think about. It was very rare for a teen-age boy to have his life laid out in front of him so clearly.

Jane sat quietly for a few minutes. Finally, she spoke. She said, "In a few days, I still would like to have you meet with Felicia. She has special gifts. She may be able to answer the bigger questions such as "Why You?""

Nate asked, "Can she be trusted?"

Jane said, "Yes. If she were to tell this tale to anyone, it would only further the claims that she is a witch." She paused briefly then said, "I think that we should give Felicia the written stories and let her review them for a few days. After that, we will set up a day for us to meet her." Nate begrudgingly agreed. After a few day's rest, they would meet with Felicia.

FELICIA

J ANE HAD MET with Felicia and told her the entire story. She had left her with the written stories. They agreed that Felicia, Jane, and Nate would meet the following Saturday. This meant that Nate would have to get his chores done ahead of schedule. Saturday was a big day on the Farm. He told his parents that he needed to meet with Jane to complete his writing project.

They arrived at Felicia's house shortly before nine o'clock the following Saturday morning. Nate had seen this house many times. It seemed overrun with growth. She had many plants that he was unfamiliar with. There also was very unique artwork. The designs were very intricate and religious in nature. Jane knocked on the door, and Felicia very warmly welcomed them. Once they entered Felicia's home, Nate noticed many Christian symbols everywhere he looked. There were Crucifixes, statues of Mary the Mother of Christ, and sayings from the New Testament everywhere. This conflicted with the impression that she was a witch.

She simply was misunderstood. She was a bit of a hermit and only rarely left her home for supplies. Most people just didn't have the chance to get to know Felicia. Their opinion of her would have likely been different.

Felicia served them tea and bread. They made small talk, and Nate could tell that she was a very kind-hearted person. Felicia seemed to know Nate's life story. Even beyond the written stories of his Dreams. Felicia explained, "I can see people's auras. It usually tells the whole story about that person. Also, I have been blessed with the ability to speak with the spirit world. I discovered these skills shortly after my younger sister died from Small Pox." She went on to say, "My sister's death enabled me with a skill that is inherent to all of us. Suddenly I was able to communicate with other spirits. These spirits assured me that my sister was doing great and that she was very happy." She continued, "Oddly enough, I have never been able to talk to my sister. I have seen images of her where she is smiling, though." She paused briefly, then continued, "I know that sooner rather than later, I will be joining her. This brings joy to my heart."

Nate asked, "Why can't you speak with her?"

She responded, "I don't know why, but there seems to be rules and guidelines in the afterlife. You will understand as we move forward. There are beings that are guardians of the Spirit world. Some call them Angels. Others say that they are beings that give direction to wayward spirits. They have one thing in common, though, they all praise the creator. Everything that you have learned in the Bible is true. Some powerful people have changed the written word for their own benefit. When you join the spirit world, you will understand everything. You will come to know Jesus, and you will understand the mission of your soul." She asked me, "Do you understand what the soul is?"

Nate said, "I understand that the soul is what leaves our body after death and goes to Heaven."

She said, "That is correct in a general sense. I will start at the beginning. There is a concept known as reincarnation, where your soul leaves your body at the time of death and can be reborn into a new body. This can happen immediately or can happen several hundreds of years later. The soul has a specific task that it must complete before going to heaven and sitting with Jesus for eternity. Sometimes, souls can complete their mission after just a few lives, and sometimes they may be reincarnated thousands of times. To expand on this concept, souls often work in concert with other souls. For example, in this life, these souls can be your sibling or a perfect stranger. In the next life, the souls may be your mother or father. Sometimes there are lifetimes where not all souls join in. Maybe the circumstance dictates that they are not needed. However, they are still there. Some refer to them as Guardian Angels. Sometimes they speak to us through what we call intuitions. Sometimes there are other souls that work against you. They have a similar mission, but are working for a different outcome. For the fortunate ones, they have a soulmate. This means that they have been with a special soul on most or all of the journeys. They usually are a wife or husband. Somehow in every life, they seem to find each other. At a very deep level that a human cannot understand, there is a magnetism that draws these souls to each other. When they find each other, there is an extraordinary love that is beyond words. When we are born into a new body, at some point, we have intuitions, or even more strongly, Dreams that guide us. One of the most misunderstood concepts is Dreams. Some think they are meaningless drifting that the mind goes through. What people don't understand is that many of our Dreams are memories from a past life. Sometimes they make sense, but most of the time, they don't. In your case, I believe that your Dreams are very forcefully trying to guide you. I believe that you are part of an ancient and sacred mission that involves many other souls. I have learned a very effective technique called Hypnotism that allows me to speak with your inner being. Sometimes, it allows me to speak with the Masters who guide your soul. I assure you that it will not cause you any harm. You probably won't even remember being hypnotized. Your Sister will be here to witness the entire thing. I believe that it will bring you answers."

Nate looked at Jane, and she nodded that it would be okay. Jane said, "You know that I will not let anything bad happen to you. Also, I trust Felicia. She is the kindest person that I have ever met." So Nate agreed to let Felicia hypnotize him.

They moved into her living room, where she guided Nate to her couch. She said, "Sometimes it is easier if you lay down."

Nate said, "I can't promise you that I won't fall asleep, but if I start to snore, please wake me up. My brothers claim that I snore all of the time."

Felicia laughed and said, "You need not worry about snoring." That was the last thing that Nate remembered.

Seemingly two minutes later, Felicia woke him up. Nate asked, "How long was I asleep?"

Jane responded, "Roughly an hour and a half."

Nate asked Felicia, "Did it work?"

She nodded yes and said, "I will let Jane explain to you what we discovered."

Nate said to Jane, "Please tell me everything that happened."

Jane said that she would. She seemed troubled by what she had heard. She began, "Felicia instructed you to look up at the sky as if you were looking through a see-through cathedral ceiling. Then she asked you to look down at your feet and tell me what you see. You responded in a voice that wasn't yours that you are wearing a white tunic with a red cross. She asked you your name, and you responded, "Jacques Courtier." The words came out of your mouth, but it wasn't your voice. She asked him what his mission was, and he responded in a heavy French accent that his mission was to be a Guardian of the Secret of Eden. Then she asked him several questions in French that I couldn't understand. He seemingly responded. Then she requested to speak with Ian MacIntyre. Suddenly, a Scottish voice came forward. She asked him what his mission was, and he gave the same response. "I am the Guardian of the Secret of Eden." She asked him about his mission to the New World. He recanted the story exactly as they had recorded it.

Felicia asked Ian if Clara was with him, and he responded that she is always with him, but he said, "Just as I am on my next mission, so is she. We will be together again soon. Then Felicia startled me by asking for Jeremiah Briggs. Just hearing his name sent a shiver down my spine. It brought back memories of our father telling us his tales. Now I am about to hear his voice."

Jane recalled the exchange. She said, "Felicia asked, "Are you, Jeremiah Briggs?"

He responded with a hint of a British accent, "Yes."

Felicia asked, "Do you understand that you are speaking through your Great Grandson Nathaniel right now."

He responded, "Yes. Nathaniel will be a very important person on this mission."

Felicia then asked, "Is there any guidance that you can give Nathaniel?"

The voice responded, "Everything was recorded in my Diary."

Felicia then asked one final question, "Is the Secret of Eden still hidden?" The voice responded, "Yes, but we moved it from its resting place in New Scotland. It is recorded in the Diary. Nathaniel will need to learn the code. But he needs to beware that others are on a mission to stop him."

Jane said, "After this last couple of questions, Felicia woke you up."

Nate sat quietly for several minutes. He was trying to digest what he had just heard.

He asked Felicia, "Am I part of this mission? Am I safe? Is my family safe? Do I have a soulmate currently walking this Earth? Am I to carry on the mission of Jacques, Ian, and Jeremiah?"

Felicia then shocked Nate to his core. She said, "My dear boy. You are not only here to carry on their mission. You are Jacques, Ian, and Jeremiah. You are all the same soul."

They all sat very quietly for several minutes when Jane finally spoke. She said, "Our great grandfather left a diary?"

The
Saga
Continues